'A fabulously gripping r̶ ̶ ̶ ̶ ̶ ̶ ̶ ̶
With a Pearl Earring and ̶ ̶ ̶ ̶ ̶ ̶ ̶ ̶ ̶ ̶
inely new voice'

'Glittering, suspense-powered . . . This is a sumptuous book in every sense . . . the plot seems to twist and buck with every passing page. Truly, it's thrilling' *Metro*

'Highly accomplished and enthralling . . . Burton has clearly done her research and writes with skill, impressively evoking the oppressive society of the Dutch Golden Age'
Mail on Sunday, novel of the week

'Atmospheric and fascinating . . . An original story that keeps you gripped right to the unexpected conclusion' *The Times*

'Incredibly well-written, beautifully plotted' *Evening Standard*

'Gripping and gorgeous . . . Finely crafted' *Daily Telegraph*

'It grabs you from the off . . . Like nothing you've read before'
Glamour

'Preoccupying, to the final sentence' *Vogue*

'Exquisite . . . Mesmerizing and suspenseful, Nella's story deals with themes like obsession, perception and truth, and brilliantly describes how she learns to be the mistress of her own destiny in a constrained, claustrophobic world. Unmissable' *Psychologies*

'Gorgeously written'   *Good Housekeeping*

'Like Tracy Chevalier, Burton is skilled at evoking place . . . Wonderful'   *Guardian*

'A compelling, atmospheric literary thriller'   *Sunday Times*

'In this lushly written debut, it's as though figures from old Dutch masters come to life . . . Feisty yet tender, Nella is a heroine to suit a modern readership'
                        RACHEL HORE, *Independent*

'Gripping . . . Full not only of beautiful historical details but of rounded characters that are easy to care for. It is a delight to read such an intelligent page-turner'   *Glasgow Herald*

'A deftly plotted mystery, a feminist coming-of-age drama and a probing investigation of marriage. Burton evokes the sights, sounds and smells of seventeenth-century Amsterdam as she brings to life a cast of sensitively rendered characters, each longing to be free . . . This fine historical novel mirrors the fullness of life, in which growth and sorrow inevitably are mingled'   *Washington Post*

'An old-fashioned page-turner, with sudden twists, cliff-hangers at the close of every chapter and an absorbingly unfamiliar and rich period setting . . . The reader is never allowed to relax for too long before the ground once again shifts under their feet'   *Financial Times*

THE MINIATURIST

Jessie Burton

PICADOR

First published 2014 by Picador

First published in paperback 2014 by Picador

This edition first published 2015 by Picador
an imprint of Pan Macmillan, a division of Macmillan Publishers Limited
Pan Macmillan, 20 New Wharf Road, London N1 9RR
Basingstoke and Oxford
Associated companies throughout the world
www.panmacmillan.com

ISBN 978-1-4472-8466-6

Dolls' house of Petronella Oortman, anonymous, c. 1686 – c. 1710, Rijksmuseum

3 5 7 9 8 6 4 2

A CIP catalogue record for this book is available from the British Library.

Printed and bound by CPI Group (UK) Ltd, Croydon, CRO 4YY

Visit **www.picador.com** to read more about all our books
and to buy them. You will also find features, author interviews and
news of any author events, and you can sign up for e-newsletters
so that you're always first to hear about our new releases.

For

Linda,
Edward
& Pip

Petronella Oortman's cabinet house,
The Rijksmuseum, Amsterdam

The term VOC refers to the Dutch East India Company, known in Dutch as the Vereenigde Oost-Indische Compagnie (the VOC). The VOC was founded in 1602 and ran hundreds of ships trading across Africa, Europe, Asia and the Indonesian archipelago.

By 1669, the VOC had 50,000 employees, 60 bewindhebbers (partners), and 17 regents. By 1671, VOC shares on the Amsterdam Stock Exchange were reaching 570% of their nominal value.

Owing to the positive agricultural conditions and financial strength of the United Provinces of the Netherlands, it was said that their poor ate much better than their counterparts in England, Italy, France and Spain. The rich ate best of all.

Take ye the spoil of silver, take the spoil of gold:
For there is none end of the store and glory out of all
the pleasant furniture.

Nahum 2:9

And as he went out of the temple, one of his disciples
saith unto him,
Master, see what manner of stones and what
buildings are here!
And Jesus answering said unto him, Seest thou these
great buildings?
There shall not be left one stone upon another, that
shall not be thrown down.

Mark 13:1–2

*(All excerpts come from marked passages in the
Brandt household Bible)*

The Old Church, Amsterdam: Tuesday, 14th January 1687

The funeral is supposed to be a quiet affair, for the deceased had no friends. But words are water in Amsterdam, they flood your ears and set the rot, and the church's east corner is crowded. She watches the scene unfold from the safety of the choir stall, as guildsmen and their wives approach the gaping grave like ants toward the honey. Soon, they are joined by VOC clerks and ship's captains, regentesses, pastry-makers – and him, still wearing that broad-brimmed hat. She tries to pity him. Pity, unlike hate, can be boxed and put away.

The church's painted roof – the one thing the reformers didn't pull down – rises above them like the tipped-up hull of a magnificent ship. It is a mirror to the city's soul; inked on its ancient beams, Christ in judgement holds his sword and lily, a golden cargo breaks the waves, the Virgin rests on a crescent moon. Flipping up the old misericord beside her, her fingers flutter on the proverb of exposed wood. It is a relief of a man shitting a bag of coins, a leer of pain chipped across his face. What's changed? she thinks.

And yet.

Even the dead are in attendance today, grave-slabs hiding body on body, bones on dust, stacked up beneath the mourners' feet. Below that floor are women's jaws, a merchant's pelvis, the hollow ribs of a fat grandee. There are little corpses down there, some no longer than a loaf of bread. Noting how people shift their eyes from such condensed sadness, how they move from any tiny slab they see, she cannot blame them.

At the centre of the crowd, the woman spies what she has come for. The girl looks exhausted, grief-etched, standing by a hole in the floor. She barely notices the citizens who have come to stare. The pall-bearers walk up the nave, the coffin on their shoulders balanced like a case for a lute. By the looks on their faces, you might have thought a few of them have reservations about this funeral. It will be Pellicorne's doing, she supposes. Same old poison in the ear.

Normally processions like this are in tight order, the burgomasters at the top and the common folk beneath, but on this day no one has bothered. The woman supposes that there's never been a body like it in any of God's houses within the compass of this city. She loves its rare, defiant quality. Founded on risk, Amsterdam now craves certainty, a neat passage through life, guarding the comfort of its money with dull obedience. I should have left before today, she thinks. Death has come too close.

The circle breaks apart as the pall-bearers push their way in. As the coffin is lowered into the hole without ceremony, the girl moves towards the edge. She tosses a posy of flowers down into the dark, and a starling beats its wings, scaling up the church's whitewashed wall. Heads turn, distracted, but the girl does not flinch, and neither does the woman in the choir stall, both of them watching the arc of petals as Pellicorne intones his final prayer.

As the pall-bearers slide the new slab into place, a maid-servant kneels by the vanishing dark. She starts to sob, and when the exhausted girl does nothing to check these rising tears, this lack of dignity and order is noted with a tut. Two women, dressed in silk, stand near the choir stall and whisper between themselves. 'That kind of behaviour is why we're here in the first place,' one murmurs.

'If they're like this in public, they must behave like wild animals indoors,' her friend replies.

'True. But what I wouldn't give to be a fly on that wall. *Bzz-bzz.*'

They stifle a giggle, and in the choir stall the woman notices how her knuckle has turned white upon the moral misericord.

With the church floor sealed once again, the circle dissolves, the dead at bay. The girl, like a stained-glass saint fallen from the church's window, acknowledges the uninvited hypocrites. These people start to chatter as they exit towards the city's winding streets, followed eventually by the girl and her maid, who move silently, arm in arm along the nave and out. Most of the men will be going back to their desks and counters, because keeping Amsterdam afloat takes constant work. Hard grind got us the glory, the saying goes – but sloth will slide us back into the sea. And these days, the rising waters feel so near.

Once the church is empty, the woman emerges from the choir stall. She hurries, not wanting to be discovered. *Things can change*, she says, her voice whispering off the walls. When she finds the newly laid slab, she sees it is a rushed job, the granite still warmer than the other graves, the chiselled words still dusty. That these events have come to pass should be unbelievable.

She kneels and reaches in her pocket to complete what she has started. This is her own prayer, a miniature house small enough to sit in the palm. Nine rooms and five human figures are carved within, the craftsmanship so intricate, worked outside of time. Carefully, the woman places this offering where she had always intended it to lie, blessing the cool granite with her toughened fingers.

As she pushes open the church door, she looks instinctively for the broad-brimmed hat, the cloak of Pellicorne, the silken women. All have vanished, and she could be alone in the world were it not for the noise of the trapped starling. It is time to leave, but for a moment the woman holds the door open for the bird. Sensing her effort, instead it flaps away behind the pulpit.

She closes away the church's cool interior, turning to face the sun, heading from the ringed canals toward the sea. Starling, she thinks, if you believe that building is the safer spot, then I am not the one to set you free.

ONE

Mid-October, 1686
The Herengracht canal, Amsterdam

Be not desirous of his dainties:
For they are deceitful meat.

Proverbs 23:3

Outside In

On the step of her new husband's house, Nella Oortman lifts and drops the dolphin knocker, embarrassed by the thud. No one comes, though she is expected. The time was prearranged and letters written, her mother's paper so thin compared with Brandt's expensive vellum. No, she thinks, this is not the best of greetings, given the blink of a marriage ceremony the month before – no garlands, no betrothal cup, no wedding bed. Nella places her small trunk and birdcage on the step. She knows she'll have to embellish this later for home, when she's found a way upstairs, a room, a desk.

Nella turns to the canal as bargemen's laughter rises up the opposite brickwork. A puny lad has skittled into a woman and her basket of fish, and a half-dead herring slithers down the wide front of the seller's skirt. The harsh cry of her country voice runs under Nella's skin. '*Idiot! Idiot!*' the woman yells. The boy is blind, and he grabs in the dirt for the escaped herring as if it's a silver charm, his fingers quick, not afraid to feel around. He scoops it, cackling, running up the path with his catch, his free arm out and ready.

Nella cheers silently and stays to face this rare October warmth, to take it while she can. This part of the Herengracht is known as the Golden Bend, but today the wide stretch is brown and workaday. Looming above the sludge-coloured canal, the houses are a phenomenon. Admiring their own symmetry on the water, they are stately and beautiful, jewels set within the city's pride. Above their rooftops Nature is doing her best to keep up, and clouds in colours of saffron and apricot echo the spoils of the glorious republic.

Nella turns back to the door, now slightly ajar. Was it like this before? She cannot be sure. She pushes on it, peering into the void as cool air rises from the marble. 'Johannes Brandt?' she calls – loud, a little panicked. Is this a game? she thinks. I'll be standing here come January. Peebo, her parakeet, thrills the tips of his feathers against the cage bars, his faint cheep falling short on the marble. Even the now-quiet canal behind them seems to hold its breath.

Nella is sure of one thing as she looks deeper into the shadows. She's being watched. *Come on, Nella Elisabeth*, she tells herself, stepping over the threshold. Will her new husband embrace her, kiss her or shake her hand like it's just business? He didn't do any of those things at the ceremony, surrounded by her small family and not a single member of his.

To show that country girls have manners too, she bends down and removes her shoes – dainty, leather, of course her best – although what their point has been she can't now say. *Dignity*, her mother said, but dignity is so uncomfortable. She slaps the shoes down, hoping the noise will arouse somebody, or maybe scare them off. Her mother calls her over-imaginative, Nella-in-the-Clouds. The inert shoes lie in anti-climax and Nella simply feels a fool.

Outside, two women call to one other. Nella turns, but through the open door she sees only the back of one woman, capless, golden-headed and tall, striding away towards the last of the sun. Nella's own hair has loosened on the journey from Assendelft, the light breeze letting wisps escape. To tuck them away will make her more nervous than she can bear to seem, so she leaves them tickling her face.

'Are we to have a menagerie?'

The voice sails sure and swift from the darkness of the hall. Nella's skin contracts, for being right about her suspicions can't banish the goosebumps. She watches as a figure glides from the shadows, a hand outstretched – in protest or in greeting, it is hard to tell. It is a woman, straight and slim and dressed in deepest black, the cap on her head starched and pressed to white perfection. Not a wisp of her hair escapes, and she brings with her the vaguest, strangest scent of nutmeg. Her eyes are grey, her mouth is solemn. How long has she been there, watching? Peebo chirrups at the intervention.

'This is Peebo,' Nella says. 'My parakeet.'

'So I see,' says the woman, gazing down at her. 'Or hear. I take it you have not brought any more beasts?'

'I have a little dog, but he's at home—'

'Good. It would mess in our rooms. Scratch the wood. Those small ones are an affectation of the French and Spanish,' the woman observes. 'As frivolous as their owners.'

'And they look like rats,' calls a second voice from somewhere in the hall.

The woman frowns, briefly closing her eyes, and Nella takes her in, wondering who else is watching this exchange. I must be younger than her by ten years, she thinks, though her skin's so smooth. As the woman moves past Nella towards the door frame, there is a grace in her movements, self-aware and unapologetic. She casts a brief, approving glance at the

9

neat shoes by the door and then stares into the cage, her lips pressed tight together. Peebo's feathers have puffed in fear.

Nella decides to distract her by joining hands in greeting, but the woman flinches at the touch.

'Strong bones for seventeen,' the woman says.

'I'm Nella,' she replies, retracting her hand. 'And I'm eighteen.'

'I know who you are.'

'My real name is Petronella, but everyone at home calls me—'

'I heard the first time.'

'Are you the housekeeper?' Nella asks. A giggle is badly stifled in the hallway shadows. The woman ignores it, looking out into the pearlescent dusk. 'Is Johannes here? I'm his new wife.' The woman still says nothing. 'We signed our marriage a month ago, in Assendelft,' Nella persists. It seems there is nothing else to do but to persist.

'My brother is not in the house.'

'Your brother?'

Another giggle from the darkness. The woman looks straight into Nella's eyes. 'I am Marin Brandt,' she says, as if Nella should understand. Marin's gaze may be hard, but Nella can hear the precision faltering in her voice. 'He's not here,' Marin continues. 'We thought he'd be. But he's not.'

'Where is he then?'

Marin looks out towards the sky again. Her left hand fronds the air, and from the shadows near the staircase two figures appear. 'Otto,' she says.

A man comes towards them and Nella swallows, pressing her cold feet upon the floor.

Otto's skin is dark, dark brown everywhere, his neck coming out from the collar, his wrists and hands from his sleeves – all unending, dark brown skin. His high cheeks, his chin, his wide brow, every inch. Nella has never seen such a man in her life.

Marin seems to be watching her to see what she will do. The look in Otto's large eyes makes no acknowledgement of Nella's ill-concealed fascination. He bows to her and she curtsies, chewing her lip till the taste of blood reminds her to be calm. Nella sees how his skin glows like a polished nut, how his black hair springs straight up from his scalp. It is a cloud of soft wool, not flat and greasy like other men's. 'I—' she says.

Peebo begins to chirp. Otto puts his hands out, a pair of pattens resting on his broad palms. 'For your feet,' he says.

His accent is Amsterdam – but he rolls the words, making them warm and liquid. Nella takes the pattens from him and her fingers brush his skin. Clumsily she slips the raised shoes onto her feet. They are too big, but she doesn't dare say it, and at least they lift her soles off the chilly marble. She'll tighten the leather straps later, upstairs – if she ever gets there, if they ever let her past this hall.

'Otto is my brother's manservant,' says Marin, her eyes still fixed on Nella. 'And here is Cornelia, our maid. She will look after you.'

Cornelia steps forward. She is a little older than Nella, perhaps twenty, twenty-one – and slightly taller. Cornelia pins her with an unfriendly grin, her blue eyes moving over the new bride, seeing the tremor in Nella's hands. Nella smiles, burnt by the maid's curiosity, struggling to say some piece of empty thanks. She is half-grateful, half-ashamed when Marin cuts her off.

'Let me show you upstairs,' Marin says. 'You will want to see your room.'

Nella nods and a look of amusement flickers to life in Cornelia's eyes. Blithe pirrips from the cage bounce high up the walls, and Marin indicates to Cornelia with a flick of her wrist that the bird must go to the kitchen.

'But the cooking fumes,' Nella protests. Marin and Otto turn back to her. 'Peebo likes the light.'

Cornelia takes up the cage and starts swinging it like a pail. 'Please, be careful,' says Nella.

Marin catches Cornelia's eye. The maid continues to the kitchen, accompanied by the thin melody of Peebo's worried cheeps.

⧯⧯

Upstairs, Nella feels dwarfed by the sumptuousness of her new room. Marin merely looks displeased. 'Cornelia has embroidered too much,' she says. 'But we hope Johannes will only marry once.'

There are initialled cushions, a new bedspread and two pairs of recently refreshed curtains. 'The velvet heaviness is needed to keep out canal mists,' Marin observes. 'This was my room,' she adds, moving to the window to look at the few stars which have begun to appear in the sky, placing her hand upon the windowpane. 'It has a better view, so we gave it to you.'

'Oh no,' says Nella. 'Then you must keep it.'

They face each other, hemmed in by the mass of needlework, the abundance of linen covered in *B* for Brandt, encircled by vine leaves, entrenched in birds' nests, rising out of flower beds. The *B*s have gobbled up her maiden name, their bellies fat and swollen. Feeling uneasy but duty-bound, Nella brushes a finger over this bounty of wool, now bearing on her spirits.

'Your grand ancestral Assendelft seat, is it warm and dry?' Marin asks.

'It can be damp,' Nella offers as she bends over and tries to adjust the large pattens strapped awkwardly to her feet. 'The dykes don't always work. It's not grand, though—'

'Our family may not have your ancient pedigree, but what's that in the face of a warm, dry, well-made house,' Marin interrupts. It is not a question.

'Indeed.'

'*Afkomst seyt niet.* Pedigree counts for nothing,' Marin continues, prodding a cushion to emphasize the word *nothing*. 'Pastor Pellicorne said it last Sunday and I wrote it in the flyleaf of our Bible. The waters will rise if we're not careful.' She seems to shake herself out of a thought. 'Your mother wrote,' she adds. 'She insisted she would pay for you to travel here. We couldn't allow that. We sent the second-best barge. You're not offended?'

'No. No.'

'Good. Second-best in this house still means new paint and a cabin lined in Bengal silk. Johannes is using the other one.'

Nella wonders where her husband is, on his best barge, not back in time to greet her. She thinks about Peebo, alone in the kitchen, near the fire, near the pans. 'You only have two servants?' she asks.

'It's enough,' says Marin. 'We're merchants, not layabouts. The Bible tells us a man should never flaunt his wealth.'

'No. Of course.'

'That is, if he has any left to flaunt.' Marin stares at her and Nella looks away. The light in the room is beginning to fade, and Marin sets a taper on the candles. They are tallow and cheap, and Nella had hoped for more fragrant beeswax. The choice of this meat-smelling, smoky variety surprises her. 'Cornelia seems to have sewn your new name on everything,' Marin says over her shoulder.

Indeed, thinks Nella, remembering Cornelia's baleful scrutiny. Her fingers will be red ribbons, and who will she punish for that?

'When is Johannes coming – why is he not here?' she asks.

'Your mother said you were keen to begin your life as a wife in Amsterdam,' Marin says. 'Are you?'

'Yes. But one needs a husband in order to do so.'

In the frost-tipped silence that follows, Nella wonders where Marin's husband is. Maybe she's hidden him in the cellar. She smothers her desperate impulse to laugh by smiling at one of the cushions. 'This is all so beautiful,' she says. 'You didn't have to.'

'Cornelia did it all. I am no use with my hands.'

'I'm sure that is not true.'

'I've taken my paintings down. I thought these might be more to your taste.' Marin gestures to the wall where a brace of game-birds has been captured in oil, hanging from a hook, all feather and claw. Further along the wall is a portrait of a strung-up hare, a hunter's prize. Next to it a painted slew of oysters are piled on a Chinese patterned plate, shadowed by a spilt wineglass and a bowl of over-ripened fruit. There is something unsettling about the oysters, their exposed openness. In her old home, Nella's mother covered the walls in landscapes and scenes from the Bible. 'These belong to my brother,' Marin observes, pointing at a brimming vase of flowers, harder than life, coloured in excess, half a pomegranate waiting at the bottom of the frame.

'Thank you.' Nella wonders how long it will take her to turn them to the wall before she goes to sleep.

'You'll want to eat up here tonight,' says Marin. 'You've been travelling for hours.'

'I have, yes. I would be grateful.' Nella shudders inwardly at the birds' bloodied beaks, their glassy eyes, promising flesh puckering away. At the sight of them, she is taken by the desire for something sweet. 'Do you have any marzipan?'

'No. Sugar is – not something we take much of. It makes people's souls grow sick.'

'My mother used to roll it into shapes.' There was always marzipan in the pantry, the only predilection for indulgence in which Mrs Oortman echoed her husband. Mermaids, ships and necklaces of sugared jewels, that almond doughiness melting in their mouths. I no longer belong to my mother, Nella thinks. One day I will roll sugar shapes for other little clammy hands, voices baying for treats.

'I will ask Cornelia to bring you some *herenbrood* and Gouda,' Marin says, drawing Nella out of her thoughts. 'And a glass of Rhenish.'

'Thank you. Do you have an idea of when Johannes will arrive?'

Marin tips her nose into the air. 'What *is* that smell?'

Instinctively, Nella's hands fly to her collarbone. 'Is it me?'

'Is it you?'

'My mother bought me a perfume. Oil of Lilies. Is that what you smell?'

Marin nods. 'It is,' she says. 'It's lily.' She coughs gently. 'You know what they say about lilies.'

'No?'

'Early to ripe, early to rot.'

With that, Marin shuts the door.

Cloak

At four o'clock the next morning, Nella is still unable to sleep. The oddness of her new surroundings, gleaming and embroidered, wreathed with the smell of smoking tallow, forbids her to be easy. The paintings in their frames remain exposed, for she had not the courage to switch them to the wall. Lying there, she lets the events that have led to this moment swirl through her exhausted head.

When he died two years ago, they said in Assendelft that Seigneur Oortman had been a man who fathered breweries. Though Nella loathed the suggestion that her papa was nothing more than a sozzled Priapus, it proved depressingly true. Her father tied them up with his knot of debts – the soup thinned, the meat got scraggier, the servants fell away. He'd never built an ark, as all Dutchmen were supposed to, fighting the rising sea. 'You need to marry a man who can keep a guilder in his purse,' her mother said, taking up her pen.

'But I have nothing to give in return,' Nella replied.

Her mother tutted. 'Look at you. What else do we women have?'

The statement had stunned Nella. To be reduced by her own mother caused her a new sort of distress, and grief for her father was replaced by a sort of grief for herself. Her younger siblings, Carel and Arabella, were allowed to continue outside, playing at cannibals or pirates.

For two years, Nella practised being a lady. She walked with new poise – though there was nowhere to walk to, she complained, feeling for the first time a desire to escape her village, ignoring the enormous skies, seeing only a bucolic prison already developing fine layers of dust. In a newly tightened corset she improved her lute, moving her neat fingers on the fretboard, concerned about her mother's nerves just enough not to rebel. In July this year her mother's enquiries, through the last of her husband's connections in the city, finally fell on fertile ground.

A letter arrived, the handwriting on the front neat and flowing, confident. Her mother didn't let her read it – but a week later, Nella discovered she was to play for a man, a merchant called Johannes Brandt, come to the country from Amsterdam. As the sun lowered over the browning Assendelft flatlands, this stranger sat in their gently crumbling house and listened to her play.

Nella thought he seemed moved, and when she'd finished he said that he'd enjoyed it. 'I love the lute,' he told her. 'A beautiful instrument. I have two hanging on my wall, but they haven't been played for years.' And when Johannes Brandt – thirty-nine, a true Methuselah! Carel crowed – had asked for her hand, Nella decided to accept. It would have seemed ungrateful and certainly stupid to say no. What other option was there but – as Marin puts it – life as a wife?

After the Assendelft ceremony in September, their names entered in the church register, they had a brief dinner at the Oortman home and Johannes left. A shipment needed to be delivered to Venice, he'd said, and he had to do it himself. Nella and her mother had nodded. Johannes was so charming, with his crooked smile, his suggestion of such power. On her wedding night, the newly married Nella slept as she had for years, top to toe with her wriggling sister. But it was all to the good, she thought, picturing herself rising from the flames of Assendelft like a new woman – a wife, and all to come—

Her thoughts are interrupted by the sound of dogs in the hall. Nella hears a man – Johannes' voice, she is sure. Her husband is here, in Amsterdam – a little late, but here. Nella sits up in her wedding bed, blearily rehearsing. *I am so pleased. Was your journey safe? Yes? So happy, oh so happy.*

But she dares not go down. Struck with nerves, the excitement of seeing him is not quite enough to overcome. Waiting, apprehension blooming in her stomach, she wonders how to begin. Finally she shucks on her pattens, pulls a shawl over her nightgown and creeps along the passageway.

The dogs' claws skitter across the tiles. They bring the sea air in their fur, their tails thwack the furniture. Marin has got to Johannes first, and Nella can hear them talking.

'I never said that, Marin,' Johannes says. His voice is deep and dry.

'Forget it now. Brother, I am glad to see you. I have prayed for your safe return.' As Marin moves out of the shadow to survey him, the light of her candle dips and dances. Craning over the banister, Nella watches the unfamiliar bulk of Johannes' travelling cloak, the surprising butcher's fingers. 'You look worn out,' Marin goes on.

'I know, I know. And autumn in London—'

'Is gruesome. So that's where you have been. Let me.'

With her spare hand, Marin helps remove his cloak. 'Ah, Johannes. You are thin. You have been away too long.'

'I am not thin.' He moves away. 'Rezeki, Dhana,' he calls, and the dogs follow him like familiars. Nella digests the odd sounds of their names. *Rezeki, Dhana*. In Assendelft, Carel called their dogs Snout and Blackeye, unimaginative but perfect reflections of character and appearance.

'Brother,' says Marin. 'She's here.'

Johannes stops but he does not turn. Shoulders dropping, his head inclines a little lower to his chest. 'Ah,' he says. 'I see.'

'It would have been better for you to be here when she arrived.'

'I'm sure you coped.'

Marin pauses, and the silence grows between her pale face and the closed bulk of her brother's back. 'Don't forget,' she says.

Johannes runs his fingers through his hair. 'How could I?' he replies. 'How could I?'

Marin seems about to say something else, but instead she folds her arms across her body. 'It's so cold,' she says.

'Then go to bed. I have to work.'

He shuts his door, and Marin swings her brother's cloak onto her shoulders. Nella leans further over, watching Marin bury her face in the long folds of material. The banister creaks and Marin whips off the cloak, peering up into the darkness. When Marin opens a cupboard off the hallway, Nella creeps back to her room to wait.

Minutes later, at the sound of Marin's bedroom door closing at the end of the corridor, Nella sidles down the main staircase. She stops by the hall cupboard and expects to find the cloak hanging, but it is crumpled on the floor. Kneeling down to pick it up, she finds it has a damp scent of a tired man and the cities he's seen. After placing it on the hook, Nella approaches the door behind which her husband disappeared, and knocks.

'For God's sake,' he says. 'We'll speak in the morning.'

'It's me. Petronella. Nella.'

After a moment, the door opens and Johannes stands there, his face in shadow. He is so broad-shouldered – Nella hadn't remembered him being this imposing at the half-empty church in Assendelft. '*Esposa mía*,' he says.

Nella does not know what this means. As he steps back into the candlelight she sees his face is tanned and beaten by the sun. His irises, grey like Marin's, are almost translucent. Her husband is no prince, his hair greasy at the scalp, a dull metallic. 'I'm here,' she says.

'So you are.' He gestures to her nightgown. 'You should be asleep.'

'I came to greet you.'

He comes forward and kisses her hand, his mouth softer than she imagined. 'We'll talk in the morning, Nella. I am glad you arrived safely. I'm so glad.'

His eyes rest on nothing for long. Nella considers the conundrum of his energetic fatigue, noticing a musky tang in the air, intense and unsettling. Retreating into the yellow glow of what looks to be his study, Johannes shuts the door.

Nella waits for a moment, looking up the main staircase into the pitch black. Marin must surely be asleep, she thinks. I'll just take one look, to be sure my little bird's all right.

Tiptoeing down the stairs to the kitchens, she finds her parakeet's cage hanging by the open stove, the dying embers gently illuminating the metal bars. 'All maids are dangerous,' her mother had said, 'but the city ones are worse.' She hadn't explained exactly why, but at least Peebo is alive, on his perch, feathers up, hopping and clicking in acknowledgement of Nella's presence. More than anything she wants to take him upstairs, but she thinks of what Marin might do if she's disobeyed, Cornelia arranging a dinner of two little drumsticks with a garland of green feathers. 'Goodnight, Peebo,' she whispers.

Through her bedroom window the mists rise off the Herengracht, the moon above a faded coin. Drawing the curtains and gathering her shawl around her, Nella takes a seat in the corner, still wary of her giant bed. Her new husband is a rich man in Amsterdam, a city power-broker, a lord of the sea and all its bounty. 'Life's hard if you're not a wife,' her mother had observed. 'Why?' Nella asked. Having witnessed her mother's constant annoyance at her father turn to panic on the news of his posthumous debts, she asked why Mrs Oortman was so keen to shackle her daughter to a possibly similar risk. Her mother looked at her as if she was mad, but this time she did explain. 'Because Seigneur Brandt is a city shepherd, and your father was only a sheep.'

Nella looks at the silver ewer on the side, the smooth mahogany writing desk, the Turkey rug, the voluptuous paintings. A beautiful pendulum clock makes its gentle measure of time. There are suns and moons on its face, its hands are filigreed. It is the most beautiful clock Nella has ever seen. Everything looks new, and speaks of wealth. Nella has never learned this particular language, but she thinks it will be necessary. Picking up the fallen cushions on the floor, she mounts them on the coverlet of deep red silk.

The first time Nella bled, aged twelve, her mother told her that the purpose of that blood was 'the security of children'. Nella never thought there was much to feel secure about, hearing the cries through the village of women in their labour pains, the coffins sometimes marched to church soon after.

Love was much more nebulous than stains on linen rags. Her monthly blood never seemed connected to what Nella suspected love could be – of the body but beyond it. 'That's love, Petronella,' Mrs Oortman said, observing how Arabella held the puppy Blackeye tight until she nearly choked his canine life away. When musicians in the village sang about love, they sang indeed of pain concealed in the bounty. True love was a flower in the gut, its petals unfurling inside out. You would risk all for love – blissful, never without its drops of dismay.

Mrs Oortman had always complained there were no suitors good enough for miles – 'hay-chewers', she called the local boys. The city, and Johannes Brandt, held her daughter's future.

'But – *love*, Mother. Will I love him?'

'The girl wants love,' Mrs Oortman cried theatrically to the peeling Assendelft walls. 'She wants the peaches and the cream.'

Nella was told it was right that she leave Assendelft, and God knows that by the end to escape was all she wanted. She had no desire to play shipwrecks with Carel and Arabella any more, but this doesn't stop the disappointment flooding in now, sitting by her empty wedding bed in Amsterdam like a nursemaid to a patient. What is the point of being here if her husband will not even greet her properly? Clambering up on the blank mattress, she burrows amongst the cushions, thwarted by the scornful look in Cornelia's eyes, the edge in Marin's voice, Johannes' indifference. *I am the girl*, Nella thinks, *who hasn't had a single peach, never mind the cream.*

The house still seems awake despite the unforgiving hour. She hears the sound of the front door being opened and shut, and then another door above her. There is whispering, footsteps padding across the corridor, before an intense quiet wraps the rooms.

She listens, desolate, a hairline crack of moonlight glinting over painted hare and rotten pomegranate. It is a deceptive quiet, as if the house itself is breathing. But she doesn't dare leave her bed again, not on her first night. Thoughts of last summer's lute playing have gone, and all Nella can hear running through her head is the herring-seller's words – *idiot*, *idiot*, screeching her country voice.

New Alphabet

After opening the curtain to let in the morning sun, Cornelia stands at the end of Nella's rumpled bed. 'The Seigneur's arrived from London,' she says to the small foot poking through the bedclothes. 'You'll breakfast together.'

Nella's head shoots up from the pillow, her face puffy as a cherub's. She can hear every maid along the Herengracht, their mops clanking in buckets like muted bells as they wash the filth from their front steps. 'How long have I been asleep?' she asks.

'Long enough,' replies the maid.

'I could have been in this bed for three months, under a spell.'

Cornelia laughs. 'What a spell.'

'What do you mean?'

'Nothing, Madame.' She offers her hands. 'Come. I have to dress you.'

'You were up late.'

'I was, was I?' Cornelia's tone is impudent, and this confidence makes Nella falter. None of her mother's maids spoke to her in such a way.

'I heard the front door in the night,' she says. 'And one above me. I'm sure of it.'

'Impossible,' replies the maid. 'Toot locked it before you went up.'

'Toot?'

'It's what I call Otto. He thinks nicknames are silly, but I like them.' Cornelia takes an undershirt and puts it over Nella's head and rigs her into a blue gown shot with silver. 'The Seigneur paid for this,' she says, her voice full of admiration. Nella's excitement at the gift quickly fades – the sleeves are too long, and however tightly Cornelia ties her in, her ribcage seems to shrink within the oversized corset.

'Madame Marin sent the seamstress your measurements,' Cornelia tuts, pulling the stays tighter and tighter, dismayed by the acres of ribbon left over. 'Your mother put them in a letter. What will I do with all this spare material?'

'The seamstress must have got it wrong,' says Nella, looking down at her swamped arms. 'I'm sure my mother knows my size.'

❦ 3.2 ❦

When Nella enters the dining room, Johannes is talking with Otto, murmuring over some lengthy documents. On seeing his wife he bows, an amused expression on his face. The colour of his eyes has solidified, from fish to flint. Marin sips lemon water, her eyes fixed on the gigantic map on the wall behind her brother's head, pieces of land suspended in gaping paper oceans.

'Thank you for my dress,' Nella manages to say. Otto moves to the corner and waits, hands full with Johannes' paperwork.

'This must be one of them,' replies Johannes. 'I ordered several. But it does not look as I imagined it would. Is it not a little large? Marin, is it not a little large?'

Marin takes a seat, tidying her napkin into a perfect white square, a loose tile on the black expanse of her lap.

'I fear it may be, Seigneur,' says Nella. The quiver in her voice is embarrassing. Where was it, along the line of communication between Assendelft and Amsterdam, that her bridal body was shrunk to parody? She looks at the map on the wall, determined not to pick at the ludicrous length of her sleeves. There is Nova Hollandia, palm trees fringing its coast, turquoise seas and ebony faces inviting the onlooker in.

'Never mind,' Johannes says, 'Cornelia will trim you down.' His hand wraps round a small glass of beer. 'Come and sit, eat something.'

A hardened loaf and a slim fish lie on a plate in the centre of the damask tablecloth. 'We are eating frugally this morning,' Marin explains, eyeing her brother's glass. 'A gesture of humility.'

'Or privation as a thrill,' Johannes murmurs, taking up a forkful of herring. The room is silent except for the sound of his gentle mastication, the bread a block between them, dry, untouched. Nella tries to swallow her fear, staring at her empty plate, noticing how the aura of sadness so quickly gathers around her husband. 'Think of the things you'll eat, Nella,' her brother Carel had said. 'I heard in Amsterdam they scoff strawberries dipped in gold.' Now how little impressed he'd be.

'Marin, have some of this fine ale,' Johannes says eventually.

'It gives me indigestion,' she replies.

'The Amsterdammer's diet of money and shame. You can't trust yourself. Go on, be defiant. Bravery in this city is so rare these days.'

'I just don't feel well.'

Johannes laughs at this, but Marin's face is pinched in humourless pain. 'Papist,' she says.

During the self-improving breakfast, Johannes does not apologize for failing to attend his new wife's arrival the day before. It is to his sister he talks, whilst Nella is forced to roll up her shirtsleeves in order not to drag them through her piece of oily fish. Otto is dismissed and he bows, his fingers clasped carefully around the sheaves of paper. 'See to it, Otto,' Johannes says. 'With my thanks.' Nella wonders whether the men Johannes trades with also have a servant like Otto, or whether he is the only one. She scrutinizes Otto's face for any expression of discomfort, but he seems sure and deft.

Bullion prices, paintings as currency, the carelessness of some of the cargo-packers moving his stock from Batavia – Marin devours Johannes' far tastier titbits. If he ever seems reluctant, Marin snatches them, an honour which might evaporate. She takes his snippets of tobacco sales, those of silk and coffee, of cinnamon and salt. He talks of the shogunate's new limitations of transporting gold and silver from Dejima, of the long-term damage this might cause, but how the VOC are determined that profit must come before pride.

Nella feels drunk with all this new information, but Marin's head seems steady. What news of the pepper treaty with the Sultan of Bantam, and what does that mean for the VOC? Johannes tells her of the clove-planters' rebellions in Ambon, their land over-populated with trees at the VOC's behest. When Marin demands the exact nature of their unrest, he grimaces. 'By now, the situation will have changed, Marin, and we'll know nothing.'

'And that, Johannes, is too often the problem.' She asks him about some silk due to a tailor in Lombardy. 'Who won the import right?'

'I forget,' he says.

'Who, Johannes? Who?'

'Henry Field. A merchant with the English East India,' he replies.

Marin thumps her fist. 'The *English*.' Johannes looks at her, saying nothing. 'Think of what this means, brother. *Think*. The last two years. Allowing it to wander to another man's purse. We haven't—'

'But the English buy up our Haarlem linen.'

'With their tight fists.'

'They say the same of us.'

From bullion to sultans via the English, Marin's lexicon is a serious astonishment. Johannes is surely crossing a forbidden boundary – for what other woman knows this much about the ins and outs of the VOC?

Nella feels quite invisible and ignored – it is her first day here and neither of them has asked her a single question, though at least the mercenary debate gives Nella an opportunity to inspect her new husband under lowered lids. That suntanned skin – she and Marin are ghostly in comparison. Nella imagines him with a pirate's hat, his ship beating the dark-blue waves of a faraway sea.

She goes further – picturing Johannes without his clothes, imagining the thing he has underneath the table waiting for her. Her mother has told her what wives can hope for – a rising rod of pain, the chance it won't go on too long, the wet clam dribble between your legs. There are enough rams and ewes in Assendelft to know exactly what happens. 'I don't want to be just that kind of wife,' she told her mother. 'There is no other kind,' came the reply. Seeing her daughter's expression, Mrs Oortman had softened slightly, taking Nella in her arms and patting her stomach. 'Your body is the key, my love. Your body is the key.' When Nella asked what exactly she was supposed to unlock, and how, her mother had demurred. 'You'll have a roof over your head, thanks be to God.'

For fear the other two might see these memories cross her face, Nella stares at her plate. 'Enough about all that,' Marin says. Nella jumps, as if her sister-in-law has read her mind. Johannes is still talking about the English, swilling the amber ale at the bottom of his glass.

'Have you spoken to Frans Meermans about his wife's sugar?' Marin interrupts. His silence makes her grim. 'It's just *sitting* in the warehouse, Johannes. It arrived from Surinam over a week ago and you still haven't told them what you're going to do with it. They're waiting.'

Johannes puts down his glass. 'Your interest in Agnes Meermans' new wealth surprises me,' he says.

'I'm not worried about her wealth. I know how Agnes wants to breach these walls.'

'Always your suspicions! She wants me to distribute her sugar because she knows I'm the best.'

'Well, sell it and be done with them. Remember what is at stake.'

'But of all the things I might sell, you push for this! What about *lekkerheid*, Marin – the craving craze for all things sweet

– what might your Pastor say?' Johannes turns to his wife. 'My sister thinks sugar is not good for the soul, Nella, but she wants me to sell it anyway. What do you make of that?'

Nella, remembering her rebuffed request for marzipan, feels grateful for his sudden attention. Souls and purses, she thinks, these two are obsessed with souls and purses.

'I'm merely keeping my head above the flood,' Marin says, her voice tight. 'I fear my God, Johannes. Do you?' Marin grips her fork like a small trident. 'Please just sell the sugar, brother. It is to our advantage that there is no Guild of Sugar-sellers. Our own prices, to whom we want. Get rid of it and soon. It would be best.'

Johannes stares at the untouched loaf still resting in the middle of the damask. Nella's stomach rumbles and she clutches it instinctively as if her hand will keep it quiet. 'Otto would not approve of our new kind of free trade,' Johannes says, his eyes flicking to the door.

Marin drives her fork tines into the damask cloth. 'He's a Dutchman. A pragmatist. He's never even seen a cane plantation.'

'He nearly did.'

'He understands our *business* as well as we do.' Her grey eyes bore into his. 'Wouldn't you agree?'

'Do not speak for him,' Johannes says. 'He works for me, not you. And this tablecloth cost thirty guilders, so kindly stop making holes in everything I own.'

'I was at the docks,' Marin snaps. 'The burgomasters drowned three men yesterday morning, one after the other. Hung weights on their necks. Put them in sacks and threw them in the water.'

Somewhere in the hallway, a plate clatters. 'Rezeki, bad dog!' comes Cornelia's cry, but Nella notices both Johannes' dogs are in the corner of this room, fast asleep. Johannes closes his eyes, and Nella wonders how drowning men have anything to do with stocks of sugar, or Otto's opinions, or Agnes Meermans trying to breach their walls.

'I know how a man drowns,' he murmurs. 'You seem to forget I've had to spend most of my life on the sea.'

There is a warning in Johannes' voice, but Marin keeps going. 'I asked the man clearing the dockside why the burgomasters had drowned them. He said they didn't have the guilders to appease their God.'

Breathless, she stops. Johannes seems almost bereft, sagging in his chair. 'I thought God forgives all, Marin?' he says. He doesn't seem to want an answer to his question.

The air is hot, the atmosphere a bruise. Red-faced, Cornelia appears and clears the plates, and Johannes rises from his chair. The three women look at him expectantly, but he moves out of the room, batting the air with his hand. Marin and Cornelia seem to know what this means, Marin taking up the book she has brought with her to breakfast. Nella eyes the title – Hooft's play, *True Fool*.

'How often does he go away?' Nella asks.

Marin puts the book down, tutting in displeasure as a page bends the wrong way on the table. 'My brother leaves. He comes back. He leaves again,' she sighs. 'You'll see. It's not difficult. Anyone could do it.'

'I didn't ask if it was difficult. And who is Frans Meermans?'

'Cornelia, how is Petronella's parakeet this morning?' Marin asks.

'He's well, Madame. Well.' Cornelia avoids Nella's eye. Today there are no giggles, no sly remarks. She seems tired, as if something is bothering her.

'He needs clean air,' says Nella. 'The kitchen must be so full of cooking fumes. I'd like to fly him round my room.'

'He'll peck at something valuable,' says Marin.

'He won't.'

'He'll fly out of the window.'

'I'll keep it closed.'

Marin slams her book shut and walks out. The maid straightens, narrowing her blue eyes in her mistress's wake. After a moment's hesitation, she too leaves the room. Nella slumps back in her chair, staring sightlessly into Johannes' map. The door is still open, and she can hear Marin and Johannes whispering outside the study.

'For the love of Christ, Marin. Have you got nothing better to do?'

'You've a wife now. Where are you going?'

'I also have a business.'

'What business do you have on a Sunday?'

'Marin, do you think this house is run by magic? I'm going to check the sugar.'

'I don't believe you,' Marin hisses. 'I won't allow this.' Nella feels the tension condensing between the siblings, a second, silent language filling to the brim.

'What other man lets his sister speak to him like this? Your word is not the law.'

'Perhaps. But it's closer than you think.'

Johannes strides out of the front door, and Nella hears the velvet suck of air, the outside once more shut away. She peers round the door and observes her new sister-in-law in the hallway. Marin has covered her face, and her shoulders hunch; a pose of misery.

Trompe l'Œil

As Marin turns upstairs and her footsteps echo away, Nella creeps down to the lower ground floor, where Peebo clicks for his mistress. To her surprise, Peebo's cage is now hanging in the best kitchen. No cooking takes place here – that exertion is saved for the working kitchen, across the corridor. The best kitchen is a room used solely to display the Brandt collection of China-ware, free of spattering pots and pans, the walls unstained. Nella wonders how long Peebo has been breathing clean air, and more intriguingly, who committed this act of charity.

Otto sits at a small side table, slowly buffing the silver cutlery they will be using for dinner. He is not tall, but his shoulders are wide and he looks too big for his chair. On seeing her at the threshold, he points towards Peebo's cage. 'He's a noisy little thing,' he says.

'I'm sorry. I'd have him in my room—'

'I like his noise.'

'Oh. Good. Thank you for putting him there.'

'It wasn't me, Madame.'

Madame. It feels lovely when he says it. His shirt is immaculate, neatly pressed, no loose threads or stains. His arms beneath the calico move with unconscious grace. How old is he? Thirty, perhaps a little younger. His boots shine like a general's. Everything about him is so fresh, so unfamiliar. To be called Madame in her own house by a servant in such perfect clothes is suddenly the apogee of her very being. Her heart swells with gratitude but Otto doesn't seem to notice.

Blushing, Nella walks to the cage and begins to stroke her parakeet through the bars. Peebo makes a gentle ick-ick sound, and runs his beak through his feathers as though in search of something.

'Where's he from?' Otto asks.

'I don't know. My uncle bought him.'

'Not born from an egg in Assendelft, then?'

Nella shakes her head. Nothing so bright and otherly would ever be born in Assendelft. She feels awkward but giddy – Otto knows the name of her village. What would her mother, the grandfathers in the town square, the little schoolchildren, make of this man?

As Otto picks up a fork and runs a soft cloth through each of the tines, Nella presses on the cage bars until her fingertips turn white, craning her neck as she follows the polished wall tiles, right up to the ceiling. Someone has painted a trick of the eye upon it – a glass dome pushes up beyond the plaster towards an impossible sky.

'Seigneur Brandt had that made,' says Otto, following the direction of her gaze.

'It's clever.'

'It's a trick,' he replies. 'It'll peel off soon enough in the damp.'

'But Marin told me that this house is dry. And that pedigree counts for nothing.'

Otto smiles. 'Then she and I must disagree.'

Nella wonders to which of Marin's two statements Otto is referring. She surveys the enormous shelves built into the wall, where three huge glass panes protect various plates and pieces of porcelain. She has never seen such a large collection. At home, they had a small array of Delftware and little else, for most of it had to be sold.

'The Seigneur's world in a set of plates,' says Otto. Nella listens, trying to tell his voice for pride or envy, but hearing neither. Otto's tone is studiedly neutral. 'Delft, Dejima, China,' he goes on. 'Spanning the seas in crockery.'

'Isn't my husband rich enough for someone to travel for him?'

Otto frowns at the knife blade he's buffing. 'You have to keep your wealth afloat and no one will do it for you. It'll run through your fingers if you don't take care.' He finishes, folding his soft cloth into a neat square.

'So he works hard?'

Otto makes a spiral motion with his finger, to the fake glass dome above their heads, toward the illusion of depth. 'His shares have gone up and up.'

'And what happens when they get to the top?'

'What always happens, Madame. Things will spill over.'

'And then?'

'Why then,' he says, 'I suppose we sink or swim.' Picking up a large soup spoon, Otto looks at his warped features shrunk into the convex silver.

'Do you go with him to sea?'

'No.'

'Why not? You are his servant.'

'I no longer sail.'

Nella wonders how long he's lived upon this man-made land, shored up from the marshes with deep polders and determination. Marin called him a Dutchman. 'The Seigneur's spirit belongs on the seas,' Otto says. 'And mine does not, Madame.'

Nella pulls her hand out of Peebo's cage and takes a seat next to the fireplace. 'How do you know so much about my husband's spirit?'

'Haven't I ears and eyes?'

Nella is startled. Such boldness was not expected – but then Cornelia too feels this free to speak her mind. 'Of course you do, I—'

'The sea is something the land can never be, Madame,' Otto says. 'No patch stays the same.'

'Otto.'

There is Marin, standing at the doorway. Otto rises, his cutlery laid out like an arsenal of gleaming weapons. 'He's working,' Marin says to Nella. 'With much to do.'

'I was only asking him about the Seigneur's—'

'Leave that, Otto,' Marin says. 'You need to send those scrolls.'

Marin turns away and disappears. 'Madame,' Otto whispers to Nella under the receding footfall. 'Would you kick a hive? It'll only get you stung.'

Nella cannot tell if this is a piece of advice or an order. 'I'd keep that cage shut, Madame,' he adds, nodding at Peebo. She listens to his step up the kitchen stairs; perfectly measured and soft.

The Gift

For the next two nights in the house, Nella waits for Johannes to put his hands on her and start her life anew. She leaves her bedroom door ajar, the key hanging off the thick oak panel – but when she wakes in the morning, it is, like her, untouched. He seems to be working late. At night, she hears the front door creak open, and often in the early morning when the sun cracks low along the sky. The dull light seeps into her eyes as she sits up, followed by the realization she is yet again alone.

Once dressed, Nella wanders aimlessly around the rooms on the ground and first floors. At the back of the house, further away from any possible guests, the rooms are plainer, for all grandeur has been saved up for the ones whose windows overlook the street. These front chambers seem at their most beautiful when no one is in them, wearing their furniture down or placing muddy footprints on their polished floors.

She pokes her head round marble pillars and empty fire-places, roving an untrained eye over the paintings – so many paintings! Ships with crucifix-like masts rising to the sky, hot-looking landscapes, more dying flowers, upturned skulls like brown root vegetables, broken-stringed viols, sprawling taverns and dancers, gold plates, enamelled seashell cups. To stare quickly at them all has a sickening effect. The gold-leaf leather wallpaper on the walls still smells vaguely of pig, reminding her of the Assendelft farmyards. Turning away, unwilling to be reminded of a place she thought she was so keen to leave behind – Nella is confronted with vast Bible tapestries hanging from the panels; Mary and Martha with Jesus, the wedding at Cana, clever Noah and his sturdy ark.

In the best kitchen, Nella notices Johannes' two lutes that Cornelia keeps polished and hanging on the tiles. Reaching up to take one off its hook, Nella jumps with shock, for a restraining hand is already on her shoulder.

'It's not for playing,' snaps Marin. 'It's a piece of craftsmanship that will be ruined by your plucking.'

'Are you following me?' When Marin does not reply, Nella taps the lutes. 'Their strings are sagging. From lack of care.'

She turns on her heel and stalks upstairs. Marin's room at the end of the first floor corridor has remained unexplored, and she eyes its distant keyhole, wondering what bare cell must lie within. Her fury almost propels her in. Who is Marin to tell her no? She is the mistress of this house, after all.

But Nella goes back to her own room, instead staring in dismay at the bloodstained feathers of the painted birds, their lizardish beaks and curving nostrils. Good God, Marin even hates music! Doesn't she know that lutes weren't made to hang up on a wall?

Marin will usually not converse with her unless it is an instruction, or a homily plucked out of the family Bible, usually designed to crush. When she gathers the household in the hallway to hear passages from the Holy Book, Nella is surprised to see this is Marin's job. At home, when her father was sober he undertook it – and now Carel, aged thirteen and well practised, reads to his sisters and mother.

Other times, Marin sits on a green velvet chair in the salon, working on her ledger book. Nella's new sister-in-law seems so diligent with the household accounts, the vertical columns a natural stave for her, the numbers her musical notes where their money trips a silent melody. Nella wants to ask more about her husband's business, about Frans and Agnes Meermans' sugar, but conversation with Marin is never easy.

On the third day, however, she creeps into the salon where Marin is sitting, head bent as if in prayer. The household ledger is, as usual, open on her lap.

'Marin?'

Nella has not used Marin's first name to her face before; she feels the strange raw daring of it, her stab at intimacy falling short.

'Yes?' Marin snaps her head up. She makes a show of resting her pen upon the open pages, placing her hands on the elaborate leaf carving of the chair. From the hard look in Marin's grey eyes, Nella supposes that the exchange over the lute is not forgotten; feeling the scrutiny of her sister-in-law's gaze, her panic rises. A blot of ink has leaked from Marin's nib.

'Will it always be like this?' Nella blurts.

The bald question charges the atmosphere, stiffening Marin's spine. 'Like *what*?'

'I – never see him.'

'If you mean Johannes, I can assure you, he exists.'

'Where is it that he works?' Nella shifts the conversation to where Marin must give her a more solid answer. Her question has an almost stranger effect than the first; Marin's face becomes a mask.

'In several places,' Marin replies, her voice controlled and tight. 'The bourse, the docks, the VOC offices on the Old Hoogstraat.'

'And – what exactly does he do in these places?'

'If I knew that, Petronella—'

'But you do know. I know you know—'

'He turns mud to gold. Water to guilders,' Marin snaps. 'He sells other men's stock at better prices. He fills his ships and puts them out to sea. He thinks he's everybody's favourite. That's all I know. Pass me the brazier, my feet are like icebergs.'

Nella believes that may be the longest string of sentences Marin has ever spoken to her. 'You could always light a fire,' she replies, shunting one of the small hot braziers towards Marin, who secures it with a stamping foot. 'I'd like to see where he works. I will go and visit him soon.'

Marin closes the ledger book, the pen still trapped inside, and stares at its battered leather cover. 'I wouldn't do that.'

Nella knows she should stop asking questions, because she only gets told no. But she cannot help herself. 'Why not?'

'He's busy.'

'Marin—'

'Surely your mother told you it would be like this?' Marin cries. 'You haven't married the local notary.'

'But Johannes—'

'Petronella! He has to work. And you had to marry someone.'

'You haven't. *You* haven't married anyone.'

Marin's jaw tightens and Nella feels a little spark of triumph.

'No,' Marin replies. 'But I've always had everything I wanted.'

❦

The next morning, Marin chooses a proverb, a brimstone story from Job, and finishes with the clear waters of Luke.

> *But woe unto you that are rich! for ye have received your*
> *consolation.*
>
> *Woe unto you that are full! for ye shall hunger.*
>
> *Woe unto you that laugh now! for ye shall mourn and weep.'*

She's quick about it, unmusical, as if embarrassed to hear her own voice ringing out over those interminable black and white tiles, her hands holding the lectern like a raft. Nella shifts her eyes up as her sister-in-law intones, wondering why Marin is still here, unmarried, no gold band enclosing her finger. Perhaps there was no man with heart stout enough to take the battering? Nella relishes the pleasure of a vicious thought.

Is *this* my new family? she asks herself. It seems impossible that any of these people have ever laughed except for a hidden giggle in a sleeve. Cornelia's chores seem endless. If she is not downstairs boiling a sturgeon, she's polishing the oak and rosewood furniture, or sweeping the acres of floor upstairs, beating the sheets, polishing pane upon pane upon pane of glass. Everyone knows that toil makes you virtuous – that it keeps all good Dutch from the grasp of slovenly and dangerous luxury – and yet, something about Cornelia does not seem so pure.

43

Otto has a thoughtful expression on his face as he listens to the words. Catching Nella's eye, he looks hastily away. Human contact in such a moment of spiritual reflection does seem almost sinful. Johannes chooses to clasp his hands into a fist of prayer, his eyes upon the door.

Nella returns to her room and attempts to write a letter to her mother, explaining her predicament. But the words she chooses withhold their best qualities, they refuse to match the way she feels inside. Nella cannot describe her bafflement, her exchanges with Marin, her husband who speaks in all tongues save that of love – nor the servants whose worlds are hidden, whose laughter is another language too. Instead she doodles names – *Johannes*, *Otto*, *Toot*, and draws a picture of Marin with a giant head, screwing up the paper in a ball and throwing it short of the fire.

An hour later, the sounds of men's voices, barking dogs and Johannes' laughter come up the main staircase. Nella looks out of the window onto the canal path and sees three strong journeymen with ropes slung over their shoulders. They are stepping out of the house, their sleeves rolled up.

By the time Nella has left her room, Marin is already in the hall. 'Johannes,' she hisses. 'What on earth have you *done*?'

Nella moves quietly along the landing, and gasps when she sees what the three men have left in the hallway.

In the middle of the tiles is a cabinet – an enormous, looming structure, measuring nearly half Johannes' height again; a huge cupboard supported by eight curved and sturdy feet, two mustard-coloured velvet curtains drawn across its front.

Having shunted the Bible lectern into the corner to make room, Johannes stands by its side. One hand rests upon it; he gazes up at the gleaming wood, his smile unrelenting. He seems refreshed, more handsome than Nella has ever seen him.

Marin approaches the cabinet with caution, as if it might fall on her, or start to move of its own accord. Rezeki backs away with a deep growl. 'Is this a joke?' asks Marin. 'How much did it cost?'

'For once, sister, let us not talk of money,' Johannes says. 'You told me to find a distraction—'

'Not a monstrosity. Is that *saffron* dye in those curtains?'

'A distraction?' Nella echoes, standing on the stairs. Marin spins round to face her, her expression aghast.

'Something for you,' Johannes calls. 'A wedding gift.' He pats the side of the cabinet, and its curtains seem to twitch.

'What is it, Seigneur?'

'Made of oak and elm. Elm is strong,' Johannes says, as if this is the explanation his new wife has been waiting for. He looks at Marin. 'It's used for coffins.'

Marin's mouth sets in a thin line. 'Where did you get it, Johannes?'

Johannes shrugs. 'A man at the docks said he had some cabinets left over from a dead carpenter's business. I had it improved with a tortoiseshell veneer and pewter inlays.'

'Why have you done this?' Marin says. 'Petronella has no need of such a thing.'

'It's for her education,' Johannes replies.

'My what?'

Johannes reaches out for Rezeki but the dog bucks away from her master. 'Hush, girl. Hush.'

'She doesn't like it,' says Cornelia, who has followed Nella down the stairs. Nella wonders whether Cornelia is referring to her or the dog. Both of us, by the look of it, she thinks, watching Rezeki's hackles rise. Cornelia holds her broom like a staff in front of herself, as if expecting an attack.

'Education?' Marin scoffs. 'What does Petronella need with education?'

'I should say she has very great need,' Johannes says.

No I don't, thinks Nella. I'm eighteen, not *eight*. 'But what is it, Seigneur?' she asks, trying to hide her dismay.

Finally, Johannes reaches for the curtains, and with an extravagant flourish, he pulls them aside. The women gasp. The inside of the cabinet is revealed, divided into nine sections, some lined with gold-embossed wallpaper and others with wooden panels.

'Is it – this house?' Nella says.

'It's your house,' Johannes corrects her, pleased.

'It's a lot easier to manage,' says Cornelia, craning to see into the upper rooms.

The accuracy of the cabinet is eerie, as if the real house has been shrunk, its body sliced in two and its organs revealed. The nine rooms, from the working kitchen, the salon, up to the loft where the peat and firewood are stored away from damp, are perfect replicas. 'It's got a hidden cellar too,' Johannes says, lifting the floor up between the working and best kitchens, to reveal a concealed empty space. The ceiling in the best kitchen has even been painted with an identical trick of the eye. Nella remembers her conversation with Otto. *Things will spill over*, he'd said, pointing his finger to that unreal dome.

Rezeki growls and circles the cabinet. 'How much was this, Johannes?' Marin demands.

'The frame was two thousand,' he says placidly. 'The curtains brought it to three.'

'Three thousand guilders? Three *thousand*? Invested properly, a family could live off that for years.'

'Marin, *you* have never lived off two thousand guilders in one year, for all your herring dinners. And with Meermans' deal, what is there to worry about?'

'Well, if you were doing something about it, I wouldn't be worrying—'

'For once in your life, *be quiet*.'

Marin reluctantly stands away from the wooden construction. Otto appears from the kitchen and eyes the new arrival with interest. Johannes seems slightly deflated, as if sensing his gesture is beginning to backfire.

The tortoiseshell casing reminds Nella of autumn in Assendelft, oranges and browns caught in motion, of Carel taking her by the hands and spinning her around beneath the garden trees. Pewter has indeed been embedded through like metal veins, fine and flowing over the entire surface, even the legs. There is an odd thrill in the wood and shell. Even the touch of the velvet curtains suggests a certain power.

In Assendelft, Nella knew richer children who'd been given cabinet houses, but none so grand as this. Before her father had drunk away their money there might have been a chance she'd have one too – smaller than this, a practice-instrument so she might learn to manage her larders, her linen, her servants and furnishings. Now she's married, she'd like to think there is no need.

Nella catches Johannes watching her. 'The hallway floor is identical,' she offers, gesturing beneath their feet to where the black and white tiles span out. She places her finger delicately on the correspondent, miniature squares.

'Italian marble,' says Johannes.

'I don't like it,' says Marin. 'And neither does Rezeki.'

Johannes snaps. 'Well, that's a bitch's taste.'

Marin's face flames red, and she storms to the front door, slamming it behind her.

'Where's she going?' asks Cornelia, sounding panicked. She and Otto watch their mistress's progress from the front window.

'I thought it would be a good surprise,' Johannes says.

'But, Seigneur,' says Nella. 'What must I do with it?'

Johannes looks at her, slightly blank. He rubs the velvet curtains between forefinger and thumb before drawing them shut. 'You'll think of something.'

Johannes disappears into his study with the click of a lock. Otto and Cornelia make a quick descent to the lower ground floor, towards the working kitchen. Alone except for Rezeki whimpering around the hallway walls, Nella considers her gift. Her heart sinks. I am too old for this, she thinks. Who will see this piece of work, who will be able to sit on those chairs, or eat the waxen food? She has no friends, no family in this city to come and exclaim at it – it is a monument to her power-lessness, her arrested womanhood. *It's your house*, her husband had said – but who can live in tiny rooms, these nine dead ends? What sort of man buys a gift like this, however majestic its casing, however beautifully made?

'I don't need to be educated,' she says out loud. Rezeki whines. 'Nothing to be frightened of,' Nella tells her. 'It's just a toy.' Perhaps the curtains could be cut into a hat, she thinks, pulling them apart.

As Nella stands before the exposed interior, it begins to make her uneasy. Its hollow carapace of elm and tortoiseshell seems to watch her back as if its rooms are eyes. From the working kitchen she can hear raised voices – Cornelia talking most, Otto's quieter replies. She places a tentative hand over the wood again. It has a cooling effect compared to the velvet, hard as polished stone.

With Marin out and those two downstairs in the working kitchen, I could fetch Peebo and give him a fly, Nella thinks. Johannes wouldn't notice, and it would be good to see my Peeblet soar. But as she turns from the cabinet towards the main staircase, her thoughts catch again on Marin's distant keyhole, upstairs at the corridor's end. Forget this insult of a dolls' house, Nella cajoles herself, drawing its mustard-coloured curtains shut. You can go wherever you like.

Blood thumping, leaving Johannes' present stranded on the tiles, Nella makes her way upstairs towards Marin's room, Peebo quite forgotten. But her hallway bravado begins to feel flimsy. What if I'm caught? she wonders, her imagination surging once again as she scuttles along the corridor as quick as her skirts will allow. What happens to me then?

But Nella pushes open the heavy door and on the edge of Marin's sanctuary, she is caught short, the extraordinary sight within vanquishing all caution.

Trespasses

Still on the threshold, Nella cannot believe what she is seeing. Nun-small, the room's contents could fill a convent. She wonders how willingly Marin gave up the dimensions of her old chamber for this overflowing cell of fantasy.

Dangling from the ceiling is the shed skin of a huge snake, draped like a pennant, papery to touch. Plumes of all patterns and shapes, once attached to the most exotic of birds, brush against her outstretched fingers. Instinctively Nella looks for a green feather, relieved to find none that resemble Peebo's. A butterfly, wider than her palm, is pinned to the wall, the sky blue of its wings overwritten with swirls of black. The room is full of smells. The strongest is of nutmeg, but there is also a sandalwood tang, and clove and pepper imbuing the very walls, such scents of heat and warning.

Nella moves further in. Along the simple wooden shelves is a miscellany of yellowing animal skulls, belonging to creatures she can't even guess at – long jaws, snub craniums, strong, sharp teeth. Beetle carapaces, shiny as coffee beans, iridescent in the light, glow black with a tinge of red. An upturned tortoise shell rocks gently at her touch. Dried plants and berries, seed pods, seeds themselves – the source of these intoxicating scents – are everywhere. This room is not from Amsterdam, though it shows an Amsterdammer's drive for acquisition. This is the republic's reach, in four small walls.

There is a map of the African continent, huge, so much unknown. Ringed in the centre of the western coastline is a place called Porto-Novo. There are questions written over it, in Marin's neat hand. *Weather? Food? God?* There is a map of the Indies, with many more circles and arrows, marking from where the flora and fauna found in this room have come. *Molucca 1676, Batavia 1679, Java 1682* – all voyages Marin has surely never made herself.

On the table by the window is an open notebook, and it appears to contain a detailed categorization of all these things. Marin's handwriting flows better than her speech, and Nella recognizes it from the envelope that was sent to her mother earlier this year. She feels again the trespasser's tension – desperate to stay and find out more, but dreading the trap she has wilfully set herself. I'm no more mistress of this house than little Arabella back in Assendelft, she thinks.

Further along the shelf is a strange-looking lamp, with the wings of a bird and a woman's head and breasts. Nella reaches out to touch its cool, thick metal. Next to the lamp is a pile of books, and their pages emanate a loamy mix of damp and pigskin. Nella lifts the top one off the pile, too curious about Marin's reading habits to think about anyone coming up the stairs.

The first book is a travel journal entitled *The Unfortunate Voyage of the Ship Batavia*. Most people in the United Provinces are familiar with the story of Corneliszoon's mutiny, the infamous onboard enslavement of Lucretia Jans and her implication in the murders of survivors. Nella is no exception, but her mother hated the more salacious aspects of the story. 'It's because of that Jans woman that ladies no longer sail so much, and a good thing too,' Nella's father had observed when he was still alive. 'Women on board bring bad luck.'

'They only bring the luck men give them,' Mrs Oortman had retorted.

Nella closes the book, puts it back and runs her fingers delicately over the uneven bump and jut of the spines. There are so many books here – and as much as she would like to read all the titles, she knows she cannot dawdle. Marin must spend a good guilder on this habit, Nella supposes, rubbing the luxurious paper.

Beneath *The Unfortunate Voyage* is a book by Heinsius, who everyone knows is banished from the country for manslaughter. It is almost a crime to own it, and the fact that Marin has a copy astonishes Nella. There is also a folio edition of Saeghman's *Almanac*, *Children's Diseases* by Stephanus Blankaart and Bontekoe's *The Memorable Accounts of the Voyage of the Nieuw Hoorn*. Nella flicks through. Bontekoe's accounts are tales of voyage and peril, full of brilliant woodcuts, ribs of shipwrecks, great sunrises and swallowing seas. One woodcut depicts a shoreline, waves in the background cushioning a large vessel. In the foreground, two men face each other. The first man has his arms and legs filled in with fine black lines, a ring through his nose and a spear in his hand. The other is dressed in the old-fashioned style of a Dutchman. Their expressions are the same, however. Impassive, trapped in their own closed orb of experience, the gap between them wider than the sea beyond.

The spine is flexible, the book has been used often. As Nella moves to put it back on the pile, a piece of paper covered in writing falls from its middle pages. She scoops it from the floor and the words charge her blood.

I love you. I love you. From back to front, I love you.

Nella feels a tingling sensation in the roof of her mouth. In a daze, she puts the book back, unable to let go of the extraordinary note. There are more words on the scrap of paper – hasty, dancing words not in Marin's handwriting.

You are sunlight through a window, which I stand in, warmed. One touch lasts a thousand hours. My darling—

Pain shoots through Nella's arm – someone grips it tightly and won't let go. Marin looms, white-faced, turning Nella around like a rag doll. The note flutters to the floor, and Nella covers it with her foot as Marin drags her away. 'Did you look at my books?' Marin hisses. 'Did you?'

'No – I—'

'Yes you did. Did you open them?'

'Of course not—'

Marin adjusts her grip, her hand shaking from the pressure. 'Marin—' Nella gasps. 'It hurts. You're hurting me.'

For a couple more seconds, Marin does not let go, then Nella wrenches herself free. 'I'll tell my husband,' she shouts. 'I'll show him what you've done!'

'We don't like traitors,' Marin hisses. 'Go. *Now.*'

Nella stumbles away, straight into the snakeskin in her hurry to escape. 'These things don't belong to you!' Marin calls after her. She slams her door and the scent of spice evaporates.

Safely on the island of her own bed, Nella murmurs to her pillow, her mouth dry and mind incredulous. *One touch lasts a thousand hours.* That ink was secret nectar, for Marin isn't married.

The writing was scrawled but Nella is sure it was not Marin's. I should never have gone in there, she thinks. Perhaps Marin was even waiting in the darkness, to catch me in the act? She imagines her sister-in-law stringing her up on one of the ceiling beams, pattens falling off her swinging feet among the feathers, her cold body warmed by poetic sunlight through a window.

Marin starts to shift in Nella's mind. From her drab black clothes, Marin rises like a phoenix, enveloped in her nutmeg scent – no lily for her, no floral nicety. Covered in the symbols of the city, Marin is a daughter of its power – she is a secret surveyor of maps, an annotator of specimens – an annotator of something else as well, not so easy to slot into a category. Nella imagines the smell of spice on Marin's skin, hearing her across the damask tablecloth, telling her brother exactly how to trade. Who is this woman? *From back to front, I love you.*

The next day, just before dawn, she tiptoes down into the best kitchen. The house is wrapped in quiet – even Otto and Cornelia are still asleep. Unhesitant, determined, Nella scoops up Peebo's cage. She takes him to her room, thinking of those hanging feathers, convinced that from now on she must keep her parakeet close.

Smit's List

Above Nella's head, Peebo flaps and chirrups in delight around her room, his black eyes glittering. 'Marin might behead you,' she tells her little bird, drawing her shawl close against the morning chill, trying the threat for size. In daylight, it now seems ridiculous, but the rules of this house are written in water. I must either sink or swim, Nella thinks. Her bruise, day-old, like a small splash of wine, truly hurts when she presses it. It is staggering, really. Does Johannes not see his sister? He has done nothing to tame Marin, despite her obvious dislike of his new bride.

A sharp knock at the door makes Nella's stomach flip. 'Come in,' she says, irritated by how apprehensive she sounds.

Marin appears on the threshold, looking pale. Nella stands and drops her shawl to expose the darkening mark. Stiffening, Marin stares instead at the parakeet, now perched on the end of the bed. She has a book clutched close to her chest, and her slender fingers tighten round it.

'I will keep him in my room,' Nella says.

'Here,' is all Marin's reply, her voice cracked, hand outstretched, offering the book.

'What is it?'

'*Smit's List*. A register of all craftspeople and businesses in this city.'

'And why would I need *Smit's List*?' Nella asks, prising it from Marin's grasp.

'To decorate your house.'

'Which one, Marin?'

'If you leave that cabinet empty, you'll turn Johannes' gift into a crime of profligacy. You must do something with it.'

'I don't have to do anything—'

'Here,' Marin rushes on, 'these are promissory notes with my brother's stamp and signature.' She pulls out a sheaf from the book, her fingers tangling them in a fluster. 'Any seller you buy from can take their note to the Stadhuis and have it exchanged. You just fill in the amount and countersign.' Marin extends the promissory notes towards Nella as if she's keeping the devil at bay. 'No more than a thousand guilders per note.'

'Why are you doing this, Marin? I thought the Bible says it doesn't pay to flaunt your wealth,' Nella says, but she feels excited about the money. She is not as far as she would like to be from that awful day when her papa died, when Arabella found nothing in the coin jar but a button and an upturned spider. Marin would never understand such relief, she thinks.

'Just take them, Petronella.'

Aggression spreads between them, a familiar stain. When Nella duly lifts the promissory notes from Marin's hand, she notices how miserable her sister-in-law looks. If this is a game, we've both lost, she thinks, but as she rubs her fingers over the notes she can feel their invisible power.

'And what will my husband say about this?'

Exhaustion blooms on Marin's face. 'Don't worry. My brother knows the danger of having nothing to do.'

❦

After Marin has gone, Nella attempts to put all thought of her sister-in-law and the love note aside. She carries *Smit's List* to her writing desk and opens it up. The book is neatly laid out in alphabetical order of trade. Apothecaries, astronomers, chandlers, chocolate-makers, librettists and locksmiths are but some of the sundry craftsmen paying Marcus Smit a fee to appear. The advertisements are self-penned, with no restriction on how they are written.

Outside her window, the canal is full of life. Boatmen call to one another about the winter nip in the air, on a far-off corner a bread-seller cries his wares, and two children holler with a hoop and stick. Within, however, all is quiet and still, the only sound in her room the light tock of the golden pendulum. As Nella continues to flick through the book, an entry under *M* catches her eye:

MINIATURIST
Residing at the sign of the sun, on Kalverstraat
Originally from Bergen
Trained with the great Bruges clockmaker, Lucas Windelbreke
ALL, AND YET NOTHING

It is the only entry under *Miniaturist*, and Nella likes its brevity, its odd ring. She has no idea where Bergen is, nor what a miniaturist does, nor indeed that clockmakers could be considered great. The miniaturist is certainly not from Amsterdam, that much is clear. Therefore he cannot be a member of its city guilds – and it is illegal to undertake work for which registered citizens could earn money. Her father taught her that. He was from Leiden, and claimed the draconian guild laws were more to blame for his downfall than the flagons of beer. Not that there can be a guild for miniaturists, surely? Nella is surprised the advertisement is in *Smit's List* at all.

Free from the pressure of Marin's presence, Nella can feel her defiance solidifying. Marin didn't even apologize for pinching her as if she were a naughty child. Marin, with her maps and bossiness, Johannes and his ever-closing door, Cornelia and Otto – their shared sanctuary, their silent language of chopping, polishing, the slop of mop and flash of knife—

Nella jumps up, desperate to be rid of her own thoughts, what Marin calls the danger of having nothing to do. She cannot care for the cabinet – it is an insult to her womanhood. And yet, when she fans the promissory notes, she's never seen so much potential money in her entire life.

As Peebo circles Johannes' expensive paintings, Nella takes up her pen at the desk and explodes her fury in a burst of scrawl:

Dear Sir,

I have seen your advertisement in Smit's List, *and wish to solicit your help.*

I have a house of nine rooms, on a miniature scale, that is to be displayed in a cabinet. I venture these three requests to you and await your response. I cannot guess but that you are trained in the art of small things. The list is by no means exhaustive, and I am amply able to pay.

Item: One lute, with strings

Item: One betrothal cup, filled with confetti

Item: One box of marzipan

In advance gratitude,

Petronella Brandt, at the sign of the dolphin, Herengracht

Her new surname seems so truncated, so brusque compared to the one she's had for eighteen years. Writing it still feels uncomfortable, like donning a particular costume that's hers but doesn't fit. She crosses it out and puts instead the words *Thank you, Nella Oortman*. He'll notice that, Nella thinks. And he'll probably laugh. She tucks the letter into her pocket along with a promissory note of three hundred guilders, and goes down to the working kitchen to see if she can quickly swipe a late breakfast from Cornelia's scarred worktop. A roll, a slice of meat, anything but herring.

Cornelia appears to be stuffing a goose with a carrot, not scrimping on the brutality of insertion. Behind her, Otto is sharpening pins and using them to prick holes in walnuts. Nella wonders why he's doing it, but doesn't ask, supposing that the answer will be his usual generous evasion. Over the fire, a sauce bubbles. Cornelia and Otto look for all the world like a married couple in their cottage, handling their daily meal. Again, Nella feels their comfortable closeness, and it makes her wretched. She grips the letter in her pocket, trying to gain strength from her subversion of Johannes and Marin's attempt to tame their new arrival. Oh, I will decorate my house, Marin, Nella thinks – with all the things that you detest.

'Does it hurt, Madame?' Cornelia asks, carrot peelings now suspended in her hands like muddy orange streamers.

Nella pulls her shawl around her. 'What do you mean?'

'Your arm.'

'Were you *spying*?'

Otto glances at Cornelia, but the maid laughs. 'She's like a crab coming out of her shell for a nip, Madame! We ignore it and so should you.' Cornelia lays the peelings down. 'You took your bird,' she says, looking almost impressed. 'I'll tell you a thing. Madame Marin only wears black, but underneath's a different story.'

'What do you mean?'

'Cornelia,' Otto says, a warning in his voice.

'The *lining*,' Cornelia carries on, seemingly determined to offer Nella this crumb. 'Sable fur and velvet, under every dress. My mistress – who quotes us Ezekiel – "*I will put an end to the pride of the mighty*" – walks around in secret furs.'

'Really?' Nella laughs, overwhelmed by Cornelia's offering. Encouraged, she yanks down her shawl to show her wound.

Cornelia whistles. 'That's going to be pretty,' she says, glancing at Otto. 'But it'll fade. Like everything else.'

Nella, who had hoped for a more motherly reaction, now feels foolish. 'Were you up late again last night?' she asks, concealing her bruise.

'Why, Madame?' Cornelia chucks the carrot skins in the fire and picks up her mop.

Nella can feel the friendly atmosphere ebbing away with every question she asks.

'I'm sure I heard voices.'

Cornelia stares into the bucket of dirty water.

'We're too tired to hear voices,' Otto says.

Dhana trots out of the gloom, nuzzling Nella's hand. She rolls on her back and offers her belly, a small black marking on the fur. Cornelia considers this display of affection. 'She doesn't do that to anyone,' she says, a sliver of admiration in her voice. Nella turns and makes her way up the stairs. 'Here, Madame,' Cornelia calls. Her palm is outstretched. A hot roll, buttered; Nella takes it. Peace offerings in this house come in rather strange shapes.

'Where are you going, Madame?' Otto asks.

'Out. That's *allowed*, isn't it? I'm going to the Kalverstraat.'

At this, Cornelia shoves her mop into the bucket. The water slaps against the side, its surface like a broken mirror.

'Do you know where that is, Madame?' asks Otto, gently.

Nella feels drops of butter running down her wrist. 'I'll find it,' she says. 'I have a good sense of direction.'

Otto and Cornelia exchange another, longer glance; Nella catches the almost imperceptible shake of Otto's head.

'I'll come with you, Madame,' says Cornelia. 'I need some air.'

'But—'

'You'll want a coat,' says Otto. 'It's very cold.'

But Cornelia grabs her shawl and ushers Nella out.

On the Kalverstraat

'Sweet Jesu,' mutters Cornelia. 'Otto was right. This winter is going to be awful. Why do you want to go to the Kalverstraat?'

'To leave a message for somebody,' Nella replies, piqued at the ease with which Cornelia interrogates.

'Who's somebody?'

'No one. A craftsman.'

'I see.' Cornelia shivers. 'We'll need to get our meat in soon, stretch it out till March at least. It's odd he hasn't sent us a cut.'

'Who hasn't sent us a cut?'

'Never mind,' Cornelia says, looking towards the canal and linking her arm through Nella's. '*Somebody*.' The young women huddle close, walking swiftly up the Herengracht towards the centre of the city. The cold is not quite unbearable yet – but its force is coming, Nella can tell. Feeling Cornelia's arm through hers, she reflects on the oddness of their touching limbs. In Assendelft, maids and manservants were never so friendly with their actions. Most of them were actively unwilling.

'Why didn't Otto come?' Nella asks. When Cornelia says nothing, she persists. 'I saw him, he refused.'

'He stays where it's easiest,' Cornelia replies.

'*Easiest*?' Nella laughs.

The maid scowls and Nella hopes she that she isn't going to be given another *never mind*. But no; when it comes to Otto, Cornelia is expansive.

'Toot calls his luck a double-edged sword,' she says. 'He's here – and yet he isn't.'

'I don't know what you mean.'

'He was put on a Portuguese slave-ship, Madame – bound from Porto-Novo in Dahomey to Surinam. His parents were dead. The Seigneur was visiting the West India Company at the time, selling them copper for their cane refineries.'

'What happened?'

'The Seigneur saw the state of Toot and brought him back to Amsterdam.'

'Johannes bought him.'

Cornelia bites her lip. 'Guilders sometimes work quicker than a prayer.'

'Don't let Marin hear you say that.'

Cornelia ignores this comment; it appears the window for gossip about Marin and her pincers has been closed. 'Otto was sixteen when he arrived,' she says, 'and I was twelve, as new to the house as him.'

Nella tries to picture them both arriving on the doorstep as she had. Was Marin lurking in the shadows of the hallway even then? What world had Otto left behind? She longs to ask him, but wonders if he'd want to tell. Nella has heard of a palm tree, but she cannot imagine the heat of Porto-Novo, the world of Surinam. All of it – exchanged for brick walls and canals, and a language he didn't speak.

'He's quite the Dutch gentleman,' Cornelia says, 'but

people think differently.' Nella detects a new edge in her voice. 'When he arrived he didn't speak for a month. Just listening, always listening. That coffee-bean skin. I see *you* looking,' she adds, a little sly.

'I don't,' Nella protests.

'Everyone does. Most people have never seen a man like him. When they still visited, the ladies rested their songbirds in his hair as if it was a nest. He hated it.' Cornelia pauses. 'No wonder Madame Marin can't stand your parakeet.'

They walk on, the canal paths strangely muted, the slow brown water between them forming a thin veneer of ice around the edges. Nella tries to grasp at this image of the young black man, his head filled with birdsong, the women's fingers pawing at his hair. She feels ashamed that her fascination with him is so obvious. Johannes treats him just like any other man, and Otto is just that – but his voice, his face – no one back in Assendelft would believe it. 'Why don't the ladies come any more?' she asks.

But there is no answer to this, for Cornelia has stopped outside a confectioner's shop, the sign of two sugar loaves and the name *Arnoud Maakvrede* above the door. 'Madame,' Cornelia urges. 'Let us stop in here.' Though wishing to exert just one drop of authority, Nella smells the baking and cannot resist.

Within is a delicious heat. Through an arch at the back of the shop, Nella spies a rotund middle-aged man, red-faced and sweating from the stove. On seeing them, he rolls his eyes. 'Hanna, your friend's here,' he shouts into the air.

A woman appears, slightly older than Cornelia, her cap

neatly pressed, flour and sugar dusting on her dress. Her face lights up. 'Cornflower!' she exclaims.

'*Cornflower*?' says Nella.

Cornelia blushes. 'Hello, Hanna.'

'Where've you been?' Hanna motions for them both to take a seat in the coolest corner of the shop floor. She puts up a sign saying *Closed*, a waft of cinnamon in her wake.

'What by all the angels are you doing, woman?' cries the man.

'Oh, Arnoud. Five minutes,' Hanna says. The couple stare at each other, and he returns to the stove to bang an angry rhythm with his trays. 'Honeycomb this morning,' Hanna murmurs. 'And marzipan in the afternoon. He's best avoided.'

'But to avoid him now is to see much more of him later,' says Cornelia, the concern etched on her face.

Hanna throws her a glance. 'Well, you're here now and I want to see you.'

Nella looks around at the shining wooden floors, the scrubbed counter, the pastries adorning the shop window, piled like irresistible presents. She wonders why Cornelia has brought her here instead of taking her straight to the Kalver-straat, but the smell of sweet cakes is so delicious. Who is Cornflower – this softer, sweeter person conjured by the wife of a confectioner? The verbal baptism is sudden and strange, unsettling Cornelia's essence. She remembers something Cornelia said the first morning, about calling Otto Toot. *He thinks nicknames are silly, but I like them.*

The paper used to wrap the cakes looks expensive, and comes in a variety of colours: scarlet, indigo, grass-green, cloud-white. Cornelia looks meaningfully at Hanna, gives her a dip of the chin that the older woman seems to understand. 'Please, Madame,' Hanna says to Nella. 'Do have a look around.'

Dutifully, Nella roams the shop, looking over the waffles, the spiced biscuits, the cinnamon and chocolate syrups, the orange and lemon cakes, the fruit rolls. As she watches Arnoud through the arch, bashing the cooled stubborn trays of honeycomb, she tries to listen to Hanna and Cornelia as they keep their voices low.

'Frans and Agnes Meermans wanted only the Seigneur to distribute it,' Cornelia says. 'They know how far his business spreads abroad. And Madame Marin's encouraging it. Even though she hates sugar, even though it belongs to *them*.'

'It could make them all a lot of money.'

Cornelia sniffs. 'It could. But I think there's other reasons.'

Hanna ignores this, more interested in the business side of things. 'But why not sell it here? With no guild to control these rapscallions, so much of this city's sugar is cut at the cheap refineries with flour, chalk and God knows what. There are pastry chefs and bakers along the Nes and the Street of Buns who can do with better product.'

Arnoud curses loudly, finally dislodging the honeycomb.

'Try something,' Hanna calls brightly to Nella. She reaches over the counter and comes back with a little crinkled parcel. Nella, confused to see pity in the older woman's eyes, unwraps the offering and discovers a fried ball of dough, covered with sugar and cinnamon.

'Thank you,' she says, returning her gaze to Arnoud firing up his oven, pretending her attention is solely on the fat confectioner.

'Hanna, I think it's happening again,' Cornelia whispers.

'You were never sure the first time.'

'I know, but—'

'You can do nothing, Cornflower. Head down, that's what they taught us.'

'Han, I wish—'

'*Shh*, take this. It's nearly the last of it.'

Nella turns in time to see a packet pass between the women, disappearing swiftly from Hanna's fingers into Cornelia's skirts.

'I have to go,' says Cornelia, standing up. 'We must pay a visit to the Kalverstraat.' She weights the word, a shadow passing her face.

Hanna squeezes Cornelia's hand. 'Well, give the door a kick from me,' she says. 'My five minutes is up. I must go and help Arnoud. Anyone would think he was hammering armour the way he bangs those trays.'

Back outside, Cornelia hurries along. 'Who is Hanna?' Nella asks. 'Why does she call you Cornflower? And why are we kicking a door?'

But Cornelia is morose and mute; the talk with Hanna has released an unexpected gloom.

The Kalverstraat is a long, busy street away from the canal, where many sellers ply their trade. They no longer sell calves and cows there, but the manure from horses lends it a meaty, pungent atmosphere amidst the print and dye shops, the haberdashers and apothecaries.

'Cornelia, what's wrong?'

'Nothing, Madame,' comes the eventual, sullen reply. But

Nella has already spotted the sign of the sun. A small stone sun has indeed been engraved on a plaque, embedded in the brickwork. Painted freshly gold, it's a heavenly body come to earth; bright stone rays shoot from a glowing orb. It is so high up in the wall that Nella cannot touch it. Beneath the sun, a motto has been engraved: *Everything Man Sees He Takes For A Toy*.

'*Thus is he always, forever a boy*,' Cornelia says wistfully. 'I haven't heard that saying for years.' She looks up and down the street as though in search of something. Nella knocks on the small, plain door, barely noticeable amidst the noise and bustle, and waits for the miniaturist to reveal himself.

There is no reply. Cornelia stamps her feet with cold. 'Madame, there's no one there.'

'Just wait,' Nella says, knocking again. There are four windows looking onto the street, and she thinks that perhaps there is a shadow at one of them, but she cannot be sure. 'Hello?' she shouts, but no answer comes.

There is nothing for it; she slips her letter and the promissory note as far under the door as possible. Only then does Nella realize that Cornelia is no longer with her. 'Cornelia?' she calls, scanning the Kalverstraat.

The maid's name dies in Nella's throat. Several feet away from the miniaturist's door, a woman is watching her. No, not watching – staring. She stands still amidst the milling crowd, her eyes fixated on Nella's face. Nella experiences the unprecedented sensation of being impaled – the woman's scrutiny is like a beam of cold light dissecting her, filling her with an awareness of her own body. The woman does not smile, but she drinks Nella in, her brown eyes nearly orange in the weak midday light, her uncovered hair like pale gold thread.

A chill, a sharp clarity, enters Nella's bones. She draws her shawl tight, and still the woman keeps staring. Everything seems brighter, thrown into relief – yet the sun is still behind cloud. Nella supposes it could be the old bricks, the damp stone accounting for the sudden lack of warmth. It could be, but those eyes – no one has ever looked at Nella like that before in her life – such a calm, transfixing curiosity.

A boy with a barrow trundles past, almost running Nella over. 'You nearly broke my foot!' she shouts after him.

'Never did!' the barrow-boy yells back.

When Nella looks back, the woman has gone. 'Wait!' she calls, making her way up the Kalverstraat, spying the back of a head the colour of shining wheat. But the sun comes out from behind the clouds, obscuring Nella's vision. 'What do you want?' Sure she has seen the woman disappearing up a narrow passage, Nella begins to push harder through the crowd. Plunging down this dark alleyway, her heart leaps to see a figure up ahead – but it is Cornelia, alone at the end, pinch-faced, trembling at a large front door.

'Where is she? What are you doing?' Nella asks. 'Did you see a woman with blonde hair?'

Cornelia aims a swift kick on the panel of the door. 'Every year,' she says. 'Just to remember how lucky I am.'

'What?'

Cornelia closes her eyes. 'My old home.'

The noise of the shoppers on the Kalverstraat is now muffled by the tight walls of the passage. Nella steadies herself against the kicked door. A plaque depicting children dressed in city colours of black and red, grouped around a giant dove, has been placed above the architrave. Beneath it, the words span out a humourless rhyme:

> We're growing in numbers and our walls are groaning
> Please give what you can to stop our masters moaning.

'Cornelia, an orphanage?'

But the maid is already walking back up the passage, towards life and light and noise. Nella can only pursue her, still hollowed by the fair-haired woman's gaze.

On returning to the Herengracht, Nella discovers that Marin has arranged for the cabinet to be put in her room. Too wide to fit through the bedroom door, it has been winched up the front of the house.

'It couldn't stay in the hall,' Marin says, drawing open the mustard-coloured curtains to reveal the nine empty rooms. 'It's far too large. It was taking up the light.'

Aside from the intrusive presence of the cabinet, Nella's room now also stinks of lily. That night, she discovers her perfume bottle from Assendelft, knocked on its side, the oil pooled to the floor in a viscous mess beneath her bed.

'It was the delivery men,' Marin says when Nella shows her the glass shards and asks for an explanation. Unconvinced, Nella throws some of the embroidered wedding cushions onto the stain. Glad not to be reminded of those taunting marriage emblems, she hopes their bulk will absorb the smell.

Lying back, listening to Peebo clicking in his cage, the air tinged with the ill-advised gift from her mother, Nella thinks about Otto and Cornelia. The slave boy, the orphan girl. How did Cornelia get from there to the Herengracht? Was she 'rescued' like Otto? Were you rescued too? Nella asks herself. So far, life here feels the opposite of escape.

In the dark of her room, she conjures the white-blonde head and unusual eyes of the woman on the Kalverstraat. It was as if she was skinning Nella, like one of those animals in Johannes' paintings, and then dismantling her body bit by bit. And yet, simultaneously, Nella felt so *concentrated*. Why was the woman there, on the busiest street in the city, just standing, staring – had she nothing better to do? And why was she looking at me?

As Nella drifts to sleep, she imagines great silver dishes and Johannes spinning them, his face turned to his counterfeit ceiling, towards the depth that doesn't exist. Ascending into this restless, spiral nightmare she is woken by a short, high cry that sounds like a dog in pain. Perhaps it's Rezeki, she thinks, wide awake, her heart hammering.

The silence descends again, heavy as damask, and Nella turns to the empty cabinet. Monumental, almost watchful, as if it has always stood there, in the corner of her room.

Delivery

Three days later, Cornelia is with Marin at the meat market. 'Can I come?' Nella had asked. 'It's quicker with two of us,' came Marin's swift reply. Johannes has gone to his VOC offices on the Old Hoogstraat, and Otto is in the back garden, planting bulbs and seeds for next year's spring. The garden is his domain. He is often out there, making new hedge patterns, conversing with Johannes about the dampness of the soil.

As Nella crosses the hallway with some pilfered nuts for Peebo, a rapid set of knocks on the front door makes her jump. Pocketing the nuts, she draws back the bolts and pulls the heavy door.

A young man stands before her on the top step, a little older than herself. Nella's breath catches in her throat. His long legs are wide apart as if he's trying to take up all the space. Dark tousled hair crowns a pale face, and his cheeks are carved with symmetrical precision. His clothes are fashionable but messily arranged. Cuffs spill from the arms of his rich leather coat, and a pair of boots, even newer than the coat, cling to his calves as if they don't want to let go. His shirt laces are loose, and a triangle of skin at the top reveals a few freckles. His body is a story in itself, starting sharp with an uncertain end. Nella holds on to the door frame, hoping that she is shining back at him, as he seems to know he's shining at her.

'Delivery,' he says with a smile. Nella is surprised by his voice. The accent is unusual – unmusical, flat. He knows the Dutch word, but it's clearly not his mother tongue.

Rezeki bounds up and starts barking at this boy, growling when he tries to pat her head. Nella looks at his empty hands. 'You're supposed to use the lower door for deliveries,' she says.

He smiles again. 'Of course,' he says. 'I always forget.' Nella, unsettled by his beauty, wants to touch those cheek-bones if only to push them away. Sensing a presence behind her, she turns. Johannes is upon them, ploughing forward and standing between Nella and the boy.

'Johannes? I thought you were at work,' she exclaims. 'Why are you—'

'What are you doing here?' Johannes asks the boy, his voice constricted, almost whispering. He ignores Nella's puzzled expression and pushes a snarling Rezeki back into the house.

Although the young man puts his hand nonchalantly under his jacket, he has straightened up a little, drawing his legs together. 'Just come with a package,' he says.

'For whom?'

'For Nella Oortman.'

The boy weighs out the word of Nella's maiden name with care, meeting Johannes with a level look, and Nella feels her husband tense. The young man holds a parcel aloft, and she can see it has been inked with the sign of a sun. Has the minia-turist already made my pieces? she wonders, scarcely quelling the urge to snatch the packet and run upstairs.

'Your master works quickly,' she observes, wishing to scrape back some modicum of poise. This was my delivery, she thinks, not my husband's.

'What master is she referring to?' demands Johannes.

The young man laughs, handing her the parcel, and Nella holds it close to her body. 'I'm Jack Philips. From Bermondsey,' he says, taking Nella's hand. His kiss is dry and soft, and leaves a shiver of sensation.

'Ber-mond-sey?' she echoes. Nella has no image she can fix to this unusual word – no meaning in fact, for this unusual boy.

'Just outside the City of London. I sometimes work for the VOC,' Jack says. 'Sometimes for myself. I was an actor back home.'

From the hallway, Rezeki barks and her noises echo in the cloudy sky. 'Who paid you to do this?' asks Johannes.

'People all over the city pay me to deliver, Seigneur.'

'Who paid you this time?'

Jack takes a step away. 'Your wife, Seigneur,' he says. 'Your wife.' He bows to Nella, sauntering down the steps and away.

'Come, Nella,' Johannes says. 'Let us close the door on prying eyes.'

Back inside, they find Otto waiting at the top of the kitchen stairs, a rake in his hand, the sharp prongs glinting in the light. 'Who was it, Seigneur?' he asks.

'No one,' Johannes says, and Otto nods.

Johannes turns to Nella, and she shrinks from his size, seeming larger to her now in the confines of the hall. 'What is in the parcel, Nella?'

'Something for the cabinet you bought,' she says, wondering what he'd say if he saw the lute, the marzipan, the cup to celebrate betrothal.

'Ah. Excellent.'

Nella waits for more curiosity, but none is forthcoming – in fact, Johannes seems nothing but agitated. 'Shall I open it upstairs? You could come and see,' she offers, hoping he will join her. 'You could see how your wedding gift might grow.'

'I must work, Nella. I'll let you to your privacy,' he replies with an anxious smile, waving a hand towards his study.

I don't want my privacy, she shouts in silence. *I'd throw it away in an instant if you would pay me some attention.*

But Johannes has already gone – Rezeki, as ever, trotting behind.

⋘ ⋙

Still unsettled by the vision of Jack Philips from Bermondsey, Nella climbs onto her giant bed and sits with the parcel. Bulky, the width of a dinner plate, it has been wrapped in smooth paper and string. A sentence has been written round the sun in black capitals:

*EVERY WOMAN IS THE ARCHITECT
OF HER OWN FORTUNE*

Nella reads it twice, puzzled, a feather-thrum of excitement in her belly. Women don't build anything, let alone their own fates, she thinks. All our fates are in the hands of God – and women's in particular, after their husbands have passed them through their fingers and childbirth has put them through the wringer.

She pulls out the first object and weighs a tiny silver box in her palm. On the top, an *N* and an *O* have been carved, with encircling flowers and vines. She carefully prises open the lid,

76

the miniature hinges well-oiled, silent. Inside lies a neat block of marzipan about the length of a coffee bean, and her taste buds come alive at the prospect of the sweet almond sugar. She probes with a fingernail and puts it on the tip of her tongue. The marzipan is real, even scented with rosewater.

Nella removes a second object. Here is a lute, no longer than her forefinger – with real, tuned strings, its wooden body swelling to hold the sound of notes. Never has she seen things like this – the craftsmanship, the care, the beauty of these objects. She plucks tentatively, astonished as a quiet chord sings out. Remembering the skeleton of the tune she played Johannes in Assendelft, Nella now plays it again, alone.

The next dive in reveals the requested betrothal cup. Made of pewter, a man and a woman with their hands entwined around the rim, its diameter is no wider than a grain. All newly married couples drink from these cups in their republic, just as she and Johannes should have done, back in September. Nella imagines them both taking a sip of the Rhenish wine, standing in her father's old orchard, rice and petals showered on their heads. This little cup is a memento of something that never actually occurred. What she had intended as a rebellion against Marin now makes Nella feel strange and pathetically sad.

She picks up the wrappings in order to discard them, then realizes there are more things inside. This cannot be correct, she thinks, her gloom warping into curiosity. Everything I asked for is already on the bed.

She tips the packet up, and three wrapped items fall onto the coverlet. Nella fumbles with the material encasing the first, and discovers two exquisite wooden chairs. Lions the size of ladybirds have been carved on their arm-rests, the backs are covered with green velvet, studded with copper nails. On each of the arms, sea monsters writhe in acanthus leaves. Nella realizes she's seen these chairs before. Last week in the salon downstairs, Marin was sitting on one of them.

Beginning to feel uneasy, she unwraps the next item. Something small but bulky waits in the folds of cloth, and she wrenches it free. It is a cradle, made of oak, with intricate floral inlays, tin runners and a fringe of lace at the hood. A quiet miracle of wood, its tiny presence nevertheless makes Nella's throat constrict. She places it in the middle of her palm, where it rocks in a perfect motion, almost of its own accord.

This has to be a mistake, she thinks – these pieces are intended for someone else. Chairs, a cradle – perhaps the usual things a woman might ask for a replica of her house – but I didn't. I *definitely* didn't. She rips apart the wrapping on the third package, and beneath another layer of blue material is a pair of miniature dogs. Two whippet bodies no larger than moths, covered in silky grey fur, with skulls the size of peas. Between them, there is a bone for them to chew, a shank of clove painted yellow – the smell is unmistakeable. Nella picks up the animals and peers closer, her blood charging round her body. These dogs are not any dogs. They are Rezeki and Dhana.

Nella drops them quickly as if they have stung her, and jumps off the bed. In the dark and unlit corner of the room, the cabinet waits for its new deliveries. Its curtains are still pulled open, like unseemly lifted skirts. She allows herself a brief glance down to the whippets' scattered bodies. The same curve and colour of their flanks, their wonderful streamlined ears. 'Come on, Nella Elisabeth,' she says to herself. 'Who says they're the same whippets curled up by Cornelia's stove?'

She holds both miniature dogs up to the light. Their bodies are slightly spongy, their joints articulated, covered in grey mouse-skin and soft as an earlobe. When Nella turns them over, her blood slows to an uncomfortable thump. On one of the dog's bellies is a small black spot, in exactly the same place as Dhana's.

Nella stares around the room. Is someone here? She tries hard to be reasonable. Of course not, Nella, she thinks – you've never felt more alone. Who might want to trick her? Cornelia wouldn't have the money to play such games, nor time to think of them. Nor would Otto – and surely he would not willingly write to a stranger?

Nella feels a sense of invasion, as if she is being closely observed in her bridal foolishness. It's Marin, she thinks. Marin is taking revenge for Johannes' marriage and me getting in her way. She spills my lily perfume, she forbids me marzipan, she pinches me hard on the arm. *She* was the one who gave me *Smit's List*. Why wouldn't Marin pay the miniaturist to frighten me? For her, it's just another idle amusement.

And yet. *Idle* and *amusement* are not words one might associate with Marin Brandt, and even as she thinks of her sister-in-law, Nella knows it doesn't make sense. Marin eats like a mouse and shops like a nun, except for her books and her specimens probably purloined from Johannes' travels. This can't be Marin's doing, because it involves spending money. But as Nella looks over the unasked-for pieces again, part of her actually hopes it's her sister-in-law. Because if it's not

Marin, she wonders – what other sort of strangeness have I invited in?

Someone has peered into Nella's life and thrown her off centre. If these items aren't sent in error, then the cradle is a mock to her unvisited marriage bed and what's beginning to feel as though it's an eternal virginity. What sort of person would dare such impertinence? The dogs, so particular; the chairs, so exact – the cradle, so suggestive – it's like the miniaturist has a perfect, private view.

Climbing back onto her bed, Nella registers the disturbance these pieces have created, how her curiosity churns with a cusping terror. This will not do, she thinks. I will not be bullied from afar as well as near.

As she listens to the constant tock of the gold pendulum, surrounded by these inexplicable deliveries, she writes a second note to the miniaturist.

> *Sir,*
>
> *I thank you for the items I requested, delivered today by Jack Philips of Bermondsey. Your craftsmanship is exceptional. You work miracles with your fingertips. The marzipan is particularly good.*

Nella's pen hovers, but before she can change her mind, the nib meets the paper in a fever of words.

> *However, you expanded the delivery in a way I did not foresee. The whippets, whilst accurate, might suggest a lucky guess, Seigneur, for many people in the city own such dogs. Yet I am not many people – and these dogs, the cradle and chairs, are not mine. As wife of a high-ranking VOC*

*merchant, I shall not be intimidated by an artisan. Thank you
for your work and time, but I will curtail our transactions
forthwith.*

> *Yours in good faith,*
>
> *Petronella Brandt*

She hides the pieces under her coverlet and calls for
Cornelia, placing the newly drafted, sealed note in the maid's
hands before she can change her mind. She will admit that the
possibility is quite real. Perhaps I have rejected something
here, she thinks – a challenge, a hidden purpose to these surprise pieces, never to be discovered. Will I have a sliver of
regret? No, Nella corrects herself. That's just your imagination.

Cornelia reads the address. 'The craftsman again?' she says.
'The somebody?'

'Don't open it,' Nella orders and the maid nods, for once
muted by the urgency in her younger mistress's voice.

It is only after Cornelia has gone to the Kalverstraat that
Nella realizes she has not returned the miniaturist's unasked-
for pieces. One by one, she pulls them from under the coverlet
and places them in the cabinet. They look perfectly at home.

Barge

The next day, Cornelia seems reinvigorated. 'Come, Madame,' says the maid, bounding in, Marin on her heels. 'Let me tidy those wisps of hair. Tuck them under, hide them away!'

'What are you talking about, Cornelia?'

'Johannes is taking you to a feast at the Guild of Silver-smiths tonight,' Marin says.

'Was it his idea?'

Marin looks over at the cabinet, its curtains now shut from prying eyes. 'He loves a feast,' she replies. 'He thought it appropriate you should attend.'

Now the adventure is surely to begin, Nella thinks – my husband is launching his little raft into the storm-tossed seas of Amsterdam's finest society – and he, the best of sailors, will be there as my guide. Putting the miniature whippets and the cradle out of her mind, Nella leans under her bed, takes a smear of lily oil on her fingers, and in full view of Marin, rubs it on her neck.

After Marin has left, Nella asks Cornelia what happened at the Kalverstraat. 'No one answered again,' the maid says. 'So I slipped it underneath the door.'

'At the sign of the sun? You saw no one?'

'Not a soul, Madame. But Hanna sends her greetings.'

'Marin, why aren't you coming?' Johannes asks that evening, waiting for their barge. He is wearing an exquisite suit of black velvet, a starched white shirt and collar and a pair of calfskin boots polished to mirrors by Otto, who waits with a clothes-brush in one hand.

'All things considered, I think you should be seen with your wife,' Marin replies, fixing him with a stare.

'What do you mean, "all things considered"?' Nella asks.

'Talk to people, Johannes,' Marin says. 'Show her off—'

'I'll introduce you, Nella,' Johannes interrupts, frowning at his sister. 'I think that's what Marin means.'

'And speak with Frans Meermans, brother. He'll be there tonight,' Marin persists, her expression grim. 'Invite them both to dine.'

To Nella's surprise, Johannes nods. Why does he let his sister talk to him like this?

'Johannes, do you promise—'

'*Marin.*' Johannes finally snaps at the sound of her voice. 'When have I ever got my business wrong?'

'You haven't,' she sighs. 'At least, not yet.'

❧ ❦

Nella's mouth feels dry but her stomach is a creel of fish. The boat journey to the Guild of Silversmiths is the first time she and her husband have been alone outside the house. She thinks the silence will drown her, but the voice inside her head is so loud she's convinced Johannes can hear it too. She wants to ask him about Marin's room of maps, Otto and his slave-ship – she wants to tell him about the tiny whippets, the cradle, the beautiful miniature lute. She won't tell him about the woman on the Kalverstraat, staring at her – that feels like something she wants to keep to herself – but at any rate, her mouth won't move.

Johannes begins cleaning his nails absentmindedly. The discarded crescents of dirt float to the floor of the boat, and he catches her looking.

'Cardamom,' he says. 'It gets caught under the nail. As does salt.'

'I see.'

Nella inhales the air in the boat, the hint of the places he's been, the scent of cinnamon stuck in his very pores. He smells vaguely of that musky tang she smelled in his study the night he first came home. Her husband's brown face and his too-long hair, bleached and toughened by sun and wind, trigger an awkward longing – the desire not necessarily for him, but to know how it will feel when they finally lie together. The gift of the cabinet, and now this trip together to the Guild – perhaps it will happen tonight after the feast? Both of them, wine-flushed – they will get it done.

The water is so smooth and the boatman so expert that it feels as if the houses are moving and not the barge. Nella, more used to riding on a horse, is unsettled by the sedate pace, supposedly tranquil when she feels anything but. She tries to press away her agitation between the palms of her hands. *How do I begin to love you?* – the question, enormous, impossible to ignore, goes round and round in her head as she stares at him.

She tries to focus on how the silversmiths' hall will look, a room full of watery light, plates like giant coins, the diners reflected on every surface.

'What do you know of the guilds?' Johannes asks, breaking her thoughts.

'Nothing,' she replies.

Johannes absorbs her ignorance with a nod, and Nella watches it sink into him, wishing she could sound more clever. 'The silversmiths' guild has a lot of money,' he says. 'One of the richest. Guilds offer protection in hard times, apprentice-ships and a means to sell, but they also determine their workload and control the market. It's why Marin's so keen on selling the sugar.'

'What do you mean?'

'Well, like chocolate and tobacco – and diamonds, silk and books, the market is open. There's no guild for them. I can name my price – or Frans and Agnes Meermans can.'

'So why are we going to the silversmiths' guild?'

He grins. 'Free meal. No, I jest. They want me to increase my patronage, and it's good to be seen doing just that. I'm the crack in the wall that leads to the magic garden.'

Nella wonders how magic his garden is, how much he can truly afford to stretch his purse strings open. Marin seemed so uneasy about his expenditure on the cabinet house, and what was it Otto said? *Things will spill over.* Don't be silly, she thinks. You live on the Herengracht now.

'Marin seems very keen for you to sell Frans Meermans' sugar,' she dares, immediately regretting her decision. There is a long pause, so long, that she believes she would rather die than endure it any longer.

'It's Agnes Meermans' plantation,' Johannes says eventu-ally. 'But Frans has taken over the managing of it. Agnes' father died last year with no sons – though not for want of going at it till his final breath.' He stops himself on seeing Nella's blushes. 'My apologies. I did not mean to be coarse. Her father was an awful man – and yet Agnes inherited his acres of cane fields – a woman's name on the papers, despite all her father's best efforts. And now she's handed them to Frans. Overnight these cones of sugar have made them both quite venal. It's what they've been waiting for.'

'*What* have they been waiting for?'

He grimaces. 'A good opportunity. I'm storing the cones in my warehouse, and have agreed to sell them. My sister constantly doubts I will.'

'Why?'

'Because Marin sits indoors and has ideas, but does not understand the nuances involved in actual trade. I've been doing this for twenty years – for too long,' he sighs. 'One must tread carefully, and yet she crashes like an elephant.'

'I see,' Nella says, though she has no idea what an elephant is. It sounds like an elegant flower, but Johannes didn't seem to be paying his sister a compliment. 'Johannes, is Marin – *friends* with Agnes Meermans?'

Johannes laughs. 'They have known each other a long time, and sometimes it's hard to love a person you know too well. There's your answer. Don't look shocked.'

The observation lodges in Nella like a shard of ice. 'Do you really think that, Johannes?'

'When you have truly come to know a person, Nella – when you see beneath the sweeter gestures, the smiles – when you see the rage and the pitiful fear which each of us hide – then forgiveness is everything. We are all in desperate need of it. And Marin is – not so forgiving.' He pauses. 'There are –

ladders in this society. . . and Agnes loves to climb them. The problem is, she never loves the view.' His eyes glitter on an invisible joke. 'Anyway. I'll bet you a guilder Frans is wearing the biggest hat in the room, and Agnes will have made him wear it.'

'Do wives often attend these feasts?'

He smiles. 'Women are usually *proibidas*, except for special occasions. Though there is a freedom among Amsterdam ladies that the French and English lack.'

'Freedom?'

'Ladies can walk alone on the street. Couples can even hold each other's hands.' He pauses again, looking through the window. 'It is not a prison, this city, if you plot your path correctly. The foreigners may tut, with their *well-I-nevers* and *alors*, but I'm sure they're envious.'

'Of course,' Nella replies, again not understanding his alien words, not seeing at all. *Proibidas*. Over her short stay in the house Johannes has often spoken in other languages, and it mesmerizes her when he does it. He doesn't seem to be show-ing off – it's more a reaching for something his own tongue can never achieve. Nella realizes that no man – no person, in fact – has ever talked to her the way he has tonight. Despite the mysterious allusions, Johannes treats her like an equal; he expects her to understand.

'Come here, Nella,' he says.

Obediently, with a little fear she moves towards him and he tips her chin gently to lengthen her neck. She stares back at him and they size each other up like slave and master at a market. Taking her face in his hands, he brushes the contour of her young cheek. She leans forward. The tips of his fingers are roughened, but this is what Nella has waited for. Her head thrums at the feel of his touch. She closes her eyes, remembering her mother's words – *the girl wants love. She wants the peaches and the cream.*

'Do you like silver?' Johannes asks.

'Yes,' Nella breathes. She will not babble this moment away.

'There's nothing more beautiful in the world than silver,' Johannes says. His hands drop from her face, her eyes snap open and she feels a swoop of embarrassment at her craned position. 'I'll have a necklace made for that throat.'

His voice sounds far away from the roar of her thoughts. Nella pulls back, rubbing her gullet as if bringing it back to life. 'Thank you,' she hears herself say.

'You're a wife now. We're supposed to dress you up.'

Johannes smiles, but the sentence is brutal to Nella, and a stone of fear hardens in her gut. She finds she has nothing to say.

'I will not hurt you, Petronella.'

Nella looks through the window towards the unending flow of house-fronts passing by. Closing her legs together tight, she imagines the moment of penetration – is there something in her that will rip, will it feel as painful as she fears? Whatever the sensation, she knows she cannot avoid it, that it must be overcome.

'I am quite serious,' Johannes says. 'Quite serious.' Now it is his turn to lean towards her. The smell of trapped salt and cardamom, his strange maleness, threatens to overpower her. 'Nella, Nella, are you listening?'

'Yes. I am, Johannes. I – you will not hurt me.'

'Good. You have nothing to fear from me.'

As Johannes says this, he withdraws, staring at the canalside houses. Nella thinks of the picture in Marin's travel book, the native and the conqueror, acres of misunderstanding between their bodies. Night has fallen fully. She looks at the lights of the smaller boats, and feels completely alone.

Marriage Parties

The Guild of Silversmiths' feast chamber is large and full of people, whose faces blend into a blur of eyes and mouths and feathers bouncing off the brims of hats. Around them, the sound of silverware on silverware builds, male laughter hitting the walls to a subtler counterpoint of women's titters. There is an almost monstrous presence of food. Long tables draped in white damask have been lined up, piled with plates of chickens, turkeys, candied fruit, five-meat pies and twisted silver candelabra. Johannes links his arm tight through Nella's and they skirt the dizzying array, keeping close to the dark mahogany panelling. It seems that whispers and snickering run the room in their wake.

The other wives glide to their places, seeming to know where to sit. They are all in black, the skin above their bosoms covered with lace jabots, a sliver of white flesh on show. One woman in particular darts her eyes, glittering like jet in the candlelight, focusing their intent on Nella. Her stare couldn't be more different than that of the woman on the Kalverstraat. 'Smile, and sit with me,' Johannes says, proffering the woman a hard-boiled grin. 'Let us put something in our stomachs before facing the masses.' Nella thinks she might be eaten alive were it not for the food.

They take their seats at a table where a first course of crab has been laid.

'I find much of myself in food,' observes Johannes, holding his crabbing fork aloft. Nella, staring at the shining silver chargers and the doughty jugs of wine, wonders what he means. In the presence of these other people, his problems with Marin are forgotten. Johannes is genial, aware of the gazes of the gathered company, chatting to his junior bride as if they've spent two decades together weathering the seven seas.

'Cumin seeds, studding a new cheese, remind me that I am capable of delight,' Johannes says loudly. 'Delft butter – so fine and creamy, so different from the others, gives me enormous satisfaction. I sell China-ware plates in Delft and pick it up in pats. And Cornelia's marjoram and plum beer makes me happier than a successful deal. She must make you some.'

'My mother makes it,' Nella replies, the chomping, clattering noises of the feast beginning to daunt her. She feels drained by the chamber's energy, as crystallized as the chunks of sugar-dusted fruit.

'Figs and sour cream for an early breakfast in summer,' Johannes goes on, oblivious. 'A particular joy, taking me back to childhood, only the taste of which I now remember.' He looks at her. 'You remember yours, no doubt, for it was not so long ago.'

Nella wonders if this sharp point is deliberate, or a symptom of his nerves, being out here in company, under its scrutiny. At any rate, she wants to disagree. Right now, her childhood feels incredibly distant. It has been replaced with uncertainty, a low level of constant dismay. The stone of fear splits into a sick anxiety in her stomach; she hates the room's cacophony, the timbre of this conversation, the invasion of the unfamiliar.

'I left my cradle long ago,' she murmurs, thinking of the miniaturist's unwanted nursery offering and feeling even more at sea.

'Memory through food,' Johannes says. 'Food is a language in itself. Parsnips, turnips, leeks and endives – and yet I crunch when no one else can hear. And fish! Flounder, sole, dab and cod are my favourites, but I'll eat anything else offered up by the seas and rivers running round my republic.'

Nella senses there is something protective in the way he is talking, as if he hopes his words will keep her mind from straying to worry. 'What do you eat when you're on the oceans?' she asks, summoning the courage to play along.

He puts his fork down. 'Other men.'

Nella offers a laugh, a shy burst that falls between them and lands on the tablecloth. Johannes pops another piece of crab into his mouth. 'Cannibalism is the only way to survive once the food runs out,' he says, 'but I'd rather have potatoes. My favourite tavern in this city is on the Eastern Islands, by my warehouse. Their hot potatoes have the fluffiest flesh.' He prods the crab on his plate. 'It is my secret place.'

'But you've just told it to me.'

He lays his fork down. 'So I have,' he says. 'So I have.' He seems caught by her observation, and looks away towards his crab. With nothing to say, Nella also examines the splayed and perishable flesh, its pincers the colour of ink, its shell turning angrier shades of red. Ripping off a leg and using his fork to scoop out the last of the fibrous whiteness, Johannes calls a greeting to one of the silversmiths. Nella manages a small mouthful of her own crab. It tastes salty, and it sticks in her teeth.

Johannes leaves her after his crab is fully scooped. 'I won't be long,' he says with a sigh. 'Business.' He makes it sound a chore, installing himself in a corner with a group of men.

Nella feels wholly exposed without him, but watches with fascination as her husband appears to transform. If Johannes is tired of talking about work, commissions, the state of trade, he manages to hide it. How handsome he is compared to the others, despite their own fine coats and leather boots. Laughter rises above their hats, heads are thrown back – and amongst the tipped-up moony faces and russet cheeks, the beards flecked with tiny bits of crab, Johannes is in the centre, tanned and smiling.

I could love him, Nella thinks. It should be easy to be the wife of a man like that. And love has to come, otherwise I cannot live. Perhaps it will grow slowly, like one of Otto's winter seeds.

Apprentices begin to approach Johannes, showing him what they have made, and he holds each piece up, handling the silver ewers and vases with delicate respect. A compliment from him sends the young men away delighted. The other merchants step back, watching Johannes with shrewd eyes as he opens the floor to artistic debate, the merits of seascape engravings over floral. He appears knowledgeable, observant, unusual to his core. He takes down names, pockets a silver box, tells an apprentice to see him at the VOC.

Nella is looking at her second course, a bowl of scallops drizzled in mutton broth and onion sauce, when the woman with the darting eyes moves forward. She is straight-backed, her fair hair twisted into an elaborate coif crowned by a black velvet band, seed pearls sewn along its curve. Silently, Nella thanks God for His small miracles, for Cornelia's deft sewing that has made her dress fit.

The woman stops at the table, curtseying low. 'Well, they said that you were young. Has he abandoned you?'

Nella grips the side of her bowl. 'I'm eighteen.'

The woman stands up straight, her eyes scanning the room. 'We wondered what you would look like,' she carries on in the same quiet voice. 'But now I see Brandt keeps the same standard of wife as he does everything else. The Oortman name is *very* old. And what does it say in Ecclesiastes? A good name is better than precious ointment!' Her tone is solicitous, admiring – but there is something within it that prods at Nella's vulnerability.

Nella attempts to extricate herself from the bench, but the table top and her large skirt conspire to wedge her in. The woman waits patiently for a curtsey, eyeing Nella's struggle. Finally free from the narrow gap between trestle and bench, Nella bends low, her face close to the woman's black brocade skirt, spanning out before her like the wings of a smothering crow.

'Oh up, child,' says the woman. *Too late*, *Madame*, thinks Nella. 'I'm Agnes, wife to Frans Meermans. We live at the sign of the fox on the Prinsengracht. Frans adores hunting, so he picked it himself.'

This offered intimacy holds awkwardly in the air, and Nella merely smiles, having learned already from Marin that silence is a marginal advantage.

Agnes pats her coif and Nella sees what she's supposed to – the rings adorning every one of her fingers – small rubies, amethysts and the mineral green flash of emerald. It is rather un-Dutch, all those precious stones for everyone to see – most women wear any jewel buried deep under the folds of their clothes. Nella tries to imagine Marin's hands glittering this way.

In the face of Nella's silence, Agnes gives a tight smile and continues. 'We are practically neighbours, part of the same *gebuurte*.'

Agnes Meermans has a strangely laboured way of speaking, her words unspontaneous, as if she has been practising her gracefulness in front of a mirror. Nella stares at the collapsed halo of seed pearls circling the woman's haughty head. The pearls are the same size as milk teeth, glinting in the candelabras' dancing light.

Agnes is perhaps a little older than Marin, but her slim, plain face is unworked – no moles or sun patches, no dark half-moons beneath her eyes, no sign of toil or children. She seems ethereal, un-lived in – except for those dark eyes, which blink in quick succession and then half-close in feline laziness. Agnes takes in Nella's silver dress, her narrow waist. 'Where are you from?' she asks.

'Assendelft. My name is Petronella.'

'A popular name, shared by many in this city. Did you like Assendelft?'

Agnes' teeth, Nella notices, are slightly stained. She considers the best answer to give this woman, who seems to be testing her. 'I have been from it for eleven days, Madame, and it could have been a decade.'

Agnes laughs. 'Time is such a stubborn candle in the young. And how did Marin find you?'

'Find me?'

Again Agnes laughs, cutting Nella off – a light expulsion of air, an aspirated disdain. This is not a conversation, it is Agnes sending out darts and watching them pierce. There seems to be a permanent lilt of amusement in her voice, but Nella is sure there is something else working away beneath this propped-up confidence, something she senses but cannot name. She looks straight at Agnes and smiles, defending her distress with whiter, younger teeth.

Around them the smells of cooked chicken, the stewed fruit and the sloshing sounds of wine jugs threaten to encroach upon their little circle, but Nella's magnetic attraction to Agnes repels all else.

'A bride for Johannes Brandt,' says Agnes with a sigh, drawing Nella down gently but insistently by the arm to sit with her on the bench. 'It's been *such* a long time. Marin must be so pleased; she always said he must have children. But Brandt was so infuriating about heirs.'

'I'm sorry?'

'No sure bet, he said. "Ugly from a beauty's legs, rude under decent care, and stupid despite their clever parents." Funny to a point, of course – Brandt always is. But one does have to pass it all on.'

It seems so disrespectful, so irreverent of Agnes to use only Johannes' last name, to talk of him so freely. Nella feels affronted, mute, unable to imagine in what circumstance Johannes would ever talk about heirs to this peculiar woman.

Agnes lifts a jug and pours them two glasses of wine. For a few moments they sit in silence, surveying the steady inebriation, the splash of port on damask cloth, the glint of clearing platters, the last of the food ladled in. 'The Golden Bend,' says

Agnes, her eyes sorting through Nella as if she was a pack of cards. 'Coming from Assendelft, it must seem as far away as Batavia.' She tucks an imaginary hair behind one ear, her ringed fingers glinting once again.

'A little.'

'But a love match like my own – so rare! Frans spoils me,' she whispers conspiratorially. 'Much like Brandt will spoil you.'

'I hope so,' Nella replies, feeling ridiculous.

'My Frans is a good man,' Agnes says.

The uninvited observation hovers like a challenge, and Nella wonders at its odd defiance. Perhaps this is fashionable conversation – combative and unsettling, passing for casual talk.

'And have you met the Negro?' Agnes continues. 'A *marvel*. There are hundreds on my Surinam estate, but I've not met a single one.'

Nella takes a sip of her wine. 'You speak of Otto. Have you been to Surinam?'

Agnes laughs. 'How sweet you are!'

'So you haven't?'

Agnes' smile drops. She looks almost mournful. 'The whole estate being given to us was a wonderful example of God's beneficence, Madame. No brothers lurking, you see – just me. I could never risk my life on a three-month voyage, now God has charged me with Papa's sugar loaves. How could I honour his memory if I was stuck somewhere on a ship?'

Nella's wine goes up her nose. Agnes leans in closely. 'I suppose the Negro is not perhaps a slave in the *strictest* sense,' she says. 'Brandt would not have us call him *that*. A couple of regentesses I know have one here in Amsterdam. I'd like one that plays music. The Receiver-General has *three*, and one of them's a woman, *and* she can play the viol! Proof now you can buy anything under the sun, I suppose. What can it be like for him? We all wonder. Just like Brandt to bring him home—'

'Agnes,' says a voice, and Nella hastens to stand. 'Please,' the man before them says, gesturing to reassure her that curt-seying in heavy taffeta is not required.

Agnes' deft fingers twine in her lap. 'My husband, Seigneur Meermans,' she says. 'And this is Petronella Oortman.'

'Petronella Brandt,' he says, looking round the room. 'I know.'

For a moment, this scene – this man standing, the woman sitting by his side, dressed in their wealth, bound by invisible ties – is the most perfect image of a marriage Nella has ever seen. The unity of it is intimidating.

Frans Meermans is slightly younger than Johannes, and his large face has not been roughened by wind or sun; five scallops could be eaten off that clean, wide jaw. He is holding a hat, the brim of it wider than anyone else's in the room. *One guilder to you, Johannes*, Nella thinks, wondering what other sorts of bets her husband wins.

Meermans is the sort of man who will soon get fat, she imagines. And he's likely to, given the food they serve in these places. He smells a little of wet dog and wood smoke, wilder than the fruity pomade of his wife. He leans forward and picks up a shining spoon. 'Are you a silversmith?' he asks.

Agnes smiles tightly at the weak joke. 'Will we speak with Brandt tonight?' she says.

Instinctively, Meermans lifts his head and scans the room.

Johannes has moved away from the group near Nella's table and is nowhere to be seen. 'We will,' he says. 'The sugar has been in his warehouse nearly two weeks.'

'We – you – must agree upon the terms. Just because *she* will not have anything sweet, doesn't mean that others won't.' Agnes offers the air her unamused *ha*; pouring herself another glass of wine, her hand makes a tiny tremble.

Nella stands up. 'I must find my husband.'

'He's coming now,' says Agnes primly. Meermans grips the brim of his hat. Agnes offers a deep, slow reverence at Johannes' approach. Meermans' spine stiffens, he puffs his chest.

'Madame Meermans,' says Johannes. The two men do not greet each other with a proper bow.

'Seigneur,' breathes Agnes, her dark eyes drinking in the expensive cut of his coat. It seems to Nella as if Agnes is doing her very best not to reach out and caress his velvet lapel. 'I see you are working your usual magic this evening.'

'Not magic, Madame. Just me.'

Agnes glances at her husband, who appears to be concentrating on the tablecloth. As if he can feel her eyes on his neck, Meermans speaks. 'We wanted to discuss the sugar . . . ' He trails off, and Nella sees the cloud on his half-hidden face.

'When will it sell?' Agnes asks, her question jabbing the air.

'I have it in hand, Madame.'

'Of course, Seigneur. I would never doubt—'

'Van Riebeeck's corruption at the Goede Hoop, these bloody little emperors at our far-flung outposts,' Johannes says. 'Batavian back-handers, black markets in the east – people are craving good product, and I'm telling them it's coming from you, Madame. The West Indies will end up saving us all, I imagine – but I will not take your sugar to the bourse. The trading floor is a circus, the brokers like crazed harpies. This sugar requires careful, controlled release abroad—'

'But not the English,' Agnes interrupts. 'I hate the English. The trouble they caused my father in Surinam.'

'Never the English,' Johannes assures her. 'It's well stored,' he adds smoothly. 'You can go and check it if you want.'

'You are most unusual, Seigneur, in insisting you sell abroad,' Meermans observes. 'Most good Dutchmen would keep such treasure to themselves, and given the quality of it, it would fetch a handsome price.'

'I find such *amour-propre* self-defeating,' Johannes says. 'It helps no one. We are seen abroad as untrustworthy. I have no desire to be such a thing. Why not spread your sugar's reputation?'

'For better or worse, we have put our trust in you.'

'I'm keeping a sugar loaf at home,' Agnes interrupts, pouring balm on heated water. 'It's so – beautifully *solid*. Hard as a diamond, sweet as a puppy. That's what my father used to say.' She fiddles with the lace at her neck. 'I can hardly bear to break it.'

Nella sways, staring at the dregs in her wineglass, slightly drunk.

'I will sail to Venice for you both,' Johannes says. 'Plenty of buyers there. It is not the best time for your sugar to arrive, but be assured there are Venetians who will want to buy.'

'Venetians?' Agnes gasps. '*Papists?*'

'Her father worked very hard, Seigneur Brandt,' Meermans snaps, 'not to fill Catholic stomachs.'

'But a guilder from any pocket is just as useful, is it not? A true businessman knows that. Venice and Milan eat sugar like we Dutchmen breathe—'

'Come, Agnes,' Frans says. 'I'm tired. And full.' He jams his hat back on his head like a stopper on his thoughts. Agnes stands waiting as the awkward silence grows.

'Goodnight, then,' says Johannes finally, his broad smile unable to mask the fatigue behind his eyes.

'God be with you,' Agnes says, snaking her arm upon her husband's. As the couple make their way along the mahogany panelling, the massacred tablecloths, the tipped-over silver jugs and scraps of food, Nella feels a spreading sense of worry.

'Johannes,' she says. 'Marin said we must invite—'

He puts his hand on her shoulder, and she sags at his weight. 'Nella,' he sighs, 'with people like that, you must always leave them wanting more.'

But when Agnes looks over her shoulder and throws her a haughty glance, Nella is not so sure.

Study

On their way back, Johannes lies stretched like a beached seal inside the barge.

'You know lots of people, Johannes. They admire you.'

He smiles. 'Do you think they'd talk to me if I wasn't rich?'

'Are we rich?' she asks. The words come out of her before she can stop them, the worry in her voice too obvious, the question mark too loud and accusatory.

He turns his head to her, his hair trapped on the bench beneath his cheek. 'What's wrong?' he asks. 'Ignore Marin, the things she says. She loves to worry.'

'It isn't Marin,' Nella replies, but then she wonders if it is.

'Just because someone tells you something with a bit of passion doesn't mean it's true. I have been richer. I've also been poorer. It never seems to make a visible difference.' His voice slows, drugged by food and the exhaustion of the evening. 'You cannot really touch my wealth, Nella. It is in the air, swelling, diminishing. Growing again. The things it buys are solid but you can put your hand through it like a cloud.'

'But, husband, surely there is nothing more solid than a coin?'

As he yawns and closes his eyes, Nella pictures her husband's money, no more than moisture, dissolving and re-forming without prediction. 'Johannes, there is something

I should tell you.' She pauses. 'There was – a miniaturist I hired—'

But looking over, she sees he has succumbed to the oblivion of a full stomach. Nella wants him to wake up, so she can ask him more questions. Unlike Marin, he always gives her an interesting answer. He seemed restless after Frans and Agnes left, his grey eyes shifting over private thoughts, locking her out once more. Why did Meermans seem so much less enthusiastic than his wife in dealing with Johannes? Why did Johannes not invite them to the house?

Nella smells the residue of Agnes' floral pomade on her hands. Her stomach mewls under her lace petticoat and she wishes she'd eaten more. Johannes' age is showing in the way his eyelids droop and his chin draws to his chest. He looks craggy, at thirty-nine a face from a fairy tale. She thinks about the silences that follow on from his bright chattiness, before he moves once more into darker distraction. She closes her eyes, putting her hand on the flat plane of her stomach. *Much like Brandt will spoil you.*

The love note hidden in Marin's room comes back to her. Where has it come from, how many days – or years – has it lain there in her pages? Nella wonders how Marin reads it – with pleasure or disdain? The soft touch of sable in the severity of her plain black bodice, her bridal bouquet a yellowing skull propped upon her shelves. No. Nobody would ever spoil Marin. She wouldn't let them.

Nella lifts her hand in the semi-darkness, looking at her wedding ring, her nails like faint pink shells. In Assendelft, there may have only been one town square, but at least the people sitting in it would listen to her. Here she is a puppet, a vessel for others to pour their speech. And it is not a man she has married, but a world. Silversmiths, a sister-in-law, strange acquaintances, a house she feels lost in, a smaller one that frightens her. There is ostensibly so much on offer, but Nella feels that something is being taken away.

When they enter the house, she turns, determined to speak – but now Johannes is bent over in commune with Rezeki. She is clearly his favourite, and Johannes runs a tight palm over the dog's skull. Rezeki bares her teeth in unaggressive pleasure. No one has lit the candles in the hall. The space is so dark, no moon through the high windows.

'Have they fed you, my beauty?' he asks, his voice gentle, full of love. The whippet responds by thumping her muscular tail on the tiles, and Johannes chuckles.

The chuckle irritates Nella, the attention she wants given to an animal. 'I shall go to bed, then,' she says.

'Do, do,' he replies, straightening up. 'You must be tired.'

'No, Johannes. I am not tired.'

She holds his gaze until he looks away. 'I must make notes on those men I met.' He walks towards his study and the dog follows immediately.

'Does she keep you company?' Nella calls. Eleven days alone as a wife, she thinks. Longer than it took God to make the world.

'She helps me,' he replies. 'If I try and solve a problem directly, I can't do it. If I tend to her, the answer comes.'

'She is useful then.'

Johannes smiles. 'She is.'

'And how much did you pay for Otto – is he useful?' she asks, her voice cold and shrill with nerves.

Johannes' expression clouds and Nella feels the blood pounding in her face. 'What did Agnes say to you?' he says.

'Nothing,' she replies, but it is true that Agnes' words have crept under her skin.

'I merely paid Otto's first wages in advance,' he says, his voice level.

'Does Otto think you set him free?'

Johannes sets his jaw. 'Does it bother you, Petronella, living here with him?'

'Not at all. It's just – I've never – I mean—'

'He's the only manservant I've ever had,' Johannes replies. 'And ever will.'

He turns away. Don't go, Nella thinks. If you go then I will become invisible, right now in this hallway, and no one will ever find me again. She points to the dog, sitting obediently at his side. 'Is that Rezeki or Dhana?' she asks.

Johannes raises his eyebrows, patting the animal with a loving hand. 'You have been paying attention. This is Rezeki. Dhana has a spot on her belly.'

I know she does, Nella thinks, picturing the little dog upstairs, waiting in the cabinet. 'They have strange names.'

'Not if you're from Sumatra.'

'What does Rezeki mean?' She feels young and stupid.

'Fortune,' he replies, slipping into the study and closing the door.

Nella peers into the darkness of the hall, a cold draught blowing towards her as if another door has opened somewhere beyond the expanse of marble tiles. The hairs on the back of her neck rise up. Someone is in the shadows.

'Hello?' she calls.

From deep in the kitchen come faint voices, urgent mutterings, the occasional clang of a pan. The sensation of being observed diminishes slightly, and these sounds, however distant, are a comfort. The house makes Nella lose her sense of proportion, and as if to reassure herself, she puts her hand out and touches the solid wood of Johannes' door frame. When she hears what she believes is an intake of breath behind her, and something brushes against the hem of her dress, Nella hammers with both fists on the study door.

'Marin, not now.'

'It's Nella!'

Johannes doesn't reply, and Nella stares down the darkness, trying not to let her terror win. 'Johannes, *please*. Let me in.'

When the door opens, the yellow glow is so welcoming that Nella could almost cry.

What strikes her is that the study feels so much more lived-in than anywhere else she has been in the house. This is a room with a firm purpose. It knows itself, and it is the closest Nella has felt to her husband. As she steps inside and he closes the door, she tries to shake away her hallway fright.

'There's no one out there, Nella,' he says. 'It's just the dark. Why don't you go to bed?'

Nella wonders how he knew her fear, just as he knew how Agnes had ruffled her over Otto. Being observed by Johannes is like being watched by an owl, she thinks. You feel pinioned.

Outside it has begun to rain, a gentle night patter, rhythmic and familiar. There is a tangy, papery smell in the small room, a high wooden table hinged to the wall, a mess of scrolls and an inkstand made of gold. Candle smoke covers the low ceiling with black welts, and the swirling design of a deep Turkey rug is scarcely visible for loose sheets covered in unfamiliar languages. Bits of red wax seals are scattered everywhere, and some have been ground into the wool.

There are maps on all the walls, more than Marin has. Nella looks over the shapes of Virginia and the rest of the Americas, the Mare Pacificum, the Moluccas, Japan. Each one is scored with fine lines shooting off in diamond patterns. These are items of precision, not dotted with wishful questions. Beneath the window is a huge padlocked chest, carved from a dark wood. 'That's where the guilders are stored,' Johannes says, sitting up on his stool.

Nella wishes Johannes would be more wolfish than owlish. It would give her the sense of a proper role, if not her wifely cue. 'I wanted – to thank you,' she falters. 'For my cabinet. I have such plans—'

'You do not need to thank me,' he says, batting the air with his hand again. 'It is the least I can do.'

'But I wanted to show you my thanks,' she says.

Nella attempts to mimic the physical grace of Agnes Meermans, giving a caress of his shirtsleeve with her trembling hand. She wants that unity, that image of a marriage to be made real. He does not react. Her fingers paw him like a tugging child's.

'Yes?' he says.

She lowers her hand and rests it upon the top of his thigh. Never in her life has she touched a man like this, never mind someone so imposing. She can feel the muscular bulk of his leg through the thick wool. 'When you speak those languages, you fascinate me,' she says.

Immediately, she knows she's said something wrong. He pulls himself off the stool. 'What?' he says.

Johannes looks so dismayed that Nella puts her hands to her mouth as if to wipe away the words. 'I just – it was just—'

'Come here,' he interrupts. To Nella's surprise, he strokes her hair with rough movements.

'I'm sorry,' she says, though she does not know for what she is apologizing. He leans down, holding her narrow arms, and kisses her on the mouth.

The shock of it – the alarming hot residues of wine and crab – assaults her, and it takes all her might not to tense up in his grip. She parts her lips a little, if only to release the pressure from his mouth. He keeps holding her – and she decides quickly before fear gets the better – to bring her hand down to the front of his breeches. If this is what all women have to do, she thinks – then practice must make it vaguely pleasurable.

Nella can just make it out, the snug bulge she has no knowledge of. But it isn't the rod her mother promised, it's more of a curled worm, a—

Her fingers seem to set off a spring, and Johannes drops her, jumping back into the edge of his desk. 'Nella,' he says. 'Oh, God.'

'Hus—'

'Go!' he cries. 'Get out.'

Nella stumbles away to a single admonishing bark from Rezeki, and Johannes slams the door. She hears his key turn in the lock, and as the terror of being out in this darkened hallway floods back, she runs upstairs to her room.

The cabinet is in the corner, and she pulls its curtains back, the cradle within glowing like an insult in the moonlight. Nella kicks the cabinet's leg, but the wood and tortoiseshell do not yield, and she hears the crack of bone. Yelping in pain, she refuses to cry. She limps round the room, turning her husband's paintings to the wall. Caught hare and rotten pomegranate, every single one.

Steps

'Why are the paintings all topsy-turvy?' Cornelia asks, turning the one nearest her back to its normal position. A painted caterpillar, crawling from the pomegranate, creeps towards the edge of the frame. The maid shudders, glancing at the cabinet. 'You can learn to live here, Madame,' she says quietly. 'You just have to want to do it.'

Nella watches her with one eye open, last night's humiliation flooding in. It pins her to the bed and she pushes her face in the pillow. Was it Cornelia down in the hall last night, listening to the disaster unfold? Then why didn't she comfort me? The thought of her wifely failure being overheard is devastating.

Johannes' rejection coats Nella's spirit like a film. She'd dash her own head if it meant she could remove these foolish ideas of true love, of marriage beds, laughter and children. As Cornelia turns another painting, the splayed oyster on a dark indigo background, Nella feels the walls closing in, their magnifying images of dead game and overblown blooms.

'I think Marin tried to slip the worst pictures over to you,' Cornelia says. Another crumb, at least – this grin, Cornelia's little offering of information, Marin and her cunning betrayed by someone slyer.

Cornelia pulls open the curtains and the late-October

morning light throws everything into stark relief. She grimaces as she shucks off one of her pattens, jutting out a small foot. 'Believe it or don't believe it, Madame,' she says, 'but my feet get tired too.' Balancing herself against the wall, she begins rubbing her sole. 'Bloody tired. Like a dead man's.'

Nella sits up. Back in Assendelft, there was never a maid like her. This sense of freedom Cornelia has, to do and say things she wouldn't anywhere else. Cornelia's voice is brightly conversational; the pleasure of feet-rubbing appears too great to worry what her mistress thinks. Perhaps it is something in this house, Nella thinks, some permissiveness I do not understand. Life here is indeed topsy-turvy – seeming wrong, but shining a light upon them all. How darned Cornelia's stockings are, a criss-cross of stitches, a rash of wool. Can't Marin give her better ones? Nella remembers Johannes' comment on his cloudy, untouchable wealth.

The vague touch of Johannes – pouched and unresponsive, comes back to her. Nella shudders. Watching as Cornelia turns back the painting of the strung-up hare, she feels a resentment prickling on her skin. *You have no idea*, she wants to say. *You try being married.*

'Cornelia,' she says. 'Why is Marin so intent on selling Agnes' sugar? Are we poor?'

Cornelia gapes at her. 'Madame, don't be ridiculous. *Poor?* Women all over the city would give their right arm to be where you are—'

'I don't need a *lesson*, Cornelia. I asked a question—'

'To have a master who treats you with respect, who takes you to feasts and buys you dresses and three-thousand-guilder cabinets? He feeds us, he asks after us. Otto will tell you the same.'

'Otto told me that things would spill over.'

'Well, there is much to admire in the Seigneur,' Cornelia replies, her words propulsive, urgent. 'He raised Toot like a son. Who else would do that? A manservant who can speak French and English? Who can plot a map, check the quality in a bolt of Haarlem wool—'

'But what can Otto do with all of that, Cornelia? What can any of us *do*?'

Cornelia looks uncomfortable. 'From where I'm standing, Madame, your life has only just begun. Here.' The maid reaches in the main pouch of her apron and places a large parcel on Nella's bed. 'It was left outside on the step, addressed to you. What's wrong?'

'Nothing,' Nella falters. Inked with the sign of the sun, the uninvited package rests on the coverlet.

'No herrings today, you'll be pleased to hear,' Cornelia goes on, eyeing the parcel. 'Winter jams and creamed butter. The Seigneur requested supper early.' She scoops up her errant patten and pushes it back over her shoe.

'I'm sure he did,' says Nella. 'Apparently he finds much of himself in food. I'll be down soon.'

Once the door is closed, Nella takes the parcel gently in her hands. I didn't ask for this, she thinks. My letter expressly told the miniaturist to cease. But even as she remembers this, Nella's fingers rip the paper. Who would not open such a parcel? she reasons. She remembers her letter clearly. *As wife of a high-ranking VOC merchant, I shall not be intimidated by an artisan.*

A note flutters out, and upon it, the words:

I FIGHT TO EMERGE

'Oh, do you, Mr Miniaturist?' Nella says out loud.

She tips up the rest of the package and an array of minuscule domestic items fall out. Irons as long as two barley grains, tiny baskets, woven sacks, a few barrels and a mop, a brazier for drying clothes. There are pots and pans, tiny fish knives and forks, an embroidered cushion, a rolled-up tapestry that reveals a portrait of two women and a man. Nella is convinced that is the same as the stitched story hanging on Johannes' wall downstairs – Martha and Mary, arguing over Jesus. Fear starts to mingle with her indignation.

In a small gold frame, a vase of flowers has been painted in oils, complete with a crawling caterpillar. It's a common motif, Nella tells herself, trying to keep calm, looking at the life-size version that Cornelia has just flipped over on the wall. There are a few exquisitely bound books, some no bigger than a stuiver coin, covered in unreadable handwriting. She flicks through their pages, half-expecting to find a love note – but there is none. There are two small maps of the Indies, and a Bible with a big B upon the front.

A separate package catches Nella's eye, glinting through the cloth. Nestling in the folds she finds a tiny golden key, hanging on a ribbon. She swings it in the cold morning light. It is beautiful, no longer than her little fingernail, intricately wrought with a carved pattern running down its neck. Too small to open any door, Nella thinks. Useless but ornate.

There is nothing else in the package – no note, no explanation, just the strange motto of defiance and this flurry of gifts. Cornelia swore she delivered the letter telling the minia-turist to desist. So why didn't he obey me?

But as she looks at these pieces – their extraordinary beauty, their unreachable purpose, Nella wonders if she really wants the miniaturist to cease. The miniaturist himself clearly has no desire to do so.

Tenderly, Nella places the new items in the cabinet, one after the other. She feels a fleeting sense of gratitude that takes her by surprise.

❦

'Where are you going?' Marin asks as Nella crosses the hall-way an hour later.

'Nowhere,' Nella replies, her mind already on the sign of the sun, on the explanations which lie behind the miniaturist's door.

'I thought so,' Marin says. 'Pastor Pellicorne is preaching at the Old Church and I assumed you would want to attend.'

'Is Johannes coming?'

Johannes is not coming, having claimed the need to be at the bourse, attending the latest figures being bandied on the trading floor. Nella wonders whether it is worship that her husband is avoiding.

Desperate to visit the Kalverstraat, Nella deliberately lags behind Marin, whose feet are pounding the canal paths as if they have done her a personal disservice. Rezeki, never that happy without her master, is at the bourse with Johannes. Not wanting to leave Dhana behind, Nella walks with the second whippet, the dog trotting obediently at her side, wet black nose tipped up towards her new-adopted mistress.

'Do you usually take dogs to church?' Nella asks Cornelia.

The maid nods. 'Madame Marin says they can't be trusted on their own.'

'I could bring Peebo.'

'Don't be ridiculous,' says Marin from over her shoulder, and Nella marvels at her ability to eavesdrop.

It is a brilliant day, the terracotta rooftops almost vermilion, the temperature cold enough to dilute any stench from the canal. Carriages clatter by, the waterways full of vessels loaded with men, women, bundles of goods, even a few sheep. They walk up the Herengracht, up Vijzelstraat and over the bridge onto the Turf Market leading towards the Old Church. Nella looks longingly towards her original destination, before Cornelia reminds her that unless Madame looks in the direction she is going, Madame will trip upon the cobbles.

From the boats, from their windows, from the canal path, the people stare. With every step they take past the tall and slender silk merchants' houses on the Warmoestraat, past the shop windows selling Italian maiolica, Lyons silk, Spanish taffeta, porcelain from Nuremburg and Haarlem linen, the Amsterdammers impress upon them a selection of looks. For a moment, Nella wonders what it is they have done, then she sees the muscles tense in the back of Otto's neck. He calls to Dhana to put her on the lead. 'It speaks!' Nella hears someone say to a peal of laughter.

When Otto passes there's hardly a face that doesn't open in surprise to see him walking with these women. Some expressions curdle to suspicion, others to disdain or outright fear.

Some are blankly fascinated, others seem unbothered, but it doesn't make up for the rest. As the party drops down off the Warmoestraat approaching the back of the Old Church, a man with smallpox scars, sitting on a low bench at a door, calls out as Otto passes by. 'I can't find work, and you give that animal a job?'

Marin wavers but Cornelia stops walking. She strides back and raises her fist inches from his cratered skin. 'This is Amsterdam, Hole-Face,' she says. 'The best man wins.'

Nella makes a strangled, nervous laugh which dies as the man lifts his own fist to Cornelia's face. 'This is Amsterdam, bitch. The best man knows the right friends.'

'Cornelia, hold your tongue,' calls Marin. 'Come away.'

'He should have his cut out!'

'*Cornelia!* Sweet Jesu, are we all of us animals?'

'Ten years Toot's been here, and nothing's changed,' the maid mutters, coming back to her mistress. 'You think they'd be used to it.'

'*Hole-Face*, Cornelia. How could you?' Marin says, but Nella hears a distinct note of approval in her voice.

Otto gazes towards a horizon far beyond the buildings of Amsterdam. He does not look at Hole-Face. 'Dhana,' he calls. The dog finally stops, perks her head up and trots towards him. 'Don't go too far, girl,' he says.

'Me, or the dog?' Cornelia sighs.

Though people continue to goggle, no one else offers their commentary. Nella notices how they look at Marin too. Unusually tall for a woman, with her long neck and head held high, Marin is like the figurehead on the bow of a ship, leaving waves of turning faces in her wake. Nella sees her through their eyes, the perfect Dutchwoman, immaculate, handsome and walking with a purpose. The only thing missing is a husband.

'How it looks, that Johannes does not come to church,' Nella hears Marin observing to Otto. In the face of his silence, Marin turns back to the girls. 'Did he invite the Meermanses to dinner?' she asks Nella.

Nella hesitates, on the cusp of a lie. 'Not yet,' she replies.

Marin stops, unable to hide her fury, her mouth held in an undignified O of shock as she accuses Nella with a flash of her grey eyes.

'Well, I couldn't *make* him invite them,' says Nella.

'My God,' Marin cries, stepping in a puddle of slop. She strides ahead, leaving the other three behind. 'Must I do it all?'

Boom and Bloom

Nella has never been in the Old Church before. 'Who's Pelli-corne?' she whispers to Cornelia. 'Don't we have enough of the Bible at home?'

Cornelia grimaces, for Marin has overheard. 'One must also worship in public, Petronella,' Marin says.

'Whatever you have to endure?' mutters Otto.

Marin pretends not to have heard. 'Pellicorne,' she breathes, as if referring to a particularly favourite actor. 'And the civitas is watching.'

They have a smaller church in Assendelft and this building is enormous in comparison. Soaring white stone columns divide the arches around and up the middle of the nave. Painted scenes from the Bible are in several of the windows, and through their stained-glass saints the sunlight floods the floor in watery red and gold, pale indigo and green. Nella feels she could dive in, but the names of the dead embedded in the floor remind her that the water is actually stone.

The church is busy; the living are staking their claim. Nella is surprised by the permitted level of noise, the fathers and mothers, the gossip and pleasantry, the unleashed dogs and little children. Barks and infant chatter scale the whitewashed walls, the sounds only lightly absorbed by the wood above. One dog is relieving itself nearby, its leg cocked jauntily against a pillar. There is light everywhere Nella looks, as if for one hour, God has turned his sole attention to this soaring chamber and the hearts that beat within it.

As Nella lowers her gaze to the people milling inside the church, her heart sends a hot thump of blood into her stomach.

The strange woman from the Kalverstraat is here. She sits alone in a chair near the side door, the sun through a plain window catching the top of her blonde head. Again, she watches Nella. There is nothing neutral in this gaze; it is active, enquiring and curious – but she is so still that Nella believes she could be one of the stained-glass saints, fallen from the church's pane.

Succumbing to the sensation of being measured and found not entirely whole, Nella is powerless to resist the stare. This time, however, the woman's gaze glides over Otto, Cornelia and Marin, even Dhana – taking all five into her understanding. Nella lifts her hand in greeting and Marin's voice interrupts her. 'She's too old to be out.'

'What?' Nella says, dropping her hand.

'The dog,' says Marin, bending over, trying to move Dhana, from where the animal has placed her rump firmly on the floor. Dhana refuses to budge, whining, her snout up in the direction of the woman, her claws clattering the stone. 'What on earth is wrong with her?' Marin straightens, massaging the base of her spine. 'She was fine a minute ago.'

Nella looks back to where the woman is sitting, but all she sees is an empty chair. 'Where did she go?'

'Who?' asks Cornelia.

Despite the light from the sun, the church seems very cold. The hubbub rises and falls and rises again, the people continue to mill, and the woman's chair remains untaken. Dhana starts to bark.

'Nothing,' says Nella. 'Be quiet, Dhana, you're in a house of God.'

Cornelia giggles. 'You're both too loud,' Marin says. 'Please remember that people are always watching.'

'I know they are,' says Nella, but Marin has moved away.

True to Calvinist form, the pulpit is in the middle of the nave, where the murmuring crowd congregates in clusters. 'Like flies upon a piece of meat,' says Marin disapprovingly, as they catch up with her, gliding with slow dignity up the nave. 'We shall not sit in the crowd. God's word reaches far. They don't need to clamber like four-year-olds to see Pastor Pellicorne.'

'The more they try to look holy the less I am convinced,' says Otto.

A tiny smile forms in the corner of Marin's mouth, dying quickly as Agnes and Frans Meermans come into view.

Billowing a cloud of intense, flowery fragrance, Agnes swims in her great skirts across the freezing grave-slabs. 'They've brought the savage,' she whispers in earshot to her husband, her eyes riveted on Otto.

'Seigneur and Madame Meermans,' Marin says, retrieving her psalter from a pouch at her waist, passing it from palm to palm as if she's weighing it up as a missile. The women curtsey. Frans Meermans bows, watching Marin's slender fingers move nervously over her well-worn leather book.

'Where is your brother?' asks Agnes. 'The Day of Judgement—'

'Johannes is working. He offers thanks to God a different

way today,' Marin replies. Meermans snorts. 'It is quite true, Seigneur.'

'Oh yes,' he says. 'The bourse is known to be a haven for the godly.'

'There was an oversight at the Guild of Silversmiths,' Marin says, ignoring his tone. 'My brother meant to invite you to eat with us, but so many duties distract his mind.' She pauses. 'You must come and dine at our house.'

Meermans sniffs. 'We don't need—'

'We are honoured, Madame Brandt,' Agnes interrupts, her dark eyes sly with undisclosed excitement. 'Though should not his wife be issuing this invitation?'

Nella feels her cheeks go red. 'Dine with us tomorrow,' Marin says, her voice tight.

'Tomorrow?' Nella is unable to help herself. It seems unlike Marin to be so hasty. 'But—'

'And do bring a sugar loaf. We will taste it and toast your fortune to come.'

'You wish to *taste* our Carib treasure?' Agnes buries her chin in her ostentatious fur collar, jet irises boring into Marin.

Marin smiles, and Nella notices how attractive she is when she does so, even if it is pretend.

'I do,' says Marin. 'Very much.'

'Agnes,' says Meermans, and his wife's name becomes a note of caution. 'Let us take our place.'

'We will come tomorrow,' Agnes adds, 'and will bring such sweetness the like of which you've never tasted.'

They drift off, calling greetings, waving and nodding as they go.

'I could kill him,' Marin murmurs, her eyes on their

retreating backs. Nella wonders whom she means. 'Carib treasure my eye. Why did Johannes ever agree to this?'

'But don't we need it, Madame?' Cornelia murmurs. 'You said so yourself—'

Marin snaps her head round. 'Don't parrot me my own words, girl. Listening at doors – you know nothing. Just make sure there's a decent supper tomorrow.'

Cornelia shrinks back, bending down to busy herself with the dog, her face a mask of hurt pride. Marin rubs her temples, eyes closed in pain. 'Are you quite well?' Nella asks, feeling the need to intervene.

Marin looks at her. 'Quite well.'

'We must take our seats,' Otto says. 'There's room in the choir.' He looks marooned among the barely whispered commentaries that accompany his every move.

Pastor Pellicorne goes up to the pulpit. He is tall, over fifty, clean-shaven, his grey hair short and neat, his collar wide and sparkling white. His appearance suggests he has an attentive set of servants.

Pellicorne does not bother with introductions. 'Foul practices!' he booms over the dogs and children, the scuffling feet and mewling of the gulls outside. A silence falls, all eyes on him but those of Otto, who bows his head, focused on the knot of his intertwined hands. Nella looks over at Agnes, whose face is turned upwards to the pastor like a mesmerized child. She is so odd, Nella thinks. One minute so glib and haughty, the next so infantile and striving to impress.

'There are many closed doors in our city through which we cannot see,' Pellicorne continues, hard and unrelenting. 'But do not think you can hide your sin from God.' His tapering fingers grip the edge of the pulpit. 'He will find you out,' Pellicorne calls across their heads. 'There is nothing hidden that will not be revealed. His angels will look through the windows and keyholes of your heart, and He will hold you to your acts. Our city was built on a bog, our land has suffered God's wrath before. We triumphed, we turned the water to our side. But do not rest easy now – it was prudence and neighbourliness that helped us triumph.'

'Yes,' calls a man in the crowd. A baby begins to wail. Dhana whimpers and tries to get under Nella's skirts.

'If the reins of our shame are not held tight,' says Pellicorne, 'we all will return to the sea. Be upright for the city! Look into your hearts and think how you have sinned against your neighbour, or how your neighbour is a sinner!'

He pauses for effect, breathless in his righteousness. Nella imagines the congregation pulling open their ribs, staring into the beating mess of their sinful hearts, peering into everyone else's before slamming their bodies shut. In the corner of the church, a starling beats its wings. Somebody should let it out, she thinks.

'They're always getting trapped,' Cornelia whispers.

'Let us not allow his fury to harm us again.' There are several grunts of assent from the congregation, and by now, Pellicorne's voice is slightly quavering with emotion. 'It is greed. Greed is the canker we must cut out – greed is the tree and money the deep-lying root!'

'It also paid for your nice collar,' Cornelia mutters. Nella feels breathless with trying not to giggle. She risks a glance at

Frans Meermans. Whilst his wife's attention is drawn to the pulpit, he is watching the Brandts.

'We must not fool ourselves that we have harnessed the power of the seas,' Pellicorne modulates his voice to an insistent, lulling hum before sticking in the knife. 'Yes, the bounty of Mammon has come to us – but one day it will drown us all. And where will you be on that fateful day? Where? Up to your elbows in sugared sweets and fat chicken pies? Swamped in your silks and strings of diamonds?'

Cornelia sighs. 'If only,' she murmurs, 'if only.'

'Take care, take care,' warns Pellicorne. 'This city thrives! Its money gives you wings to soar. But it is a yoke on your shoulders and you would do well to take note of the bruise around your neck.'

Marin has screwed her eyes tight as if she's going to cry. Nella hopes it is merely a sort of spiritual bliss, an abandonment to the power of Pellicorne's holy warning words. Meermans is still staring. Marin opens her eyes and notices this; her knuckles tighten on her psalter. She shifts in her seat, misery writ across her waxen face. Nella's throat feels dry but she dares not cough. Pellicorne is reaching his climax and the bodies of the congregation draw together, solidifying, alert.

'Adulterers. Money-men. Sodomites. Thieves,' the pastor cries. 'Beware them all, look for them! Tell your neighbour if the cloud of danger is approaching. Let not evil pass your doorstep, for once the canker comes it will be hard to take away. The very ground beneath us will break apart, God's fury will seep into the land.'

'Yes,' says the man in the crowd again. 'Yes!'

Dhana barks with increasing agitation. 'Shut *up*,' Cornelia whispers.

'What can you do to make it go away?' booms Pellicorne, back to his full volume, arms aloft like Christ himself. '*Love*. Love your children, for they are the seeds that will make this city bloom! Husbands, love your wives, and women, be obedient, for all that is holy and good. Keep your houses clean, and your souls will follow suit!'

He is finished. There are sighs of release, sounds of agreement, an awakening and stretching of legs. Nella is beginning to feel lightheaded. The light is shining on the grave-slabs. Be obedient. Husbands, love your wives. *You are sunlight through a window, which I stand in, warmed. My darling.* The baby wails again and Nella and Marin look up together as its mother unsuccessfully tries to hush it, absenting herself from the congregation and slipping out through the side-door of the church.

Nella follows Marin's gaze, both staring enviously at the brief square of golden sunlight afforded by the mother's exit. In this intense new world of Amsterdam, in this cold city church, one hour of worship feels like a year.

❧

That night in Nella's room, the moon illuminates her cabinet in patches. The tock of the pendulum clock beats the air like a muffled pulse, seeming to grow louder in her ears. She thinks of the woman in the church, observing her in silence.

'Why didn't you speak to me?' Nella asks out loud, watching the spaces of her nine dark rooms. 'What do I have that you want?'

No answer comes, of course, and the pieces inside the cabinet give off a shifting silver radiance. Tomorrow, Nella thinks, I will go to the miniaturist to settle their unwanted presence once and for all. It is not right, surely, to be sent things you didn't ask for? It is a staking of forbidden territory.

Nella is glad to be out of Assendelft, true – but home is nowhere – it is neither back there in the fields nor here in the canals. Adrift, she feels shipwrecked between the idea of her marriage and its actual state, and the cabinet, beautiful and useless, is a horrible reminder of it all.

Johannes' diffidence towards her has begun to pierce deeply. He has disappeared many times to the bourse, to the VOC, to his warehouse by the eastern taverns, where the potatoes have the fluffiest flesh. He takes no interest in her, he doesn't come to church. At least Marin notices me enough to give me a bruise, Nella thinks. How ridiculous this is, to be grateful for a pinch! Her anchor has dropped but found no place to hold – and so it goes through her, massive, unstoppable and dangerous, plunging through the sea.

The sound of whispering rouses her from self-pity. Sitting up, Nella can still smell lily oil hanging on the air. Even I am beginning to dislike it, she thinks. She creeps across her room, straining her ears as she opens her door. The corridor is freezing, but there are definitely two voices in the hallway, words winnowing from urgent breath. They seem excited or fearful – certainly careless, their whispers coming up the house.

Nella wonders if her imagination is betraying her as the voices pause, two doors are shut, and the house falls again to quiet. She moves along the corridor, pressing her forehead between the spindles of the banister, listening vainly. But there is only silence, as if the speakers have vanished into the panelling of the wall.

When the scrabbling starts up, the hairs rise on the back of Nella's arms. Her guts swill as she looks down to where the noise increases – but it is only Rezeki, Rezeki, peering up at her before slinking low across the tiles. The animal moves like spilled liquid, masterless, a chess piece rolling out of place.

The Wife

By midday, Cornelia has already spent hours in the working kitchen preparing for the Meermans' dinner. The feast is to be sumptuous; a spread of winter fare, spiced to the hilt with treats from Johannes' deals in the East.

Nella finds her sitting at the table chopping a pair of huge cabbages. 'Hungry?' the maid asks, looking up at her young mistress, who hovers on the bottom step, Dhana at her side.

'Like a dog,' Nella replies, trying to trace signs of a sleepless night on Cornelia's face. The maid looks more flustered than anything.

'Talk about short notice!' Cornelia says. 'You've got dried bread and herring until I've finished all my dishes – Madame Marin insists. This cabbage needs a dress.' On seeing Nella's face, Cornelia relents. 'Oh, here. Have a puffert. They've just come out of the pan.' She pushes a plate towards her, piled up with small fried pancakes dusted in sugar.

'What did Hanna give you, in her husband's shop?' As Dhana moves to her bed by the stove, Cornelia's hand hovers over the remaining cabbage. Her skin is red-raw, her fingernails white from all the soap.

'You're eating it,' Cornelia says, leaning in. How round and blue her eyes are, her irises ringed in black. 'The last of Arnoud's best sugar. Hanna's right. So much for sale in this city is terrible. It's a shame the Seigneur is selling all of Agnes' abroad.'

Cornelia's act of sharing has cracked a carapace, and Nella feels within a sense of rising warmth. Even the cabbage seems to glow, a green orb in the friendly firelight of the open stove.

❦

Taking a deep gulp of cold air, Nella coughs on the tinge of sewage. In summer this canal will be hell, she thinks, walking up the Golden Bend. But for now, walking alone feels wonderful – and unaccompanied women, as her husband observed on the barge, are not such a rarity that Nella feels any scrutiny. Passing through Vijzelstraat, crossing Reguliersdwarsstraat and onto Kalverstraat after asking for directions, Nella quickly finds the sign of the sun with the motto underneath: *Everything Man Sees He Takes For A Toy*. She knocks on the heavy door. The street is not busy – people want to stay inside where it is warm. Nella's breath turns into moisture on the air as she knocks again.

'Hello?' she calls. Please answer, she thinks. '*Hello?* It's Nella Oortman. Petronella Brandt. I need to speak with you. You sent some things I didn't order. I like them, but I don't understand why you did it.'

Nella puts her ear to the dense wood, straining vainly for the sound of feet. She stands back, looking up into the panes. No candles are lit from within and all is still – yet the place has the unmistakeable air of occupation.

When the face at the window appears, Nella stumbles back into the middle of the Kalverstraat, a shock of recognition stopping the breath in her throat. The glass may be thick and warped, but that hair is unmistakeable. It is the woman who watched her at church.

Her face a pale coin, blonde locks beaming through the dark glass shadows, the woman rests her palm upon the windowpane. She remains motionless in that position, casting a calm regard down onto the street.

'You!' Nella says. But the woman doesn't move. 'Why—'

'She won't come out,' interrupts a man's voice. 'However hard you try. I've got a good mind to report her to the authorities.'

Nella swivels towards the speaker. He is a little way off from her, sitting outside what appears to be a wool shop. Nella swallows. It's smallpox man – *Hole-Face* – the one who called Otto an animal, whom Cornelia yelled at in the street. Up close, his skin is like a sea-sponge, full of pinkish craters.

Nella looks back to the window. The woman has gone, the pane empty, and the house has a sudden deadened aspect, as if no one lives there at all. She rushes to the door and starts hammering, as if to beat the building back to life.

'I told you, she doesn't answer. She's a law unto herself,' Hole-Face remarks.

Nella spins round and presses her back against the door. 'Who is she? Tell me who she is.'

He shrugs. 'She doesn't talk much. Funny accent. Nobody knows.'

'*Nobody*? I don't believe you.'

'Well, we're not all civic-minded, Madame,' he says. 'She keeps herself to herself.'

Nella pauses for breath. 'In *Smit's List*, a miniaturist advertised under this address. Are you telling me, Seigneur, that the only person who lives here is a woman?'

Hole-Face brushes wisps of wool from his trousers. 'I am, Madame. And who knows what she's getting up to in there?'

'All and yet nothing,' Nella replies.

'Is *that* what you ladies call it.'

It cannot be possible that a woman lives alone in the heart of Amsterdam, under the eye of the burgomasters, the guilds, the hypocritical puritans like Hole-Face. What thoughts whir under her pale hair, why does she send out these breathtaking, unasked-for pieces?

I just want to know, thinks Nella, closing her eyes, remembering the inexpressible sensation of the woman's gaze in the church and before that, out here on the Kalverstraat. This is too wonderful to be believed – a woman! Shame courses through Nella for what she wrote in her second letter – *Sir . . . I will curtail our transactions forthwith*. But it hasn't seemed to matter. The woman seems to enjoy disobeying rules.

'A woman alone like that can only mean one thing,' Hole-Face goes on. 'She's a strumpet. And the boy who came to take her parcels was another foreigner. Those goings on should be kept for the Eastern Islands. Honest people who just want to work and live well shouldn't have to—'

'How long has she been here?'

'Three or four months, I suppose. Why's she so important to you?'

'She's not,' says Nella, the fib jarring in her mouth. It feels the same as a betrayal. She girds herself, feeling protective towards the woman but not knowing exactly why. 'She isn't important at all.'

From one of the higher windows Nella thinks she sees movement, but it's muddled by the reflection of another woman in the window above the wool shop, beating a rug into the street and looking irritated by the fuss outside her door.

'Seigneur, if you speak to her—'

'I won't be doing that,' Hole-Face interrupts. 'She's got the devil in her.'

Nella fumbles for a guilder, placing it in his filthy palm. 'If you do speak to her,' she turns and calls up to the window. 'Tell her Nella Brandt is sorry! And to ignore her last letter. I only want to know why. And tell her – I'm looking forward to what she sends next.'

Even as she shouts these words up to the window, Nella wonders if they are exactly truthful. Only widows and whores live alone, some happily, others unwilling – so what exactly is the miniaturist doing up there, sending out her pieces, wandering the city alone? Nella has no idea what she's playing with, but it certainly doesn't feel like a toy.

She drags her heels back up the Kalverstraat. The miniaturist's extraordinary existence is wasted on people like Hole-Face, she thinks. And it *will* be extraordinary – whatever it turns out to be – those eyes alone, that stare, these incredible packets full of clues and stories. The back of Nella's neck prickles and she turns quickly, believing herself connected to that house at the sign of the sun.

But the Kalverstraat is once again quiet, unaware of the presence hiding in its heart.

Nella returns home and rushes upstairs to the cabinet, running her fingers over the miniaturist's pieces. They are charged with a different energy, laden with a meaning she cannot penetrate, yet even more addictive in their mystery. She's chosen me, Nella thinks, glowing with this discovery, yearning to know more.

Cornelia's voice and approaching footsteps pull her from her reverie. Hastily, she draws the cabinet's curtains as the maid pokes her head round the door. 'The Meermanses are coming within the hour,' Cornelia gabbles, 'and the Seigneur still isn't home.'

Downstairs, Cornelia and Otto have exhausted themselves with extra polishing, sweeping, mopping, beating the curtains, pummelling the cushions, as if the house is out of shape and needs a realignment which cannot be achieved. The faience and China-ware glitter in the best kitchen, the mother-of-pearl winks from inlays, and seeing how all the tallow candles have been replaced with those of beeswax, Nella takes the chance to inhale their lovely scent.

'Chores over chaos will only go so far,' Otto murmurs to himself as he passes by, and she wonders what he means.

Marin has dressed in her finest black. Not stooping so low as perfume but armed with a shield of voluminous skirts, she now paces the salon, her stride long and regular as the pendulum clock. Her slender fingers worry her psalter, her hair screened off her face by a stiff white lace headband, handsome features stern. Nella sits, dressed by Cornelia in another of her altered gowns, this one the colour of gold. 'Where is Johannes?' she asks.

'He'll be here,' Marin says.

With every restless footfall Marin makes across the polished floor, Nella wishes she could go back upstairs and search her miniatures for some clue as to what might come next, if anything, and what the mottoes mean.

By the time the Meermanses arrive, the cold blast of canalside air shooting behind them into the hall, Johannes has still not returned. All the windows have been washed by Otto and the panes catch the reflection of twenty burning candles winking in the early twilight, their honey scent mingling with the sharper tang of vinegar and lye.

If Agnes notices the effort Marin has exerted on her servants, she makes no comment. Gliding in, her poise perfect now, all traces of the childlike girl at church are quite evaporated. They curtsey to each other, their silence broken only by the crush of their wide skirts towards the floor. Frans comes forward, a look of strain upon his face. Marin raises her hand and he takes it, the gold of his wedding ring gaudy on her pale skin. Time appears to slow, the lights twinkling in the air around them.

'Seigneur,' says Marin.

'Madame.'

'Come in, both of you, please.' She extricates her hand and leads them to the salon.

'Is your Negro here?' Agnes calls, but Marin pretends not to hear.

It takes the women a few minutes to arrange themselves in the chairs around the fire, due to the amount of material that swathes them. Meermans stands by one of the windows, looking out. Nella eyes the green velvet seats – their copper studs and carved wooden lions – and thinks about their shrunken doubles upstairs in the cabinet. How on earth did the miniaturist know to send me those? she wonders, desperate to know.

But a pulse of fear beats inside her. She has chosen me, but for what? Who is this woman, watching from afar, who comments on my life? Instinctively, she turns to the windows, thinking she might see a face there, peering from the street. But the light outside has darkened further, and Meermans' bulk would scare a person off.

'Cornelia should draw the curtains,' Marin says.

'No,' says Nella.

Marin turns to her. 'It's cold, Petronella. It would be best.'

'Sit by me,' says Agnes, interrupting.

Nella obeys, rustling over in her golden dress. 'You look like a coin!' exclaims Agnes – and the ridiculous comment, thrown hard and bright in the air, falls to the floor with a thud.

'Where's Johannes?' asks Meermans.

'He's coming, Seigneur,' says Marin. 'He's been delayed by unexpected business.'

Agnes glances at her husband. 'We are rather tired.'

'Oh?' Marin replies. 'Why is that, Madame?'

'Oh, Agnes, call me *Agnes*. Marin, I don't know why, after twelve years, you can't do it.' Agnes laughs, the *ha* that makes Nella wince.

'Agnes,' says Marin quietly.

'Feasts, mainly,' Agnes goes on, sounding conspiratorial. 'So many weddings before the winter. Did you know Cornelis de Boer has married *Annetje Dirkmans*?'

'I do not know the name,' says Marin.

Agnes demurs, jutting her lower lip. 'Always the same,' she

says to Nella, her tone a mix of playful admonishment and deliberate barb. 'I *love* a wedding,' she goes on. 'Don't you?'

Neither Marin nor Nella say anything. 'Marriage is—' Agnes stops deliberately, considering her audience.

Marin's hands are so still in her lap, they could be carved upon a tomb. Nella feels the jangle of this conversation, the dead ends of it and the unsaid words forming a knot in her mind. The only sound is the crackling of the fire and the occasional creak of Meermans' leather boots as he shifts his weight at the window. From the working kitchen, the smells of Cornelia's cooking waft, capons in mace and rosemary, a parsley pigeon in ginger.

'I have to know,' Agnes announces. Marin turns to her, alarm in her eyes. 'What *did* Brandt buy you for your wedding gift, Nella?'

Nella's eyes meet Marin's. 'A house,' she says.

'How *wicked* of him! Is it a hunting lodge? We're buying a lodge in Bloemendaal.'

'This one is enamelled with tortoiseshell,' Nella says, beginning to enjoy herself, as Agnes' eyes saucer in their sockets. 'You . . . couldn't possibly live inside it.'

Agnes seems puzzled. 'Why not?'

'It is this house, shrunk to the size of a cabinet,' says Marin. From the window, Meermans turns.

'Oh, one of *those*,' Agnes tuts. 'I thought you meant a real house.'

'Do you have one, Agnes? Petronella's is shot through with pewter,' Marin says.

Agnes' girlishness rises up once again, a momentary defiance flickering over her face. 'Of course I do. Mine is covered in *silver*,' she replies.

Her hard boast melts to a raw fib, pooling between the silent women. Each of them examines the material of her dress, unable to look up. 'Whom did you pay to furnish yours?' Agnes finally asks.

Nella falters. The thought of Agnes going to the Kalverstraat, of her having a connection with that woman, of her knowing she even exists, feels insupportable. It would feel as if her secret knowledge had been plucked, its best bits pecked away.

As if she senses weakness, Agnes leans forward. '*Well?*'

'I—'

'My mother left me some childhood pieces. Petronella has been using those,' Marin says.

'What, Marin?' says Agnes. 'You had a childhood?'

'I must fetch the Rhenish wine,' Marin adds, ignoring both this and the gratitude which beams from Nella's face. 'Otto has failed to put it out.'

Marin disappears from the room, calling Otto's name. Agnes watches her exit, leaning back against her chair. 'Poor thing,' she breathes. 'Poor thing.' She turns to Nella, concern etched on her face. 'I don't know why she's so unhappy.' She leans ever closer, scooping Nella's hand in both of hers. Her fingers are damp, like a pond-pulled frog. 'Our husbands, Nella, used to be such good friends.' She squeezes tight, the stones of her twisted rings indenting Nella's palm. 'They made it through some of the worst storms the North Sea has ever seen.'

'You are too interested in the past, my darling,' her husband calls from the window. 'Is not today more interesting?'

Agnes laughs. 'Oh, Frans. Nella, your husband must have told you, they met when they were twenty-two, working in the VOC ships? Over the Equator they went – missing the Carib storms because the north-east trade wind was pushing them on.' Agnes recites it like a fairy tale, learned by years of repetition.

'My dear—'

'They were so talented, working for the glory of the republic! Of course, Frans found his calling at the Stadhuis in the end, but the brick walls of Amsterdam could never hold Brandt.'

When her husband stops at the door, Agnes' gaze follows him like a hawk. 'Has Brandt told you his tales of Batavia?' she asks Nella.

'No.'

'He sold his stock and *quadrupled* the money he went with. He practically talked the guilders into his pocket and came back with a crew of his own.'

Agnes' admiration, laced with an indefinable scorn, is hypnotic. Although this information seems to cause Meermans some discomfort, Nella is eager for more.

'That was seventeen years ago, Agnes,' says Meermans, his voice forcefully hearty. 'These days he's happier down on the Eastern Islands stuffing himself with potatoes.'

He walks out of the room as if he lives here and knows where he's going. She hears the pause of his heavy clump across the hallway and imagines him sitting in one of the hall chairs, seeking a moment of relief – but from what exactly, she cannot tell.

He's right about one thing, though – Agnes is the only person Nella has met who likes to bring up the past. It pained her mother, it made her father weep. The rest of Amsterdam seems to want to move forward, building ever upwards despite the boggy land that might well sink them all.

Agnes looks breathless, slightly wild. Opening her hands with a shrug, she picks absently at an invisible mote of dust on her skirt. 'Men are men,' she says, oblique and adult once again.

'Of course,' Nella replies, thinking that two men couldn't be more different than Frans Meermans and Johannes Brandt.

'I've given a loaf of our sugar to your maid,' says Agnes. 'Frans said we'll try it after dinner. Do you think Marin will have a spoonful?' She closes her eyes. 'All those perfect loaves! Frans has been – *wonderful*. The refining process has gone very smoothly.'

'It was your sole inheritance, am I correct?'

Agnes blinks. 'In the act of submission, Madame Brandt,' she murmurs, 'one always gains much more.'

Nella instinctively rejects this offered confidence. Disappointed by the curdling silence between them, Agnes straightens up. 'Although there may be more sugar to come, it is important your husband does well by us,' she says. 'The weather is not always kind to Surinam, and foreigners are constantly attacking my father's – that is to say, our land. This crop could be our only fortune for many a year.'

'Yes, Madame. We are highly honoured you have selected us.'

Agnes visibly softens a little. 'Have you ever been to your husband's office?' she asks.

'Never, Madame.'

'I go quite frequently to the Stadhuis. It is pleasant for Frans when I pay him visits. Such a thrill to see his achievements in regulating this republic. He is an exceptional man. But tell me,' Agnes continues. 'Has Marin made you eat her herring dinners, those culinary massacres of self-improvement?'

'We—'

'One-herring dinners and plain black gowns!' Agnes places a hand on her heart, closing her eyes again. 'But in *here*, Madame, God sees our truest deeds.'

'I—'

'Do *you* think Marin looks unwell?' Agnes snaps her eyes open, adopting her previous pose of concern.

Nella doesn't know what to say, exhausted by the woman's mercurial conversation. Unhappiness seems to roll off Agnes in uneven waves, and yet, she can be so convincingly confident that it makes for such confusion. She hungers for something, and Nella cannot sate her.

'Marin always used to be the strongest,' Agnes observes, a faint wisp of spite.

Nella is saved from replying by the sound of Rezeki's bark.

'Ah!' says the guest, rearranging her dress. 'Your husband is finally home.'

Exchanges

The meal, for all of Nella's hunger and Cornelia's cooking talent, is excruciating. Over the downy white expanse of cloth, Agnes drinks three glasses of Rhenish and talks of Pastor Pellicorne's excellent sermons and his piety, of the importance of always being grateful – and what about those petty thievers with their severed hands she's seen being let out of the Rasphuis?

'What is the Rasphuis?' Nella asks.

'The male prison,' Agnes replies. 'The Spinhuis is where wicked women are sent, the Rasphuis where they tame the wild men. It's where the lunatics live,' she continues, craning forward and boggling her eyes in some approximation of madness. It is a shocking sight and when Agnes persists in it, Frans stares into the tablecloth. 'Abandoned by their families, paid for with a stipend to the prison to keep them safe.' She points a ringed finger at Nella. 'But the *really* wild men get sent to the torture chamber in the bottom of the Stadhuis, next to the storerooms for the city's gold.'

Marin says little, throwing glances at her brother, who matches Agnes glass for glass and then one extra by the time Cornelia removes the first course.

Johannes holds himself together, but he is glassy-eyed, his stubble unshaved silvering his tanned face. He considers his plate with extra concentration, plunging his fork into the chunks of pigeon slicked in ginger sauce. As Agnes becomes more foolish, Meermans takes over, trying to impress with his mercantile talk. He wants to discuss cane juice and copper equipment, sugar loaves, the degree to which one must punish a slave. Johannes chomps on his carrots with a barely muted ferocity.

Eventually, the plum pie and thick cream has been fought with and swallowed down, the meal is done, and the real reason for their being there can be avoided no longer. At a nod from Marin, Cornelia comes in with the sugar loaf on a China-ware plate, as tentative as if she were carrying a newborn child. Behind her, Otto enters with a tray of spoons.

Nella examines the sugar loaf, a conical, glittering structure the length of her forearm, the crystals tightly compacted.

'Half of the crop was loaved before it shipped,' Meermans says. 'The other half has been refined in Amsterdam.'

'Spoons?' says Johannes, handing them out. Everyone takes an implement. 'Cornelia, Otto, you should try,' he says. 'You're the likely experts.'

Agnes' nostrils flare and she purses her lips. Gingerly, Cornelia accepts a spoon and passes one to Otto. As Johannes pulls out a small flick-knife and stands to make the first incision, Meermans rises from his chair and draws a dagger from his belt. 'Allow me,' he says, brandishing the blade. Johannes smiles and sits back down. Marin remains rigid, both hands resting on the damask cloth.

The first white shaving lands in a curl at the base of the cone. 'For you,' says Meermans, handing it with a flourish to his wife. Agnes beams. He hands out more shavings, leaving

Johannes and Otto till last. '*Incroyable*,' he says, popping his own curl in his mouth. 'Your father may not have been blessed with sons, my dear, but in his sugar he got the prize.'

Nella feels the shaving melt in her mouth, sweet and granular, vanished in a moment. It leaves a sheen of vanilla behind, and tacks her tongue onto her palate. Marin holds her spoon, her eyes averted from the waiting sweetness. Agnes' eyes never leave her as Marin's knuckles tighten on the handle, her mouth barely opening as she swallows it quickly.

'Exceptionally good,' Marin says; a thin smile.

'Another taste, Madame?' says Agnes.

'Cornelia, what do you think of it?' Johannes asks. Marin throws the maid a warning glance.

'Very good, Seigneur. Delicious.' Cornelia's voice is the most timid Nella has ever heard.

'Otto, what do you think?' Johannes asks.

'Now God be thanked, but you are going to make our fortunes, Brandt!' Agnes interrupts. Johannes smiles, accepting another white curl from the glistening loaf. Nella watches Otto wipe his mouth delicately, every move one of controlled economy.

'When are you going to Venice?' asks Meermans. 'All those palazzos and gondolas – it'll be home away from home.'

Marin, who had been trying another shaving, puts down her spoon. 'Venice?' she says.

'What is a gondola, dearest?' Agnes asks her husband, her voice stupid, her eyes shining with Rhenish wine and a desire to be loved.

'*C'est un bateau*,' he replies.

'Oh,' says Agnes.

'I'll be gone within the month,' says Johannes. 'Perhaps you would like to join me, Frans? Ah,' he adds, putting up a finger. 'I forget how hard you find the water.'

Meermans sniffs. 'Very few men bear choppy waves.'

'True.' Johannes drains his glass. 'But there are always those who can.'

Marin rises from the table. 'Petronella, will you play the lute?'

'The lute?' With Marin's warning not to pluck her brother's strings rising in her mind, Nella cannot conceal her surprise.

'That is what I said.'

Their eyes meet for the third time that evening. Nella, seeing the fatigue in Marin's face, refrains from any protest. 'Of course I will, Marin,' she says. 'Of course.'

❧

It is a pleasure to play the lute, but an even greater one to see her audience's faces as the hastily re-tuned strings lend themselves to her fingers. For once, Nella is the object of appreciative attention, playing for forty minutes in a horse-shoe of chairs. Even Otto and Cornelia come to listen.

The contentious, now-diminished sugar loaf is back in Agnes' pouch, and a quiet descends, strung together moment by moment with simple notes and a cracked song of lost love. Johannes watches his new wife with something akin to pride. Marin stares into the fire, listening, and Agnes nods out of time whilst her husband shifts his buttocks in his seat.

The Meermanses leave soon after, with promises to check with Johannes on his progress through November. Marin closes the door. 'God be thanked they've gone,' she breathes. 'Clear it all in the morning,' she tells Cornelia, who cannot hide her shock at being excused a night's worth of plate-cleaning.

Exhilarated from her triumph, Nella cradles the lute in her hands, leaning up against the hallway window. Agnes and Frans are making their way down the front steps.

'*Tortoiseshell*, Frans.' Agnes barely bothers, or is unable after all that wine, to keep her voice down. 'With *pewter*.'

'Agnes, be quiet.'

'What a strange wedding gift – the way these great minds work! I'm having one of my own, Frans. We can afford it soon. And I want mine to be better than hers.'

'I wouldn't say his mind was precisely great—'

'And, God be praised – did you see Marin's face when she ate our sugar? *Weeks* I've been waiting for that. Fransy, the Lord has been merciful—'

'Oh, just hold your insufferable tongue.'

As they walk away, Madame Meermans falls to a silence that does not break again.

The Deserted Girl

Cornelia has already lit a fire by the time Nella comes to the next morning. Nella dresses herself, not bothering with the constriction of a stomacher, preferring a shirt and waistcoat to all the whalebone Cornelia would inflict.

'Are there any deliveries for me?' she asks Otto downstairs.

'No, Madame,' he replies. He sounds relieved.

Agnes' observation still rings round Nella's head. *It is pleasant for Frans when I pay him visits.* Though Nella had felt buoyed from the lute-playing, the whole evening has left a residue of discontent.

Whilst Nella has no desire to copy Agnes Meermans in anything – she *does* know more about marriage than anyone in this household. I must be seen to encourage Johannes, Nella thinks, to praise him at his tasks. In turn, perhaps, he will soon praise me. Her plan is to surprise Johannes at his place of work, and after that, to return to the sign of the sun. If Hole-Face isn't hovering, perhaps the miniaturist will want to speak.

Though all the rooms are now once more immaculate, the whole house has a muted feel, an air of exhaustion after a fight. Johannes' study door is open, and Nella can see his maps and papers scattered on the floor.

She wanders into the dining room and stops at the sight of

Marin. Not fully dressed, wearing her house coat over a blouse and skirt, Marin draws it close. Her light brown hair is loose and tumbles past her shoulders, giving off the vague scent of nutmeg. It is like seeing Marin, but through a softer and enriching lens.

'Has Johannes already gone to the Old Hoogstraat?' Nella asks.

Otto comes to pour two cups of coffee, and the bitter smell sharpens her senses. A few drops fall from the spout, spreading on the cloth like virgin islands on a map. He keeps his expression focused on the stains that he has made.

'Why?' asks Marin.

'I wanted to ask him where Bergen is.'

'It's in Norway, Petronella. Don't bother him.'

'But—'

'And why do you want to know about Bergen, of all places? All they do there is trade fish.'

In the hallway, Cornelia is brushing the black and white tiles around the front door, her head dipped in concentration. Otto continues down to the kitchen, the waft of the coffee pot in his wake. The weak October light is dim through the windows, and the tallow candles, newly rescued from their hiding place, are already lit. Nella pulls back the bolts and opens the door. Cornelia stops and straightens as the outside air comes in. 'Madame, it's only eight o'clock,' she says, her head erect, hands gripping the broom like a spear. 'Where are you going so early?'

'I'm running errands,' says Nella. Her temper swells at Cornelia's unconvinced look. She feels imprisoned again, the fledgling sense of power imbued by the lute already faded. 'Ladies don't have errands, Madame,' Cornelia says. 'They should know their place.'

It feels like a slap, an outrage that no servant would ever dare commit in Assendelft.

'You should stay here,' Cornelia persists, looking almost wretched. Nella turns to breathe the air of the outdoors, away from the smoky scent of the candles and Cornelia's watchful face. 'Wherever it is, you shouldn't go alone,' the maid murmurs, more gently this time, putting a hand on Nella's arm. 'I'm only—'

'Unlike *you*, Cornelia, I can go wherever I want.'

⟡

It will be interesting to see her husband in his place of work, to witness his efforts at solidifying his wealth. It is a way to understand him. Nella turns onto the Kloveniersburgwal, within reach of the sea-smell, the masts of the tall ships in the middle distance. As she walks along the canal, she even considers showing Johannes the models of his precious dogs. Surely they would please him.

She walks through the main arch of the Old Hoogstraat entrance to the VOC house, near the armoury, where shields and breastplates are clanked and sorted for size. This place is the hub of the whole city, some might say the whole republic. Her father once told her that Amsterdam had funded over half the entire country's war chest. He'd sounded suspicious of the city's wealth and power, but mingled with that wariness was a wistful awe.

Nella walks the perimeter of the first courtyard, dizzied by the repetitive brickwork. Two men are talking in the far corner and as she passes them, they drop to low bows. She curtsies and they consider her with curiosity.

'We never see women at the VOC,' the first man says.

'Except at night,' his friend chimes in, 'with the fragrance of vanilla musk.'

'I'm looking for Johannes Brandt,' she replies, her voice tight with anxiety at their suggestive manner. A spray of red pimples covers the second man's forehead. He's little more than a boy. God has been malicious with his paintbrush.

The men exchange a glance. 'Go through that arch, into the second courtyard, and there's a door on your far left,' says the first. 'It's confidential up there,' he adds. 'No women allowed.'

Nella can feel their eyes on her back as she walks under the second arch. No one answers when she knocks on the far-left door, and with impatience she pushes it open. Salt has infused the sparse furniture and walls, making the room dank. At the back is a spiral staircase and Nella begins to climb it, up and up, until she reaches an airier floor, a long corridor at the end of which is another large oak door.

'Johannes?' she calls.

I am always calling after him, she thinks. Always waiting at his doors. She runs towards his office, fleet-footed as a cat, her excitement growing as she thinks of his surprise.

The handle at the end of the corridor is stiff, and as Nella pushes it hard and the door bursts open, her husband's name mangles in her throat.

Lying at the back of the room, Johannes is stretched out on a couch, eyes closed, naked, so naked, unable to move for a head of dark curls that hovers over his groin.

The curls seem stuck there on her husband. And then Nella sees that the head is moving, up and down, up and down. The head is attached to a body, a lean torso, a pair of kneeling legs, half hidden behind the couch.

Johannes' eyes open on the sound of the door slam, widening in horror as he sees his wife. His body starts to buck. The head of curls lifts and it's Jack Philips, mouth open, eyes shocked, turning his pale face towards her. He rears upright on the other side of the couch, his slicked bare chest drawing Nella's horrified gaze.

Moving as if underwater, Johannes does not, or cannot cover himself. He is slow and seems unable to breathe. His thing, his *worm*, is a mast – so meat-like, so upright, so glistening wet. He pushes Jack away and rises like a burly courtesan from his bower, his broad chest so hairy compared to the younger man's.

The day's grey light is a pallor on them all.

'Nella,' her husband says, but her head is on fire and she can barely hear him. 'You're not supposed. You're not—'

The spell breaks as Jack tosses Johannes his shirt. They fumble – arms, fingers, knees – both ungainly, both of them panicking, and as she watches their hasty dance, Nella's own knees begin to give way. From the floor she looks up and sees that her husband has managed to stand. He reaches out – for her, for Jack, for clothes, she cannot tell – it's as if he's grasping at invisible ropes in the air. And there is Jack from Bermondsey, topless, running his fingers through his curls. Is he grinning or grimacing or both at once? The idea dies in the roar of her head and her hands fly up to her eyes.

The last thing she sees is Johannes' penis, beginning to loll, long and dark against the top of his thigh.

The silence bellows down Nella's ears, pain bursts from the centre of her heart. Humiliation spreads from one black spore to thousands, and the hurt that has been hibernating finally finds a voice.

She doesn't know if he can hear her, if words are coming out. '*Idiot, idiot, idiot,*' she whispers, her eyes shut tight. Her legs are leaden, her skin hot, her body heavy as a millstone. She feels men's hands upon her, and, lifted, her head lolling, she sees the five white toes on one of Johannes' feet. It is the first time since Marin's pinch that anyone has touched her.

'Nella,' says a familiar voice.

It is Cornelia. Cornelia has come. Nella allows herself to be dragged from the room, fumbled rapidly down the endless corridor, as if the two of them are running from a wave.

Johannes is calling her name. Nella can hear him, but she can't answer, and would she want to even if she could? Her mouth won't make words. They choke upon her tongue.

Cornelia descends with her down the last steps, orders her to move one foot in front of the other, Jesus Christ, Madame, just walk, please just walk so we can get you home. They pass the same men still standing in the courtyard. Cornelia has to drag her, shielding Nella's head so no one can see the devastation smacked across her mistress's face.

As they move up the Kloveniersburgwal, Nella's distress surges and she retches. Cornelia puts a firm hand over her mouth, for a cry will attract too much unwelcome attention on these close and watchful streets.

They reach the house. The door swings open as if by its

own accord, but then Nella sees Marin and Otto waiting in the shadows. Hiding her face, she allows Cornelia to be her barrier, helping her up the stairs. Nella climbs onto her bed, and pulls at the bridal sheets, trying to breathe, choking on her tears.

Then, from deep within, the howl comes – a scream which rips apart the air.

Nella feels someone stroke her forehead, again and again, holding her, forcing a drink down her throat. She can hear her howling start to fade, the last noise dying. Otto, Marin and Cornelia lean like Magi over the crib, their faces full-moons of concern.

I am the wrong one, Nella thinks. *Idiot*. I was not sup-posed—

The faces disappear and Nella falls, the image of her naked husband vanishing beneath a darkened pool.

TWO

November, 1686

Doth a fountain send forth at the same place
sweet water and bitter?

James 3:11

Inside Out

An irresistibly sweet smell wakes her up. Nella opens her eyes and sees Marin at the end of her bed, deep in thought, a plate of wafers in her lap. Marin unawares looks so much softer, her grey eyes lidded low, her mouth a dejected line. For seven days she has come to sit at the end of Nella's bed, and on every one of those days Nella has pretended to sleep.

The image of Johannes and Jack Philips thrummed for days inside Nella's skull, like a moth with constantly beating wings. Through the force of her own will Nella has made it flight-less. She has stupefied it and removed its wings. But it has not disappeared.

What else did the two men do before she arrived in that office – their bed a rolled-out atlas, gods above their paper world? I am not capable of this life in Amsterdam, Nella thinks, wishing herself far away. I feel younger than eighteen but burdened as an eighty-year-old. It is as if her entire life has come at once, and she is wading through a sea of suppositions with no way of bailing. How foolish I was, to imagine I could make Amsterdam my own, that I could ever match Johannes Brandt! I have pulled my own wings off. I have no dignity.

The cabinet house, unpeopled, looms in the corner. Some-one has opened its curtains, and it seems to grow as the rays of sunlight illuminate its frame. It captures Marin's attention too

– she places the plate of wafers on the floor and walks slowly towards it, putting her free hand inside the miniature salon. Pulling out the cradle, she rocks it back and forth across her palm.

'Don't touch that,' Nella snaps, the first words she has spoken in a week. 'Those things don't belong to you.'

Marin jumps and puts the cradle back. 'There are rose-water wafers for you,' she says. 'With cinnamon and ginger. Cornelia has a new griddle.'

Nella wonders what Cornelia has done to deserve a new griddle. The fire has been lit, bright and cheering in the grate. Outside, winter has made its true arrival, and within the room she can feel a trace of cold.

'I thought you said an empty belly was better for the soul?' she says, although she has been accepting the bowls of *hutspot* and the slices of Gouda Cornelia has been leaving outside the door. She feels the accusations boiling up inside her, ready to burst forth.

'Eat,' says Marin. 'Please. Then let us talk.'

Nella takes the plate, a Delft pattern of flowers and intricate leaves. Marin plumps her pillows, resuming her perch at the end of the bed. The wafers are gold and crisped to perfection and the rosewater mingles with the warming ginger. From the corner Peebo squawks in his cage, as if he senses Nella's reluctant pleasure.

What will Marin say, she wonders, when I tell her what I've seen?

'Perhaps you would like to get out of bed?' Marin sounds like a queen trying to be friends with a peasant.

Nella points towards the cabinet. 'I suppose you'd be happier to see me in there.'

'What do you mean?'

'My life here is over.'

Marin stiffens at this, and Nella pushes the plate of unfinished wafers towards her sister-in-law. 'No more of your orders, Marin. I understand it all.'

'But I wonder if you do?'

'I do.' Nella takes a deep breath. 'There is something you must know.'

Blood flushes into Marin's pale face. 'What?' she says. 'What is it?'

Nella, made momentarily powerful by her withheld knowledge, crosses her hands on the coverlet and stares into Marin's grave eyes. Her body feels heavy, anchored to the bed.

'There's a reason I've stayed in here all week, Madame. Johannes – your brother – no, I can barely say it.'

'Say what?'

'Johannes is – your brother is – a *sodomite*.'

Marin blinks. The hardened image of Johannes and Jack bursts to fresh life in Nella's mind. A flake of pastry sticks in her throat. Still Marin does not speak, examining instead the embroidery of the bedcover, the fat *B*s swirled amongst the foliage and woodland birds.

'I'm very sorry you are upset, Nella,' Marin says in a quiet voice. 'Johannes is unlike most husbands, I admit.'

At first, Nella does not understand. Then Marin's face opens towards her, a book showing its pages. A prickling sensation runs over her. It pinks her cheeks, it rushes through her blood.

'You knew? You *knew*?' She feels the sob come – this is almost worse than seeing her husband naked on his office couch with Jack. 'Dear God. I *am* your fool – I've been a fool since the moment I arrived.'

'We have not laughed at you, Petronella. Ever. You are no one's fool.'

'You've humiliated me. And I've seen it with my own eyes now. The disgusting, awful thing he did with – that boy—'

Marin stands up and walks to the window. 'Does Johannes disgust you in his entirety?'

'What? *Yes*. Sodomites – *beware them all*, Pellicorne said. *God's fury will seep into the land*. I'm his wife, Marin!' Words pour out of her, words she never thought she'd say. Letter by letter, she feels lighter, as if she might take off.

Marin spreads her fingers wide against the windowpane until the tips go white. 'Your memory of that sermon is prodigious.'

'You knew that Johannes would not love me!'

When Marin speaks, her voice is cracked. 'I wondered how he could not. I – do not always understand.' She pauses. 'He likes you.'

'Like a *pet*. And he likes Rezeki more. I cannot forgive this trick, this shame – you knew what this would be for me. The nights I waited—'

'I did not see it as a trick, Nella! It was an opportunity. For everyone.'

'*You*? Did Johannes even pick me himself?'

Marin hesitates. 'Johannes was – reluctant. He did not want – but – I made enquiries. One of your father's friends in the city mentioned your family's financial predicament he'd left behind. Your mother was more than enthusiastic. I thought it would satisfy everyone.'

Nella pushes the plate onto the floorboards where it breaks in three pieces. 'And what opportunity have *I* had, Marin?' she cries. 'You've controlled everything. You've ordered my clothes, you hold the ledger book, you drag me to church, you push me into guild feasts where everyone stares at me. I was so grateful when you let me play the lute. Pathetic. *I'm* supposed to be the wife in this house but I'm no better than Cornelia.'

Marin covers her face with her hands as the air thickens between them. Nella feels her own vitality surge as she watches Marin's struggle to remain composed.

'Marin, stop pretending to be so calm! This is a disaster.' Tears bubble up and Nella wills them to stop, but they run down her face despite her. 'How can I be happy with a man who is going to burn in Hell?'

Marin's face turns into a mask of rage. 'Be quiet. Be *quiet*. Your family had nothing but your name. Your father left you paupers. You would have ended up a farmer's wife.'

'There's nothing wrong with that.'

'You say that in ten years' time when the dams break, when your hands are raw and ten children are running around your feet, needing to be fed. You needed security, you wanted to be a merchant's wife!' Nella stays silent. 'Petronella? What are you going to do?'

As the panic in Marin's speech intensifies, it begins to dawn on Nella that some real power is finally hers. Does Marin think I'm going to the burgomasters? She stares in wonder at Marin's contorted, pale features, feeling giddy that she – an eighteen-year-old from Assendelft – could go and tell the fathers of Amsterdam that her respectable merchant husband is possessed by the Devil.

Oh, you could do it, Nella tells herself. Right now, she feels like doing it. You could report Jack Philips, too. Who could stop you, if you wanted to go? You could crush this woman's life in one sentence and free yourself of all humiliation.

As if she has read her mind, Marin speaks again. 'You're part of this family, Petronella Brandt. Its truth sticks to you like oil on a bird. What do you want, a pauper's life again? And what would happen to Otto and Cornelia if you let our secret out?'

She spreads her arms wide like wings, and Nella feels her own body contract into the bed.

'We can do nothing, Petronella – we women,' Marin says. '*Nothing.*' Her eyes burn with an intensity Nella has never seen in her before. 'All we can do if we're lucky is stitch up the mistakes that other people make.'

'Agnes is happy enough.'

'*Agnes*? Oh, Agnes plays her role, but what will happen when her lines run out? That plantation was her father's and now she's handed it to her husband. It astonishes me how she can feel so *clever* about it. And some of us can work,' Marin cries, 'back-breaking work, for which they won't even pay us half of what a man could earn. But we can't own property, we can't take a case to court. The only thing they think we can do is produce children who then become the property of our husbands.'

'But you have not married, you do not—'

'There are some women whose husbands don't leave them *alone*. Baby after baby till their body's like a wrinkled sack.'

'I'll be a wrinkled sack if it means I'm not alone! *A public wife, a private life* – isn't that the way the motto goes?'

'And how many women die on the birthing bed, Petronella? How many girls become a housewife corpse?'

'Stop shouting at me! There were funerals at Assendelft too, you know – I understand the danger.'

'Petronella—'

'Did my mother know what he was? Did she?'

Marin, breathless, stops. 'I do not think so. But she told me that you were a girl with imagination – strong and capable – and that you would thrive in the city. "Nella will find a way", she wrote – "Assendelft is too small for a mind like hers." I was happy to believe it.'

'That may be,' Nella says. 'But to decide that I was never going to live as a proper woman was not your choice to make.'

Marin's sneer scrapes Nella's skin. 'What do you mean – a *proper* woman?'

'A proper woman marries – she has children—'

'Then what does that make me? Am I not a proper woman? Last time I looked I certainly was.'

'We neither of us are.'

Marin sighs, rubbing her forehead. 'God's blood. I do not mean to lose my temper. It slips from me and I cannot catch it. I'm sorry.'

The true quality of this apology creates a moment of peace. Exhausted, Nella lies back on her bed and Marin breathes deeply. 'Words are water in this city, Nella,' she says. 'One drop of rumour could drown us.'

'Did you and Johannes sacrifice my future,' Nella says, 'because your own were in such peril?'

Marin closes her eyes. 'The marriage has benefited you, has it not?'

'Well, I wouldn't have drowned in Assendelft.'

'Yet your life there was like one underwater. A few cows, your draughty house, and boredom. I thought this marriage might give you – an adventure.'

'I thought you said women don't have adventures,' Nella snaps. Even as she says this, she thinks about the miniaturist on the Kalverstraat. 'Are we in danger, Marin? Why do we need that sugar money? Johannes wouldn't sell it if he didn't have to.'

'Keep your enemies close.'

'I thought Agnes Meermans was supposed to be your friend.'

'The sugar profits will protect us,' Marin replies, looking back out of the window. 'In Amsterdam, God, for all His glory, only goes so far.'

'How can you say such a thing? You, who are so pious—'

'What I believe has nothing to do with what I can control. We are not poor, but the sugar is a dam against the rising waves. And you protect us too, Petronella.'

'*I* protect you?'

'Of course. And believe me, we are grateful.'

Marin's awkward gratitude blooms in Nella's blood, swelling her with self-importance. She tries to hide her pleasure, concentrating on the swirling design of the coverlet.

'Marin, tell me – what would happen if Agnes and Frans found out about Johannes?'

'I hope they would have mercy.' Marin pauses, finding a chair. 'But I suspect that they would not.'

In the heavy silence, Marin collapses slowly like a puppet, her legs folding beneath her, arms and neck slack, chin to chest. 'Do you know what they do to men like my brother?' she says. 'They drown them. The holy magistrates put weights on their necks and push them in the water.' A wave of devastation seems to draw down Marin's body. 'But even if they dragged Johannes back up and cut him open,' she says, 'they still wouldn't find what they wanted.'

'Why not?'

Tears start to strand on Marin's pale cheeks. She presses her hand to her chest as if to ebb her grief. 'Because, Petronella – it's something in his soul. It's something in his soul and you cannot get it out.'

Decisions

Nella opens her door an hour later, holding Peebo in his cage. The sun shines a thin light through the landing window, turning the wall before her pale lemon. She can hear Johannes in Marin's tiny room, the low rise and fall of their hushed voices. Leaving Peebo's cage at the top of the stairs, she creeps along the corridor.

'Why can't you keep away from that man? I think how this might end and I cannot bear it.'

'He has no one, Marin.'

'You underestimate him.' Marin sounds exhausted. 'He has no loyalty.'

'You think the worst of everyone.'

'I see him, Johannes. He'll bleed us dry. How much have you paid him now?'

'He's helping guard the sugar. It's a fair exchange. At least it stops him making deliveries and coming round here.'

Nella measures the beats of Marin's silence. 'With what blind eyes you view the world,' she finally says, her voice holding down her fury. 'Why is your warehouse any less exposed than this house? He should be kept as far away as possible from anything to do with us. What if Petronella tells her mother – or the burgomasters?'

'Nella has a heart—'

'Whose existence you've barely acknowledged.'

'Not true. Not fair. I've bought that cabinet, those dresses, I took her to the feast. What else am I supposed to do?'

'You know what else.'

There is a long pause. 'I believe,' Johannes says, 'that she's the lost piece in our puzzle.'

'Which you are in danger of losing. The damage you've done, so careless with other people's needs—'

'*Me*? Your hypocrisy is breathtaking, Marin. I warned you back in August that I couldn't—'

'And I warned you, that if you didn't stop with Jack something terrible was going to happen.'

Nella cannot bear to hear any more. She walks back to the staircase and picks up Peebo's cage. As she goes downstairs she realizes never has she felt more powerful, nor more frightened. She pictures Johannes disappearing underwater, a face distorted, hair swirling like grey seaweed. Her hand could be the doing of it. They have been protected by these walls and that heavy front door for years – but they opened it and let Nella in, and now look what has happened. *We don't like traitors* – Marin's words come back to her, a reminder of the strange unity of these people to whom Nella half-belongs, waiting to see where her loyalty lies.

On the last stair, she sits and puts the cage beside her. Peebo is on his perch, gripping it obediently. Nella begins to tug at the door and it swings open with a light clang. Her little bird jumps in shock, his head twitching with curiosity, blinking at her with his bead-like eyes.

He is tentative at first, but then he takes his chance, and flies. Round and round the giant hall, up and up, swooping and flapping at the great space, his droppings falling abundant on the floor tiles. Let them fall, Nella thinks. Let him cover these blasted tiles with shit.

She leans back, watching Peebo's upward spiral, shivering from the front window, left ajar. The bird flits from one side of the hall to the other. Nella can feel the displacement of air as his wings beat – the papery flap of bone and feather, the riffling of pinions as he finds a perch in the rafters his mistress cannot see.

Whatever her mother's warnings – the women buried too soon in the Assendelft churchyard – Nella has always assumed that one day a baby would come. She touches her abdomen, imagining a curve there, a balloon of flesh hiding a child. Life in this house isn't just preposterous, it's a game, an exercise in fakery. Who is she now? What is she supposed to do?

'Hungry?' asks a voice.

Nella jumps as Cornelia appears from under the stairs, looking pale and apprehensive. She doesn't bother to question what the maid is doing hovering there. No one is ever truly alone in this house; there will always be someone watching or listening. Doesn't she herself listen – to footsteps, closing doors, those hurried whisperings?

'No,' she says, but she is hungry. She could eat that whole feast from the silversmiths' now, and never stop – consuming every morsel to make her feel she has some substance.

'Are you going to leave him flying around?' asks Cornelia, pointing to the brief glimpse of green feathers as Peebo flies low before moving off again into the shadows.

'I am,' Nella replies. 'He's been waiting for this moment since the day he arrived.'

She hunches over and the maid kneels down and places both her hands on Nella's knees. 'This is your home now, Madame.'

'How can this house of secrets ever be called a home?'

'There's only one secret in this house,' Cornelia says. 'Unless you have one too?'

'No,' Nella says, but she thinks of the miniaturist.

'What's in Assendelft for you, Madame? You never talk of it, you can hardly miss it.'

'No one ever *asks* me about it, except for Agnes.'

'Well, from what I've heard, it's got more cows than people.'

'*Cornelia.*'

But Nella relents with a nervous giggle, musing on the distance she now feels from that crumbling house, that lake, those childhood memories. She does wish people wouldn't be so rude about it. I could find my way back, she supposes – Mama would have to forgive me eventually, especially when I told her the truth. And if I stay, Johannes will still have his escapes, running his risks with pastors and magistrates, the prospect of eternal damnation diminishing in the face of his desires. I, on the other hand, will have almost nothing. No promise of motherhood, no shared secrets in the night, no household to run – except the one inside a cabinet where no living soul can thrive.

And yet, Nella thinks to herself. *I fight to emerge*, that's the message the miniaturist sent me. Assendelft is small, its company is limited, mired in the past. Here, in Amsterdam, the cabinet's curtains have opened a new world, a strange world, a conundrum she wishes to solve. And most of all, there is no miniaturist in Assendelft.

The woman who lives on the Kalverstraat is nebulous, uncertain. She is possibly even dangerous – but right now, she is the only thing Nella can call her own. If she went back to the countryside, she would never know why the miniaturist had chosen to send her these unexpected pieces, she would never discover the truth behind the work. She knows she wants these deliveries to continue more than she wants them to stop. In a fanciful moment, it occurs to her that their very existence might keep her alive.

'Cornelia – you followed me that day. At Johannes' office.'

The maid looks sombre. 'I did, Madame.'

'I don't like being followed. But I'm glad you did.'

Tales

In the working kitchen, the maid hands Nella a *kandeel* of hot spiced wine, pouring one for herself. 'Peace at last,' she says.

'I don't want peace, Cornelia. I'd rather have a husband.'

'My pasties will be ready,' the maid replies, wiping her hands on her apron as a log in the fire breaks open with a shower of glowing sparks. Nella lays her *kandeel* down on the oiled surface of the little chopping table by her knee. *I will not hurt you, Petronella,* was Johannes' promise, made in the barge on their way towards the Guild of Silversmiths. She has always thought that kindness was an active thing. But the not doing of something, an act of restraint – could that be kindness too?

She was taught that sodomy was a crime against nature. In that respect, there is little difference between the doctrine of an Amsterdam preacher and a childhood priest in Assendelft. But how right is it to kill a man for something that is in his soul? If Marin is right, and it cannot be removed, then what is the point of all that pain? Nella takes a sip from the *kandeel* and lets the taste of hot spices carry her away from the awful image of Johannes under a cold black sea.

'I put dried peas in them too. A new idea,' Cornelia says as heat rushes out of the stove door, filling the room. She puts the pasty on a plate, drizzling it in grape juice, mutton-stock and butter before handing it over to Nella.

'Cornelia, was there someone Marin once loved?'

'*Loved*?'

'That's what I said.'

Cornelia's fingers tighten on the plate. 'Madame says love is best a phantom than reality, better in the chase than caught.'

The flames of the fire arch and disappear. 'She might say that, Cornelia. But – I found something. A note. A love note, hidden in her room.'

The colour drains from Cornelia's face. Nella hesitates, then takes the risk. 'Did Frans Meermans write it?' she whispers.

'Oh, by all the angels,' Cornelia breathes. 'It can't possibly – they never—'

'Cornelia – you want me to stay, don't you? You don't want me to make a fuss?'

The maid tips up her chin and peers at Nella down her nose. 'Are you *bargaining* with me, Madame?'

'Perhaps I am.'

Cornelia wavers, then pulls a stool near and places her hand on Nella's heart.

'Do you swear, Madame? Do you swear not to speak of this to a soul?'

'I swear.'

'Then I'll tell you now,' the maid says, lowering her voice. 'Agnes Meermans has always been a cat to hide her claws. All those airs and graces – but look closer, Madame. Look at the worry in the middle of her eye. She can't ever hide her feelings about Marin – because Marin stole her husband's heart.'

'What?'

Cornelia stands up. 'I can't tell you all this without having something to keep my hands busy. I'll make some *olie-koecken*.' She gathers together a bowl of almonds, a handful of cloves and a cinnamon jar. As she starts crushing the nuts and cloves, the maid's whispering, her air of secrecy and conviction tastes more delicious to Nella than the pasty on her plate.

Cornelia checks the stairs to see no one is coming. 'Madame Marin was a lot younger than you when she first met Meermans,' she says. 'He was the Seigneur's friend when they worked as clerks at the treasury. The Seigneur was eighteen, and Madame Marin must have been about eleven.'

Nella tries to imagine Marin as a child, but Agnes had it right; it is impossible. Marin is who she surely always was. Something rises in Nella's mind, a jarring note. 'But Agnes said that Frans and Johannes met at the VOC when they were twenty-two.'

'Well, she was making that up – or else Meermans lied to her. He never worked at the VOC. He met the Seigneur at the Amsterdam treasury and ended up making laws at the Stadhuis. Not very impressive, is it – to stay in the office when your friend is out at sea with the republic's greatest company. He gets seasick, Madame. Can you imagine a seasick Dutchman?'

'Well, I prefer horses to ships,' Nella says.

Cornelia shrugs. 'And both can throw you out the saddle. Anyway, Meermans first met Madame Marin on the feast of St Nicholas. Music filled the place, citterns, horns and viols – and Madame Marin danced with Meermans more than once. She thought he was a prince, so handsome. He eats too much now, but he was everyone's favourite then.'

'But how do you even know this, Cornelia? Were you even *born*?'

Cornelia frowns, dropping in her wheat-flour and ginger, thickening her batter with a whisk. 'I was a baby in the orphanage then. But I've put it together, haven't I? *Keyholes*,' she whispers, fixing her blue eyes on Nella with a knowing look. 'I've worked her out.' She draws a small bowl of apples close, peeling each one with a single rotation of her knife. 'There's something about Madame Marin. She's a knot we all want to untie.'

But Nella wonders if there are any fingers sharp or deft enough to pick at Madame Marin. With her moodiness, her moments of shy generosity dashed by an unkind comment, Marin is the most tightly bound of them all.

As Cornelia resumes her whisking, Nella's heart feels as if it's swelling in her ribs. This girl came to Johannes' office to save me, she thinks. And if that is true, then she's the first real friend I've ever had. Nella can hardly bear it – any moment she's going to stand up and throw her arms round this strange child from the orphanage, whose talent with food has given her the power to console.

'The Seigneur and Meermans were good friends,' Cornelia says. 'So he would often be calling at the house to play a game of *verkerspeel*. Love came into it later – what did Madame Marin know of love, at eleven years old?'

'I'm nearly nineteen, and a married woman, Cornelia. And yet I can make no more claim on love than if I were a child.'

Cornelia blushes. Growing older, Nella realizes, does not seem to make you more certain. It simply presents you with more reasons for doubt.

'Their parents died when Madame Marin was fourteen,

and the Seigneur left the treasury to join the VOC,' Cornelia continues. 'Meermans moved to the Stadhuis.'

'How did their parents die?'

'Their mother was always sickly, and weakened by her labours. She barely survived after Madame Marin was born. There were more babies than just the Seigneur and Madame Marin, of course – but none of them lived. A year after their mother died, their father went of the fever, and the Seigneur took his first VOC ship out to Batavia. Madame Marin turned fifteen. Frans Meermans was working in the Stadhuis, but without a chaperone, she couldn't meet him.'

Nella pictures her husband under boiled blue skies, upon hot sands laced with tinkling shells and shed blood. Piracy and adventure, whilst Frans and Marin were marooned amidst the mahogany furniture and smothering tapestries, the sluggish canals and the peal of bells to worship.

'The Seigneur tried to encourage him into the VOC. Told him to seize the opportunity. "Don't criticize Frans," Madame Marin said. "Not everyone has had your chances, Johannes, and you like it that way." '

Cornelia swirls a bowl of soaked raisins with the end of her wooden spoon. 'Problem was, Meermans couldn't match the Seigneur. Couldn't open the right doors, didn't inspire the men – had only modest success, while the Seigneur got very rich. And then five years later, when Marin was twenty, Meermans called by without her knowing. He'd saved his money up and asked the Seigneur if he could have her hand in marriage.'

'He waited *five years*? And what did Johannes say?'

'The Seigneur said no.'

'What? Five years waiting to be given a no – but why? Meermans didn't have a bad reputation, did he? And he must have truly loved her.'

'The Seigneur never does anything without good reason,' Cornelia says defensively, dropping her first strip of batter into a pan of sizzling oil.

'Yes, but –'

'Meermans was handsome, if you like that type,' Cornelia says, 'but he didn't have the best of reputations.' She pauses. 'He had a temper on him, he always wanted better than what he had. And after that snub, he never came back. Until now.'

She draws out the new doughnut and lays it gently on the tray of prepared sugar. 'I shaved the top of Agnes' sugar cone,' she adds, a little sly.

'Perhaps Johannes wanted to keep Marin where he needed her,' Nella says. 'A puppet wife – and look! Now he has two.' Cornelia makes a face. 'Oh, Cornelia. She's still mistress of this household. You see how strict she is, keeping us all in order. That's supposed to be my job. Although – have you noticed how distracted she can seem?'

Cornelia is silent for a moment. 'I've noticed no difference, Madame,' she says.

'Did Marin find out what Johannes had done?'

'Eventually, but by then Meermans had gone and married one of Madame Marin's friends. *Agnes Vynke*.' Cornelia enunciates the name like the parts of a wasp. 'Agnes' father worked with the West India Company and had got rich in the New World. He'd forbidden her from marrying any man not wealthy enough. He was a monster, Seigneur Vynke – trying to sire sons at eighty to make sure she didn't inherit! Agnes' marriage to Meermans was her first and last rebellion. She adores Frans like a sickness. She turned the other guild wives against Madame Marin, just to be sure that chapter was closed. Agnes wanted a little power, but then her father died and left her all those fields.'

Nella remembers the ladies Cornelia described, visiting the house, putting songbirds in Otto's hair – was Agnes Vynke one of them, ordered by Marin never to return?

'It was a huge wedding feast,' Cornelia goes on, 'paid for by Frans with all the guilders he'd borrowed, no doubt. Always in debt, that one. The party lasted three days. But you know what they say about big weddings. They cover up a lack of appetite.'

Nella blushes. If the reverse was true – after their measly ceremony, she and Johannes should never have left their bed-chamber.

'Frans and Agnes have been married twelve years – and still no children,' Cornelia says. 'And then comes Agnes' sugar plantation, straight into his lap! For him, it's better than an heir. He may be counting on that sugar to make a legacy, but it doesn't change his love for Madame Marin.'

She hands Nella the first *olie-koeck*. It is still warm, and the fried crust breaks apart under Nella's teeth, releasing the perfect blend of almond, ginger, clove and apple. 'And Marin still loves him?' Nella asks.

'Oh, I'm sure of it. He sends her a gift every year. Pigs and partridges – once a haunch of deer. And Madame Marin won't send them back. It's like a silent conversation they want to maintain. Of course, I'm the one who has to deal with it all. Pluck, chop, stuff, fry, boil. A necklace would be easier.' Cornelia wipes out the batter bowl with a damp cloth. 'That's how

Madame Marin found out that the Seigneur had rejected Frans' proposal. It was soon after Agnes' wedding when the first gift came.'

'What was it?'

'I'd just arrived. I remember Madame Marin quite clearly, holding up a salted piglet in the hallway. She looked so unhappy. "Why is he sending me a present, Johannes?" she asked, and the Seigneur took her to the study, where I suppose he had to explain.'

'My goodness.'

Cornelia looks grim. 'And Meermans has sent something ever since. Although he never puts his name, we all know it's him.' She rubs her forehead. 'But a love note's different,' she says. 'A love note's dangerous. Oh, close your eyes to it, Madame Nella, and pretend you never saw.'

❧

Nella goes back upstairs to give Peebo the leftover crumbs of the *olie-koeck*, her head filled with images of a young Marin, throwing blushed glances in the direction of princely Meermans. It is like trying to imagine her parents as young people, falling in love. I'd prefer to rise in love, she thinks – lifting up to the clouds, not plunging to the earth. She pictures herself, weightless and adored, delirious in ecstasy.

The rafters are empty. She wanders through the ground-floor rooms, calling Peebo's name, her arm out, expecting him to beat the air and land upon her, his familiar body, his beady little eyes. She walks up to the first floor, even checking that he hasn't climbed inside the cabinet house for shelter. 'Peebo?' she calls. Marin's room is shut; she's trying to sleep. A sudden nightmare of a plucked corpse, feathers hanging, crosses Nella's mind.

Johannes' sparsely furnished chamber is also empty. 'Peebo?' Nella calls again. Dhana bounds up, sensing in her voice there is some problem to be chased. Nella imagines the parakeet mauled in the dog's teeth, a chance snap, Nature following her cruellest course. A sense of dread charges through her stomach and she runs down the stairs. 'Cornelia?' she calls. 'Do you know where—?'

And then she sees it. The hall window, no longer ajar but swinging open, the cold air rushing in.

Eight Dolls

All afternoon and into evening, Cornelia and Nella have called up and down the canal for the bird, to no avail. Indoors, the rafters are empty, no thrum of wings. Disorientated and freezing cold, it is impossible Peebo will last long. The temperature has dropped overnight, ice is forming a thin veneer over the Heren canal, and the last thread of her old life has unravelled across the sky. 'I'm sorry,' Nella whispers. 'I'm so sorry.'

Exhausted from worry and lack of sleep over Peebo's disappearance, Nella finds a small posy of bright red and blue flowers with a note the next morning, left outside her door. She is gripped with the hope that it's from the miniaturist, but to her surprise, a large capital letter of her name launches the missive, the handwriting rushing forward, a keen slant towards the full stop.

Nella:

Blue periwinkle for early friends, Persicaria for restoration —
I would buy you a new bird, but it would pale in imitation.

   Johannes

Nella smells the flowers in the semi-darkness of her room, their gentle scent battling with her grief and resurging feelings of humiliation.

What will it mean, for the rest of her life, married to this pleasure-loving, complicated man – but without a marriage bed? Johannes will include her in his social gatherings, his guild parties and feasts. He even wants to be her friend. But there will be all those endless nights of loneliness, those day-times filled with longing, as love is sealed up for good. She hopes the miniaturist sends her something soon. The fear of what it might be is worth the distraction alone.

Nella twines two of the periwinkles behind her ear. She has never envisaged a lifetime of being untouched, and yet deep inside, a tiny voice rises to be heard. *You're relieved he isn't going to do it*. She admits the shock of witnessing Johannes naked. Since arriving, a great part of her has urged, even attempted, to transform herself into what she has long assumed is a real wife, a *proper woman*. She has spent so long craving this transformation, solidifying it in her mind, she has become oblivious to its ambiguity. Now, the *proper woman* loses all her meaning. Nella's solid desire is fragmenting, a mist inside her head. What does it even *mean*, to be a real wife?

A knock on the door rouses her from the wandering circle of her thoughts. 'I've asked Otto,' Cornelia says, peering her head round the door. She hesitates at the sight of Nella's puffy eyes. 'He didn't leave the window open, and it wasn't me—'

'I'm not blaming anyone, Cornelia.'

'He might fly back.'

'He won't. I was a fool.'

'Here,' Cornelia says, proffering a parcel inked with the sign of the sun. 'It was left outside for you.'

Nella's blood sings. It's as if she hears me, she thinks, even when I'm silent. What is she trying to say?

'Was it – Jack who delivered this?' she asks, her fingers trembling lightly on the package, desperate to pull it apart.

Cornelia winces at the name, her eyes on her mistress's shaking hand. 'It was there when I went to wash the front step,' she says. 'I dare say that Englishman's keeping away. Madame – what is *in* these parcels?'

Nella knows she is not ready to share the woman on the Kalverstraat. Having rejected the idea of privacy, now she craves it, desperate to be alone with what the miniaturist has to show.

'Nothing. Pieces I've ordered for my cabinet,' she says.

'Pieces?'

'You may go.'

Once Cornelia has left with one last glance over her shoulder, Nella tips out the package on her bed. Nothing prepares her for what she sees.

Eight dolls are laid out on a strip of blue velvet. So lifelike, so delicate; they are items of such humanly unreachable perfection. Nella feels like a giant, picking one up as if it might break. Johannes lies in her palm, a cloak of dark indigo slung over his broad shoulders, one hand balled into a fist. The other hand is open, palm offered and welcoming. His hair is longer than Nella has seen it, reaching just below his shoulders. Dark-eyed, the shadows on his face make him look weaker than he is in real life. At his waist is a heavy bag of coin, nearly the length of his leg, and he is thinner. The bag burdens the joints in his hips, weighing him crookedly to one side.

The hair of Nella's own doll escapes its cap, as in reality it is wont to do. Wearing a neat grey dress, her miniature stares straight up, a look of faint surprise across her frozen face. In one of her tiny hands is an empty birdcage, its door swinging open wide. Nella feels a strange sensation in her body, as if pins are pricking the inside of her skin.

In the doll's other hand, is a minuscule note written in neat black capitals:

THINGS CAN CHANGE

Unable to look any longer at her miniature self, Nella moves on to Cornelia, marvelling at the maid's blue eyes, which appraise her with a hint of merriment. Cornelia's hand is raised to her face, and on closer inspection, it appears she has her finger to her lips.

Otto is next, his hair made from dyed lamb's wool. Looking more agile than Johannes, he too is thinner than in real life. Nella touches his arms; his simple servant outfit belies the carved muscles underneath. Her fingers spring away. 'Otto?' she says out loud, feeling foolish when the doll does not reply.

Then comes Marin, her grey eyes fixed on some invisible horizon. It is undoubtedly her – the slim face, the solemn mouth holding a thought desperate to burst. Her clothing is accurately sombre; black velvet, a capacious plain lace collar. Mesmerized, Nella runs her fingers up Marin's thin wrists, her slender arms, the high forehead and rigid neck. Remembering what Cornelia told her about the secret, softer lining of Marin's sober clothes, Nella feels beneath the bodice. Her fingers light on a fine pelt of sable.

Good God, she thinks. What is happening here? For this is further than the miniaturist has ever gone. A little gold key, a rocking cradle, two dogs – these could all arguably constitute the pleasant aspects of life in a merchant's house. But this –

these dolls – are different. How does the miniaturist know what Marin wears against her skin, or that Peebo has flown away?

You thought you were a locked box inside a locked box, Nella tells herself. But the miniaturist sees you – she sees *us*. Tracing a shaking finger over Marin's skirt (what looks like the best black wool on the market), Nella hides her sister-in-law's doll in a far corner of the miniature salon, behind a chair where no one can see her.

Next out is a male figurine, slightly shorter than Johannes, wearing a big brimmed hat and a sword, dressed in the livery of the St George Militia. His face is large, and despite the reduced articulacy of his full-barrelled body, it is quite clearly Frans Meermans. Agnes follows, with her waspish waist and rings on her fingers made from tiny shards of coloured glass. Her face is narrower than Nella remembers it, but the familiar seed pearls are dotted in white on her black headband. A large crucifix hangs round her neck, and in one hand she holds a conical loaf of sugar, no longer than an ant.

The eighth and last doll falls from the velvet cloth, making Nella cry out. Picking him up from the floor, it is plain to see Jack Philips, his leather jacket and white shirt with spilled cuffs, his legs encased in a pair of leather boots. Hair wild, mouth a cherry red. Why would the miniaturist want to remind me of this awful boy? Nella wonders. Why must I have him in my house?

No answer comes from the dolls, who stare up at her, such powerful diminishments. Nella tries her best to look calmly at these characters, lying on their velvet cloth, made with care and observation. She places them one by one in dark corners in the miniature house.

Surely there is no malice in them? She tries very hard to convince herself – but this is something that seems to go beyond the normal, there is a commentary here she cannot place her finger on. It is more than plain mimicry.

There is one black cloth parcel left, smaller than the others. Nella barely dares to open it, but the impulse is too strong. When she unwraps the cloth she thinks she might be sick. Lying there is a miniature green bird, looking up at her with bright black eyes, his feathers real, purloined from a less fortunate creature. His tiny claws are made of wire and covered with wax, and can be manipulated to perch anywhere.

Her world is shrinking, and yet it feels more unwieldy than ever.

She whirls round – is the miniaturist here in the room, hiding under the bed? Nella crouches to look, pulling the curtains away from the wall in a quick sweep as if to catch her unawares, even looking behind the curtains on the cabinet. All she finds are empty spaces that mock her desire to believe. You're Nella-in-the-Clouds, she reprimands herself – you with your fancies and your imagination running wild. You were supposed to leave that Assendelft girl behind.

Through the window, people are walking along the path. The Herengracht is busy today, for ice has prevented easy travel on the canal. The herring-seller is stamping her feet on the corner to keep warm, ladies and gentlemen walk with their servants, all wrapped against the bitter cold. A few glance up at Nella as they pass, faces turned like snowdrops towards the winter sky.

Nella looks away towards the bridge. A flash of pale hair, she is sure of it. Her skin begins to prickle again, she feels her bowels go weak. Is it her? There is quite a crowd at this end of the Herengracht, crossing the bridge. Nella leans further out of the window. It *is* her – that shining head of hair, masked by the shoal of darker figures, moving fast against the cold.

'Wait!' Nella shouts from the window. 'Why are you doing this to me?'

Someone titters on the path. 'Is she a lunatic?' a woman asks. Nella feels the burn of this unjust and awful scrutiny.

But the pale hair has disappeared, leaving both unanswered questions ringing in the air.

Written in the Water

Nella rushes down the main staircase, the new, miniature Peebo jammed deep into her pocket. Her indoor pattens still on her feet, she heads for the front door, but the intensity of Marin's and Johannes' voices in the dining room stops her dead. She hovers, torn between going after the miniaturist and listening to the siblings' storm.

'You said you would go, Johannes, and you must.' Marin's voice is low and strangely raw. 'I've ordered a barge to take you to the harbour. Cornelia has packed you a trunk.'

'What? I'll go in a couple of weeks,' Johannes replies. 'There's plenty of time.'

'It's November, Johannes! Think of all the pastries and parties that require sugar this season. To go in December will be too late, and the warehouse damp will not be doing that sugar any good—'

'What about the damp in my bones, hopping from boat to boat in this weather? You've no idea of the monotony of greasing palms, the exhaustion of speaking Italian, dinners with cardinals who can talk of nothing but the size of their Tuscan palaces.'

Marin sniffs. 'You are correct, I do not. But all things considered, it would be – prudent for you – to be away.'

'Prudent – why?' Johannes' voice warms with teasing. 'What are you plotting when I'm not here?'

'No plot, Johannes. I will collect my scattered thoughts. And so will Petronella.'

'I'm tired, Marin. I'm nearly forty.'

'You were the one who wanted to sell it abroad. And if you bothered to visit your wife's bed – then in fifteen, sixteen years' time, you could hand all this to your son. You could spend your dotage in a tavern, for all I care.'

'What did you say? My *son*?'

Nella can almost taste the silence which follows. It falls between them, Johannes and Marin in the room and her outside it, like a dense blanket of snow a man might trip in and disappear. She rests her cheek against the wood, waiting. Was that longing she heard in her husband's voice, or was it merely surprise? How correct had Agnes really been, that night at the silversmiths'? No sure bet, was Johannes' reported view on heirs. If things can change, Nella thinks, running her fingers over the miniature bird in her pocket – then maybe that means people too.

'Marin,' Johannes sighs, breaking Nella's thoughts, the snow of reverie melted. 'These perfect lives you'd have us lead, plotted on maps that take us nowhere! In fifteen years I'll probably be dead.'

'Oh, I see our destinations clearly, brother. That is what pains me.'

'If I go I must take Otto with me.'

'We need Otto here,' says Marin. 'Just three women, and no man to lug the firewood? The ice is coming in.'

'You want to run my business, but you can't lift a log? In that case,' Johannes sniffs, when Marin offers no rejoinder, 'there is only one other assistant I could take.'

'If you're even considering—'

Nella barges into the room. It is the first time she has seen her husband since the moment in his office. An expression of pain flickers over Johannes' face as he rises from his chair, awkwardly scraping its feet across the floor. 'Nella,' he asks, 'were you—'

'What's that?' Nella interrupts, pointing to where Marin is poring over a map.

'De'Barbari's map of Venice,' says Marin, gazing at the petals of the periwinkle nestling by Nella's ear.

'Did you have any luck with your parakeet?' Johannes asks.

Nella jams her hand in her pocket. 'No. I did not.'

'Ah.' He pauses, rubbing his chin in meditation, looking at her carefully. He glances at Marin. 'I have decided I must go to Venice, to set up talks regarding Agnes' sugar.'

'Venice?' Nella echoes. 'Will you not be here at Christmas?'

'I cannot guarantee it.'

'Oh.' To her surprise, Nella hears the feather-breath of disappointment in her voice. Marin looks up.

'We thought it would be best,' Johannes says.

'For whom?'

'For the sugar,' he replies.

'For all,' says Marin.

As Marin intended, Johannes boards the VOC barge from outside the house. It will take him towards the docks, where he will board his ship. Standing on the threshold of the house, Nella shivers as he holds up a reluctant hand towards her. She mirrors him, her own palm facing the cold air, not waving, just held in goodbye.

'You put the flowers in your hair,' he says.

'I did.' She takes in his sun-tanned skin, the grizzled lines around his eyes, the sweep of silver stubble. 'For restoration.'

At her words, Johannes seems unable to speak, and in that brief, held moment between them, Nella feels as if she has grown taller, as if dignity is something she can grasp in her hand.

Rezeki bounds out of the house, barking her displeasure at being left behind.

'Do you have the sample loaves?' Marin asks.

'My word is enough, Marin,' Johannes replies, but his words are eliding with emotion.

Who is this man, Nella wonders, so moved by my good-bye?

'Why don't you take her?' Marin says.

'She'll get in the way,' Johannes replies. 'Just keep her safe.'

Nella prays they're talking about the dog. Marin sounds so frosty towards her brother, it's hard to keep up. He's going isn't he – isn't that what she wants? Perhaps the miniaturist will send me something soon to elucidate this strange woman, Nella wonders. The doll of Marin holds no clues. Tonight, she tells herself. Tonight I go to the sign of the sun.

Marin moves slowly back inside, as if the cold has seized her joints. Cornelia scrutinizes her mistress's halting progress. Standing by Otto, Nella watches her husband's figure grow smaller as his barge moves up the Golden Bend. 'Didn't you want to go to Venice?' she asks.

'I've been, Madame,' Otto replies, his gaze on the wake of the water. 'Once is enough for the Doge's palace.'

'I would like to see it,' Nella says. 'He could have taken me.'

She catches Cornelia and Otto exchanging one of their glances. As they turn back to the house, the three of them see Jack Philips standing by the higher bend of the canal. Nella's stomach shifts. Jack's hands are in his pockets, his hair as wild as ever, and he scowls at Johannes' vanishing barge. Otto propels Nella back up the steps, and she sags at the contact, letting him guide her, hearing a soft thud behind as Cornelia closes the door.

⋰⋱

Outside, the winter night has darkened. The sky is a deep river of indigo, the stars pricked like lights in its flowing stream. Nella sits at her window, the miniature Peebo in her lap. Jack has long gone from his post. Where is Johannes now – will he take one of those mysterious gondolas, will he return to the Doge's palace? Of course he will, Nella thinks. It's Johannes. She turns to her cabinet and places Peebo gently on top of one of the velvet chairs. *Things can change.* She tries not to picture her real bird, out in a night like this, prey to hawks and owls. Perhaps the miniaturist has kept him safe – though from where else did these shortened little feathers come? The thought that the woman would pluck at him and do him harm is unbearable.

It's time to find out. The Kalverstraat will be freezing at this hour, Nella thinks, pulling on her travelling cloak. And who knows how long it will take to persuade the miniaturist to come outside?

189

She drapes the small gold key the miniaturist sent around her own doll's throat, placing her little self neatly on the real bedcovers. 'I am not frightened,' she says out loud, turning to see a brief gleam on the doll's tiny clavicle. And yet, she cannot erase the thought that this gesture towards her miniature is the only thing that guarantees her safe return.

Nella has never gone out after dark in her entire life. In Assendelft, she'd only meet an errant fox breaking into a coop of chickens. The foxes in Amsterdam might take very different forms. Quietly opening her door, she inhales a lovely scent of lavender, diffusing in the passageway as steam moistens the air. The rest of the house is silent except for the sound of slopping water coming from the end of the corridor. Marin, who keeps her secrets like weapons, who wears sable dresses but eats old herring, appears to be having a midnight bath.

A bath at any time of day is a sumptuous thing to do, and Nella wonders at such nocturnal indulgence. Unable to resist, she moves silently down the corridor and puts her eye to the keyhole.

Marin has her back turned, blocking Nella's view of the bath, which takes up most of the spare space left in her tiny room. Who put it there for her, filling it to the brim with hot water – surely not Marin herself? Her sister-in-law is not as slender as Nella thought she'd be. From behind there is a fleshiness to her thighs and buttocks, usually all hidden under her skirt. Marin's clothes come before her, they tell the world who she wants to be.

But Marin unclothed is a different creature, her skin pale, limbs long. As she leans over to test the bath temperature, Nella sees that her breasts are not small. Marin clearly straps them down in the most unforgiving corsets. They are fuller and rounder, like they should belong to someone else. That this is Marin's body at all is oddly unsettling.

Marin lifts a leg into the copper bath, then the other, sliding slowly in as if she aches. Her head leans back, she closes her eyes, the water covers her. She stays under for several seconds, seemingly kicking her leg against the side of the bath before coming up for air. As the dried lavender buds skate the surface of the water and release their scent, Marin rubs her skin until it turns pink.

The damp curls at her neck look girlish, unbearably vulnerable. Before her on the shelf next to all the books and animal skulls, Nella spies a small bowl of candied walnuts, gleaming like jewels in the candlelight. She cannot remember a single time Marin has publicly eaten a fritter, a waffle or bun – nothing, except Agnes' sugar which she could barely swallow. Has Marin purloined these from the kitchen – has Cornelia colluded in her mistress's secret appetite?

It is just like you, Marin, Nella thinks – to hide candied walnuts in your room and criticise me for loving marzipan. Sugar and herrings – Marin's commodities beautifully define her infuriating contradictions.

'What have you done?' Marin suddenly asks the air. 'What on earth have you done?'

Marin seems to wait, looking into the nothingness where no answer comes. Nella keeps her eye to the keyhole, terrified that the folds of her travelling cloak will rustle too loudly. After a while, Marin gets out of the bath with some difficulty, drying each leg and arm slowly. She looks well fed for someone who eats like a bird, who tells the world she denies herself the pleasures of sweets. Dressing in a long linen shift, Marin sits on her bed to the left of the bath, scanning the spines of her books.

Nella cannot draw her eyes away. Gone are her sister-in-law's perfect skirts, her black stomachers, the white half-haloes of her headbands. Now Nella knows what lies beneath; she is witnessing the skin. Marin reaches out, pulling a piece of paper from one of the books. It is the love note, Nella is sure – and now Marin is shredding it into tiny pieces until there is no paper left, just white petals spilling on the surface of the bath. Then she puts her head in her hands and begins to weep.

Seeing her like this should make me feel powerful, Nella supposes, as Marin's sobs flood her ears. Yet even now she eludes me. Like her idea of love, Marin is best witnessed in the chase – for caught like this, she is even more ungraspable. How would it feel, Nella wonders, to have Marin's trust, to take this pain from her and help extinguish it?

Suddenly saddened, Nella turns away. That will never be. The naked intimacy of this moment pulses through her, quelling the desire to face the outside dark and cold. She wants to sleep. Tomorrow, Nella tells herself. For now, she will take up her smaller self from off the bedcover, garlanded with the golden key, and place it back in the cabinet.

As Nella draws her cloak close and heads towards her own room, a shadow shifts near the top of the stairs. The back of a foot, a heel aloft, gone into the darkness again.

The Boy on the Ice

A dead body has bobbed to the surface of the Herengracht, a man without his arms or legs, just a trunk and head. Men hack at the ice to remove it as Marin watches, hiding herself behind the front door. The canal is a year-long dumping ground and as it solidifies with the cold, past deeds rise to be scrutinized by the rest of the city. Johannes' absence stretches into its second week, and more prosaic items emerge as the water freezes harder; broken furniture, chamber pots, ten kittens in a tight and pitiful circle. Nella fantasizes about warming them up, watching them come alive again, the torture they suffered nothing but a dream. When the authorities carry the man's body away like a severed haunch, Marin predicts that his murder will remain unsolved.

'These things were done in the dark in order to stay there,' she observes. Nella can almost smell again the lavender of Marin's bath. Marin seems distracted, looking out of the windows, wandering through the rooms.

Alone in her own room, wrapped up in two shawls, Nella holds the doll of Jack Philips in her hands. It seems easier to do this, now Johannes is away. Jack has a physical springiness and his leather coat has been tooled beautifully. Nella pulls lightly at his hair, wondering if wherever Jack is, he can feel the ache on his skull. It seems possible. I hope he can, Nella thinks. A feeling of power rushes through her, a desire to destroy. Resisting, but exhilarated, she returns him to the top of the cabinet house, where he lolls to one side.

Outside, enterprising street-urchins skate on the frozen canal, their light bodies no threat to the new ice crust. They remind Nella of Carel, skidding and sliding, whooping in joy. She opens the front door, hearing them call to one another – Christoffel! Daniel! Pieter! Nella steps out, instinctively searching the sky for a beloved flash of green, but there is none.

One of the skaters is the blind boy, the one who stole from the herring-seller the first day Nella arrived. The others call him Bert. Bert looks underfed, but seems at least to enjoy the reprieve the skating gives him, swooping around with his friends. Nella marvels at the way he skates as fast as the rest – one arm out, ready for a fall. The slipperiness of the environment is a great leveller. He skates off, up the unending frozen beam of light.

Every time Nella plans to go to the Kalverstraat, Marin finds something for her to do. Nothing has been delivered since the dolls and the miniature Peebo, and Nella finds herself impatient. Johannes has been away two weeks when December arrives, and she declares she must go and buy her family some festive gifts. She goes shopping through the Amsterdam streets, choosing a Milanese riding crop for Carel and a China tulip vase for her mother, items to tell the tale of a successful merchant's wife. But on the Street of Buns with Cornelia, shopping for the tastiest gingerbread for her sister, she looks around constantly for a pale blonde head of hair, those cool and watchful eyes. Nella almost wants to be spied on. It would make her feel alive.

She wants to go to the Kalverstraat, but Cornelia contrives it that they end up in Arnoud Maakvrede's shop, saying that Arabella deserves Amsterdam's best baking.

'Gingerbread has been banned,' Hanna says, her face grim. 'At least, in shapes of mankind. I thought Arnoud was going to lay an egg, he looked so angry. We've had to crush entire families and sell them on as crumbs.'

'What? Why?'

'The burgomasters,' she says, as if that explains all. Cornelia shudders.

Arnoud confirms that the forms of men and women, boys and girls, have indeed been banned, as have the doll-seller booths on the Vijzeldam. The reason has something to do with the Catholics, he says. False idols, the importance of the invisible over the tangible. 'Puppets are funny things,' Cornelia sniffs.

'That doesn't make the Church right,' says Arnoud. 'Think of the cost.'

'We'll just have to make them in the shape of dogs,' says Hanna, ever-enterprising.

Instead of gingerbread, Nella buys Arabella a book of insect prints. She supposes her sister would prefer Arnoud's finest biscuits, but better, she thinks, that Arabella should have a book and learn a little. You wouldn't have thought such a thing back in August, Nella tells herself. She feels differenced, as if something is working on her and she has taken the bait.

Back home, Marin sizes up the riding crop. 'How much did this cost? He's only a child.'

'It's what Johannes did with my cabinet,' Nella observes, giddy with her purchases, feeling powerful and rich. 'I'm only following suit.'

By the third week of Johannes' absence, icicles hang off every door frame, every windowsill, even off the spiders' webs in the garden, like tiny crystal needles. The four of them wake up cold and they all go to bed shivering. Nella yearns for spring, for blossom, the smell of turned earth, new animals, the vivid oily tang in the root of lamb's wool. She waits at the door for something to arrive from the miniaturist, but nothing comes. Remembering Hanna's comment about the burgomasters, the banning of puppets at Christmas, she wonders whether the miniaturist will ever send anything again.

Returning to her room, she finds Marin with her hands in the cabinet. It is a shock to see her there, and Nella rushes over, trying to pull the curtain across.

'You didn't ask to come in!'

'No, I didn't,' Marin replies. 'I wonder how that feels.' She has something in her hand, and she seems agitated. 'Petronella, did you tell someone about us?'

Please, God, Nella thinks. Let her not have found her own doll. Marin opens her palm and on it Jack Philips lies, as beautiful as his real self. 'What are you trying to do to us?'

'Marin—'

'The limited appeal of furniture and dogs I can just understand. But a puppet of *Jack Philips*?'

To Nella's astonishment, Marin yanks open the window and throws Jack through it. She runs to the casement to witness his flailing journey. He lands right in the middle of the iced canal, inert and marooned in the mass of white. A fear thrills through her. 'You shouldn't have done that, Marin,' she says. 'You really shouldn't.'

'Don't play with fire, Petronella,' Marin snaps.

I could say the same to you, Nella thinks, looking miserably at the stranded doll. 'It's my cabinet, not yours,' she calls, as Marin closes the bedroom door.

Jack remains outside on the ice. Nella tries to coax Rezeki to bring the doll back in her jaws, but the dog growls at the sight of it, skittering, her hackles raised. Nella wants to cross the frozen canal herself, but she is not as light as Bert and the other urchins, and they are no longer around to ask. She pictures herself falling through and drowning, all to save a puppet – compelled to protect it though she doesn't know why. Keeping Jack closer to the cabinet just seems like the safest thing to do, where she can keep an eye on him. Reluctantly Nella goes back in, cursing Marin in her head.

That night, Nella falls into a restless sleep, the words of Marin's ripped-up love note floating in her mind. Jack is speaking it, his English accent hitting the words like a skiff on choppy waves. *You are sunlight through a window, which I stand in, warmed. From back to front, I love you. A thousand hours.* Jack runs through the corridors of Nella's mind, wet from the ice, wearing one of Marin's animal skulls upon his curly head. Nella wakes up with a jolt, her dream so vivid that she's convinced Jack is in the corner of the room.

The next morning is St Nicholas's Day, the sixth of December. When Nella pulls open her curtains and looks below, her breath stops in her throat. Jack's doll is sitting up against their door post, taking in the frosty light.

The Rebel

When Nella sneaks out to pick up the frozen puppet from the front step, the street is still empty. Mists rise like swirls of breath above the ice.

'Where is everyone?' she asks at breakfast, Jack hidden in her pocket. Marin says nothing, delicately dismantling a herring.

'The burgomasters have succeeded once again,' Otto says heavily, carrying in a board laden with *herenbrood* and a deep disc of yellow Gouda for Nella. His weariness for the bureaucracy of state sounds almost fond – almost like Johannes.

Marin abandons her herring and stirs a bowl of compote, the tips of her fingers bluish on the spoon. She stirs and stirs, staring at the glistening maceration of plum. 'It has been publicly stated that dolls and puppets are forbidden,' she says. Nella can feel Jack's frozen doll against her leg, the offending item making a dark, damp circle on the wool. 'Papistry,' Marin continues. 'Idolatry. A heinous attempt to capture the human soul.'

'You sound frightened of them,' Nella says. 'Almost like you think they'll come to life.'

'Well, you can never be sure,' observes Cornelia. She, like the other two women, is wrapped up in layers of clothing, swaddled tightly in her Haarlem shawls.

'Don't be ridiculous,' Marin snaps. Nella imagines tiny sugar crumbs gathered like snow in the corner of her sister-in-law's solemn mouth as she weeps in another bath. Wearing her hidden fur, eating her secret stash of candied walnuts, protecting her unholy brother, Marin lives in two worlds. Is her deathless public propriety really a fear of God, or a fear of herself? What lies beating in that carefully protected heart?

Freezing air whistles through the crevices of the dining-room walls. The house does feel colder – as if the air from the night seeped in and hasn't shifted. 'The fires are lit,' Nella says. 'But it doesn't make the slightest bit of difference. Have you noticed that?'

'It's because our wood supplies have thinned,' says Otto.

'It does us no harm to experience the cold,' Marin replies.

'But must experience always be endurance, Marin?' Nella asks.

They all turn to Marin. 'In suffering we find our truest selves,' she says.

Nella follows Cornelia down to the warmth of the working kitchen, Jack still in her pocket. Cornelia clatters the plum compote jar and brandishes a rolling pin to attack some pastry for a pie. Otto follows, taking up a cloth to polish a battalion of Johannes' spring boots lined up along the kitchen door. 'Otto, will you sneak some peat from the attic? Madame Marin won't notice.' He nods, distracted. 'She loves her privations, but we are feasters to our core,' Cornelia observes. 'Behind closed doors, I will bet you my entire set of pans that gingerbread men are being gobbled into women's stomachs, no matter what the burgomasters say.'

'Or husbands, nibbling effigies of their wives,' Nella adds. Her joke is heavy, hanging undigested in the air; this talk of wives, of edible men to be held in the hand. Never to be nibbled, Nella flushes with shame. To distract herself, she imagines cheerier scenes behind doors other than theirs. Celebrations turned inwards – houses draped in paper chains and fir branches, buns fresh from the stove, laughter and *kandeels* of cinnamon wine. It is happening all over the city today, St Nicholas' Day, the patron saint of children and sailors celebrated in a carnival of hidden defiance. Sinterklaas belongs to them. As does their gluttony, so does their guilt.

It is hard right now to imagine the Magi in the boiling desert, travelling to worship the soon-to-be-Christ. Nella wants the doors and windows open, to let in the spirit of revelation. An open window might maintain an open mind. 'Christmas soon,' Cornelia says, 'and then – *Epiphany*.' Her voice hints at a private bliss.

'What's so special about Epiphany?'

'The Seigneur lets Toot and me dress up like lords and eat at his table. No chores all day. Of course,' Cornelia adds, 'I still have to make the food. Madame Marin doesn't let it go that far.'

'Of course not.'

'I'll make a King's Cake too,' Cornelia says. 'Hide a coin in the mix. Whoever bites it will be king for a day.'

Otto laughs, a sound with a bitter edge. It makes Nella's head turn, it sounds so unlike him. And when she looks at him, he will not meet her eye.

'This came for you,' Marin says, making her way down the kitchen stairs.

Nella's heart lifts that something new has come from the miniaturist, but the writing on the front flushes a melancholy through her before the letter is even opened. It is her mother's wiry hand, inviting her daughter and son-in-law to spend some of the festive season back in Assendelft. *Carel misses you.* The loops and lines are a painful reminder of a life which for Nella no longer exists.

'Will you leave?' Marin asks.

The pleading note in her question comes as a surprise. Something has slipped in Marin over these three weeks, and amidst her flashes of ill temper she has a new vulnerability. She really seems to want me to stay, Nella thinks – and could I even bear to go back, my flat stomach wrapped in a dress of Bengal silk, no growing child to brag of, my marriage a hollow victory? Johannes could perform the role of loving husband without much fuss. He is complacent when it comes to keeping his wits. But I would let mine go – they would fall from my grasp the moment I saw my mother's hopeful face.

'No,' she replies. 'I think it best that I stay here. I'll send the gifts I bought. We'll go next year.'

'We'll have a feast of sorts,' Marin offers.

'No herrings?'

'None at all.'

The women's two pledges flit between them like a pair of moths, charging the air with a new sort of energy.

Nella reinstates Jack in the cabinet house with mixed feelings. It still seems better to have him where she can keep an eye on him, although his presence remains unnerving. Later in the evening, some illicit musicians come to risk a song outside for money, and Nella leans out of the hallway window to hear their low singing. Otto and Cornelia hover, looking half-desperate to see the musicians, half-terrified of what Marin might say. 'The St George Militia might come,' Cornelia says. 'You should see their swords. They patrol to keep the peace but there might be blood.'

'Smashed violins? I look forward to it,' says Nella, drily.

Cornelia laughs. 'You sound like the Seigneur.'

Marin says Nella should shut the window and draw the curtains. 'People will see you, hanging out the window like a washerwoman – or worse,' she hisses as Cornelia scurries away. She paces behind Nella in the dark of the unlit hall, but as Nella keeps listening to the musicians, so does Otto, standing a little further off.

As the recorder pipes faster, the drummer beats a heady, insistent rhythm on the taut pigskin, thumping in response to Nella's heart. Otto said she shouldn't kick a hive, but part of her will always be a country girl. She thinks of Jack upstairs – all of them, wedged in those miniature rooms, waiting for something to happen. No, Nella decides. I'm not afraid of anything that comes with a sting.

The Fox Is Feverish

The next morning, refreshed by her musician rebellion and her decision to stay for Christmas, Nella plans to make her way to the Kalverstraat with her longest letter yet for the miniaturist.

Dear Madame (I know you are Madame – you have neighbours willing to talk),

I thank you for the eight dolls, and the miniature of my parakeet. I am sure it was you on the Herengracht bridge, watching my despair as I realized I had lost my childhood's last surviving link. Is the reappearance of my little bird an offer of comfort or a sharp lesson?

Do you know what your delivery boy has done, the unhappiness he's caused? I assume it was you who returned the Englishman's puppet back to our front step – be you proud artisan or pesterer, I cannot tell. I am sorry that your excellent work was hurled upon the ice, but your intentions remain a mystery, and some people are unnerved.

They tell me the burgomasters have banned images of people in all forms. I wonder whether you fear their wrath – the worlds you make, your tiny idols which have crept into my mind and plan to stay. You have not sent me anything for a while, and though it is true that I worry what you might send, my greater concern is that you will cease completely.

*I assume I still have it in my power to request items, do
I not? Therefore, kindly make for me a* verkeerspel *board,
my favourite game of strategy and chance. I am not returning
to my childhood home for Christmas, and my life is short of
such amusements. Therefore, content me with a miniature
version.*

*One day, we will meet, you and I. I insist upon it. I am sure
that it will happen. I feel you are guiding me, bright star, but
there is terror in my hope that your light is not benign. I will
not rest until I know more of you, but in the meantime, written
missives must take the place of better understanding.*

*Enclosed is another promissory note, for five hundred
guilders. Let that be the oil on your front door's stubborn
hinges.*

With thanks and anticipation,

Nella signs the letter: *Petronella Brandt.*

She looks out of her window to admire the white stretch of ice.
The city is beautiful tipped in frost like this, the air thin, the
bricks redder and the painted windowframes like pristine eyes.
To her surprise, she sees Otto hurrying along the canal path.
It piques Nella's curiosity, so not bothering with breakfast or
putting on a coat, she puts the letter in her pocket and follows
him quickly, slipping out of the house unseen.

Otto crosses Dam Square, past the looming new building
of the Stadhuis, where Frans Meermans has a post and may be
working even now. *Sell his wife's sugar, Johannes,* Nella thinks,
sending him a silent message as she skips over the sand which
has been scattered for easy passage on the cobbles. Again, she

remembers Marin in her bath, questioning the air, 'What have you done?' It would be better if the Meermanses were not in their lives at all.

After the suppression of St Nicholas's Day, the people of Amsterdam seem to be taking full advantage. The sun is high, the Old Church bells ring to the sparkling rooftops, and the sound is magnificent. Four high bells peal to the skies, ringing the coming birth of the Holy Child, and one lower bell – God's voice, deep and true and long – strikes under their clamour. In the name of communal obedience, it seems some music can play loud.

The smell of cooking meat fills the air, and Otto walks past a spiced-wine stall which has been erected, flagrantly facing the front entrance to the church. Pastor Pellicorne shoos the vintners away, whilst Amsterdammers look longingly at the trestle bowing under the weight of the wine-tureens.

'Tighter than a piglet's arse, that one,' a man mutters. 'The guild arranged it, the burgomasters gave permission!'

'God before guilds, my friend,' replies his friend, putting on a haughty voice.

'That's what Pellicorne wants us to think.'

'Cheer up. Look,' says the second man, revealing under his coat two small flagons of steaming red liquid. 'Even got a piece of orange in it.'

They hurry off to less salubrious surroundings and Nella feels pleased they have got away, even more pleased that they don't stop to gawp at Otto. Pellicorne's glance rests on her, but she pretends she hasn't noticed.

Otto enters the Old Church, his head down. Nella shivers as she steps inside, for the church seems colder than the air.

Even though she's supposed to be following Otto, she can't help looking round for a bright blonde head, a gold beacon among the plain brown and white of the church interior. She pats the letter in her pocket. At this festive time, might not the miniaturist make another visit – to remember her family in Norway, to pray for clemency from the Burgomasters? The threads of Nella's imagination begin to spool, embroidering conversations, patches of which it stitches loosely together. Who are you, why are you, what do you want? The problem is this – heading straight towards the miniaturist seems to make her disappear. And yet, she is so often there, watching and waiting. Nella wonders which one of them is hunter, which one prey.

She keeps her eyes on Otto. The chairs clustering the pulpit are mainly empty, save for a single person here or there who perhaps has nowhere else to be. Normally, of course, worship is done communally, people making sure everyone else sees them at prayer as if this will make the prayer more pure. Otto takes a seat, and unseen by him, Nella moves round and watches him from behind a pillar.

His lips move in a fever. This is no serene prayer – this is almost distraught. It's astonishing that Otto should be here, alone – what has driven him such a need to be witnessed in the house of God, given who he is, and what might happen? Nella sees the twisting of Otto's hands, the panic in his body. Something stops her going towards him. It would not be right to interrupt someone in that state.

Nella shivers, her gaze straying over the chairs, along the white walls, up onto the ceiling covered with old Catholic pictures. She wants so much for the miniaturist to reveal herself. Maybe she's hiding here right now, watching them both?

Behind her the organ starts up, a booming that shakes Nella to her very core. She doesn't like thundering organs, preferring the lighter pluck of the lute, the recorder's reedy ease. A cat, who has come in to shelter from the cold, slinks over the graves, its fur standing to a point. Its movement makes Otto look up and Nella ducks behind the pillar. She covers her ears from the booms of the organ and closes her eyes, dizziness taking her.

A hand touches her sleeve. Nella screws her eyes tighter, not daring to look. It is the moment – it is the woman, she has come.

'Madame Brandt?' says a voice.

Nella opens her eyes. Agnes Meermans stands before her, looking thinner than last time, her plain face narrowed, glowing white amidst a muffle of rabbit and fox. She retains her grasp on Nella's sleeve. 'Madame Brandt?' she repeats. 'Are you quite well? You aren't even wearing a coat. For a moment I thought the Holy Spirit was upon you!'

'Madame Meermans. I came – to pray.'

Agnes links her arm through Nella's. 'Or to keep an eye on your savage?' she whispers, motioning beyond the pillar where Otto sits. 'Very wise. You cannot be too careful, Nella. What's wrong with him that he looks so distracted?' Agnes emits her dry *ha*. 'Come,' she says, draping one of her foxes around Nella, pulling it too tight. Nella can smell that fruity pomade again. The fur is wetly cold.

'We have not seen Marin much at church,' Agnes observes, patting down the fur round Nella's neck. She cannot seem to keep her fingers still, and Nella notices how blank they are, devoid of rings. Their absence makes Agnes seem half-naked. The organ stops suddenly, and Agnes is uneasy, as if something is cracking deep beneath her well-polished veneer. 'Nor have we seen Brandt,' she continues. 'Nor you.'

'My husband is travelling.'

Agnes' nostrils flare. 'Travelling? Frans didn't say.'

'Perhaps he didn't know. I believe he is working on your behalf, Madame. He has gone to Venice.' She tries to pull away. 'I must go back, Madame Meermans. Marin isn't well.'

Though she wants to escape, Nella immediately regrets her excuse. Agnes' eyes widen. 'Why?' she says. 'What's wrong with her?'

'A winter malady.'

'But Marin's never sick,' Agnes says. 'I could send round my physician, though Marin never trusts them.'

The organ's notes begin again, falling one upon the other, to Nella's ears a crashing anti-harmony. 'She will be well, Madame. It is the season for colds.'

Agnes places her hand on Nella's sleeve again. 'This might spring Marin from her sick bed. You tell her this: my *entire* inheritance is still in his warehouse on the Eastern Islands.' She's almost hissing. 'Those cane-fields are unreliable, Madame – who knows when the next crop will come? Your husband hasn't sold a single loaf of what we've managed to refine. And now it seems he's gone to Venice *empty-handed*? We need that money.'

'He will dispatch it, I'm sure. His word is enough—'

'Frans went to the warehouse. He saw with his own eyes. I could barely believe it when he told me. Piled up to the ceiling! It won't be long, Agnes, he said. It will crystallize. Our money will rot before we've even plucked it.'

The organ notes vibrate in Nella's ribcage as she absorbs Agnes' growing agitation. She looks around the pillar for Otto, but he is nowhere to be seen. 'Be assured, Madame—'

'My husband won't be taken for a fool!' Agnes snaps. 'He wondered whether Johannes Brandt was the best man for the task, but I insisted. Me. The Brandts think they can have it *all*, but they can't. Don't laugh at him, Madame. Or me.' As quickly as she gripped, Agnes pulls away. Nella watches her hurry up the church, hunched over and unusually graceless. Opening the small side door, Agnes disappears.

Nella decides the best thing is to go home and tell Marin about this unsettling exchange. Yet again, the miniaturist languishes unvisited. I will send Cornelia with my letter, she thinks, her head spinning from Agnes' fury. She turns out of the church and back towards the Herengracht.

As she approaches the house in a rush to tell Marin, she knows that something is wrong. The front door is wide open, a gaping maw onto the unlit hall. She can hear the sounds of the dogs barking, but no human voices. She hesitates, then moves soundlessly up the steps to the side of the door.

It is his boots she sees first. Softest calfskin leather, by now a little scuffed. The sight of them slides her stomach. Horrified, she watches Jack Philips, fevered-looking, the malice written on his face, stride across the hallway tiles.

Cracks

They face each other. Jack is unshaven, underfed, his skin is dull where once it seemed so lustrous. Purple smudges smear the lower curve of his staring eyes. But he still has a presence, in his leather coat, those boots now broken in. The last time Nella saw Jack this close he was topless, slicked in her husband's sweat, and the memory of it makes her breathless.

Cornelia rushes up from the kitchen stairs and tries to push him through the front door.

'Wait, I've got something for you, Madame,' Jack cries, holding his hands up, the innocent. Nella remembers his strange English accent, his inability to cling to the roll and strut of Dutch. He reaches under his jacket and Cornelia tenses like a cat. 'I'm back on deliveries,' he says.

'What? You're supposed to be guarding our sugar,' says Nella. 'Johannes said—'

'Oh, you squeal like a mouse.'

He stands with his hand outstretched, as if the parcel he's offering will gloss his insult. The package is smaller than the last – but there it is – the unmistakeable black ink sign of the sun. Nella snatches it from him, not wanting his fingers anywhere near it.

Cornelia scurries upstairs, her face white with fear. 'I need to see him,' Jack says. 'Is he returned? Johannes, are you here?' he calls down the passage towards the study door.

Upstairs, a door clicks open and Nella hears Cornelia's hissed whispering.

'Is it true he's gone to Venice?' Jack says. 'Typical.'

Nella blushes, perceiving the intimacy between the men, something she's denied. 'He exchanges our Dam Square for the Rialto,' Jack grins. 'More fresh fish.' He approaches her, a lulling insistence in his voice. 'Did you believe him, when he said he was going there to work?'

'How dare you come—'

'I know more about him than you ever will, Madame. No one works in Venice. Milan, maybe. But Venice is dark canals and courtesans, and boys like moths, flying to the brightest flame.'

Nella's own body feels light, hypnotized by Jack's voice. He might have been a good actor, in his own language. Her heart feels the size of a pea bouncing around inside her ribs.

'What's happening here?' Marin's voice rings with authority from the top of the staircase. 'Why is the front door still open?'

Jack steps into the light at the sound of her, opening his arms wide. He is really so beautiful, Nella thinks. So wild. She cannot take her eyes off him. 'Petronella, close the door,' Marin orders.

'I don't want to be locked in—'

'Just close it, Petronella. *Now.*'

Her hand trembling, Nella shuts the front door. The hallway becomes a half-lit arena – for what exactly, she cannot bear to think. She wonders if Johannes is glad to be away from this rough boy, or whether he misses his mesmeric presence, that jumping voice. A sound of something being gutted makes Nella turn.

Jack has plunged a long and narrow dagger through the canvas of a still life. Its profusion of flowers and insects flaps open like a wound, the petals hanging awkwardly. Cornelia, standing on the stairs behind Marin, utters a nauseous moan.

'Stop that!' Nella shrieks. *Control your voice*, she thinks – *he's right. You're a mouse. You're not the mistress of this house.* Her stomach swills, her mouth goes dry. 'Otto,' she tries to call, but her voice is not much more than a whisper.

'Mr Philips!'

The ice in Marin's voice, in contrast, slides all the way down the stairs, making Jack freeze. Clearly Jack is not the only actor in the room. Marin transforms herself, focused entirely on this dark-haired boy entering her realm.

'How many times have I told you to keep away?' she asks. Her words echo, multiplying the menace of her presence.

Jack backs into the middle of the floor and Marin comes to stand at the bottom of the staircase, ignoring the painting entirely. He lets the dagger hang loose in his hand, and spits onto the floor.

'Clean that up,' she says.

Jack brandishes the dagger in front of her body. 'Your brother would fuck a *dog* if the price was right.'

'Mr Philips—'

'They say he gives it to you too – that he's the only man who will.'

Marin holds up her hand. 'What a tired old insult,' she says, bringing her open palm closer and closer to the tip of his dagger's blade. Jack backs away slightly, but there is no more than an inch between the sharp tip of his weapon and Marin's flesh. 'How brave are you, really, Jack?' she wheedles. 'Do you dare draw my blood? Is *that* what you want to do?'

Jack grips the dagger tighter and when Marin places her palm directly on the tip, he swings the blade away. 'Bitch,' he says. 'He told me I couldn't work for him any more. And whose decision was that?'

'Come, Jack,' Marin says, her voice quiet and reasonable. 'We've been here before. Stop being such a child, and tell me what it will cost to make you go away.'

'Oh, I don't want your money. I'm here to show what happens when you meddle.' With a cry Jack lifts the dagger towards himself, and almost before Nella can register it, Marin shoots out her hand and slaps him on the cheek. He drops his arms and stares at her, agog.

'Why are you so weak?' Marin hisses, though Nella can see that she herself is trembling. 'You can't be trusted for one hour.'

Jack rubs his face, collecting himself. 'You made him get rid of me.'

'I did no such thing,' Marin says. 'Johannes is a free man and you chose to believe what he told you. That belonged to my father,' she adds, pointing to the dagger.

'Well, Johannes gave it to me.'

From her pocket, Marin produces a crumpled set of guilder notes. She hands them over, her fingers brushing his palm. 'There's nothing for you here,' she says.

Jack pats the guilders thoughtfully. Without warning he pulls Marin towards him and kisses her hard on her mouth.

'Oh, God,' Nella whispers.

Both Cornelia and Nella move towards Marin, of one mind to pull them apart – but Marin puts her hand up as if to say, *Keep away – this transaction must take place.*

Cornelia stops, in horrified disbelief. Marin, rigid, does not put her arms around the boy, but the kiss seems to last for ever. Why is he doing this? thinks Nella – and why is Marin letting him? Yet a small part of her cannot help wondering how it must feel to be Marin in this moment: the touch of such a lovely mouth.

The front door swings open. Otto, returned from church, stops on the threshold, his whole body stupefied by the entwined figures of Marin and Jack. Something in him seems to snap – he rushes towards them – 'He has a knife!' Nella cries, but Otto doesn't stop.

At Nella's cry, Jack breaks away from Marin, who staggers back towards the main staircase. 'The old hag tastes of fish,' he sneers in Otto's face.

'Go,' hisses Otto. 'Before I kill you.'

Jack hops over to the front door. 'You might dress up as a lord, but you're nothing but a savage,' he says.

'Filth.' Otto's voice booms like Pastor Pellicorne's.

Jack freezes. 'What, boy? What did you say to me?'

Otto advances towards Jack. 'Otto,' Marin cries.

'He's going to get rid of you, savage,' says Jack. 'He knows you've done something and he's going to—'

'*Toot!* Keep away from him! Don't be a fool.'

'Someone close the door!'

'—he says a nigger can't be trusted.'

Otto lifts his fist. '*No!*' screams Cornelia as Jack shrinks away.

But all Otto does is place his palm gently on Jack's chest. An iron feather that pins, his hand rising and falling with the Englishman's ragged breath. 'You're nothing to him, *boy*,' Otto murmurs. 'Now go.'

Otto removes his hand just as Rezeki bounds back into the hall, a shaft of the weak light from outside turning her the colour of a pale mushroom. She snarls at Jack, her ears flattening on the top of her skull. Crouching low to the tiles, she warns him off. 'Rezeki!' Otto calls. 'Get away!'

The flash of panic in Jack's eyes compels Nella. 'Jack,' she says. '*Jack*, I promise. I'll tell Johannes you were—'

But Jack has driven his dagger into Rezeki's skull.

It is as if they all are underwater, and no one can breathe. The blade rips with a sickening squeak through fur and flesh and Rezeki slumps to the floor.

A wail starts low, rising higher and higher, and Nella realizes it's coming from Cornelia, staggering across the tiles towards Rezeki's body.

Rezeki is beginning to choke. Jack has driven in the dagger so hard that Cornelia's fingers cannot pull it out. Dark blood spreads in skirts of scarlet. Tender and trembling, Cornelia cradles the animal's head. Rezeki's breath rattles; a reddened tongue lolls from her gaping mouth. As the nerves twitch to stillness in the dog's legs, Cornelia presses her tight, desperate to hold together her fading warmth. 'She's gone,' Cornelia whispers. 'His girl is dead.'

Otto closes the door and stands between Jack and the outside world, his body spread across the entrance. Jack wrenches his dagger from Rezeki's head and more blood gushes on the tiles. '*Move!*' he shouts, his head butting Otto in the chest, his blade aloft. They scuffle, there is a fumble – a moment – and then Jack staggers back. He looks down at himself with terror in his eyes.

Jack turns to Nella. His own dagger is sticking in the top of his upper chest, below the collarbone but near enough to the heart for danger. His hands flutter round the hilt. *My God*, Marin cries, far off. *No, please God!*

Jack totters like a foal, arms out, knees buckling, and as he sinks to the floor he hangs on Nella's skirts. They kneel together on the black and white, his shirt beginning to bloom a festive red, and not even the earthy smell of mingled bloods can hide the tang of his urine.

'Otto,' Nella says, but her voice comes out like a cracked whisper. 'What have you done?'

Jack pulls Nella close and she feels the solid heat of the knife handle pressed between their bodies. He weeps with pain into her ear. 'I'm bleeding,' he pleads. 'I don't want to die.'

'Jack—'

'Get up,' cries Marin. '*Get up!*'

'Marin, he's dying—'

'Madame Nella,' Jack murmurs in her ear, holding Nella tighter, as if gripping onto life.

'All will be well,' Nella says. 'We'll fetch you a surgeon.'

His voice is muffled in her cap, but Jack sounds like he is laughing. 'Oh, Madame,' he whispers. 'You little girl. It'll take more than a fucking needle to murder me.'

It takes Nella a moment to understand. Jack crawls to his feet. He lurches towards the front door, the knife still in him, his movement like a tavern roll, drunk on his performance.

She cannot marry the blood-soaked shirt, the protruding hilt and his pleadings for life with this cockiness, this morbid glee at having tricked her that he was on his way to meet his maker.

'I believed you,' she whispers.

Otto steps back, stunned. Jack opens the door and, moving slowly into the thin light, he turns to face them, bowing deep and low as his fingers fumble with the hilt. He winces, sliding the dagger from out of the wound, pleased at the expression on Nella's horrified face. 'I'll be needing this,' he says, staunching the flow with one hand, the other lifting the flash of scarlet metal. 'Attempted murder. Evidence.'

'I wish that knife had found your heart,' says Nella.

'I hide it well,' he says, giving her a winner's smile. His wild curls mat to his brow, the dagger drips in his hand. He turns, running a crooked passage down the steps.

Marin, her face smeared with the faint red mark of Jack's lips, slumps against the panelling. 'Sweet Jesu,' she whispers, her grey eyes on Otto. 'Sweet Jesu, save us all.'

THREE

December, 1686

His mouth is most sweet: yea, he is
    altogether lovely.
This is my beloved, and this is my friend,
    O daughters of Jerusalem.

Song of Solomon 5:16

Stains

'The Seigneur found Rezeki in a sack,' Cornelia says in the hallway, her voice murky with grief. She watches Nella shuck the dog's rigid body into an empty grain bag. 'Around the back of the VOC, eight years ago. They were all dead – all the puppies, except for her.'

'We need a mop, Cornelia. Lemon juice and vinegar.'

Cornelia nods. There are still red sweeps of blood across the marble tiles, but the maid doesn't move. The picture frame attacked by Jack is now propped against the panelling. Marin ordered it to be hollowed out. 'He won't care, Madame,' Otto had advised, but she insisted. 'It is not for him,' she said. 'I cannot stand to see it half-ravaged.' Otto completed Jack's handiwork, his hand shaking slightly as he carved the canvas from the wood.

Now in the kitchen, Marin and Otto talk in low voices. It's my fault, Nella thinks – I carried Jack's doll inside after Marin threw him out. There he was the next morning, laid out on the front step, an omen of what was to come. If it was the miniaturist who laid him there, a horrid presage of what was to happen in this hall – why would she do that – why insist that this poisonous creature should stay close at all? 'Cornelia,' she says, rousing herself. 'We need to clean this up.'

She tries to push Rezeki's legs into the bag, but they are too long.

When Nella and Cornelia go down to the kitchen, Rezeki's paws protruding inelegantly from the sack, an air of aftermath hangs between the gleam of pans. So near to Christmas, the killing of a master's beloved dog feels like the opening act of some macabre carnival. The dog-murderer is out there somewhere, nursing more than simply a physical wound.

Otto places his trembling hands on the ancient oak of the table. Nella's thoughts are clogged. She wants to comfort him, but he won't even look at her. Dhana is slumped by the fire, whining at the sack in Nella's hand.

'Please can we bury her now?' asks Cornelia.

There is an uneasy pause. 'No,' Marin says.

'But she'll start to smell—'

'Just put her in the cellar.'

It is Nella who places Rezeki down gently, in the dark, upon the damp loam and potatoes. 'Poor, poor girl,' she says, choking on her breath. 'Godspeed.'

'What if Jack reports what I did?' says Otto, back in the kitchen. 'He's got the knife, the wound to prove it and a tongue in his head to tell tales. He mentioned evidence, attempted murder. The militia will arrest me. And what if they ask him why he was here?'

'Exactly,' Marin says, banging her fist on the table. 'I know a bit about Jack Philips. He likes the taste of life. Jack is a bragger but he would never go to the authorities. He would be signing his own death warrant and he knows it. He's

English, he's a sodomite, and he used to be an actor. I can't think of three things our burgomasters hate more.'

'He has no money, Madame. What might a man do when he is desperate?' Otto says, his expression clouding. 'If they ask him why he came here, then the Seigneur is embroiled.'

He shakes his head and Cornelia bustles over with a basket of *herenbrood*, some pieces of chicory and a contrary, sunny wedge of Gouda. Nella cuts the cheese as the maid busies herself at the stove. There will be no potatoes or mushrooms in tonight's dish, for Cornelia cannot even bear to look at the cellar door, let alone go into the darkness. Nella clings to her sounds of determined, domestic activity – the clang of pans, the onions softening in butter, the spitting of the bacon. Their irregular but constant beat is better now than any street-musician's festive melody.

Cornelia places the slices of fried bacon in front of them, and Nella sees how blanched she is with worry.

'The Seigneur saved me,' says Otto. 'He taught me everything. And look how I've repaid him. Rezeki—'

'That was Jack's doing, not yours. And there's never been a debt to pay,' Marin says. 'My brother bought you for his own amusement.'

Cornelia drops a heavy pan into the sink and curses under her breath.

'He employed me, Madame,' says Otto.

Marin wipes a piece of bread back and forth in the bacon fat, but doesn't eat. Nella cannot work out her mood. She seems determined not to be overwhelmed by these events, yet here she is, provocative as ever.

'The boy's alive,' Marin snaps. 'You haven't killed anyone. Johannes will be more concerned with Rezeki than with you.'

This statement seems to hit Otto in the chest. 'I have endangered you,' he says. 'I have endangered all of you.'

Marin reaches out for Otto's hand. It is an extraordinary sight – their fingers, the dark and light together – and Cornelia cannot pull her eyes away. Otto withdraws and heads up the kitchen stairs, and Marin watches his departure, the colour drained from her face, her eyes exhausted. 'Petronella, you need to change,' she says, her voice barely a whisper.

'Why? What's wrong with me?'

Marin points at her, and when Nella looks down, she sees her corset and shirt are covered in the brown stains of English blood.

❧

Upstairs, Nella sits shivering in her undergarments as Cornelia sponges off the specks of Jack. Putting Nella in a robe, the maid asks to be excused. 'I'm worried about Otto, Madame. He has no one else to talk to.'

'Then you must go.'

She is relieved to be alone. Her body aches from the tension of the morning, the imprint of Jack's grip on her arms. She scoops up her own doll from the cabinet, lying inert in the miniature kitchen, and presses her little figure, as if to do so will push the pain away. Her own ribs ache as she squeezes her miniature tight, and for a brief moment she believes there is no difference between the miniaturist's minor version of herself and her own human limbs. For what am I, she wonders, but a product of my own imagination? Yet the little bean-face looks up at her, giving nothing away, whilst Nella remains in tumult and grief remains.

On Nella's bed is the parcel from the miniaturist, brought to her just hours ago by Jack. She almost left it under the chair in the hallway, unsure if she wanted to open it, and now, observing it again, a wet sort of dread spreads through her. But who else is there to open these parcels? She couldn't bear for it to be anyone but her.

If the miniaturist is a strange teacher who will not stop, Nella feels a most reluctant pupil. She has failed to catch the meaning of these lessons. She yearns for just one piece that will explain what the miniaturist wants from her. Pulling open the package, she sees there is only one item.

A tiny *verkeerspel* board nestles in her palm. The board's triangles aren't simply painted, but have been inlaid with wood – and there are counters too, in a minuscule pouch. Their scent reveals that they are coriander seeds sliced in half, painted black and red.

Nella drops the board and fumbles through the pockets of her skirt. The long letter she wrote this very morning, addressed to the miniaturist and requesting a *verkeerspel* board, is no longer there. But I *had* it, she thinks. I had it today. I followed Otto to the church, I felt it in my pocket, I spoke to Agnes and I ran home to find Jack pacing in the hall. After that, all thought of it had been forgotten.

Time has melted; the hours mean nothing when you cannot keep hold of them. Nella tips up the packet and a piece of paper flutters out.

NELLA: THE TURNIP CANNOT THRIVE
IN THE TULIP'S PATCH OF SOIL

She's used my name, thinks Nella, the personal pleasure of this dissolving quickly in the oddness of the statement that follows. She feels an embarrassment creeping in – does the miniaturist mean I'm a *turnip*? Turnips and tulips are entirely different phenomena of nature – one practical and simple in its structure, the other decorative and engineered by man.

Nella touches her face instinctively, as if the neat handwriting will transform her cheeks into a dense and rotund earthiness, a dull vegetable from Assendelft. The miniaturist is the brilliant one, graceful and colourful, her power drawing the eye. Is this her way of warning me to stay away, Nella wonders – to tell me I may never come to an understanding?

Reaching into her cabinet house, Nella takes the doll of Jack and pulls off his leather coat. Pinching one of the tiny fish knives between her forefinger and thumb, she drives it in the front of his chest like a pin, near enough to the throat that he might choke. It makes a satisfying entry, slipping into the soft body, a protruding silver dart.

Placing Jack back in the cabinet, his doll-self now more accurately reflecting their dire situation, Nella picks up the painful reminder of Rezeki's body. Johannes should have taken you with him, she tells the little doll. How will it be, telling him what has happened to his favourite pet? I will offer this miniature as a memento of her life, she thinks, as a guiltier thought enters her mind. It will remind my husband what Jack is really like.

Stroking the head, Nella's fingers freeze between the blades of the dog's neck. There, on the tiny body, is an uneven, red mark almost the shape of a cross. Nella moves to the window;

it is unmistakeable, the colour of rust. Her heart begins to throb, her throat goes dry. She cannot remember if the mark was there before today. She did not look closely enough.

Perhaps it was accidental, the miniaturist dropping a fleck of red onto the dog's head as she moved with her paintbrush? Perhaps she didn't notice her mistake, letting the thin lines spread on the skull's curve. The model of Rezeki lolls in Nella's palm, her head articulated, the mark behind it a ghoulish baptism. The room is cold, but it is Rezeki's stained body that sends a chill to Nella's tail bone.

She tries to control her thinking. The miniaturist didn't seem to know what Otto was going to do when he drove that dagger into Jack's shoulder – because Jack's doll arrived unmarked. I had to tell that story for her. So are these pieces echoes or presages – or, quite simply, a lucky guess?

You have to go to the Kalverstraat, she tells herself. No distractions this time – and this time, you will stay until the miniaturist comes out. If you have to stand there all day with Hole-Face, you will do it.

Nella puts the dog back in the cabinet, Cornelia and Marin's conversation about papist idols swimming through her mind. Cornelia said you could never be sure that these things wouldn't come to life, and right now the puppet of Rezeki seems to thrum with a power Nella cannot name. And the house itself – the wooden frame appears to glow, the tortoiseshell so rich, the interiors so sumptuous. Nella stares at her own miniature clutching the tiny birdcage, that gilded trap encasing nothing. Silently, she recites the earlier mottoes from the miniaturist – *Things Can Change. Every Woman Is the Architect of Her Own Fortune. I Fight To Emerge.*

But who is fighting to emerge here, Nella wonders, and who is the architect – the miniaturist, or me? The old, un-answered question rises up – why is this woman doing this? Unnamed, the miniaturist lives on the outside of society, not bounded by its rules – but be you a tulip or a turnip, we are all of us accountable to someone in the end. Rezeki dead and Peebo gone, Jack at large and Agnes' sugar languishing on the Eastern Islands, Nella can feel the chaos coming, and all she craves is some control.

The miniaturist must help her. The miniaturist knows. Everyone in this house is too scared to do a thing except throw puppets out of windows, but that doesn't work. Nella fetches a pen and paper.

Dear Madame, she writes.

The turnip grows out of sight, while the tulip flourishes above. The latter serves the eye's pleasure, while the former nourishes the body – but both creations enjoy the soil. Separately, they have their uses, and one is no more valued than the other.

Nella hesitates – then, unable to help herself, she writes – *And the tulip's petals will fall, Madame. They will drop long before the turnip emerges, filthy but triumphant, from the earth.*

Nella worries she's been too rude, too direct. *Tell me*, she adds. *What is it I should do?*

She lays down her pen, feeling slightly silly with all this talk of vegetables, but panicky at the thought that the miniaturist has known all along what was going to happen to Johannes' dog. Before this mark on Rezeki's neck, Nella has taken her for a watcher, a teacher, a commentator – but this, well, this is more like prophecy. What else does she know – what else can she prevent? Or worse – what is she determined must come to pass?

❦

It is almost dawn the next morning when Nella creeps out of her room, her fourth note to the miniaturist in the pocket of her travelling cloak. I'm going to keep hold of this one, she thinks, until I press it myself in the palm of her hand. She is more than a little fearful of what she might discover on the Kalverstraat, face to face at last with the woman who not only looks deep into her world, but seems to build it too.

Holding a candlestick in one hand, Nella slowly withdraws the front door bolts. Opening the door, glad for the dull light breaking in the sky beyond, she hears a light clanking noise from deep in the bowels of the house. She freezes; the clanking continues. Looking down the canal path and back then towards the kitchen, Nella feels torn in two. Always, she thinks – always when it's time to see the miniaturist, this house never fails to pull me back.

The clanking inside the house wins her natural curiosity. It is too immediate to ignore. Too long I've heard these whisperings and noises, she thinks, closing the door, tiptoeing downstairs, moving through the best kitchen in an attempt to follow the sound. The round plates – maiolica, Delft and China-ware – glow in the huge dresser like rows of opening eyes as she passes with her solitary candle.

She pauses, sniffing the air. An iron smell, wet earth; a laboured breathing sound. Instantly, she thinks of Rezeki. She's come alive. The miniaturist is in this house, she's brought Rezeki back to life. Slowly, Nella walks down the narrow corridor which separates the best and working kitchens, towards the small door at the end where the barrels of ale and pickles are kept. The smell intensifies, clogging on the back of her tongue. It's blood, unmistakeable now. The breathing has got louder.

Nella stops, her fingers on the handle – a nightmarish belief that Rezeki is behind it, that with her long legs she has dug a way out of the sack and is scratching to be free. Nella swallows and pushes on the cellar door, terrified to her core.

Marin is standing there, her sleeves rolled up, a weak lantern on the table beside her. Next to the lantern is a line of white rags, from which she appears to be cleaning blood.

'What are you doing?' Nella asks, relief flooding her body even as confusion battles with it in this strange new scene. 'What on earth are you doing?'

'Get out,' Marin hisses. 'Do you hear me? Get *out*.'

Nella backs away, shocked by the ferocity in Marin's voice, the fury stretching her face, the shocking smear of blood upon her cheek. Slamming the cellar door, she trips up the kitchen stairs into the hallway. Rezeki's red mark mingles in her mind's eye with Marin's crimson cloths, as she stumbles through the front door and down the steps into the dawn.

Sweet Weapons

The Kalverstraat, with its long strip of trade and noise, is still relatively quiet. There is the occasional fruit-seller trundling his barrow, and an enterprising ginger cat, sorting through the animal bones which didn't make it to the canal the night before. His yellow eyes shine at Nella and he stretches his fat body, witness to his forage-cunning.

Nella finds the sign of the sun. She stands before it, breathing the damp air, the residue of mist, the smell of waste covered hastily in straw. She knocks on the door, a sharp confident rap, and waits. No one comes. But I will wait, Madame Tulip, she thinks, patting the note in her pocket. I will wait and wait until I get my answer.

She takes a step back, looking up at the four windows, the golden sun and the motto engraved beneath it. *Everything Man Sees He Takes For A Toy*. It seems a taunt, and Nella bristles. *I* don't, she thinks. At least, not any more. There is nothing toylike or comforting about her miniature Peebo, or Rezeki and her blood-mark.

'I know you're in there,' she shouts despite the early hour. 'What do I have to do?'

Immediately, the door behind her swings open. Nella turns and sees a fat man in an apron, squat-faced, his gut overhanging his boots by a good foot, standing with his hands on his hips. Beyond him, a small, cool room displays long hanging yarns of undyed wool and several sheepskins nailed to the walls.

'Girl, there's no need to bellow to Antwerp.'

'I'm sorry, sir. I've come to see the miniaturist.'

The man raises his eyebrows. 'The what?'

Nella looks up at the house again and the man stamps his feet in the cold. 'Oh. Her. She won't answer you,' he says in a kindlier voice. 'There's no point trying.'

Nella swivels back to him. 'So I've been told. But I am happy to wait.'

He squints up at the house. 'Well, you'll freeze to death doing it, because no one's been in that building for over a week.'

A small desolation pitches in Nella's stomach. 'That isn't possible,' she says. 'Just yesterday, she sent—'

'What's your name?' asks the wool-seller.

'Why?'

'I might have something for you.'

'My name—' She pauses. '– is Petronella Brandt.'

'Hold on.' He dips back into the gloom of his shop. He re-emerges, holding a small packet in his hand, inked with the sign of the sun. 'Left on the doorstep opposite. I thought one of the cats might have had a go. Seems her English boy's stopped delivering, so I kept it safe.'

He places it on Nella's outstretched palm and looks up again into the burnished sun engraved above the miniaturist's door. 'What does it even mean?' he asks. '*Everything Man Sees He Takes For A Toy*?'

'It means we think we're giants, but we're not.'

He raises his eyebrows. 'I see. I should think so little of myself, should I?'

'Not at all, sir. Just that things – aren't always what they seem.'

'I'm giant enough,' the wool-seller laughs, his arms out wide. 'Pretty sure of that.'

Nella gives up, smiling wanly, looking over his shoulder into the gloom of his shop, holding her packet tight. 'Do you have someone working for you – a man with smallpox scars?'

'Oh, yes. Hauled wool for two weeks then upped and left.'

'Why did he leave?'

'He was spooked.'

'Spooked?'

'Completely terrified. Ran off in the night. God knows what happened to him.'

From the near distance comes the sound of marching, thump-thump up the Kalverstraat. The wool-seller goes back into his shop. 'The St George Militia,' he mutters, throwing down the front shutter. 'Move out of the way, girl, or you'll get crushed.'

'Wait!' says Nella, maddened. 'Where has she gone? Did you see her go?'

But the St George Militia loom on the horizon, the yellow-eyed cat scurrying away only just in time. All the guards have strapped red ribbons over their wide chests, and the colour catches the winter sunlight like a streamer of blood. Their steel-capped boots scuff the path and over-zealous weaponry clanks at their hips, pearlized pistols and hanging donder-busses for everyone to see.

Nella sees Frans Meermans among their number, his chest

puffed out, scowling at the sign of the sun. 'Seigneur?' she calls, and on seeing her he turns away, drawing his pike nearer to his chest. They are gone in a cloud of dust, marching effortlessly into the Amsterdam morning.

The street falls silent, and Nella notices how numb her toes have become in the cold. She rips the packet open, furious with Frans Meermans' rudeness, incensed with the miniaturist for eluding her yet again. Every time I search for her, she thinks, I am left with only myself.

But her frustration melts into delight, for before her inside is a collection of tiny cakes and pastries. Pufferts and cross-hatched waffles, tiny gingerbread people, *olie-koecken* dusted with white powder, round and moreish in appearance. They look as if they have been made of real pastry, yet when Nella touches them, they are hard and unforgiving. She finds another message, written on the paper beneath them:

DON'T LET SWEET WEAPONS STRAY

Nella looks up at the windows of the house. 'Sweet weapons?' she cries, pushing her own, pleading note underneath the miniaturist's door. The morning light shifts over the panes, concealing the miniaturist's secrets. Nella looks down at these inedible delicacies, almost tempted to hurl them into the nearest canal. What does the woman mean by these? No war was ever won, Nella thinks, with an arsenal of sugared treats.

The Empty Space

When Nella returns to the house, Cornelia is waiting for her at the door.

'What is it?' Nella asks, seeing the stricken look on the maid's face.

'The *Seigneur*,' Cornelia whispers. 'He's back from Venice. He's already asking where Rezeki is.'

'What?' Nella feels the quality of the air thicken, and a nub of fear lodges itself in her throat. She pictures Rezeki's blood-stained body waiting in the cellar – and Johannes, unaware, waiting for the tip-tip sound of her shapely paws.

'It has to be you who tells him, Madame,' Cornelia pleads. 'I cannot.'

Nella closes the front door quietly, scanning the floor, relieved there is no more blood to be seen. Cornelia has mopped and mopped, dousing the tiles in vinegar and lemon juice, a bath of boiling water and lye over the stains. Yet upstairs in the cabinet house, it wasn't possible to rub away the cross-like mark on Rezeki's miniature head.

'But why me, Cornelia?' she asks.

'You're strong, Madame. It's better coming from you.'

Nella doesn't feel strong. She feels ill-prepared, daunted by the story she will have to tell. *All I needed was a bit more time* to sweeten this truth to some sort of a lie, she thinks. How does anyone start such a conversation?

Johannes is standing in the centre of the salon, his gaze resting on the hollowed picture frame propped against the painted mural that stretches round the walls. He has brought two rugs back with him, thick weaves with mathematical patterns. They already have twenty, thirty of these tapestries, Nella thinks. What is the point of more? The room is freezing, and he is still in his travelling cloak.

To her surprise, Johannes' eyes light up. Her husband actually seems pleased to see her.

'Johannes,' she says. 'You are home safely. Was Venice – enjoyable?' She hears Jack's crooked Dutch in her ear – *more fresh fish*.

Johannes sniffs the air, wrinkling his nose at the lingering scent of vinegar wafting in from the hall. Nella prays that Cornelia's bubbling kitchen pots will soon overwhelm it.

'Venice was Venice,' he says. 'Venetians talk a lot. And there was too much dancing for my knees.'

To her astonishment, he takes her in a huge embrace. Nella's head only reaches Johannes' breastbone, and he presses her ear to where she feels the thump of his heart. As he digs his chin onto the top of her head, she finds the awkward hold an unexpected comfort. She has never touched this much of Johannes before. Her feet begin to lift off the floor as if she's clinging to a raft. As she closes her eyes, Rezeki's bloodied face rises into view, and no amount of scrunching her eyelids will make it go away.

'I am glad to see you, Nella,' he says before putting her down. 'Why is there no fire in this room? Otto!' he calls.

'And I am glad too, Johannes,' she replies, her mind reaching for words that simply slip away every time they feel her coming. 'I – shall we sit?'

He collapses into a chair with a sigh, and Nella finds herself still standing.

'What's wrong?' he asks, and she thinks the concern in his voice will break her.

'Nothing, Johannes. There's – I – Agnes was angry with me,' she blurts. She cannot do it – she cannot say the words. It is easier to choose the subject of Agnes Meermans over news of his beloved dog.

Johannes' expression clouds. 'And why was Agnes angry?'

'I – saw her at the Old Church. She says that all their sugar is still in the warehouse. That it might start to crystallize.'

Johannes draws his hand down the side of his face. 'She had no right to speak to you like that.'

Otto appears at the threshold of the salon, carrying a basket of peat. He hovers, barely able to look up.

'Ah, the fire,' says Johannes. 'Come in, Otto, and make us warm.'

'Seigneur. Welcome home.'

'What's Cornelia cooking?'

'Pig-liver pudding with barley, Seigneur.'

'My favourite for December! I wonder what I've done to deserve it.' Johannes smiles, sniffing the air again, running his hand over the empty frame. 'What happened here? This was one of my favourites.'

Otto seems almost grey in the half-light, and Johannes looks at him shrewdly.

'An accident,' says Nella.

'I see. Well, pile up the kindling, Otto. My feet are so cold they might fall off.'

Nella turns to see Marin, standing at the door. Her face is pinched, and she hesitates before she glides in, remaining near the wall.

'How many loaves did you sell in Venice?' Marin asks.

'Make it a big fire, Otto.'

'Brother, how many did we sell?'

From his seat, Johannes places the empty frame upright on his lap. His upper body is in the middle, and he gestures in the hollow. He picks a regent's pose, self-satisfied and ridiculous. 'It was as slow as I predicted it would be,' he says. 'It would have been better to go in the new year.'

'Then perhaps you will light such a gigantic fire when the sugar is actually sold?' Johannes' ensuing silence appears to incense his sister. 'The greedy will bring ruin to their households.'

'Your welcomes are getting worse, Marin. You're the one that pushed me out on a ship to Italy in the dead of winter. Do not speak to me of greed. And please, don't keep quoting the Bible. It becomes tiresome, given your own doubtful piety.'

Marin laughs, a strange sound which cuts the air. 'You are the constant provocator, not me,' she says, her every word straining on a leash.

He pulls off his travelling cloak and throws it in a bundle. 'And stop talking about this household as if it's yours. It belongs to Petronella.'

These words shoot through the air towards Nella like a bolt of light, but Marin stares at him in disbelief. 'Then Petronella may have it,' she says.

As easy as that? Nella thinks, turning to her. It doesn't seem possible; Marin cannot mean it.

'I've wasted my whole life keeping yours smooth,' Marin says, stepping towards her brother. 'We're nothing more than prisoners to your desire.'

Johannes sighs, holding his palms up to the fire to warm himself. 'Prisoners?' He turns to Otto, kneeling on the other side of the growing flames. 'Otto, do you feel like a prisoner?'

Otto swallows, his voice barely a whisper. 'No, Seigneur.'

'Nella, do I keep you under lock and key?'

'No, Johannes,' Nella replies. Though, she thinks, those empty nights waiting for your visits have felt like prison enough. She wants to be up in her room right now, alone, buried under the coverlet.

'This house is the only place any of us are free.' Johannes leans over in his chair and puts his head in his hands. 'And, Marin, you of all people cannot deny it.'

'Don't be a fool,' Marin snaps. This argument feels well trodden to Nella, and like the fire, its heat is rising fast. 'You are so selfish. It suits you to have me here, whilst you barely bother to hide the things you do.'

Johannes looks up at his sister. Nella sees how exhausted he is, face drawn, eyes dark. 'You think it suits me, is that the tale you tell yourself?' he says. 'Marin, against the counsel of my soul, I married a child. And I did it for you.'

'I'm not a child,' Nella whispers, finally sinking into a chair under the force of his words. And yet, she does feel childish. Johannes has transformed her in a moment, and she wants her mother, someone to notice her pain, someone else to take Rezeki's body away.

'And nothing's changed,' Marin says, oblivious to Johannes' plea. 'The careless attitude to Meermans' sugar, our future—'

Johannes kicks the empty frame and it splinters, skidding across the polished floor just as Cornelia enters, her sleeves rolled up, perspiration on her brow. Holding a tray of wine and bread, the maid stares at the broken frame and hovers by the door.

'You've never had to compromise!' Johannes says.

'It's all I've ever done. You think you can buy abstracts, Johannes. Silence, loyalty, people's souls—'

'You'd be surprised—'

'So tell me – what happens when you're actually caught? What happens when the burgomasters find out what you are?'

By the fire, Otto seems to choke on his breath.

'I am too rich for the damned burgomasters,' Johannes says.

'No.' Marin's voice is hard. '*No.* You've not been paying attention. I am the one who looks twice at the ledger books. I am the one – and let me tell you, the story they tell is a sorry one indeed.'

Johannes stands from his chair, seeming to seize up inch by inch as Marin's words plot upon him with thirty years of practised ease.

'You always thought you were different, didn't you, Marin – not marrying, interfering in my business. Do you really think, that because you have some maps of the East Indies up on your wall, some books on travelling, some rotten berries and a few animal skulls, that you know what life is like out there? What I do to keep you comfortable? You are the one who has no idea.'

Marin's eyes bore into him. 'I've got bad news for you,' she says.

No, Nella thinks. *Not like this.* Otto drops a large piece of peat onto the floorboards. Its black crumbs spray onto the wood.

'The burgomasters would scourge you for being a single woman if they could!' Johannes cajoles, coming towards her. 'The only thing you had to do, Marin – marry rich, marry well – oh, God, just to be *married* – you couldn't even manage that. We tried, didn't we? We tried to get you married, but all the guilders in Amsterdam turned out not to be enough—'

A dark and ragged sound rises up through Marin's throat, her mouth twisted, years of frustration writ large across her face. 'Are you listening to me, Johannes?'

'You've been a useless, friendless pain since the day you were born—'

'Your Englishman came knocking yesterday. Your brothel moth. And do you know what he did?'

'No!' cries Nella.

'Thanks to him, your beloved Rezeki is dead.'

Johannes doesn't move. 'What did you say?'

'You heard me.'

'What? What did you say?'

'Jack Philips rammed a dagger in her neck in the middle of your hallway. I warned you. I told you he was dangerous.'

Johannes moves very slowly back towards the chair, sitting down on it with strange caution, as if he cannot trust the touch of the wood. 'You're lying,' he says.

'If it hadn't been for Otto, he might have killed us all.'

'Marin!' Nella shouts. 'Enough!'

Johannes looks over to his wife. 'Is it true, Nella? Or is my sister lying?'

Nella opens her mouth to speak, but no words come. At the sight of her expression, Johannes covers his mouth as if repressing a scream.

Otto stands up from the fire, his eyes full of tears. 'He had a dagger, Seigneur. I thought he was going to – I never meant—'

'Jack isn't dead, Johannes. Otto showed more mercy,' Marin interrupts. 'Your little Englishman got up and walked away and your wife put Rezeki's body in the cellar.'

'Otto?' Johannes utters his servant's name like a question he can hardly bear to ask. His hand drops from his face, a raw blank space waiting the wave of grief.

'It was all so fast,' Nella whispers, but Johannes, a strange energy upon him, pushes past his sister, past Cornelia, mute with shock at the door. They hear him stumbling across the hallway, down the kitchen stairs. Nella follows him, and hears him opening the cellar. Johannes' loss echoes up the corridor. 'My sweet girl,' he cries. 'My sweet girl, my sweet girl. What has he done?'

Nella creeps along, wading against her own desire to stop, another part of her knowing she must try and give comfort. She finds Johannes on his knees, cradling the rigid dog, half-hanging out of her bloodstained sack. Rezeki's head rests on her master's arm, her wound oily in the half-light, teeth bared in a crooked grin.

'I'm so sorry,' Nella whispers, but Johannes cannot speak. He looks up at his wife, eyes wet, clinging to his love in disbelief.

The Witness

For the next two days, the house seems to nurse itself in a suspended quiet. Marin stays in her room, Cornelia plans the charity boxes they will send to the orphanages for Christmas, the cakes smaller this year, the meat pies fewer. Otto avoids them all, staying in the garden where he prods unnecessarily at the frozen soil. 'You'll disturb the bulbs, Toot,' Cornelia says, but he ignores her. Nella smells a pig's trotter pottage on the boil, and hears the chafing dishes and skimmers banging in time to Cornelia's misery.

Johannes goes out both these evenings. No one asks him where he's going, because they dread the answer. On the second evening after the argument, alone in her room, Nella stands before her cabinet house and holds up Agnes' doll to the fading light. Somewhere in the house, she can hear a person being sick, the splatter of vomit in a tin bowl, susurrations, the refreshing waft of mint tea to settle a bad stomach. She too would like to purge the worry that waits inside. She hopes Johannes is in the warehouse on the Eastern Islands, working on the sugar – although there was something so unnerving about Agnes' behaviour in the Old Church, that Nella can hardly believe the only cause for her anger is her business prospects.

As she examines Agnes' miniature, Nella feels a shudder

running up her back, her skin a sudden rash of goosebumps. The tip of Agnes' cone of sugar has turned completely black. She cries aloud, trying to scratch the spores away, but they smear the rest of the loaf like soot. She attempts to break the loaf off – thinking to bury it in the garden, to inter its power – and it snaps, taking Agnes' tiny hand with it.

Nella hurls the maimed doll to the floor, the severed hand with its ruined loaf still between her fingers. 'I'm sorry,' she mutters, unsure exactly to whom she is apologizing – to the doll, to Agnes, the miniaturist. The ruination in Agnes' tiny hand feels irrevocable, and somehow all her fault.

The poor weather could have caused these tiny spores – but the cabinet is on the first floor, where the damp is not so bad. It could be dirt from the chimney, yet the cabinet's contents are nowhere near it. All these logical possibilities; they never seem to fit. Like Rezeki's mark, was this black stain always there, minuscule and virtually unnoticeable? Or has it inexplicably appeared, spreading in response to her panic over Agnes? No, Nella thinks – don't be so ridiculous. It was simply another warning that you missed. She looks at the cabinet, at the array of baked pastries, the cradle, the paintings, the cutlery and books, wishing she'd paid more attention when the dolls and dogs first arrived. Are there more little bombs in there she cannot see, ready to explode?

Marin hates these dolls for their idolatry – but this blackened cone, this red mark on Rezeki, these extraordinary pieces of craftswomanship, are more than idolatry. They are intrusions Nella still cannot define. There is a story here and it seems like Nella's, but isn't hers to tell. She spins my life, she thinks. And I cannot see the consequences.

Nella opens *Smit's List* once more. The miniaturist's mottoes, pressed between the pages, fall from the opened spine like scattering confetti. She finds the miniaturist's advertisement. *Trained with the great Bruges clockmaker, Lucas Windelbreke. All, and yet nothing.* Every time I go to her house, Nella thinks – every time, foolishly bashing on her unopened door – I want all and I certainly achieve nothing. A different approach is required, and as she stares at the advertisement, Nella wonders why she didn't think of it before. There will be no more long letters, no more witty, semi-philosophical retorts, no more tulips and turnips or running in the cold to be embarrassed on the Kalverstraat.

She hurries to her mahogany writing table, remembering how she waited on Johannes' doorstep that first day, the people wandering up the Herengracht, the blind boy with the herring, the women laughing. Had the miniaturist known me even then? Had she known how much I looked forward to a room, a desk, a piece of paper to embellish my unhappy welcome?

Drawing out a sheet, Nella dips the pen and begins her letter:

Dear Seigneur Windelbreke,

 I am writing to enquire about an apprentice you once had.

 All I know of her is that she is female and has a tall, fair-haired appearance, and stares as if she would look into my soul. She has crept into my life, Seigneur, and the miniatures she sends are becoming more unnerving. How is it that she will not respond to me directly, yet chooses to make me the focus of her work?

Tell me how she came to you and why she left. What forces
move within her to make my life in miniature – unasked for,
exquisite, mysterious in their message? I named her my teacher
but now, God save me, I call her a prophet – but if she was once
a spying devil you had to cast out, then you must write to me.

I wait with painful anticipation,

Petronella –

There is a knock on her door. Nella shoves the letter under
a book, draws the curtains on the cabinet and gathers up the
miniaturist's mottoes.

'Come,' she says.

To her complete surprise, Johannes shuffles in. 'Did you
find him?' she asks, drawing her robe around her and pocketing the mottoes. She finds herself unable to say Jack's name
out loud, but surely that is who Johannes has been with these
two nights, though no one dared to say it.

'Alas, no,' he replies, holding his hands out like a clumsy
thief, as if Jack has slipped through his fingers.

'You're like a child, Johannes, lying about a stolen puffert.'

He raises his eyebrows, and although Nella is surprised at
her own directness, increasingly with Johannes she finds it
difficult to hide her feelings. He doesn't deny this accusation,
but tries to soften her. 'Petronella,' he says. 'I know you're not
a child.'

His kindness almost hurts more than his cruelty. 'There is
much I cannot understand,' she says, sitting up on the cover of
her bed, glancing at the closed cabinet. 'Sometimes in this
house, I see a crack of light, as if I have been given something.
And yet other days, I feel shrouded in ignorance.'

'By that measure, indeed we are all of us children,' Johannes says. 'I didn't mean what I said in the salon. When Marin – she makes me—'

'Marin just wants you to be safe, Johannes. As do I.'

'I am safe,' he replies.

Nella closes her eyes at this, feeling a deep unease. How hard it must have been for Marin all these years, caring for someone who thinks the force of his own will is enough to fight the troubles of existence! He is a citizen of Amsterdam – surely he knows he cannot survive here alone?

'This is not the marriage you imagined for yourself,' he says.

She stares at him. A glimpse of parties, a feeling of security, the dying laughter of chubby babies – it falls between them and fades to black. All that belongs to another Nella, one who will never exist.

'Perhaps I was foolish to imagine anything.'

'No,' he says. 'We are born to imagine.' He still hovers, unwilling to leave. Nella thinks again of her latest delivery from the miniaturist, the buns and cakes arranged in a tiny basket, hiding behind the mustard-coloured curtains.

'Johannes, did you manage to sell any of Agnes' sugar in Venice?'

He collapses on the end of her bed. 'It's a mountain, Nella,' he sighs. 'Literally. Metaphorically. Finding buyers, at this time of year, will take a while.'

'But did you find *any*?'

'A couple, yes. A cardinal and one of the Pope's courtesans. People seem to have less to spend these days.' He smiles sadly.

'You will have to think of something for the rest. Marin

would be bothering you even more if she knew you'd only found two buyers. You must consider yourself fortunate it's only me.'

Johannes smiles. 'I wasn't expecting the woman you've turned out to be.'

Nella's first obsession is an elusive Norwegian woman who moulds her life through miniatures, and her second is keeping Johannes' wealth from rotting near the sea. It was not the picture her mama had painted back in Assendelft.

'You only know me slenderly.'

'I was complimenting you,' Johannes says. 'You are extraordinary.' He pauses, looking embarrassed. 'Come January I'll be gone again, and I'll make their profit for them. My stock always sells.' He opens his arms wide, as if the stature and ornament of his Herengracht house should be sufficient proof.

'But do you promise, Johannes?'

'I promise.'

'I believed your vow once,' Nella says. 'I pray this time you hold it true.' In the background, the pendulum clock marks its velvet time. 'Here,' she says, lifting off the bed and gently parting the curtains of the cabinet. 'I want you to have this.'

She puts the puppet of Rezeki in his hand and Johannes looks down, blinking with tired eyes, not sure at first what he's seeing. 'Rezeki?' he utters.

'Keep her safe.'

For a moment Johannes pauses, his eyes riveted to the tiny model in his hand. Then he lifts it up, touches the silky grey fur, the small intelligent eyes, the slender legs. 'I've never seen such a thing. In all my travels.'

Nella notices that he does not comment on the red mark.

If Johannes doesn't choose to see it, she supposes, so much the better. 'Your wedding present,' she whispers. 'I know Rezeki was never human-shaped, but still – don't tell the burgomasters.'

Johannes looks at her, too moved to speak, clutching the gift like a talismanic comfort. Nella closes the door on him, listening to his quiet tread back to his own room, feeling strangely at peace.

But at dawn the next day, she finds herself woken roughly by Cornelia. The sky is split in streaks of orange and dark blue – it cannot be later than five o'clock. Nella shivers out of her dreams of red-soaked cloths and shrinking rooms, quickly conscious of the cold morning air.

'What is it?'

'Wake up, Madame, wake up.'

'I am awake. What's wrong?' she asks. As she focuses on Cornelia's looming, drawn face, fear plummets through her. 'What's happened to Johannes?'

Cornelia's hands fall from Nella's body like a pair of dead leaves.

'Not the Seigneur. It's Otto,' she whispers, her voice breaking. 'Otto's gone.'

Souls and Purses

Cornelia dances around Johannes, having to be two servants. She puts his boots on, dropping small pies into his pockets, an apple, feeding him against her fears. Johannes pushes his arms through his jacket. 'Where's my brocade?' he asks.

'Trust you to ask that now,' Marin mutters, grey with exhaustion.

'I couldn't find it, Seigneur,' says Cornelia.

'I'm going to check the docks,' Johannes says. 'Why did he run like that?'

'Check the sugar too,' calls Nella, chasing him outside.

Johannes looks at her in disbelief. 'Toot comes first,' he says. 'We cannot lose him.'

But Nella cannot help thinking of Agnes' blackened little loaf upstairs. It's a sign – the miniaturist is trying to warn them, as she warned about Rezeki. Surely there is something to be done before they lose the sugar too? But Johannes has gone, and no wife can turn up to her husband's warehouse unannounced.

There is no sign of a struggle in Otto's bed, no broken furniture, the door unforced. A bag of clothes has gone.

'He took the Seigneur's jacket, I'm sure of it,' Cornelia says.

'Maybe he'll sell it,' Nella says.

'It's more likely he'll keep it to wear. Why did he have to go?'

It strikes Nella that she has not asked Cornelia what she was doing looking for Otto in his bedroom at five o'clock in the morning. But Cornelia is literally unmanned, and to probe her now might do more harm than good.

'Cornelia,' Marin calls up the stairs. 'Come here.'

Marin is in the salon, in three jackets, a shawl and two pairs of woollen stockings, clumsily trying to light a peat fire. When she straightens, she looks so bulky, so much taller than Nella and Cornelia. 'I cannot light the peat,' she says. Her speech slides like butter in a pan.

'It's Toot's job to light fires, Madame.' It is not on the peat's thick smell that Cornelia appears to choke, tears welling in her eyes. 'I'm not very good at this.' The maid kneels before the grate, her body a folded mirror to her soul. 'I asked along the canal,' she murmurs. 'No Africans taken into the Rasphuis or the Stadhuis prison.'

'*Cornelia*,' says Marin, lowering herself into the same chair Johannes had collapsed in at the news of Rezeki. Red-eyed and worrying at her layers, Marin cannot sit still. She takes a bite from a week-old slice of apple tart that Cornelia has brought for her, then puts it to one side.

Nella sends a prayer to the miniaturist, wherever she may be at this moment – *Madame, send my husband a pair of wings. Fly him faster to the departing ships. Keep beloved Otto on this land.*

'He'll escape,' Marin says, rubbing her temples as if trying to solidify something restless shifting in her skull. 'He'll go to

London. Down by the Thames he'll have a hope of blending in.'

'You sound so sure,' says Nella.

'I told him nothing would happen,' Cornelia says. 'Why didn't he listen to me?'

'Because he was frightened,' Marin says, her breathing becoming heavier. She takes up the apple tart again and picks at it, almost talking to herself. 'Better that he is gone. By removing himself he protected us. And what would happen to a man like Otto if the burgomasters got hold of him?'

'Marin?' Nella says. 'Did you know he was going to leave?'

Marin betrays a glint of dismay at her question. 'He is a man of sense,' she replies, looking away and smoothing down her skirt.

'And was it you who told him to go?' Nella presses. The oblique answers behind which Marin hides are infuriating.

'It was the lesser of two evils,' she says. 'I may have suggested it, but I forced nobody.'

'I know how your suggestions work.'

Cornelia stares in abject horror. 'You sent him away, Madame? You said Jack wouldn't report him.'

'Jack is infinite in his capacity to surprise. He is opportunistic. Say he took a chance to attack us – Otto would have no trial, he'd have no chance to live.'

'How much you love to pull all our strings, Marin! Trial or not, Otto could die out there.'

Cornelia stands up. 'He is the Seigneur's servant.'

'Is he not my servant too?' Marin hurls her slice of apple tart against the wall, narrowly missing Cornelia. The maid jumps as the tart explodes upon the oil mural of the countryside, its currants spattering like dark bullets over the painted sheep. 'Have I not got his best interests at heart?' Marin cries. 'Johannes doesn't care.'

'He's out looking for him now!'

'Johannes loves no one but himself,' she hisses. 'And that's why we are here.' The currants slide down the mural and lie on the floor, and Marin moves slowly from the room as if weighed down by her clothes.

⚜

Christmas, like a poor relation to the promise it once held, shuffles past, with still no sign of Otto. The donations of food are sent to the orphanages, and Johannes buries Rezeki in the wintry, hibernating garden. 'I've never seen the Seigneur like this before,' Cornelia says to Nella, her face white with worry. 'He even read a passage from the Bible. It was like he wasn't *there*.'

Diminished and withdrawn, Johannes goes out daily, claiming he is making enquiries for his missing servant and working on the sale of the Meermanses' sugar. Sometimes, Nella thinks she should tell Marin that it is still all in the warehouse, that Frans is furious – but there seems little either of them could do, and Marin's mood is so unpredictable.

The spores on the miniature cone play on Nella's mind, and she checks them daily, certain they will have spread. The cone remains frozen in time, however – and Nella clings to this, by now a full believer in the prophetic power of the miniaturist. I will fight to emerge, she thinks – but the problem is that Nella has no idea where she is emerging. A dead end, she supposes. The end of a sack, a mute and feeble existence.

Otto is no place she can picture him, and his absence is a question none of them can answer. So far, his doll reveals nothing, so Nella relies on the household's speculation on his whereabouts. Marin is adamant for London, Johannes reckons Constantinople. Cornelia is convinced he is still on these shores. It is too much for her to accept that Otto would willingly stray far.

'Better for him in a port city,' Nella says. 'In Assendelft, people would shut their doors on him.'

'What, in this cold?' says Cornelia.

'I believe it,' Marin says.

'I can't believe he agreed to leave,' says Nella, staring at her, but Marin looks away. 'It just doesn't seem like him.'

'You've been here twelve weeks, Petronella,' Marin snaps. 'A lifetime isn't enough to know how a person will behave.'

Cornelia begins to slack on her vinegar and lemon juice cleans, her sweeping and polishing, her laundering, cleaning, brushing and beating. Nella sends her letter to Lucas Windelbreke in Bruges, and waits for a reply. The winter weather might slow the messenger, she thinks, but it seems like her only resort.

She decides she must ask Marin if Johannes has spoken to her about the sugar still lying in the warehouse. She finds her in the hallway, where Marin has taken to pacing, staring at the space in the salon where she argued with her brother. The candied walnuts have emerged from her room, and piled in a bowl on a side table, their half-shells glint like beetles. Nella looks at them in surprise; this is not like Marin, eating sugary fripperies in plain view. I suppose if I'd had a fight like that with Carel, she thinks, I'd eat my weight in marzipan.

'Marin, I must ask you something,' she says.

Marin winces, clutching her shawl about her.

'What's wrong?'

'The walnuts,' Marin replies. 'I ate too many.' She turns upstairs towards her room and the moment for discussion vanishes.

Cornelia and Nella spend hours in the kitchen, where it is warmest. One late afternoon, when Marin is asleep and Johannes is out, there is a hard and heavy knocking on the front door.

'What if it's the militia, coming for Toot? God save us,' whispers Cornelia.

'Well, they won't find him here, will they?' Nella would never admit her relief to Marin, but she is glad that Otto has disappeared. She imagines Jack in the middle of a gang, pointing an accusing finger.

The knocking doesn't stop. 'I'll go,' Nella says, trying to keep at least the illusion of control. This topsy-turvy house, she thinks, where the mistress is the first to greet the guests.

But through the windowpane, just one broad-brimmed hat shimmers on top of a long, full face. Nella pulls the door open, her relief that it isn't the militia only slightly subsiding as Frans Meermans removes his hat and walks straight in. The December cold rushes in with him and he bows, playing the brim through his fingers.

'Madame Brandt,' he says. 'I've come to see your husband.'

'He'll be at the bourse,' says Marin.

Nella jumps, turning to see Marin waiting on the stairs. It is as if Marin knew he was coming. The air feels charged, and Nella waits for the giveaway signs of affection between them both. None comes. Of course, Nella tells herself. Marin is well practised at keeping a surface calm.

'I've been to the bourse,' says Meermans. 'And the VOC. And several taverns. I was surprised to find he wasn't there.'

'I am not my brother's keeper, Seigneur,' Marin says.

At this, Meermans raises his eyebrows. 'And more's the pity.'

'Would you like some wine while you wait?' asks Nella, for Marin refuses to emerge from the shadows.

He turns to her. 'You told my wife at the Old Church that your husband had been selling our sugar in Venice.'

Nella can feel Marin's scrutiny on the back of her neck. 'Yes, Seigneur. He's back now—'

'I know he is, Madame. A man like that will find his every move observed. Brandt is well-returned from the Venetian papists. Christmas is gone and the New Year is almost upon us. So, I ask myself – where is my profit?'

'I'm sure it's coming—'

'He didn't write to me. So last night I went to the warehouse to find out how his Venice voyage had gone, and this time, I took Agnes. How I wish that I had not!' He spins towards Marin, fury bulging his eyes. 'Not a grain has been shifted, Madame. Not a single blasted grain. You are worse than useless – all our fortune, all our future, mouldering in the dark. I touched it – some of it was *paste*.'

Marin is visibly shocked, unable to grasp the situation and

shake it into obedience. Guilt runs through Nella as Marin flails, unarmed against his fury.

'Frans,' Marin stutters, 'that's impossible—'

'That would be reason enough to ruin Johannes Brandt, and God knows, I already had my reasons. But when we walked outside the warehouse, we saw something worse. Something much worse.'

Marin comes forward a little from the shadows. 'He *is* selling it, Frans,' she says, quietly. 'Be assured—'

'Do you know what we saw, Madame, pressed against the walls?'

Cornelia scurries up the kitchen stairs. Nella's heart is climbing out of her body. She wants to grip Cornelia's hands and form a ring around this man, to keep both him and her hammering heart under control. I should have told Marin, she thinks, the air vibrating around her as Meermans' fury builds. Marin already had her suspicions, but if I'd confirmed that the sugar was untouched, that Frans had already been to see it, maybe she could have stopped all this. She's the only one who brings us into any order.

On the staircase, Marin shrinks as Meermans advances, the opposite of a romantic vision or any tender love. As he stares her down, two images of their old story shimmer in Nella's mind, the gift of the salted piglet and Frans' beautiful note, hidden in a book. *Let Frans be kind to her*, she prays.

'We saw him,' Meermans says, his voice low and hypnotic in its intensity. 'We saw his devilry.'

'What are you talking about?' Marin says. 'What devilry?'

'I expect you've always known it,' he says. 'How he spends

his time up against the warehouse walls. And such a thing you cannot unsee.'

'*No*,' Marin says.

'Yes,' says Meermans, drawing himself up and turning to Nella. 'The world will have to know, Madame, how your disgusting husband took his pleasure – with a boy.'

Nella closes her eyes as if to stop Meermans' words entering her. But it's too late. When she opens them again, Meermans looks grotesquely pleased. Oh, you are not the first to bring me this revelation, she thinks, unable to meet his gaze. My husband gave me that, at least.

None of the women seem able to speak and Meermans seems irritated by their muteness. 'Johannes Brandt is a degenerate,' he says as if to prod their terrified stupefaction. 'A worm in the fruit of this city. And I will do my duty as a godly citizen.'

'There must be a mistake,' Marin whispers.

'No mistake. And what's more, the boy claims Johannes attacked him.'

'*What?*' says Nella.

'You're his friend.' Marin's voice is breathless, her hand slipping from the banister. 'Don't seek this punishment when you know where it will end.'

'My friendship with that man died years ago.'

'Then why did you ask him to sell your sugar? Out of all the merchants – why did you pick my brother?'

'It was Agnes who insisted,' he says, pushing his hat roughly onto his head.

'But you agreed, Frans. Why would you agree if there was not some affection there still?'

Meermans holds his hand up to stop her speaking. 'Our sugar is as abandoned as his soul. And when I saw what blasphemy he was committing, it was like Beelzebub himself had burst from the skies.'

'Beelzebub will burst on all of us, Frans, if you carry on like this! You speak of doing your duty to God but I think it's for your guilders. Money, wealth – you never used to be like this.'

It has to be Jack, Nella thinks, up against the warehouse wall. She almost wants it to be him – some constancy at least, some love perhaps, in the changing shades of this disaster. She wonders if Johannes is still there at the warehouse, unaware that he has been discovered. He needs to know, she thinks. He needs to get away.

'Did you speak to my husband?' she asks.

Meermans turns to her with a sneer. 'Certainly not,' he says. 'Agnes was – it became imperative for us to leave the scene. She is not yet quite recovered.'

'Don't seek this triumph, Frans,' Marin begs. 'You'll ruin us all. We can come to an arrangement—'

'*Arrangement*? Don't you dare talk to me about an arrangement, Madame. Johannes has arranged enough in my life.'

'Frans, we'll sell your sugar, and let that be an end—'

'No, Marin,' he says, wrenching open the door. 'I am a different man now, and I will not stem the tide.'

Escape

As Frans Meermans storms out into the freezing day, Marin's legs give way. It is disturbing to watch, like the collapse of a particularly beautiful tree. Cornelia rushes to her, trying to prop her up. 'I can't believe it,' Marin says, staring at Nella. 'Can it be true? Can he really have been such a fool?'

'To bed, Madame,' Cornelia says, trying to lift Marin up in a desperate effort. She bows under Marin's weight and her mistress shakes her off, sitting down on the hall stairs.

'Frans will go to the burgomasters,' Marin says. The words bruise the tender atmosphere Meermans has left behind. It is chilling how she looks – dead-eyed, limp, her voice bereft of any spirit. 'He didn't come here first to offer us clemency. He just came to crow.'

'Then we must take advantage of his self-importance,' Nella says. 'Johannes doesn't know that he was seen. He only has a few hours in which to escape.'

'The Seigneur too?' Cornelia says. 'But we cannot live here just the three of us.'

'Can you think of something better?' Nella asks.

The hallway falls very quiet. Irritated with her own bad mood, Nella worries Dhana's silky ears through her fingers, thinking about Agnes' blackened loaf upstairs, wondering where Johannes is. The sugar has made Meermans angry, angrier perhaps than seeing Johannes enjoying forbidden fruit. Several thousand guilders might neutralize this rage against the Brandts.

'I don't know how, but we have to sell the sugar,' she says. 'Meermans is looking for payment.'

Marin looks up at her. 'He said some of it was paste.'

'Exactly. *Some* of it. He's probably exaggerating. He likes to lie. And he might stay silent if we sell his stock.'

'Nothing will keep that man silent. Believe me. And what are you proposing? Do you know all the buyers in Europe and beyond, Petronella – the London cooks, the Milanese pastry-men, the duchesses and marquises and sultans? Do you speak five languages?'

'I am searching for the light, Marin. In the middle of all this murk.'

❧

An hour later, Nella stands before her cabinet house, staring at the rooms for some clue, some sign, of what to do. The golden pendulum clock is an awful, regular reminder that her husband has still not come home, that the minutes are ticking by. How odd it is, she thinks, that some hours feel like days, and others fly too fast. It is freezing cold outside the window, and she feels the numbing sensation in her toes, imagining her flesh made inert like that man found hacked beneath the ice. At least her breath is misting. I'm still alive, she thinks.

Moonlight creeps in through a gap in the curtain, extraordinary in its strength, showing up every swirling pattern of the pewter, turning it to quicksilver shooting through the wood. All nine rooms are illuminated, and the faces of the people inside them almost glow. Nella's betrothal cup is a pale thimble, the cradle lace a shining web. Agnes' severed hand still rests on a chair like a silver charm, the sugar loaf bone-white except for the tip. Nella tries to see if the tip has darkened any further. She cannot tell. Black spores still grimly visible, it rests in her palm like something diseased.

I am not even fortune's bricklayer, let alone its architect, she thinks. The miniaturist's elliptical mottoes and her beautiful pieces are still locked in their own world, so tactile yet so unreachable. Tonight, they seem to taunt her. The less Nella understands the miniaturist's reasons for doing all this, the more powerful the miniaturist seems. Nella prays that Lucas Windelbreke has received her letter, that some clarity will come for her to find the key.

Taking her husband's doll from the cabinet, Nella weighs him in her palm. Did the miniaturist see this coming too – Johannes discovered on the dock by his enemy? His back is still bent to the side, burdened by his bag of money. It doesn't seem to have lightened, and Nella tries to take encouragement from this, but cannot fully trust herself to intuit its true meaning.

She hears the front door, followed by the familiar click as Johannes enters his study. Putting his doll back in the cabinet, Nella runs downstairs and walks straight in.

'Johannes, where have you been?' She presses her feet into the soft wool pile of his rug, the old smell of Rezeki infused for ever in the fibres.

'Nella?'

He looks tired, and old – and this makes her feel older too. He doesn't know he's been spotted, she thinks. She can tell he has no idea. Rushing towards him, she takes him by the sleeves. 'You have to leave, Johannes. You have to get away.'

'What—?'

'But you must know this. I believe you've tried your best for me – with your cabinet, and your silversmiths' feast, and your posies and your dresses. Conversations the like of which I've never shared. I want you to know that – before you have to go.'

'Sit down, calm yourself. You look so unwell.'

'Johannes, no.' Nella stops, looking around at the maps, the paperwork, the golden inkstand – anything but the measured stare of his grey eyes. 'Agnes and Frans – they *saw* you, Johannes. At the warehouse. With a young man.'

He leans against his high stool. He looks as if the cogs inside him have broken and he is slowing to a stop.

'The burgomasters will kill you,' Nella presses on in the face of his silence, hearing her reckless words slurring into one another. 'Was it Jack? How could you? Even though he betrayed you with what he did to Rezeki—'

'It is not Jack Philips who has betrayed me,' Johannes says. His voice is harder than she's ever heard it. 'It is this city. It is the years we all spend in an invisible cage.'

'But he—'

'Any person's behaviour would mutate under such constant scrutiny, such bigoted piety – neighbours watching neighbours, twisting ropes to bind us all.'

'But you once said to me that this city wasn't a prison, if you plotted your path correctly.'

He spreads his hands. 'Well, it is a prison. And its bars are made of murderous hypocrisy. I'll leave tonight before it becomes an impossible escape.'

He is abrupt, in pain, it doesn't sound like him. Nella's bones are falling through her body, as if she's going to slide into her husband's rug and never stand again. 'Where will you go?'

'I'm sorry, sweet girl.' This tenderness is almost as unbearable. 'It is best I don't tell you. They'll ask what you know – and they have means of getting their answers.' He rifles around on the desk and hands her a piece of paper. 'I've been working on a list of names who might be interested in the sugar. Give it to Marin. She's well versed in the ledger book, so you won't have any problems there. I will give you the name of an agent I trust at the VOC.'

'More commission to share, Johannes? Any profit will be so diminished.'

'You have been paying attention.' He smiles with difficulty, lifting the lid of his chest to take a wad of guilders, and Nella notices how empty the inside looks. 'But I don't see how you can sell it without an agent.'

'Will you come back to us?'

Johannes sighs. 'This city is like no other city in the world, Nella. It is brilliant but it is bloated, and I've never called it home.'

'Then where is home, Johannes?'

He looks at the maps on his wall. 'I don't know,' he says. 'Where comfort is. And that is hard to find.'

That night, Nella is the only one to see Johannes off, draped in his travelling cloak, hunched against the cold. 'Goodbye,' he says.

'I'll – miss you.'

He nods, and she notices his eyes are wet. 'You won't be alone,' he says, rubbing the emotion away. 'You have Cornelia.'

He pauses, adjusting the strap on his bag, and he looks so vulnerable, an old man forced on an unwanted adventure. 'I have friends in many countries,' he says. 'It will be well.' His breath is like hot smoke in the freezing air, and she watches it disappear. 'I will think of you. Watch Marin. Guard her. She needs it more than you think. And don't let her feed you only herrings.'

The joke lodges inside her like a dart, a magnitude of pain she did not expect. She cannot deal with this camaraderie come too late, the sweetness of this understanding slipping out of time. 'Johannes,' she whispers, 'promise you'll come back.'

But her husband does not reply, for he has moved soundlessly up the canal path, a seasoned disappearer, the bag of money swinging from his side. I will never see him again, she thinks.

The night darkens, the stars unfriendly, the cold a knife upon her neck – but Nella waits, until she can no longer tell the difference between Johannes and the darkness that carries him away.

Horseshoe

A clanking sound outside wakes her. Nella has slept all night in Johannes's study, and her husband's rug has left an imprint on her face. At first, she thinks the noise is coming from the maids along the Herengracht, dipping their mops in buckets, washing the step, sloshing away the debris of the last day of 1686. For one moment, she forgets it all, staring at Johannes' beautiful maps. Then Meermans' anger and Johannes' escape rush into her mind, overcrowding any path to calm thought. She looks up at the ceiling, where the candle-spots are as black as the stains on Agnes' miniature loaf.

She is being called – it is Cornelia, high-pitched, hysterical – *Madame Nella! Madame Nella!* Nella rubs her eyes. The clanking has stopped. Dazed, she stands up on the trunk of guilders and looks through the window. Red ribbons over barrel chests, the flash of burnished metal, swords and pistols. The St George Militia. Then the hammering on the front door starts up. Cornelia bursts in. 'It's them,' she hisses, terrified. 'They've come.'

Nella closes her eyes and gives quick thanks that by now Johannes is on a ship, far from here. Marin is in the hallway as the hammering continues, and the three women have a rushed conference, Dhana bucking on her paws between them.

'Did he go?' Marin asks. When Nella nods, she can see the

fleeting pain in Marin's face, quickly masked. 'I cannot trust myself in front of them,' Marin says, moving up the staircase as Nella tries to control the dog.

'Marin, no—'

'I will only lose my temper, especially if Frans Meermans is among them.'

'What? You can't leave me with them—'

'I trust you, Petronella.'

Marin disappears. Cornelia opens the front door and on the top step are six guards of the St George Militia, dressed in the costume of wealthy warriors. They present their silver and pewter breastplates, their donderbusses swinging at their hips. Nella says nothing, her hands clasped, her bowels beginning to churn. She notices with relief that Frans Meermans is not among their number.

'We've come for Johannes Brandt,' states the guard nearest to the door. He has a Hague accent – his syllables staccato, not so Amsterdammish.

'He is not here, Seigneur,' Nella replies, feeling her jaw slacken. I will not ask him why he's come, she thinks. No rope, no inch, no chance to humiliate us further.

The civil guard looks her in the eye. He is tall, about Johannes' age, bald except for a beard more ornate than the others, streaked grey and worked into old-fashioned points. 'So where is he?' he asks.

'Travelling,' replies Nella, the lie as quick as breath, though her tongue feels fat and sodden and she finds it hard to sound convincing. She tries to emulate Marin's imperiousness, but she feels their collective confidence as they look down on her, their shared medals glinting, their pressed red ribbons, grim streamers of fraternity. Chests swell towards her, full-bellied, sated with the finest food.

'We know he's here,' says another man. 'You don't want to make a fuss on your doorstep.'

'Good day to you,' she says, beginning to close the door. The militiaman puts his foot out and stops her. To the sound of snickering from the other five, he pushes against the wood, and for a moment the young woman and the soldier are locked in a small war of force. He wins, easily, and the six men troop in, their heavy feet ringing on the marble tiles. They remove their helmets, looking round at the tapestries and paintings, the finely polished staircase, the wall-sconces and gleaming windows. They look less like military men than lawyers drawing up a corpse's inventory.

'Girl,' the first guard barks, spying Cornelia. 'Go and fetch your master.' When Cornelia doesn't move, he puts his hand on the hilt of his sword. 'Get him,' he says, 'or we'll take you too.'

'Let's drop her off at the Spinhuis for a dose of discipline,' says another with a laugh.

Nella wonders if these six men have ever seen a real day of battle. They seem to like their uniforms too much. *Run, Johannes*, she thinks, trying to tamp down her rising panic. *Run, run, far away.*

'I've said it once already, he isn't here,' she says. 'Now, Seigneurs, good day.'

'Do you know why we want him?' the first guard asks, approaching Nella. The other five fan out, making a loose horseshoe around her and Cornelia. 'We're here under the jurisdiction of Schout Slabbaert and the Head Burgomaster at the Stadhuis, Madame Brandt. The prison guards at the Stadhuis are looking forward to his visit.'

'Close the door,' says Nella, and Cornelia scuttles to obey, the light dimming as the maid shuts away the life outside. 'You may speak to my husband when you find him.'

'Why, have you lost him?' asks one of the other guards.

'I bet I know where he is,' replies another to a ripple of more open laughter. Nella wishes they were all dead.

'An Englishman has reported an attack on the Eastern Islands, Madame,' the first guard says. 'The English diplomat is up in arms on behalf of his king – and there's two witnesses to verify it all,' the first guard says.

The Meermanses and Jack must have worked together, Nella thinks – the boy receiving payment, no doubt, for playing another of his parts. Agnes and Frans are such improbable allies with Jack Philips, but what does that matter in the face of collective sweet revenge? Nella imagines pulling off their puppet heads – all three of them dismembered and stripped of their power.

The situation is slipping from her grasp. She looks desperately round the faces, for a drop of kindness, even of discomfort. Any point of weakness will do, and she will pulverize it. There is one guard who looks older than Johannes, but with the same tanned and open face. When their eyes meet, he looks away, and Nella pulls on what she hopes is a hanging shred of shame.

'What's your name, Seigneur?' she asks.

'Aalbers, Madame.'

'What are you doing here, Seigneur Aalbers? You're a better man than this. Go and catch your murderers, go and catch your thieves.' It isn't working, and she can hear herself, desperate and frightened. 'My husband has helped make this republic great, has he not?'

'I will make sure your husband is treated well.'

'You'll go home to your wife. And then you will forget.'

'Your husband's in trouble, Madame Brandt,' says the first guard, tramping round the glory of Johannes' hallway. 'And none of this will save him.'

Fury stings her; a careless rage. 'How dare you?' she shouts, moving towards them, and the rest break apart like a shoal of surprised fish. 'You imperfect men, dressed in borrowed glories!'

'Madame!' Cornelia pleads.

'Get out,' she hisses. 'All of you. You speak to me in my house like brutes—'

'Madame,' the first guard calls across the tiles, 'the far more brutish thing is your husband's sodomy.'

The word hangs in the air. Nella is winded by it, frozen between the hush of men. It is a word that sets dynamite under Amsterdam's buildings, beneath its churches and across its lands, splintering apart its precious life. After *greed* and *flood* it is the worst word in the city's lexicon – it means death and the guards know it. Silenced by their leader's bravado, they cannot look Nella in the eye.

From upstairs comes the almost imperceptible click of a closing door. A sound of running footsteps outside breaks the strange, suspended moment. They all turn and a young boy, no older than nine, Nella supposes, pokes his head around the front door, his face alive with glee, his mouth hanging open as he catches his breath. 'We found him,' he cries.

'Dead?' asks Aalbers.

The boy grins. 'Alive. Sixty miles upland. We've got him.'

Nella feels her stomach pitching, her knees sliding to the cold hard ground. Someone holds her before she falls – it is Aalbers, setting her gently on her feet. She sways as the boy's information forces itself into her, hardly able to breathe. She feels so alone with all these men, who do not care whether her husband receives fair justice.

'Where was he, Christoffel?' asks the first guard.

'He was on a ship, sir, up in the Texel.' Christoffel advances into the hall, his eyes on sticks at the majesty around him. 'The advance party got him. He whimpered like a kitten.' He makes a mewling sound.

'For the love of Christ,' mutters Aalbers.

'No,' Nella whispers. 'You're lying.'

The boy sneers. 'He joked he'd never been to the Stadhuis. Well, he won't be joking now.'

Aalbers slaps the boy round the head. 'Show some respect,' he shouts as the child squeals in pain.

The first guard restrains Aalbers. 'Christoffel just did the republic a great service,' he says.

'So did my husband,' Nella retorts. 'For twenty years.'

He turns to her. 'We need keep you no longer.'

They move towards the door. 'Wait,' Nella says, hardly able to muster up the words. 'What – will you do to him?'

'That's not for me to say, Madame. The Schout will examine the evidence. A hearing followed by a trial. A brief one, I expect, if what we hear is true.'

They make their way down the front steps, Christoffel a triumphant mascot between them, moving up the canal towards the city. Aalbers looks back once, giving Nella a peremptory, embarrassed nod. The militia's walking rhythm is uneven, as if the excitement of their success has overpowered discipline. Before long they are casually strolling, jostling one another, Christoffel's laughter echoing until they disappear from view.

Nella shivers in the blue air of the December day. Up and down the Herengracht, a few shadows in window casements shrink from her regard. There are many eyes watching her, it seems, but no one comes to help.

'They will kill him,' Cornelia says, hunched over on the hall-way stairs.

Nella crouches down, placing her hands on Cornelia's knees. 'Hush, hush. We must follow him to the Stadhuis.'

'You cannot do that.' Marin has emerged, wrapped in her shawl, her silhouette thrown long in the candlelight.

'What?'

'You will only draw attention.'

'Marin, we need to know what they're going to do to him!'

'They will kill him,' Cornelia repeats, beginning to shake. 'They will drown him.'

'Cornelia, for God's sake.'

Marin closes her eyes, rubbing her temples, Nella feels rage at her inertia, her reluctance to grab the scruff of the situation and shake it down into submission. 'Where is your heart, Marin? I would never abandon my brother to his fate.'

273

'But that's exactly what you did, Petronella. You left him in Assendelft and made your own escape.'

'I would not call this an escape.'

'What do you know of the burgomasters?' says Marin. 'You, who have eked your life out in fields, drinking cream from your country cows?'

'That isn't fair. What's wrong with you?'

Marin starts moving down towards Nella at the bottom of the staircase, step by step with slow and strange precision. 'Do you know what Johannes used to say to me?' she asks. The venom in her voice cuts the winter air and the hairs on Nella's arms rise up. ' "Freedom is a glorious thing. *Free* yourself, Marin. The bars on your cage are of your own making." Well, it's all very well freeing yourself, but there's always someone who has to pay.'

'Your self-pity is what keeps us from doing anything. You had your chance—'

Marin lashes out her arms and pins Nella by the wrists against the wall. 'Get off me!' Nella cries, weakened by the magnificence of Marin's fury. Cornelia staggers back in horror.

'I'm not abandoning my brother,' Marin says. 'He has abandoned me. I have kept our secrets, as he never could, I have paid his debts as much as I've paid mine – and I know you think that now you understand us, but you don't.'

'I do.'

Marin releases her. Nella sags against the panelling. 'No, Petronella,' Marin says. 'The knot's tied too tight for you.'

Hidden Bodies

Nella stands on the step of Johannes' house, the eve of new year passing with no ceremony. She wants to be splintered by the cold, transfigured by the light. The canal path is empty, the ice a ribbon of white silk between the Herengracht houses. The moon above is larger than she has ever seen it, larger even than last night; an astonishing pale circle of power. It looks as if she could reach out and touch it, that God has pushed it down from the heavens for her human hand to hold.

She hopes Johannes can see this moon through the bars of his cell, somewhere in the bowels of the Stadhuis. His attempt at escape has made him look so guilty. Where is Otto now – where is the miniaturist, still hiding from view? If it weren't for Cornelia, Nella thinks, I might run away too. While the house dwindles, occupant by occupant, the cabinet feels fuller, ever more alive.

From the open door behind her a strange smell has begun to emanate, and Nella comes back into the house. It is not coming from the kitchens. From upstairs, she hears a distant gulping, caught gasps of air. She follows the odd scent and sound up the staircase and along the dark corridor, to where a fine line of candlelight runs round Marin's door. No sweet lavender nor sandalwood this time; this is a rotting-vegetable stench that makes Nella gag.

It's some awful incense Marin's burning, she thinks, some misguided perfume block. But the gulping sound is a sob. Nella listens, bending down to look through the keyhole, and discovers it has been blocked.

'Marin?' she whispers.

There is no reply, just the sobbing. Nella pushes on the slightly open door. The rooms stinks – a tang of matted undergrowth, roots and bitter leaves macerated to release their secret properties. Marin is on her bed, holding a glass of green mixture the colour of canal water, as if the very silt off the Herengracht has been ladled in. Her collection of animal skulls has been swept to the floor, some broken into uneven shards of yellow bone. A map on the wall has been ripped in two.

'Marin? What by all the angels—'

At the sound of Nella's voice, Marin looks up, her face tear-streaked, her eyes closing in relief. Her hand goes slack and she lets Nella remove the glass. Nella places her hand on the side of Marin's face, on her neck, her chest, attempting to calm her shaking body, her unending tears. 'What is it?' she asks. 'We will save him, I promise.'

'Not him. I'm not—'

Marin cannot make a sentence. The strange pliancy of Marin's body still beneath her fingers, Nella smells the vile mixture, and it makes her feel ill. She thinks of Marin's sicknesses, her headaches, the new appetite for sugar, for apple tarts and candied nuts. Marin's tiredness, her moodiness; the hive you mustn't kick for fear of being stung. Her bulky clothes, her slower way of moving. Marin's black dresses lined with fur, her secret love note, ripped to nothingness. *I love you. I love you. From back to front, I love you.* 'What have you done?' Marin had cried into the air, lying in her lavender bath.

Marin does not stop Nella's probing hands, and so further Nella goes, slower, over her sister-in-law's full, firm breasts, to the top of her stomach, hidden deep beneath swathes of high-waisted skirts.

When she presses down, Nella utters a cry.

Time stops. There are no words. Just a hand on a womb, and wonder and silence. Marin's concealed stomach is hard and huge, full as the moon. *Marin?* Nella whispers her name, not sure if she's even spoken out loud.

She exhales as the baby turns in its tiny home, and when a small foot kicks she drops to her knees. Still Marin stays silent, head erect, eyes pouched with tiredness, fixed on an invisible horizon before her, the exertion of keeping the secret draining from her face.

This is not a small baby. This is a baby that is nearly ready to arrive.

'I wouldn't have drunk it,' is all Marin says.

❧

The walls of the room seem nothing more than the flats of a stage set, falling, and beyond them another landscape never glimpsed. An unpainted place stretching out in all directions, no signposts or landmarks; just endless space. Marin sits very still.

Nella thinks of the little cradle in the cabinet house and a shiver runs up her body. How did the miniaturist know about this? Marin's gaze is on the candle – beeswax, no burning tallow, just the pleasant smell of honey. The flame dances like a sprite, a little god of light mocking their paralysis of thought. How to start, what to say?

'You tell no one,' Marin whispers finally.

'Marin, there must be no more secrets within this house. Cornelia will have to know.'

Marin sighs. 'If she doesn't already. I've been soaking my rags in pig's blood so she wouldn't be suspicious.' Her eyes flick toward Nella. 'And you know full well this house's key-holes.'

'So that's what you were doing in the cellar. I thought you were cleaning them.'

'You saw what you wanted to see.'

Nella closes her eyes, conjuring Marin in the cellar with her reddened hands aloft. Such lengths she has gone to in the name of her secret; preparing her ghostly menstruation, keeping up the appearance that her body is just the same. Marin's profound convex is mesmerizing. She has duplicated herself – two hearts, two heads, four arms, four legs – like a monster to be recorded in a ship's log, annotated on one of Johannes' stolen maps. She's hidden it so well.

How many times has it happened, the snatched chances out of sight of Agnes, Johannes, the whole city? It is shocking, and the fact that it's Marin's deed even more so. Fornication, skin on skin, throwing the Bible out the window. But this is love, Nella thinks. This is what it makes you do.

Marin lowers her head into her hands. 'Frans,' she says, his name enough to convey all that she has hidden, the truth that could ruin her life.

'He was just angry about the sugar, Marin. He loves you.' Marin looks up, an expression of surprise blooming on her exhausted face. 'Tell him about the child. Once he knows, he won't hurt Johannes because such action will endanger you.'

'No, Petronella,' Marin says. 'This isn't one of Cornelia's stories.'

They sit in silence for a moment. Nella remembers Meermans' ugly aggression, his look of triumph when he broke the news of what he and Agnes had seen.

'People needn't know about this, Marin. We're good at hiding things.'

Marin rubs her eyes. 'I'm not so sure.' She takes a deep breath. 'If he survives, this child will be stained.'

'Stained?'

'By his mother's sin, his father's sin—'

'It's a baby, Marin, not a devil. We can go away,' Nella says more gently. 'Take you to the countryside.'

'There's nothing to do in the countryside.'

Nella bites her tongue and absorbs the barb. 'Well, exactly. No prying eyes.'

'Do you know what the word pregnant is in French, Nella? *Enceinte.*'

Nella is irritated – Marin is so like her brother, diverting the path of conversation with her foreign tongues, blanketing you with worldly overtones.

'Do you know what else it means?' Marin persists, and now Nella hears the faint note of panic in her voice. 'A surround. A wall. A *trap.*'

Nella kneels down in front of her. 'How far are you gone?' she says, wanting to be practical.

Marin exhales, resting her arms on the top of her belly. 'Seven months or so.'

'*Seven months?* I would never have known. My mother's been pregnant four times since I can remember, but I couldn't tell with you.'

'You weren't looking, Nella. I let my skirts out and bound my breasts.'

Nella cannot help smiling – even in this extraordinary situation, the act of tamping herself down, of sliding her truth away from all their gazes, makes Marin proud. 'But these days I'm finding it hard to walk. It's like bending over a globe.'

'You'll show soon. However many skirts and shawls you wear.'

'I'm tall at least. I shall just look like a glutton, the embodiment of my sin.'

Nella glances at the glass. This preparation could easily have killed her. *Preparation* – named as if it is the beginning of something, when really it is the end. A girl in Assendelft died from drinking a preparation of hellebore and pennyroyal. Her brother's friends had forced themselves upon her and one of them had 'hooked in his child' as the saying went. Her father made the mixture, and something went wrong, for they buried her the next morning.

Most countryside people can tell a poisonous mushroom, a fatal shrub. Seven months is far too late; after so much careful concealment, Marin would have perished too. Does Marin know this or not? Both possibilities disturb.

'Where did you get the poison from?'

'A book,' says Marin. 'The ingredients came from three separate apothecaries. Johannes thinks I stole all my seeds and leaves from him, but in fact half of them come from quacks in Amsterdam.'

'But why tonight? Had you never wondered before now what you were going to do?' Marin looks away, refusing to answer. 'Marin, these preparations are very dangerous if you don't drink them early enough,' Nella persists, but Marin stays silent.

'Marin, did you want this child to live?'

Marin touches her stomach, and still she doesn't speak, staring into an infinity Nella cannot see. Nella's eye moves to the stack of books. One title now stands out, *Children's Diseases* by Stephanus Blankaart, and she cannot believe she didn't consider its presence the last time she was here.

Marin focuses on the book too, and she looks frightened and strangely young. Nella takes her hand, a little pulse passing from palm to palm. 'I remember you reaching for my fingers the first day I arrived.'

'No. That isn't true.'

'Marin, I recall it quite clearly.'

'You gave me your hand as if it were a gift. You were so . . . confident.'

'I was *not*. And you proffered yours as if you were pointing me back outside. You said I had strong bones for seventeen.'

'What a ridiculous thing to say.' Marin sounds mystified.

'Especially as I was eighteen.'

It is Marin's skin that has softened; the exchange is now complete. Her body leans against Nella's, lulled into a truce. Nella cannot quite believe what the evening has brought, in this tiny room of maps. It is too large a fact to incorporate – her mind hums around the edges of it, making its way in.

She wants to ask so many questions, but doesn't know how to start.

The two of them rest in this unprecedented state, and she has a thought. This child could be proof that Johannes is the husband he's supposed to be – the creator of a good Dutch family. But looking over at Marin's pale face, Nella stops her tongue. *Give me your child, Marin, and protect your brother's fate.* They are not easy words to offer, and probably harder to receive. Marin has been making sacrifices all her life, and such a suggestion must be gently made. 'We'll have to find a mid-wife,' she says gently.

'You'll have to go to the warehouse and check the sugar,' comes Marin's reply. Her body starts to stiffen.

'But, Marin! What are we going to do with you?'

Nella marvels at Marin's ability to divide herself like this, slipping the fact of her baby like a jewel into her pocket. Marin rises unsteadily off the bed and picks her way across the scattered skulls. Without her overskirts on, Nella can see her full curve, the rising swell of her breasts. Behind the walls of Marin's anchored body a baby tumbles, possessed and possessor, its unmet mother a god to it. The child is coming – and despite Nella's hope for openness, she knows this will be the greatest secret they will ever have to keep.

The mention of the sugar unfurls a memory in her mind. 'Johannes gave me a list of names for selling the sugar,' she says, reluctantly, having no wish to let Marin divert the conversation from the question of her unborn child.

'Well, good.'

But before Nella can continue, they hear the patter of

receding footsteps along the corridor. '*Cornelia*,' Marin says. 'All her life, listening at doors!'

'I'll talk to her.'

Marin sighs. 'I suppose you must, before she fabulates another story.'

'She won't need to,' Nella says, heading for the door. 'Nothing here is more fabulous than the truth.'

No Anchor

In Nella's room, Cornelia is at first silent and stubborn, but she breaks, collapsing to the bed as if her bones are ash. 'I knew it,' she says, but her mystified face betrays her fighting talk. Nella rushes to the maid, giving her a tight embrace. Poor Cornelia, she thinks. You've been hoodwinked. But the monumental sleight of hand has been played upon all their watch. This is the greatest trick Marin has ever pulled – except it's real.

'I knew something was wrong,' says Cornelia. 'But I didn't want to believe. A *baby*?'

'She put animal blood on her rags to fool us.'

'Clever idea,' Cornelia replies, her frown changing to a grudging admiration.

'Certainly cleverer than being unmarried and getting with child.'

'Madame!' Cornelia looks outraged, and Nella realizes that she is not going to tell this orphan about Marin's mixture. Although, she thinks with a surge of fondness, I'll bet this Queen of Keyholes heard it all.

A child is on its way. Marin's secret has been released, and now Nella sees it in the curtains' swell, in the roundness of her bedroom pillows. She stares past Cornelia, to the middle of her bed. Marin has the one thing I will never have. Unbidden, the image of Meermans and Marin together enters Nella's mind. Their two bodies, the swell of him pressing between her legs, the rod of pain – him rolling down Marin's stockings, opening her, crying out in the heat of it. That is unfair, she thinks. It was probably more than that – for here is a man who believed that Marin's touch lingered for a thousand hours, that she was the sunlight which he stood in, warmed. With such poetry, how could it ever have been so underwhelming?

'What will we do with the child?' Cornelia asks.

'I suppose Marin might take it to a private orphanage.'

Cornelia jumps to her feet. 'No! We must keep it, Madame.'

'Cornelia, it isn't your choice to make,' Nella says. 'Nor mine neither,' she adds, thinking of Johannes in his cell.

The maid folds her arms. 'I would look after that baby like a lion.'

'That may be, Cornelia. But don't dream of things you can't have.'

This is too harsh, and Nella knows it, her exhaustion boiling over. It sounds like something Marin might say. Cornelia moves away from her towards the cabinet. The moon has now gone behind a cloud, and the candlelight pitches unevenly across the tortoiseshell.

Cornelia draws back the yellow velvet curtains and peers in. Nella, too ashamed by her outburst, does nothing to stop her. The maid lifts out the cradle, rocking it back and forth on her hand. 'So beautiful,' she breathes.

I should have noticed, Nella thinks – that of all the items Marin wanted to hold, the cradle was her first choice. How much else have I failed to observe? Too much, and still I keep on failing.

Cornelia has already pulled out Marin's doll. 'It's *her*,' she says, staring in disbelief at her mistress. 'As if I'm holding her in my palm!'

Marin in miniature stares up at both women, her mouth set firm, her grey eyes unwavering. Cornelia runs her hand down the seam of her mistress's skirt, the soft black wool a voluminous pleasure to touch. She holds her up in the candle-light. 'Be safe, Madame,' she whispers, clutching the doll in both hands. As Cornelia's lips meet the miniature stomach to give it a kiss, she pulls away with a jerk.

'What's wrong? Cornelia, what is it?'

'I can feel something.'

Nella snatches the doll back, lifting the skirts and then the underskirt, peeling away each layer until she reaches Marin's body of stuffed linen. When her fingers touch Cornelia's discovery, her excitement sickens. The miniaturist has beaten them again.

Unmistakeable, Marin's diminutive body holds the curve of an unborn child. A nub, a walnut, a nothing-yet, but soon-to-be. The doll appears weighed down like the woman along the corridor, full-bellied with time.

Cornelia is horrified. 'You ordered a doll of Madame Marin, carrying a *child*?' As the maid's cornflower-blue eyes shine at her with accusation, Nella's own body feels unwieldy. 'How could you betray us like this?'

'No, no,' Nella pleads. The slipping has begun, the loose brick, the hole in the dam.

'You know how rumour spreads—'

'I – I – didn't order it, Cornelia.'

'Then who did?' Cornelia looks aghast.

'I was sent it – I asked for nothing but a lute, and—'

'Then who is spying on us?' The maid spins round the room, brandishing the doll like a shield.

'The miniaturist isn't a spy, Cornelia. She's more than that—'

'*She?* I thought all those notes were going to a craftsman?'

'She's a prophetess – look at Marin's stomach! She sees our lives – she's trying to help, to warn us—'

Cornelia pulls out doll after doll, pressing their bodies for more clues, dropping them one by one to the floor. 'Warn us? Who is this woman, this *somebody*? What is this miniaturist?' She grips her own doll in her fist, staring at it in horror. 'Sweet Jesu, I've lived carefully, Madame, I've been obedient. But ever since this cabinet arrived, so many doors have opened that I've always managed to keep shut.'

'But is that such a bad thing?'

Cornelia looks at her as if she's mad. 'The Seigneur is in prison, Otto's gone and Madame Marin carries a secret shame with the man who is this household's enemy! Our world has fallen apart – and this – *miniaturist* – has been watching all this time? How has she warned us, how has she helped?'

'I'm sorry, Cornelia, I'm so sorry. Please don't tell Marin. The miniaturist has the answers.'

'She's nothing but a snooper,' Cornelia fumes. 'No one pulls my strings but God above.'

'But if we didn't know about Marin, then how did she, Cornelia?'

'We would have found out. We *did* find out. We didn't need her to tell us.'

'And look at this.' Nella shows her Agnes' blackened sugar loaf. 'It was white when it first arrived.'

'It's soot from the fire.'

'It *doesn't rub off*. And Rezeki had a mark on her head, just where Jack killed her.'

Cornelia backs away from the cabinet. 'Who is this witch?' she hisses.

'She isn't a witch, Cornelia. She's a woman from Norway.'

'A Norwegian witch turned Amsterdam spy! How dare she send you these evil things—'

'They're not evil.'

Cornelia's bile burns through Nella's heart. She feels as if she is being dissected as much as her secret miniaturist, her one possession cut apart and its innards doled out.

'I had nothing in this city, Cornelia. *Nothing*. And she took an interest. I don't understand why she's picked me, I don't always understand the messages she sends, but I'm trying—'

'What else does she know? What is she going to *do*?'

'I don't know. Please believe me – I asked her to stop, but she didn't. It was like she understood my unhappiness, and carried on.'

Cornelia frowns. 'But I tried to make it happy for you. I was here—'

'I know you were. And all I've discovered is that she was apprenticed to a clockmaker in Bruges. I've written to him, but he is as silent as her.' Nella can hear her voice pressing down into a sob, the hot tears threatening to break into her eyes. 'But what was it that Pellicorne preached? There's nothing hidden that will not be revealed.'

'No woman can be an apprentice,' Cornelia snaps. 'No

man is keen to train a woman. No guild except the seam-stresses or stinking peat-carriers would have her. And what would be the point? Men are the makers of this world.'

'She made minutes and seconds, Cornelia. She created time.'

'If I wasn't boiling your sturgeons, spicing your pies and cleaning your windows, *I* could have made time. I could have made evil puppets and spied on people—'

'You *do* spy on people. In that way, you're just like her.'

Hot and breathless, Cornelia purses her lips and shoves the doll of herself back in the cabinet. 'I am *nothing* like her.'

Nella gathers up the motley cast of characters. 'I shouldn't lose my temper, Cornelia,' she says in a small voice.

There is a pause. 'Nor I, Madame. But my world has shifted too fast these last days. It's broken up.'

'I know, Cornelia. I know.'

Nella draws the curtains across the cabinet as a means to bring some momentary peace. In silent response, Cornelia draws the main curtains of the window, and the two girls stand in the muffled half-light.

'I must see to Madame Marin,' Cornelia says, turning her back resolutely on the cabinet.

Left alone, Nella imagines the miniaturist as a younger woman. Maybe Cornelia had a point – maybe no one would buy the miniaturist's clocks, preferring those constructed by a man? She could never improve her skills, so she stopped trying to harness man's artificial rhythms, and turned inwards. At what point did she choose these more intimate, irregular jumps of an interior life and why did she pick me? Nella rests her head on the side of the cabinet, the cooling wood touching her skin like a balm. In showing me my own story, she thinks, the miniaturist has become the author of it herself. How I wish I could have it back.

FOUR

January, 1687

Behold, ye are this day as the stars in the heaven
for multitude . . .
How can I myself alone bear your cumbrance, and
your burden, and your strife?

Deuteronomy 1:10–12

Spores

The first day of the year is a time for Amsterdammers to throw open their windows in a brave ritual of letting in the cold air, dislodging cobwebs and bad memories. Nella is dressed as a servant and Cornelia helps her mistress pull on her boots, draping Johannes' warehouse key around her neck like a medal.

It is not yet Epiphany, the day of difference, but they have no time to waste. The maid looks as if she is expecting Lucifer himself and his goblins to come marching out, but has promised not to tell Marin about the secret hidden under the skirts of her doll, nor the blackened tip of Agnes' loaf. 'She needs peace,' Nella said. 'Think of the child.'

Nella draws the maid's coarse coat to her neck. She tries to stand firm, but feels herself plummeting, further than she thinks possible, deep into the bog and marsh of the city, back to the times of mud and sea.

'You shouldn't go to the Eastern Islands alone,' Cornelia says.

'We have no choice. You need to stay here with Marin. I won't be long.'

'Take Dhana with you. She can be your guard.'

Nella walks out of the house and up the Herengracht, with Dhana trotting by her side, the key lying heavy on her chest.

She wanted to see Johannes in the Stadhuis first – but in Amsterdam the guilder reigns and she must be sensible. She wonders what she's going to find on the Eastern Islands. 'Who else will do this, Marin?' she had pleaded earlier this morning. 'Johannes is in a cell. If Agnes and Frans decide to have no mercy, we might be able to bribe Jack to change his story at least.'

Marin had nodded her consent, hands on her stomach. Now her pregnancy has been acknowledged, her body seems to have grown larger. *I'm a giant loaf*, Nella's mother had once said, when she was carrying Arabella. Now it seems that Marin is also waiting to prove herself, to see if her flesh is adequate. Marin and her too-tight knot; whatever did she mean?

'I will visit Johannes afterwards, if they let me in,' Nella had added. 'Is there any message you would like me to send?'

Marin's face appeared to seize up in grief. Dropping her hands to her sides, she moved away, staring towards the salon. 'There is nothing I can say.'

'Marin—'

'Hope is dangerous, Petronella.'

'It is better than nothing.'

The cold is bitter, sharp little knives on Nella's face. Let it soon be spring, she thinks, and then wonders whether it is wise to wish this time away for Marin, for Johannes. By the time spring comes, their own republic could have crashed around their feet. Trying to shake away the gloom, she walks quickly, ten minutes or so east of the city. The miniaturist's departure from the Kalverstraat tugs on her. Nella hasn't given up hope – she still yearns on the streets for a flash of blonde hair, for a knock at the door and another delivery. But there has been only silence for so many days now. Although she had told Cornelia that the miniaturist was showing her the way, Nella feels alone, fumbling in the dark. She needs more mottoes, more miniatures, to understand what is to come and what has passed before. *Come back,* she thinks as she crosses one of several bridges towards the Eastern Islands. *I cannot do this without you.*

There is water everywhere she looks, lagoons still as glass, patched with murk like a foxed mirror when the weak sun moves behind cloud. Johannes' favourite potatoes with their fluffiest flesh are served in a tavern near here. It is unsurprising that this is his preferred area; nearer the sea, fewer people. Plenty of places to hide.

The warehouses start to loom, brick buildings towering to the sky, far wider than the houses nestling together inside the ring of the city. The Islands feel empty this morning. Most people are probably still in bed, she supposes, sleeping off the excesses of bringing in New Year. Her father was never seen until the evening after sending off the old year, then he woke to say that nothing much had changed. Not so here, Nella thinks. Nothing is the same any more. She can hear her own footsteps, the light pant of Dhana's breath as she hurries along.

Despite their peace, there is something concentrated about these separate pieces of land, for all things here have one purpose – the raw end of commerce, the storing of supplies, the repair of ships, the sustenance of sailors and captains alike. Following Marin's directions, she finally reaches Johannes' warehouse, six storeys high, a small black door at the front.

The lock is well oiled and the door opens easily. She re-adjusts Cornelia's too-large skirt and apron. They had tried to decide what would be worse – a maid caught in her master's storehouse, or his wife? Better a maid, they thought. Johannes Brandt's reputation could do without the added news that Madame Petronella was snooping on the Islands. She imagines Frans and Agnes coming here, creeping round the back of the building.

'Sit here, girl,' she orders Dhana, trying to focus on the task in hand. She pats the whippet on the head. 'And bark if anyone comes near.' We should hire a guard dog permanently, she thinks. Now Jack has disappeared.

The interior takes Nella's breath away. She feels so small, standing at the bottom of a long, spindly ladder that reaches past five busy floors of Johannes' stock. He is the man who has it all, but who has so often felt bereft of everything.

Nella begins to scale the ladder, seeking out the sugar. It feels as if she is climbing through her husband's life. Up and up she goes into the cavernous chamber, her skirts catching on the rungs, threatening her with a fall. Past bolts of Coromandel and Bengal silk, cloves, mace and nutmeg in crates marked *Molucca*, pepper labelled from Malabar, peels of Ceylonese cinnamon, tea-leaves in crates painted *via Batavia*, planks of expensive-looking wood, copper pipes, strips of tin, piles of Haarlem wool. Past Delft plates, casks of wine branded *España* and *Jerez*, boxes of vermilion and cochineal, mercury *for mirrors and the syphilis*, Persian trinkets cast in gold and silver. Gripping the rungs, she understands Marin's fascination with her brother's work. Here is real life, she thinks, out of breath and giddy. Here is where true adventures come to land.

Nella has to climb right to the eaves to find the sugar loaves. Johannes has stored them in the middle of the floorboards, covered in linen, away from the damp. This attention touches her; it almost makes her cry. Meermans would have her think he'd just thrown Agnes' loaves on the ground floor with the spare sails and untarred ropes. But it isn't true. Johannes has taken care. There are so many loaves, they touch the beams of the roof.

Scrambling off the ladder, Nella approaches the linen cape and lifts a corner gingerly. The sugar loaves are laid on top of each other like cannon. It looks like one loaf is missing, no doubt the one Agnes brought to dinner – a dubious sweetener if ever there was. If this came tumbling down, Nella thinks, I'd be crushed.

There are well over a thousand cones here. Nella kneels by the loaves which seem to have been more recently refined. They are still neat and shining bright, are indeed marked with the three crosses of the city of Amsterdam. Some of the other half, refined in Surinam, is damp to the touch, and Nella's fingers come away slightly covered in white paste. At the back of the sugar structure, tiny black spores have indeed spread over a quarter of the Surinam side. Nothing can save the precious crystals that already have the blight. But still, she thinks – Meermans has exaggerated, seen what he wanted to see. Maybe we could dry them out – part of each loaf would surely be salvageable.

Exhilarated, she tastes what has come away on her fingers. Imagine if I died from a lick of bad sugar, from the craving craze of *lekkerheid*, she thinks. Wouldn't Pastor Pellicorne love that.

She pulls out Johannes' list from her pocket, full of abundant, ornamental names. It contains the households of earls and cardinals, an infanta, a baron, people with a desire to sweeten their leisure times in London, Milano, Roma, Hamburg, even the outposts of the VOC. It is astonishing how Johannes has managed to trade with the Spanish individuals, the English, given how his country has warred with theirs. It reminds Nella of something he said to Meermans at the silversmiths'. *We are seen abroad as untrustworthy. I have no desire to be such a thing.*

There is so much more sugar than she anticipated. The reality of Johannes and Marin's current helplessness weighs on Nella's shoulders. When she suggested to Johannes that employing an agent to sail abroad for them would take up too much of their precious commission, he hadn't denied it. But they need someone nearer to hand, someone who understands, someone keen to get their hands on the sugar. Nella stands, hands on her hips, thinking hard, staring into Frans and Agnes' livelihood. And then it comes to her – a comment the first month she was in Amsterdam, sitting wide-eyed with an unwrapped cake resting in her lap. The speaker was a person Nella had immediately liked, a woman with grace and expertise. *Honeycomb this morning and marzipan in the afternoon.*

Nella crumples her husband's list. Yes, she cries silently to the brickwork and beams, the caulked timber roof of her husband's domain. I know what we must do.

Stadhuis

Nella follows a guard through the first underground passageway of the Stadhuis prison and then down a long flank of the building. She can hear the inmates' rough coughs and complaints. The place is bigger than she thought. It seems to expand inexplicably as she walks it, escaping her sense of proportion. Cell after cell, brick after brick, she cannot seem to comprehend it.

Nella starts to hear shrieks and moans, clanging bars and whimpering. She holds her head high in case they can smell her growing fear, trying to block out the cacophony of male squeals.

She and the guard walk along the side of an open courtyard, and in the middle of it Nella can see contraptions made of planks fastened with adjustable bolts. Another machine has a row of sharp spikes. The prisoners are quite literally here to be reformed. Nella averts her eyes, determined not to be cowed, touching the warehouse key hidden on her breast, her fresh idea still glowing in her mind. *Don't let sweet weapons stray.*

'Here he is,' says the guard, opening the door to Johannes' cell. He lingers for longer than is necessary, then locks the door behind her.

'Don't come back too soon,' Nella says, handing him a

guilder through the bars. The things this city has taught me, she thinks. The guard pockets the guilder and quickly his footsteps fade to silence. From outside, Nella can hear gulls wheeling far up in the sky, the distant clatter of carts on cobbles.

In the shadows, Johannes is leaning against a small table. There is no stool or chair, so she stands against the door. There's a dank atmosphere, moss covering the walls, a map of green islands devoid of latitudes. Johannes looks pensive, but his energy is powerful. Even here, stripped of his rights, he still has the capacity to impress. 'Bribing officials?' he asks.

'We should keep them as friends.' Her voice is deadened by the mineral thickness of the walls.

'You sound like Marin,' he says with a smile.

Both his eyes have been punched, and the skin around them is the colour of a dying tulip. His hair is wild like bleached seaweed, and his clothes look filthy. His arms tremble as he supports himself against the table. 'They won't let me have a Bible,' he says. 'Or anything to read, for that matter.'

From the pocket not containing the scrunched-up sugar list, Nella pulls out three slices of smoked ham wrapped in paper, half a bread roll covered in fluff and two small *olie-koecken*. She walks across the cell, her palms open and Johannes takes the offering, visibly touched. 'You'd have got in trouble if they'd found it.'

'Yes,' she says, stepping away again, sweeping the corner of the cell with her foot.

'I nearly got away.'

Nella looks towards the corner of the cell, where a family of newborn mice rustle the straw, crawling over one another in blind familiarity. She sits down heavily on the pallet, and a deep sadness diffuses inside her, fogging her will to fight. 'What have they said to you?'

Johannes points to his black eyes. 'They are men of few words.'

'When I first met you,' she says, desperate to crush her sadness, 'you did not bother with the Bible, with God, with guilt and sin and shame.'

'How do you know that I did not?'

'You did not attend church, you itched at Marin's home-prayers. And you bought such things. You ate richly, you enjoyed the delights you could take. You were your own god, the architect of your fortune.'

He smiles, gesturing to the walls around him. 'And look at the building I made.'

'But you've been free, haven't you? Think of the places you've seen.' Nella swallows, scarcely able to keep her speech afloat.

'My sister always said I was an awful combination of carelessness and determination.'

'Is that why you went back to Jack?'

Johannes closes his eyes as if the name floods him.

'He betrayed you, Johannes. Money paid and money taken—'

'I haven't given him a penny since the day he drove his dagger through my dog,' Johannes says. His words seem to drop through him like stones. 'I employed him to guard the sugar, but Marin was so worried about him that I decided to dismiss him. I saw her point, of course. He went back to making deliveries, and that's when it all went wrong. I did see Jack after he killed Rezeki.' His face softens in the dim light. 'I've never seen a body so full of remorse for what he'd done.'

Nella bites her tongue. Jack probably had no choice but to seem sorry, and Johannes in turn to believe that it was true.

'You must hold him in great store – to forgive such a thing,' she says. He is silent. 'Johannes, was it – love?'

He considers her question, and she is struck again by how seriously he always takes her. 'With Jack, it seemed as if . . . something ungraspable . . . quickly became very real. The speed of it, Nella. By telling me lies, Jack made me see truth, the way a painting can better show a thing whilst never being the thing itself. He became nearly indistinguishable to me from love,' Johannes sighs, 'but he was only ever love's painting. Do you see? The conceit of love was better than the mess it left behind.'

Johannes bestows his honesty on her like another unexpected gift. The open channel between them can be so clear and crystalline, but when Nella closes her eyes all she sees is a stagnant stream.

'Are you quite well?' he asks.

'Marin believes love is better in the chase than caught,' she says.

He raises his eyebrows. 'That does not surprise me. It is not better. But it is easier. One's imagination is always more generous. And yet, the chase always tires you out in the end.'

What are we all chasing? Nella wonders. To live, of course. To be unbound from the invisible ropes that Johannes spoke of in his study. Or to be happy in them, at least. 'Where were you going when they caught you at Texel?'

'London. I was hoping I'd find Otto. Marin was so convinced he was there. How is my sister?'

'You're powerful, Johannes.' Nella feels compelled to rush past his question, knowing that otherwise her face will let the truth about Marin slip. 'I saw you at the silversmiths' feast. You said it yourself – the burgomasters cannot touch you.'

He lowers himself onto the pallet beside her. 'It's the *crimen nefandum*, Nella. Two men together. In the face of that accusation no one has power, only God. To do nothing would be to condone it, and the burgomasters must be seen to act.'

'Then we must make Meermans change his mind!'

Johannes runs a shaking hand over the crown of his head, as if to find some answer there. 'It was years ago now,' he says, 'but I did something to make Frans very unhappy. And then I committed the greater crime of being successful. It echoes on and now comes back to haunt me.'

Nella imagines the younger Johannes turning Frans away from the house, his sister watching hidden at a window, the ugly humiliation which has now enwrapped them all.

'I had thought that accepting their commission of the sugar might perhaps bring about an *entente*,' Johannes says. 'But Frans has . . . curdled. He has waited a long time to take his revenge on the Brandts. I am everything he hates, and wants to be. And Agnes – well. Agnes will always follow the path of his poison crumbs.'

'I believe Agnes admires you.'

'Well, that will only make it worse.' Johannes' eyes glitter like two grey beads in the bad light. 'I'm so glad you've come. I don't deserve it,' he says, taking her hand.

Nella supposes it is something to be appreciated at least, if she cannot be loved. Finding substitutes for the real thing – when will that ever stop? And yet, she would rather stay next to him than be anywhere else.

'If I don't confess, there'll be a trial,' Johannes says. 'In a few weeks. Either way, I don't expect to get out of here alive.'

'Don't talk like that.'

'I'll make arrangements. You, Marin, Cornelia. And Otto, if he ever comes back.' Johannes sounds brisk all of a sudden, a notary dividing up someone else's will. 'There'll be a few men of the Amsterdam *schepenbank* at the hearing, although Schout Pieter Slabbaert will oversee it.'

'Why not just the Schout?'

'Because of the severity of the charge. Because it's me. Because the more scandalous the case, the more our goodly citizens become involved.' He pauses. 'But I imagine it will be quickly done.'

'Johannes—'

'Severe charges usually end in death.' His voice begins to catch. 'And the Schout likes to share the blame. The more people take part in a ritual, the more justified it seems.'

'I'll find Jack,' Nella says, 'I'll pay him more to change his story.' She pictures Johannes' emptying chest of guilders, the blackening sugar piled up on the sixth floor of his warehouse. 'And I've thought of a plan—'

'There's a guard,' Johannes says. 'They call him the Bloody Shepherd.' He grips her hand tighter. 'A priest by profession, by nature a monster.'

The last word hangs in the damp air, gigantic, undefeat-able. Nella touches her face. The moisture in the air has made it so cold. How has Johannes survived in here one day?

'I've seen his victims carried past,' Johannes says. 'Their bones popped out of every socket – and you can't put them back. Legs no longer legs, limbs of soggy cotton, guts like addled meat. They'll twist me open to make me say things. I'll say them, Nella, and that will be that.'

Johannes buries his face as deep as he can in her shoulder. Nella feels the plane of his nose pointing into her flesh, and she puts her arms around him. She wants to wash him from tip to toe, to make him fresh again, make him smell of spice, cardamom caught in the nail. 'Johannes,' she whispers. '*Johannes.* You have a wife. You have me. Isn't that proof enough?'

'It would never have been enough.'

Then what about a child? she wants to ask. What about a child? Marin's secret is on the tip of her tongue. More time, she thinks – all I want is more time. Who knows what story we could have told with two months' grace?

'Johannes,' she says, 'I wish I'd been enough.'

Johannes pulls back from her, and clasps the sides of her face. 'You have been a miracle.'

The light is fading in the cell, the guard will be back soon. Nella has not spent this much time alone with her husband in the whole of their four-month marriage. She remembers telling Johannes in his study how much he fascinated her. Looking at him now, those words hold true. His conversation and knowledge, his dry accommodation of the world's hypocrisies, his desire to be what he is. He lifts his hand to the candlelight, and the strong, hard ridges of his fingers are beautiful. How much she wants him to live.

This talk of transformation, how things can change, of rooms inhabited and emptied, sibling bodies stretched to reveal two such different secrets – it makes her want to tell him about the miniaturist. It seems a lifetime ago that she walked down the staircase and saw the cabinet waiting on the marble tiles. How offended she was, how angry Marin had been.

'Did Jack ever tell you who he worked for on the Kalverstraat?' she asks.

'He worked for lots of people.'

'A woman from Bergen? With blonde hair? She trained with a clockmaker.'

Johannes takes a small bite of one of the sugared doughnuts and lights a candle on his table. Nella feels his cool regard on the top of her head. 'No,' he says. 'I'd have remembered that.'

'She is the miniaturist I hired to furnish the cabinet house. She made Rezeki's puppet.'

At this, his tired eyes light up. 'A woman?'

'Yes, I believe so.'

'What extraordinary skill and observation. I'd have been her patron, given half a chance.' He reaches into his pocket, and with a captivated expression, tenderly lifts out the little dog. 'I take her with me everywhere I go. She is the greatest comfort.'

'Really?' she whispers. Johannes hands her the miniature, and respectfully, Nella takes it, with a trembling fingertip stroking the softness of Rezeki's mouse-skin head. On the dog's skull, there is not the slightest trace of red. Nella checks again, but nothing remains of the rusty mark she had once been so convinced of.

'I don't understand,' she breathes.

'Nor I. I've never seen anything like it.'

Nella peers one last time at the animal's tiny skull. Nothing. Did I even see it? she asks herself. Doubt now riots against certainty – what she has seen and not seen these past few months swirls inside her head.

'I sometimes wonder, if I sit very still in here,' Johannes says, 'if I have already died too.'

'You are alive, Johannes. You are *alive.*'

'A strange world,' he says. 'Human beings going around reassuring each other that they haven't died. We know this is not Rezeki, and yet we somehow feel it is. Thus a solid object makes a formless memory. If only it were the other way round, that our minds could conjure into being anything we wanted.' He sighs, drawing his hands down his face. 'When Otto left, for the little I recognized myself, I could have been dead.'

He pauses, putting Rezeki back in his pocket. 'This cell shall now be the compass of my waking life,' he says, spanning his arms out like a crooked windmill. 'There are horizons through the brickwork, Nella. You wait and see.'

Nella leaves him then, no longer able to bear that little room. The moss and the mice, the sounds of men screeching like birds; Johannes is locked in an aviary, her great owl surrounded by crows. Nella stumbles out into the winter sunshine, and only then does she cry – fierce, quiet tears, as she presses against the city's wall.

Verkeerspel

As she pushes open the front door, the desire to tell Marin about the state of the sugar and Johannes' condition dies in Nella's throat.

In the middle of the hallway, rocking on its tin runners, is a full-sized cradle. Made of oak, it has been inlaid with marquetry of roses and daisies, honeysuckle and cornflowers. It has a hood, lined with velvet and fringed with lace. Beautiful and shocking, it is an exact replica of the cradle upstairs in the cabinet.

Still shaken from her visit to Johannes, Nella shuts the door. What she had first taken for a mock, a cradle sent to a woman whose marriage was a farce, has become a reality. Cornelia scurries up from the kitchen.

'What is this?' Nella says. 'Do you think it came from—'

'No,' Cornelia says sharply. 'Madame Marin ordered it. It arrived in a crate from Leiden.'

Nella touches the main body of the wood. It seems to sing under her fingers, the marquetry so finely tuned. 'It's the same as she sent me.'

'I know,' Cornelia replies. 'Your somebody.'

Marin emerges from the salon. Up close, she now seems to have the girth of an oak. 'The craftsmanship is extraordinary,' she observes. 'It is just as I imagined.'

'How much did this cost to make, to transport it here?' Nella imagines Johannes' shrinking cloud of money finally evaporating into the air. 'Marin, if any of our neighbours saw this arrive, what on earth would they think?'

'Exactly the same as you.'

'What?'

'Don't think I haven't noticed your mind whirring.' Marin moves heavily towards her. 'You want to take my child for yourself.'

How does Marin understand people's thoughts quicker than anyone else? I could bluff, Nella thinks, but what's the point? I was the one who said there must be no more secrets between us.

'Marin, I don't want to take your child—'

'But you suppose he'd be convenient,' Marin persists, covering her stomach with her hands as if Nella would wrench it there and then. 'The last sacrifice? Giving up my baby for my brother – for you.'

'Johannes is in the Stadhuis prison, Marin. And if we did pretend for a while that the child is mine, would that really be so awful? We could prove Johannes has the same desires – as other men. Don't you want him to live?'

'You really cannot see.'

'See what? I see more than you.'

'Petronella, this child will be far from convenient. You can believe that.'

'I know that, Marin, I *know*. And while I'm trying to save us, you're spending money we simply do not have.'

The slap comes from nowhere, stinging Nella's face.

'I marvel how he could ever love you,' Nella says. Hot and cruel, the words rush out before she can stop them.

'He did,' Marin says. 'He does.'

'We will have to hire a midwife,' Nella says quietly. 'I cannot bear the weight of this birth alone.'

Marin snorts. 'You won't be bearing any weight at all.'

'Stop, stop,' Cornelia pleads.

'Marin, it's the law—'

'No. Absolutely not.' Marin roughly pushes the end of the cradle; it rocks back and forth, its emptiness strangely antagonizing. 'Do you know what else is the law, Petronella?' Her cheeks are flushed, her hair has loosened from her cap. 'A midwife has to write down the identity of the father. And if we don't tell her, she'll report our silence too.' She stops the cradle, breathing heavily. 'So like everything else, I will be dealing with this alone.'

Marin places her hand on her stomach, but this time she flinches, as if she's touched a burning coal.

❦

In the afternoon, Nella wanders slowly through the corridors. The quiet rooms make her feel as if there is no one in the house but her. The key to the warehouse still hangs round her neck, warmed by her skin, worth more to her than any silver necklace Johannes would have commissioned.

With a rope, Cornelia lugs the cradle up to Marin's little cell. It waits expectantly, taking up most of the free space amongst the skulls and maps and feathers. The maid's attitude towards Marin's secret has been a rapid metamorphosis; now the baby is a marvel, a crucible in which all their problems will burn. Cornelia breathes his invisible presence, gulping it like fresh air whenever she can. She has started cleaning again, opening windows despite her hatred of the cold; beeswax on bedposts, floorboards and cupboards and windowsills, lavender oil burners, vinegar on the glass, lemon juice flicked on fresh sheets. Still, Nella supposes, it is better than her gloom.

In the back room on the ground floor, away from prying eyes on the canal path, Nella can hear Marin and Cornelia setting up a game of *verkeerspel*. She thinks of the little coriander-seed counters upstairs, the miniaturist's exquisitely made wooden box, turning up like a miracle of chance. She has almost given up hoping that she will hear from Lucas Windelbreke in Bruges, a hundred and fifty miles away, on icy roads. My letter probably got lost, she thinks, creeping up to the door to spy on Marin and Cornelia.

'My whale body,' Marin sighs.

'Your little Jonah,' smiles the maid. Nella still feels bruised from their morning encounter. Marin is not dealing with everything alone, she thinks. Who went to the warehouse, the Stadhuis? But they haven't time to fight this out. Time is the latest luxury to be in short supply.

What would Agnes say if she saw Marin now? Surely Frans Meermans had thought of this eventuality. All those times spent with Marin, hidden from his wife's darting eyes. Didn't either of them worry how Nature might take her course?

'He's kicking me,' Marin says to Cornelia, looking down at her body. 'When I stand in front of the looking glass sometimes I see within myself the imprint of a tiny foot. I've not seen such a thing before.'

Nella has – when her unborn younger siblings punched at

the lining of their mother's womb. But she will not say this, for Marin in her wonderment is rather wonderful.

'I should like to see that,' she says instead, entering the room.

'If he does it again, I'll let you know,' Marin says. 'Sometimes, it's his hand. It looks like a kitten paw.'

'Do you think it's a boy?' Nella asks.

'I believe so,' replies Marin, giving the bulge of her body a peremptory tap. Her fingers hover, as if they want to caress it. 'I have been reading,' she says, pointing to Blankaart's *Children's Diseases* resting on a table.

Cornelia bobs a curtsey and makes her exit. 'It must be time soon,' Nella says.

'We'll need hot water, cloths, a stick for me to hold my teeth upon,' Marin replies.

Nella feels only pity. She remembers what Cornelia told of Marin's mother. *She barely survived after Madame Marin was born.* Has Marin any idea of the blood that is to come, the rebellion of the body, the noises and hot fear? Marin seems determined to exert her formidable will on this baby, as if, like the hermetic creature inside her, she is unaffected by the world's external tricks, as if she is immune to suffering.

'I thought we could play a game,' Marin says, lining up the *verkeerspel* counters like coins. 'You go first.'

Nella takes this as a peace offering, and plays her first counter on the *verkeerspel* board. Marin assesses her move, contemplating the sole disc, shaking the dice like two teeth in the hollow of her fist. She worries her black token, unsure of where to place it.

'Marin,' Nella says. 'You haven't asked about the ware-house.'

Marin continues to stare at the board. Against her will, Nella feels her patience slipping away. 'And you haven't asked me about Johannes.'

Marin looks up. 'What?'

'They're going – to – put him on the rack—'

'*Stop*,' Marin utters.

'If we don't—'

'Why must you torture me? You know I cannot go and see him!'

'But I need your help. Two respectable witnesses, Marin. Frans and Agnes. Think what that means.'

Marin becomes very still. 'I knew what it meant the moment Frans came to our door.'

'Then *speak* to Frans, Marin. Tell him about his child.'

Marin lays the dice down very carefully upon the *verkeer-spel* board. She looks winded, furrowing her eyebrows, twisting her mouth smaller. 'You make such a conversation sound easy,' she says. 'You know nothing of what you speak.'

'I know more than you think.' Nella stops herself, trying to collect her bad temper and shove it away up her sleeve. 'Meer-mans is a man,' she adds more gently. 'He can do something.'

'Trust me, he can do very little.'

'He has no heir, Marin—'

'What? Are you now proposing I barter my child? How do you think Agnes would greet such a piece of news?' Marin stands abruptly and begins to pace the small room. 'It would give her even more reason to bury us. You are always med-dling—'

'It isn't meddling. It's survival.'

'You know nothing of survival—'

'I know what happened, Marin,' Nella blurts. 'Cornelia told me.'

'*Happened?*'

'I know you and Frans were in love, and Johannes stopped your marriage.'

Marin puts her hand against the wall to steady herself and curves her other arm underneath her unborn child. 'What?' Her voice is extraordinary, a ferocious hiss.

'I know Frans married Agnes to spite you – how even Agnes knows that's true. I've seen the way Frans looks at you – I know about the salted piglet, the love note in your book. You keep telling me I don't see, but I do.'

'The salted piglet,' echoes Marin. She pauses, as if looking on some long-submerged memory reappearing into her mind. 'And Cornelia dared to tell you this?'

Nella glances at the door. 'Don't be angry with her. I made her tell, I had to know. It was important.'

Marin says nothing for a moment. She exhales heavily, and lowers herself into her chair. 'Frans loves his wife,' she says. When Nella starts to protest, she holds up her hand. 'You don't know what love looks like, Petronella. Twelve years together should never be underestimated.'

'But—'

'And the rest of it is a good story, patched together from listening at doors. It's more elaborate than I could have made up myself. I should have given Cornelia more chores.'

'It's not a story—'

'I come out of it well, don't I? My brother less so. However, the truth is somewhat different.' Nella notices how Marin's hands are shaking. 'Johannes did refuse Frans Meermans' proposal,' Marin says, her voice now heavy.

'I *knew* it—'

'Because that was what I wanted.'

Nella stares at the pieces of the *verkeerspel* board. They slide before her eyes. What she's hearing doesn't make sense. Marin's revelation spikes her, her certainty now misplaced.

'I did love Frans,' Marin says, her statement stiff. 'When I was thirteen years old. But I never wanted to marry him.'

Though she looks ineffably sad, another emotion rises up like a pale sun through Marin's face. It is, she senses, the bittersweet relief of confession.

And yet, Nella still cannot understand. The scenery and actors are familiar, but in roles they're not supposed to play. *I did something to make Frans Meermans very unhappy*, Johannes said in his Stadhuis cell. Why did he say nothing to Nella then – why has he never expiated himself – what is this cord of loyalty tying Marin and him together, a rope so slippery that Nella has no hope to grasp?

'By the time I was sixteen, I didn't want to give up who I was and what I had,' Marin says quietly. 'I had a household already. When Johannes was away, I was the head.'

Her tears are coming now, welling up in her grey eyes. She opens her arms wide like wings, a familiar gesture, indicating the room in which they sit. 'No woman had that, unless she was a widow. Then came Cornelia and Otto. "The bars on our cage are of our own making," Johannes said. He promised I could be free. For such a long time, I believed him. I truly thought I was.' Her hands fly towards her stomach.

'Marin, you're carrying Meermans' child—'

'And whatever his imperfections, my brother has always let me be. Alas, he cannot say the same of me.'

Marin presses her fingers under her eyes as if to do so will stop the tears. It is a futile gesture, for down they come, even as she starts to sob. 'I have taken things from Johannes that were not mine to take,' she says.

'Marin, what do you mean?'

But Marin is struggling for her words. She draws her slender hands down her face, taking a long breath. 'When Frans proposed, I didn't know how to say no. It was not a situation I had prepared for. I thought it better for him to hear I was forbidden, rather than discovering this . . . reluctance I felt. So I asked my brother to take the blame.' Her eyes are wild with distress. 'And he did it. Johannes lied, for me. I was young – we all were! I never thought it would twist—' Marin puts her hand to her mouth, unable to stop her cry. 'All friendship gone,' she says. 'All understanding. Because I couldn't tolerate being a wife.'

The Hopeful Loaf

Outside her husband's warehouse, Nella waits for Hanna and Arnoud Maakvrede, Johannes' key around her neck. Her mind rings with this new truth of Marin and Johannes; their understanding made of light as much as shadow. Love has shifted its shape; a beam of sun that sometimes clouds the heart. It seems that Marin viewed marriage as a ceding of something, whereas so many women – including my own mother, Nella realizes – see it as the only possible form of influence a woman may have. Marriage is supposed to harness love, to increase a woman's power, Nella supposes. But does it? Marin believed herself to be more powerful without it. Love has been left unharnessed, and indeed extraordinary things have happened. A child, a prison cell, yes – but also choice and the moulding of one's own fate.

After the revelation about her past, Marin had wanted some distraction, some occupation – she had practically demanded it – and Nella had taken her chance. You weren't callous, she tells herself, leaning up against the warehouse wall; it was absolute necessity. So, as Nella sat at the small table in the back room, away from the prying eyes of the canal, Marin had written a letter to Arnoud Maakvrede in Johannes' hand. She had agreed with Nella's new idea, inviting Maakvrede to taste the sugar with a proposition to sell it solely in the republic; a quicker sale to a ready audience. My marriage has afforded me a little influence at least, Nella thought wryly.

Marin's voice plays through Nella's head. 'The profit-bar is ours to set. There are fifteen hundred cones, which I estimate, if we do well, could make thirty thousand guilders. Start higher than it will sell. Remember that if they want to purchase, we'll be cutting the profit three ways now, and the bulk of the money still needs to go to Frans.'

'But what if Arnoud has heard about Johannes – what if he won't buy?'

'It's the guilder over godliness. All we can do is pray that Arnoud Maakvrede's an Amsterdammer before he's an angel.'

'He might know we want to sell the stock quickly. He might see the rot.'

'Hold your ground, Nella. Price it up, and make it seem that you're discounting it because of the spores.'

Nella could not help admiring how Marin drew up the bridge of her sadness when it really was important, how she could put herself away somewhere others couldn't reach. She wondered if she herself was too small for this big idea, that she would be swamped by it, drowned by her own ambition. And yet Marin gave her all the words she wanted to hear. 'Petronella,' she said quietly. 'You are not doing this alone. I am here.'

Across the abandoned *verkeerspel* board, Marin's hand reached out for hers and squeezed it, and in her astonishment, Nella thought her heart might burst.

Nella sees the confectioner couple approach in the cold light. She wonders if someone has told them what's happened at the

Stadhuis, but the scandal of a wealthy merchant's arrest does not yet seem to have penetrated the city streets. Cornelia has reported nothing along the canal path – perhaps Aalbers, in his decency, has managed to keep the Stadhuis prison guards silent? But it will only be a matter of time before everyone knows what's happened to Johannes Brandt. A strutting nine-year-old brat like Christoffel cannot be bridled as easily as a prison guard with mouths to feed. The surface of Amsterdam thrives on these mutual acts of surveillance, the neighbourly smothering of a person's spirit.

Outside, in the shadow of the warehouse, Arnoud looks less inflamed, his apron replaced by a neat black suit and hat. He seems a different presence to the one battering his honeycomb trays. It's as if the air has shrunk him.

'Seigneur, Madame,' Nella says, as she turns the key in the lock. 'New Year greetings. Thank you both for coming.'

'In your husband's letter, he made no mention we would be meeting you,' Arnoud says, unable to conceal his surprise at seeing Nella here alone.

'Indeed, Seigneur,' Nella replies, feeling Hanna's shrewd eye upon her. 'My husband is away.'

'And Marin Brandt?'

'Visiting family, Seigneur.'

'I see.' Arnoud is visibly perturbed by Nella's youth and sex, as if she is a trick, a play-act – but just you wait, she thinks, clenching her fists in the cuffs of her coat.

'Come this way, Seigneur, Madame. And mind your feet on the rungs.'

Leading Arnoud and Hanna up the ladder, Nella thinks of Agnes' miniature hand back home. The loaf may not have turned any blacker in the cabinet, but outside that shrunken world a day has passed, another night of weather, another night of damp. Nella can hardly guess what she will find. What was once, is now no longer. Her heart starts thumping harder as she hears Arnoud wheezing up the rungs, Hanna's neat step tapping the ladder behind him.

'Here they are,' she says, indicating the loaves when they reach the eaves.

'I hadn't expected there would be so much,' says Arnoud.

'Imagine it transformed to guilders.' He raises his eyebrows and Nella winces inwardly at her own crass patter. *Think of Marin*, she tells herself. *Be as affable as Johannes.*

Hanna approaches the Surinam side and inhales sharply. 'Rot?' she asks.

'Only on a few,' says Nella. 'The season has not been kind.'

Arnoud kneels down reverently, like a priest before an altar. 'May I?' he asks.

'Please.'

Arnoud removes a loaf from the Surinam side, and also a loaf marked with the three crosses of Amsterdam. From his pocket he produces a sharp little knife, and with an expert flick he takes a solid shaving off each cone. Breaking them in two, he hands half to Hanna. As they put the Surinam sample on their tongues, their eyes meet.

What are they saying to each other, with no words? A conversation is certainly taking place. They do the same with the Amsterdam sample, dissolving in their mouths and communing in silence. Whatever its true purpose, marriage is certainly a funny thing, Nella thinks. Who would have paired elegant Hanna with a round puffert of a man like Arnoud Maakvrede? She wishes Johannes were here. A man of many languages, he would understand the traders' silence. The image of him in that cell is too much, and Nella buries it, trying to focus on the sugar.

'There are one thousand five hundred loaves here,' she says. 'Seven hundred and fifty were refined in Surinam. The rest have been refined here in the city. We are looking to sell them all.'

'I thought Brandt traded from the east?'

'He does. But a Surinam plantation had excess stock and wanted to keep it in the republic. We have other people coming to see it later today,' she lies. 'They are very keen.'

Hanna delicately wipes the corner of her mouth. 'How much for the Amsterdam lot?'

Nella pretends to consider. 'Thirty thousand,' she says.

Hanna's eyes widen in surprise. 'Impossible,' says Arnoud.

'It is, I'm afraid,' Hanna says. 'We simply do not have that kind of money.'

'Prosperous enough,' murmurs Arnoud. 'But not stupid.'

'We are makers of cakes, not sellers of sugar,' Hanna says, frowning at him. 'There may be no guild in our way, but as pastry bakers we're still subject to the whims of the burgo-masters and their hatred of papist gingerbread idols.'

'It is excellent sugar, as I'm sure you can tell. Its quality alone will guarantee it sells. The craving craze shows no sign of abating – marzipan, cakes, waffles,' Nella says. She watches Arnoud as he thinks, staring at the cones rising to the roof. 'Your reputation would certainly increase,' she adds. 'I can only imagine what other doors such sugar might open.'

Nella isn't certain, but she thinks Hanna is hiding a smile. It is very unlikely they have thirty thousand guilders to spare, although you never know in this city. It is a preposterous sum – but what can she do? Marin said to name a high price, for Arnoud to feel he's comfortably clambering down. They need their cut, Agnes needs hers. Nella begins to feel desperate.

'We'll give you nine thousand,' Arnoud says.

'I cannot let you take all this sugar for nine thousand.'

'Very well. We will take a hundred Amsterdam loaves for nine hundred guilders and let you know how it sells. If we make a profit, we will come back for more.'

Nella tries to think quickly, as fast as Arnoud. He wants one cone for nine guilders, but she needs to be selling each one nearer to twenty. He came prepared, she thinks. 'Too low, Seigneur. Three thousand five hundred,' she says.

Arnoud laughs. 'One thousand one hundred,' he replies.

'Two thousand.'

He twists his lip. 'One thousand five.'

'Very well, Seigneur Maakvrede. But I have two other interested parties coming to see it this afternoon. I can give you three days to make your decision on the rest, but if they offer higher then your chance is gone.'

'Done,' he replies, folding his arms, looking impressed. He seems happy; it is the first time she has seen him smile. 'For a hundred loaves.'

Nella's head spins. She's not done as well as she hoped, but at least some of their stock is to be circulated – and in Amsterdam, where words are water, all it takes is one platter of delicious buns. She puts a Surinam loaf in a basket for Cornelia to experiment with drying them out.

Arnoud gives Nella one thousand five hundred guilders in crisp notes. It feels exhilarating to touch them – a sense of potential, a life raft made of paper. One thousand must go straight to Agnes and Meermans on the Prinsengracht, a sweetener to try and stop them testifying against Johannes. The other five hundred must bribe Jack Philips. They will have to think about saving anything for themselves later.

Hanna begins loading a basket with the loaves. 'How is Cornelia?' she asks.

She's frightened, Nella wants to say. She's tethering herself to her kitchen. She had left the maid in a frenzy, yanking open the tight globe of a savoy cabbage, shredding scallions and leeks. 'She's well, thank you, Madame Maakvrede.'

'Some shrink, whilst others grow,' Arnoud remarks, shaking his head at the mountain of cones.

Hanna squeezes Nella's hand. 'We will sell this sugar, and return,' she says. 'Of that I will make sure.'

⁂

Nella hurries home just as it starts to rain, feeling as if the guilder notes in her pocket are banners of small triumph. It's a beginning, and Nella trusts Hanna Maakvrede. Whilst it will not be pleasant to pay a visit to Agnes and Frans Meermans on the Prinsengracht, performance is all. She will tuck her real self away as Marin does. There is a chance that the sight of some money might soften Frans Meermans' oddly hardened heart, or waken Agnes' long-dormant generous spirit. Can they really want Johannes dead? To desire another's end – how much misery must you have stored inside yourself?

Entering the hallway and shaking off the raindrops, Nella

hears the sound of Cornelia crying. Her quiet sobs quiver from the working kitchen. She drops the basket containing the blackened Surinam loaf and runs down the stairs, almost tripping over her own skirts.

Vegetable peelings are strewn across the floor, a mess of a meal of green and white ribbons.

'What is it?' Nella asks.

Cornelia points to the note upon the table. 'Is it from her?' Nella says, her spirit lifting. Finally, she thinks, the miniaturist has returned. She rushes to the paper. As she reads the words, a sharp slice of fear cuts her, Arnoud's guilders and the excitement of the sugar evaporate to nothing.

'My God,' she cries. 'Today?'

'Yes,' the maid replies. 'Your Norwegian snoop didn't predict *this*.'

Wild Beasts Must Be Tamed By Men

The trial chamber at the Stadhuis is a square room with high windows and a viewing gallery running round the top, something between a chapel and a sunken cell. There is no gold, no velvet, no sense of indulgence, just four walls of brilliant white, the furniture dark and plain. The rest of the Stadhuis is monumental, jaw-dropping. Arches soar to gilded cornicing, and wall maps carved from marble shimmer in the light – but in this room where the law is exercised, the atmosphere is sober. Nella and Cornelia take a seat up in the gallery and look down into the chamber.

The Schout, a man called Pieter Slabbaert, and six other men begin to file in and take their seats for Johannes' hearing. 'They must be the members of the *schepenbank*,' Nella whispers to Cornelia, who nods, barely able to stop shaking. The six men are of varying ages; some look better-off than others, but none of them are cloaked and ribboned like the judging Schout. Individuality is a black mark in this city, and Nella worries that in the face of Johannes' charge, they will coagulate into a self-righteous mass, unified in loathing.

Nella can hardly look at Schout Slabbaert. The man bears more than a passing resemblance to a toad; a bulbous face, broad-mouthed and glassy eyed. The gallery around her is beginning to fill up with city spectators, among them several women and even a handful of children. Nella thinks she recognizes the little snitch Christoffel who brought the news of Johannes' capture.

'They shouldn't bring tiddlers,' Cornelia mutters. The presence of so many little fish makes her anxious, as if they're here to watch the snagging of a whale.

On the left side of the gallery from where she and Cornelia are sitting, Nella spies Hanna and Arnoud Maakvrede. So they do know, Nella thinks, nodding to them, her heart heavy. Arnoud taps his nose at her, and she tries to derive comfort from this conspiratorial gesture. Has he always known? The possibility that Arnoud *is* more Amsterdammer than angel consoles her – until she wonders if, depending on the outcome of this trial, he will come back and angle for the remaining sugar at an even more reduced rate.

On the front row of the opposite side of the gallery, Agnes Meermans is bundled up in her furs. 'What's wrong with her face?' whispers Cornelia. Agnes' features are indeed even more pronounced than when Nella saw her at the Old Church in December. She seems ill, her cheekbones and eye-sockets too prominent as she looks down into the chamber, playing with something in her lap. Agnes suddenly grips the wooden rail in front of her, her fingernails bitten to the quick. Her once perfect headband is askew, the seed pearls round it tarnished; her clothes have a thrown-on appearance. She looks like a trapped animal, eyes roving the gallery, looking for something.

'I'll tell you what it is, Madame,' Cornelia says. 'Guilty conscience, that's what.'

But Nella is not so sure. What is it that Agnes fiddles with like a little girl – what is that tiny thing she's tucking in her cuff?

Behind his wife, Frans Meermans sits under his broad-brimmed hat. Nella wonders why they are not sitting together. His large, handsome face looks damp from the rainy morning outside, and he readjusts his jacket, pulling at it as if he's too hot. Nella pats her pocket, still containing the guilders from Arnoud. She needs to persuade Meermans that money is coming, and lots of it. *Let us bury this mess, Seigneur – let us say we were mistaken – surely you see Agnes is in no fit state to bear witness.* Running through these arguments, Nella tries to catch his eye, but Meermans will not look in her direction, staring instead over his wife's head towards the arena below.

There is a sharp collective breath around the chamber when Johannes is brought in. Nella clamps her hand to her mouth, but Cornelia cannot help but cry out. 'Seigneur,' she says. 'My Seigneur!'

Johannes shakes off the guards' support, but he can barely walk. The *schepenbank* watch him, their faces tense. Johannes has clearly been put on the rack, injuring him badly but not enough to endanger his life. He stoops to one side, his ankles with barely any strength to move, dragging one foot behind him like a limp rag. Johannes said he could see horizons through the brickwork, but how changed he looks in so few days. His cloak is frayed, and yet when he takes his seat, he sweeps it behind him like a cloth spun out of gold.

But in one way, the brutality of bolts and straps has not worked. The ungainly prisoner has clearly held on to his secrets – had he not, none of them would be here now in the trial chamber. Has he told them nothing? The purpose of this hearing will be to force out some performance through a verbal humiliation instead, and this time it will be witnessed by the citizens, a different kind of brutality. What was it Johannes said in his cell? The more people who take part in a ritual, the more justified it seems.

Nella pictures him at the silversmiths' feast. The charm he had, such expertise and wit, the way he drew all people near. Where are those people now – why have only children and clerks come to see him fight?

'He should be using a stick to walk,' Cornelia whispers to her.

'No, Cornelia. He wants us to understand their brutality.'

'And test our pity too.' Hanna Maakvrede has moved to sit with them, and takes Nella's hand in hers. As the three women form a chain, Nella feels her heart might split. All this time, she'd thought Johannes had denied Marin the life she wanted, when really he'd tried to set her free. Johannes' own heart is a powerful thing, but look where it has led him.

If only Marin could repay the favour right now, when it is most needed. It might be too late to persuade Jack to change his story or sate Frans' wrath, and now the state is involved, what can stand up to the outraged machinery which has spied a possible sodomite in its midst? *You cannot really touch my wealth*, Johannes once said. *It is in the air.* But a baby is made of solid flesh. Lend us your soon-to-be child, Marin, lend us at least the charade of a normal marriage.

Picturing the miniature cradle, Marin's tiny, swollen belly, the sugar loaf in Agnes' hand and Jack's unblemished doll, Nella curses the miniaturist for not alerting her to what needed to be done, to what could have been prevented. What use is a prophetess who doesn't make clear the inevitable?

Hanna leans towards her. 'We have already promised half the loaves we took this morning, Madame. Arnoud wants to load some to the Hague where he has family. I'm sure it won't be long before we take some more – do bear that in mind when you see those other . . . interested parties.'

Nella tries to tamp down her embarrassment. She doesn't mind bluffing with Arnoud. He almost seems to invite it, but with Hanna it feels dishonourable. 'Do any of his customers know whose sugar it is?' she asks.

At this, Hanna is the one to blush. 'Arnoud is omitting to mention the source,' she says. 'But it's excellent sugar, Madame. I think if it came from Beelzebub himself, my husband would still sell it.'

Hanna's words still give Nella hope – but here, in the trial chamber, it feels as if Johannes' plight has gained a momentum out of her control. The rain is falling heavier now, a quiet roar upon the roof.

'Good people of Amsterdam, we are fortunate,' Schout Slabbaert begins. His voice is deep and fluid, and rises up to where the normal folk are sitting on their hard wooden benches. Here is a man in the prime of his life, at the peak of his legislative power, holding citizens' lives in the clam of his fist. He eats well, Nella supposes, sleeps deep. The horrors of the torture chambers below his feet are as distant to him as the isles of Molucca.

'We have made a success of our city,' Slabbaert says. The gallery ruffles with a prideful acknowledgement, and the schepenbank nod in agreement. 'We've tamed our lands and seas; we feast on its bounty. You are all righteous people. You have not wasted yourselves in the surfeit of your good luck.

'But . . .' Slabbaert pauses, holding his finger aloft before pointing to Johannes. 'Here is a man who grew complacent. A man who thought he was above his own family, above the city, the Church, the state. Above God.' Slabbaert pauses again, letting silence engorge his rhetoric with power. 'Johannes Brandt thinks he can buy anything. For him everything has a price. Even the conscience of a young man, whom he took for the pleasure of his body and tried to bribe for his silence.'

There is a ripple of excitement. Complacent, pleasure, body – these forbidden words give the people in the chamber a thrill. But Nella feels a fear unfurling, like one of Marin's poison plants.

'You cannot make such an accusation.' Johannes' voice is cracked and harsh. 'The *schepenbank* have not made their decision and you cannot make it for them. Give them some credit, Seigneur. They are sensible men.'

A couple of the *schepenbank* glow with self-importance. The rest eye Johannes with a mix of awe and disgust.

'They are good counsel,' says Slabbaert, 'but I will be the one who has the final say. You deny the charge of sodomitic attack?'

Here are the words the gallery has been waiting for. It is almost as if they move through the spectators, daring their sinews to absorb them, to taste their rare transgression.

'I do,' Johannes says. He sticks out his crippled legs. 'Despite your best efforts.'

'Just simple answers, please,' says Slabbaert, sorting through his papers. 'On Sunday, the twenty-ninth day of December last year, at the warehouses on the Eastern Islands, Jack Philips of Bermondsey, London, says you attacked and sodomized him. On God's day, he was battered and bruised until he could barely walk.'

The gallery explodes. 'Quiet,' shouts Slabbaert. 'Be quiet in the chamber up there.'

'It was not me,' says Johannes, speaking over the clamour.

'Witnesses will swear on the Holy Bible that they saw you.'

'And how do they know me to identify me?'

'You're a familiar face, Seigneur Brandt. Now is not the time to pretend humility. You are powerful, a rich leader in example. You are often by the docks, the warehouses, the wharves. The act you committed—'

'Allegedly committed—'

'Goes against all that is good, all that is right. Your behaviour towards your family, your city, your country, is that of the Devil.'

Johannes looks up to the square of white sky through the high window. The *schepenbank* fidget in their small chairs. 'My conscience is clear,' he says quietly. 'Everything you accuse me of is as false as your teeth.'

The children in the gallery titter.

'Contempt of court as well as sodomy—'

'I might as well be in contempt of court, Seigneur Slabbaert. What will you do? Drown me twice for pointing out your vanity?'

Slabbaert's toad eyes bulb, his well-fed cheeks draw down with barely suppressed rage. Be careful, Johannes, Nella thinks.

'When I ask you a question,' Slabbaert says, 'answer me

with the respect that every citizen must show to the rule of law.'

'Then ask me a question that deserves that respect.'

The *schepenbank* seem to be revelling in this exchange, their heads turning back and forth between the two men.

'You are married?' asks Slabbaert.

'I am.'

Nella shrinks back into her seat. Agnes looks over the space at her, a grimace playing on her lips.

'And what sort of husband are you?'

'I'm in one piece, aren't I?'

Some men in the gallery laugh, and Johannes looks up. He recognizes Cornelia's face leaning over the rail, and manages to smile.

'That does not answer my question,' says Slabbaert, his voice rising a little. 'Are you a good or a bad husband?'

Johannes shrugs. 'I believe I am a good husband. My wife is content. She is wealthy and secure.'

'That is a merchant's answer. To be wealthy does not mean you are content.'

'Ah, yes, I forget your spiritual agonies when it comes to money, Slabbaert. Try telling that to a journeyman – a man who keeps this republic afloat and yet can barely keep up his landlord's rent. Try telling him that to be secure should not mean to be happy.'

A few grunts of assent are heard in the gallery and a member of the *schepenbank* writes something down. 'Have you any children?' Slabbaert asks.

'Not yet.'

'Why not?'

'We're but four months married.' Cornelia clutches Nella's hand. Unwittingly, Johannes has thrown the chance of Marin's baby as a means to save him.

'How often do you lie with her?'

Johannes pauses. If he wants to make the impertinence of such a question felt, this crass invasion of his bed chamber, it does not work. The *schepenbank* crane forward, as does Frans Meermans. Agnes grips her hands on the banister, waiting like a carrion crow.

'As often as I can,' Johannes says. 'I have to travel a great deal.'

'You are late to marry, Seigneur.'

Johannes looks up to the gallery. 'My wife was worth the wait.'

His tenderness rings clear, and Nella feels a sadness ebbing through her. Two women behind her sigh appreciatively.

'You have, over the years, employed many apprentices in the various guilds,' Slabbaert observes.

'It is my duty as a citizen of Amsterdam and a senior member of the VOC. I am happy to do so.'

'Some might say too happy. Over the years, a preponderance of young men—'

'With respect, are not all apprentices young men?'

'—the number of which is greater than any other senior guild member or VOC representative has employed. I have your figures here.'

Johannes shrugs, his shoulders lifting crookedly. 'I have more money than most of them,' he says. 'People wish to learn from me. One might even argue that is the reason I'm here.'

'And what do you mean?'

'The poorest hunters always want the biggest stag. I wonder, Schout Slabbaert – who will take my business if I drown? Will it be you, dividing it up and locking it away in your Stadhuis coffers?'

'You insult the city of Amsterdam!' Slabbaert shouts. 'You disgust us with your insinuations.' The Schout looks round to the *schepenbank*. 'Taking the city as a plaything, undermining everything we work for.'

'That is not a statement of fact. That is your opinion.'

'You also have employed a Negro, have you not?'

'He's from Porto-Novo, in Dahomey.'

'You have kept him close, taught him our ways. You have tamed the savage.'

'What are you circling, Slabbaert? What do you have in your sight?'

'Merely to observe that you have a taste for the unusual, Seigneur Brandt. Many of your colleagues will attest to that. Call the plaintiff,' Slabbaert snaps and at this, Johannes' eyes widen in shock.

'The plaintiff?' Nella turns to Cornelia. 'I thought today was just to list the charge?'

But no, they hear his footsteps, and the two girls look down in horror as the guards bring Johannes' accuser through the chamber door.

The Actor

Cornelia clasps Nella's hand on seeing the Englishman again. Rezeki's killer wanders into the chamber. His wild hair has lost its lustre and he wears a bloodied bandage on his shoulder.

'That's not his blood,' Nella murmurs. 'It would have healed by now.' Jack peers up to the gallery and Nella notices how it is Agnes' turn to shrink into her seat.

At the sight of him, a real-life English devil, the *schepenbank* sit up. 'Are you Jack Philips, of Bermondsey, England?' asks Slabbaert.

Jack seems momentarily uncertain in the face of the spectators' stares and whispers. Nella, remembering his consummate performance in the hallway after stabbing Rezeki, cannot work out if he is terrified or just pretending.

'I am,' Jack replies. He throws down the two words like gauntlets at Johannes' feet, his strange Dutch echoing through the chamber. A few people in the gallery snigger openly at Jack's accent.

'Hand him the Bible,' Slabbaert intones and a court clerk stands up and brandishes a small, dense copy. 'Place your hand on it and swear you will tell the truth.'

Jack places his tremulous fingers on the top cover. 'I will,' he says.

Johannes' face is an unreadable mask and Jack does not

return his gaze. 'Do you recognize this man?' Slabbaert points to Johannes, but Jack keeps his head bowed. 'I said, do you recognize this man?'

Still Jack doesn't look. Is this guilt, or feigned fear, just one of the tricks Jack learned in the playhouses by the River Thames? 'Are you deaf?' Slabbaert says, a little louder. 'Or do you not understand me?'

'I do understand,' says Jack. His eyes flick towards Johannes, lingering on his crooked legs, his tattered-looking cloak.

'What charges do you bring to him?' asks Slabbaert.

'I bring the charges of a sodomitic attack, assault and bribery.'

The *schepenbank* rustles with excitement. 'Let me read your statement out to the assembly.' Slabbaert clears his throat. ' "*I, Jack Philips, of Bermondsey, England, lodging at the sign of the rabbit off the Kloveniersburgwal near Bethaniënstraat, was summarily seized and sodomitically abused late in the evening on the twenty-ninth of December. My abuser was Johannes Matteus Brandt, merchant of Amsterdam and bewindhebber of the VOC. I was taken against my will, and was stabbed in the shoulder for my resistance.*" Was there anything else you wished to add?' asks Slabbaert, peering over his eye-glasses.

'No.'

Cornelia turns to Nella. 'Did he just say that the Seigneur stabbed him? Does that mean Toot's safe?' she says, as if she can hardly believe it. 'One small miracle, Madame.'

But Nella cannot feel so pleased. The lie sets his servant free, yet it binds Johannes tighter to the threat of death.

'And everything in there is correct?' Slabbaert says, referring to the statement.

'Yes, Seigneur. Except that when he stabbed me, he only just missed my heart.'

'I see. And where did he seize you, Mr Philips?'

'On the Eastern Islands. I work now and then as a stower at the VOC warehouses.'

'And how did he appear to you?'

'What do you mean?'

'Well, how did Johannes Brandt behave before he – seized you?'

'He was frenzied.'

How does Jack know a word like that in Dutch? Nella thinks.

'Did you speak together?'

Jack is warming to his performance now. With a mastery of the actor's pause, he waits, letting the chamber hear nothing but their own wonderings and the falling rain.

'Did he speak to you?' Slabbaert repeats.

'He called me his little niece and asked me where I lived.'

'He called you his little niece?' Slabbaert turns to the *schepenbank*. 'On all levels of life these men are unnatural. They even steal the language of the family and turn it to mockery. Did he say anything else, Mr Philips?'

'He said he'd been watching me,' says Jack. 'He asked if he could come back and see my lodgings.'

'And how did you reply?'

'I pushed him away and told him to leave me alone.'

'And after you pushed him?'

'He took me by my coatsleeves and dragged me against his warehouse.'

'And then?' Jack goes silent. 'And then?' presses Slabbaert. 'You were abused?'

'I was.'

'You were sodomized.'

'Yes.'

Two members of the *schepenbank* explode into a fit of coughing, their chairs scraping. In the gallery, people are muttering. One of the youngest children, no more than three years old, stares between the banister spindles in horrified wonder.

The Schout leans forward to Jack, a faint flicker of delight in his amphibian eyes. 'Did he say anything as he was attacking you?'

'He said – he said he had to have me. That he would show me how much he loved his little niece.'

'And did you say anything?'

Jack throws back his shoulders, showing his bloody bandage, puffing out his chest. 'I told him he had the Devil in him. Then I told him he was the Devil, but he wouldn't stop. He said he would show a wretch like me what it was to be taken by a man like him. He said he always got everything that he wanted, and he would beat me if I didn't submit.'

'We have a surgeon's account of the plaintiff's physical state when he came to the Stadhuis with his accusation,' says Slabbaert, handing copies of it to the *schepenbank*. 'He stabbed you, my lad. Any lower and he'd have punctured your heart.'

Lad. Softening English slang – poor Jack the Lad, caught in the dark by Lucifer himself. In light of this clear declaration of where Slabbaert's sympathies lie, Johannes looks weighed down, as if his bones are made of stone.

'He did,' says Jack. At this Johannes looks up. Hastily, Jack turns to the *schepenbank*. 'And he beat me. I could barely walk.'

'This is all lies,' Johannes interrupts.

'He can't speak to me, Schout Slabbaert,' Jack says. 'Tell him he can't speak to me.'

'Silence, Brandt. You'll have your chance. Mr Philips, you are entirely sure that the man assaulting you that night was Johannes Brandt?'

'I am entirely sure,' Jack says, but his knees begin to sag.

'The boy's about to faint,' Johannes says as Jack staggers towards the floor.

'Take him out,' says Slabbaert, waving a hand at Jack. Two guards scoop him up. 'We will adjourn until tomorrow morning at seven o'clock.'

'Schout Slabbaert,' says Johannes. 'Today was just supposed to be the reading of the charges, and yet you bring out my accuser. What is the game you are playing? When will it be my turn to ask questions? You have sought to defame me and shock the crowd. I must have my say.'

'You speak too much as it is. We haven't even had the witnesses yet.'

'It is written down that it must be so,' says Johannes. 'We must both of us have our chance.' He points at the Bible. '*Do not show partiality in judging; hear both small and great alike. Bring me any case too hard for you, and I will hear it.*' 'Deuteronomy. In case you want to check.'

'You will have your moment, Brandt,' Slabbaert replies. 'But for now, we adjourn. Seven o'clock tomorrow.'

Johannes and Jack are led out through different doors. Jack keeps his head down, but Johannes turns briefly to the gallery, where Cornelia and Nella are already on their feet. She holds up her hand, and he nods at her before being bundled off.

People stretch their limbs and exchange expressions of

surprise and consternation, morbid picnickers rustling in their pockets for their bags of nuts, their curls of cheese and ham. Agnes hurries down the aisle. Nella is surprised again at the narrowness of her frame, her birdlike steps. Frans Meermans has already disappeared.

She knows she hasn't got much time. 'I won't be long,' she says to Cornelia. 'Go back to Marin.'

Immediately, Hanna looks curious, but Nella can only throw Cornelia a warning glance. Not even Hanna can know. Cornelia answers with an almost imperceptible nod.

Making her way round to where Agnes has exited, Nella notices that something has fallen on the floorboards where she was sitting, lying in the dust amid fresh orange peel. Two tiny feet poke out from under the bench, wrapped in a pair of pattens. I know those feet, she thinks, kneeling down in the dirt.

The feet belong to a small doll, dressed in gold. The face is Nella's, her hair escaping in wisps from a saffron-coloured headband. 'By all the angels,' she breathes. This version of herself looks less surprised than the doll back home in the cabinet. It is more level-gazed. Instinctively, she searches the miniature body – for wounds, she tells herself, to arm against any coming danger. But in a dark, rarely visited pocket of her mind, she knows she's doing it to find any sign of a child. There is none; no hidden bump. Nella pushes away the sadness. At least you have no cuts and breaks, she tells herself. Now is not your time.

The Guilder and the Doll

Agnes could have had this doll for months. She was jealous of my cabinet, Nella thinks – pretending she had one, giving herself away on the outside steps after the sugar party. *I want mine to be better than hers*, she'd said to Frans. And surely there can be only one place Agnes procured me? This doll is so pertinent, so accurate. It is painful to accept it's been made for someone else.

Nella puts her shining self in her pocket with Arnoud's guilders and rushes down the steps in search of Meermans. The rain has eased a little, the light is misty. Spectators hang around in the narrow street, avoiding the puddles. Nella spies the old-fashioned white ruff, the tall black smock of Pastor Pellicorne. His immaculate face, his crown of grey hair, those maddened-preacher eyes. Others have gathered round him, like burrs on wool. 'This is sin,' he pronounces as the rain patters down. 'You can smell it. Johannes Brandt has led a sinful life.'

'It's the consequence of luxury,' the woman next to him observes.

'But he's made the city money,' says a man. 'He's made us rich.'

'Who exactly has he made rich? And look what it's done to his *soul*,' says Pellicorne. He whispers the word, as if disposing with one last breath the abomination of Johannes Brandt.

Nella can hardly breathe. Smells of rotting food rise as the thick, smoky stench of tavern meat rolls down the walls. Pellicorne glides his eyes over her.

'Are you not well, girl?' asks one of the women with Pellicorne, but Nella does not answer.

'The *wife*,' someone whispers, and more heads turn.

Look at me then, Nella thinks. Look at the wife. 'Yes,' she shouts. 'I am his wife.'

'God sees through doors, Madame,' says the first woman. 'He sees it all.'

Nella walks in the opposite direction, squeezing the doll in her pocket. She tries to picture the house without Johannes. *No*, she thinks, feeling her husband's life slipping through her grip. *You cannot let him die.*

'Madame Brandt.'

She turns. Frans Meermans is standing before her. *Be calm, Nella Elisabeth.* 'Seigneur,' she says. 'I have been looking for you. Where is your wife?'

Meermans pushes his hat on his head. 'Agnes has gone home and will return tomorrow. She has been – out of sorts, ever since she saw the horror—'

'You have to stop this, Seigneur. Is it worth killing your friend for guilders?' She hesitates. 'Or making Marin this un-happy?'

Meermans puts his foot into a puddle. 'Johannes Brandt is not my friend, Madame. And Agnes is a witness before God. I am sorry for Madame Marin, but what your husband did with that boy cannot go unpunished.'

'It's not about what Johannes did with Jack, is it?' Nella whispers. 'It's what happened twelve years ago. You think my husband ruined your life. But it wasn't him.'

Meermans' chest swells. 'Madame—'

She is desperate. 'I know what happened, Seigneur. You and Marin. I understand Agnes' jealousy, but—'

'Be quiet,' he hisses. 'Keep your vicious imagination to yourself.'

'Twelve years ago, Johannes made a decision for you,' she says. 'But he didn't—'

'I will not talk of this, Madame.' Meermans looks hastily up and down the street, wincing at the rain that continues to soak the brim of his hat and the squared toes of his boots. 'Agnes is my wife.'

'But it isn't over, Seigneur Meermans. And there's something else you need to know.' Nella pulls out the thousand guilders, the little doll of herself tucked beneath. 'It's some of your money,' she says. 'Johannes sold a substantial amount of your sugar, Seigneur. To Arnoud Maakvrede.'

'One thousand guilders. Still taking me for a fool?' Meermans' countenance changes; he tenses with fear. 'And what's *that*?'

He is looking aghast at the doll. She remembers him in the Kalverstraat march of the St George Militia, staring up at the sign of the sun. 'Where did you get it?' he hisses.

'I – it's me.'

'Put it away. *Now.*'

Nella takes a deep breath. Telling him about Marin she thinks. It might be the only thing that stops this madness. 'Seigneur,' she says, 'Marin is—'

'Never show anyone that, do you hear?' Meermans sweeps his brim of rainwater, splashing Nella's dress.

Nella pushes the doll back in her pocket. 'Why not?' she asks, but he won't reply. 'Seigneur, did Agnes commission a cabinet of your house?'

'A cannonball would do less damage to my marriage than those cursed miniatures,' he snaps, snatching the money from her. 'I will count these guilders then bid you goodbye.'

'There are more to come. And perhaps then you might reconsider your plan against my husband.'

'I have no plan, Madame. It is the will of God.'

'What did the miniaturist send you?'

Meermans holds the rain-spattered guilders aloft. 'Shouldn't you be more worried about how you're going to find more of these?'

Raindrops start falling more steadily. The spectators rush past them, back into the shelter of the gallery. Nella grabs Meermans' arm to stop him from leaving.

'Did the miniaturist send you things yet to happen, Seigneur? Or things that had already passed?'

'Evil hints and vile mockery – no Dutchman should have to put up with it.' He hesitates, and then the chance to speak of it takes him over, the relief that there is one person who might believe him. 'I hid the parcels and messages, but Agnes still found them, or they found their way to Agnes. It's not jealousy that's unsettled her, Madame. It's that cabinet. If she hadn't found out about yours, none of it would have happened.'

'None of what? Is Agnes quite well?'

' "It's the truth," Agnes keeps saying – "he's telling me the truth." So I went to the Kalverstraat to have this miniaturist arrested.'

'You—'

'Your cabinet will remain unfinished, Madame, just as Agnes's has been razed to the ground. The burgomasters were very interested to know there was someone working within the city with no guild jurisdiction. Miniaturist,' he scoffs. 'It's not even a proper job.'

Fear splits Nella apart. She can't feel her body, all she can see is Meermans' large face, his pig-like eyes, the vast expanse of his jaw. 'Seigneur, what have you done to the miniaturist?'

'He'd gone, the vile little spy. But I saw to it that he won't come back. They've given Marcus Smit a hefty fine for allowing a non-Amsterdammer to offer his services on his List. And that house on the Kalverstraat will be a lodging for someone who actually belongs to this city.' Meermans holds the thousand guilders under her nose. 'You don't even realize what an insult this is, Madame, the hundreds and thousands that could have been made. My livelihood is ruined because of Brandt's neglect.'

How obsessed he is with his guilders, how careless of everything else. Nella's blood heats the ropes of her temper; they smoke and snap apart. 'I've seen Agnes' sugar loaves,' she says. 'Your borrowed glory. They're not all rotten – but you are, and so's your wife. Marin made a lucky escape when she decided to turn you down.'

At this, he staggers back.

'And I believe, Seigneur,' she says, 'I *know*, that even if Johannes had sold every one of those loaves by now – you would still be happy to see him drown.'

'How dare you. You're nothing but a little—'

'Keep those guilders,' she says and turns away, calling to the skies. 'And may the miniaturist hound both of you to Hell.'

Arrival

From the Stadhuis, she sets off quickly in the direction of the Kalverstraat, but running footsteps and Cornelia's cry stop her in her tracks. 'Madame, Madame!'

'Cornelia? I found Meermans—'

'Did you tell him about Madame Marin?' Cornelia, stricken, looks up and down the street. She appears green in the dim rainy light, her hands bunched together as if clutching a sprig of invisible flowers.

'No.' Nella feels suddenly exhausted. 'I traded with him. Guilders for a life.'

Cornelia's face falls. 'But did you persuade him to stop testifying?'

'I gave him a thousand guilders as a start for his precious sugar crystals. I cannot promise it will change anything, Cornelia. I've tried. He's done something to the miniaturist, he sent the burgomasters there. I don't know if she's—'

'You must come home.'

'But—'

'*Now.* There's something happening to Madame Marin's heart.'

'Feel it,' says Marin, waddling out of the gloom as soon as the two women arrive and close the heavy door. 'My heart's beating so fast.'

Nella puts her fingers to Marin's neck and feels the pulse jumping, surging through. Marin gasps, reaching out for her.

'What is it?'

'The pain,' she wheezes. 'It's breaking me apart.'

'*Pain*?' says Cornelia, horrified. 'You said no pain had started.'

Marin moans. On her skirts, liquid soaks the dark wool, down towards the hem in an expanding circle.

'Upstairs,' says Nella, trying to sound calm, but her own heart is thumping. 'We'll go to my room. It's nearer the kitchen to fetch water.'

'Is it my time?' Marin asks, her voice high with fear.

'I think it might be. We *have* to fetch a midwife.'

'*No.*'

'We can buy her silence.'

'With what, Petronella? You're not the only one who looks in Johannes' chest.'

'*Please*, Marin. We have enough to pay her! Be calm.'

'I don't want anyone here but you and Cornelia.' Marin grips Nella's hand, as if clinging to it will make everything all right. 'Women do this all the time, Petronella. No one but you can see.'

'I'll fetch hot water,' Cornelia says, rushing down to the working kitchen. Nella notices Blankaart's book is open on a chair.

'You do know what to do, Petronella?'

'I'll try.' Nella was four when Carel was born, nine when

Arabella was dragged out of their mother. She remembers the screaming, the panting, the lowing like a cow let loose in the house. The sheets stained red, piled up later in the garden, ready for the pyre. The weak light on her mother's clammy face, the look of marvel on her father's. There were the others of course, the children who didn't make it. She'd been older then. Nella closes her eyes, trying to remember what the midwives did, trying to forget those little corpses.

'Good,' says Marin, but she looks pale.

'When the pain was bad,' Nella says, 'my mother paced.'

For two hours, Marin paces upstairs, groaning when the rolls of thunder break inside her. Nella goes to the window, thinking of Johannes on his pallet of straw, of Jack, performing his way out of a locked box, of Meermans with his rain-spattered pride and guilders, of Agnes waiting for a message from the Kalverstraat. Where is the miniaturist now? In the corner of Nella's eye, the cabinet house lives behind its yellow curtains, full of puppets held in time. *Your cabinet will remain unfinished, Madame.*

Outside, the rain has intensified; January rain, cold and unrelenting. There is a dog scuffle, the blur of a tawny cat. A sharp stench suddenly fills the room and Nella turns from the window to see the look of pure horror on Marin's face, staring at the pile of hot, bloody faeces at her feet.

'Oh God,' Marin says, covering her face with her hands. Nella guides her back towards the bed. 'My body is not my own. I am—'

'Think no more of it. This is a good sign.'

'But what's happening? I'm falling apart. There'll be nothing left of me once the baby's here.'

Nella wipes away the mess, and puts the soiled towel into a bucket with a lid. When she turns round, Marin is curled up on her side. 'This is not how I imagined it would be,' she says, her face buried in the cushions.

'No,' says Nella, handing her a clean, damp towel. 'It never is.'

Marin crushes lavender in her fist, breathing it deeply. 'I'm so tired,' she says. 'I'm worn to my bones.'

'It'll be all right,' says Nella, but she knows they're only words. Outside in the hallway, she breathes the cool air, relieved to have escaped the bedroom's thick atmosphere, its sluggish pulse of fear. Cornelia comes up the stairs, taking Nella's hand and giving her a smile. 'It is a blessing, Madame,' she says. 'It is a blessing that you came here.'

As evening falls and the rain continues, the waves of pain come constantly. Marin seems to be spiralling through herself. It feels, she says, like a deep, rolling agony. I am a cloud full of blood, she mutters – a giant bruise, my skin being broken over and over. For her comfort, they have taken off her outer skirts and she wears nothing but a cotton blouse and petticoats.

Marin is a vessel for the pain and she is the pain itself. She is nothing she has ever been before. As Cornelia and Nella dab Marin's forehead and rub scented oils in her temples to calm her, Nella thinks of Marin as a mountain, huge and anchored, immoveable. The child inside her is a pilgrim descending her heights, in motion whilst Marin herself is paralysed. Every

step he takes, every prod of his staff in her side, every kick
gives him more power.

Marin cries out. Her hair is plastered to her forehead, her
normally smooth face looks flushed and puffy. Leaning over
the side of the bed, she vomits onto the rug.

'We should get help,' whispers Nella. 'Look at her. She
wouldn't even know.'

Cornelia bites her lip, considering Marin's sweat-soaked,
scrunched-up face. 'She would,' she whispers back, her eyes
shining with fear. 'We can't. Madame Marin wants no one
else to know.' She throws a towel over the thin liquid Marin
has expelled, watching it soak up. 'And anyway, who would we
fetch?'

'There'll be someone in *Smit's List*. We don't know what
we're doing,' hisses Nella. 'Is she supposed to vomit like that?'

'Where is he?' Marin mutters, wiping her mouth on one of
the cushions. Nella gives her the corner of a damp face cloth
to suck the moisture.

'We'll have to look under her petticoat,' she murmurs,
walking back to Cornelia.

Cornelia blanches. 'She would have my head off if I did
that. She doesn't even let me look at her bare back.'

'We have to. I don't know if this pain is normal.'

'You will have to, Madame,' says Cornelia. 'I cannot.'

Marin's eyelids flutter and she begins a low, guttural sound.
It pitches higher, rising out of her like a bugle call. When she
lets out another of these piercing exhalations, Nella hesitates
no longer and gets on her knees, lifting the hem of Marin's
petticoat. It is almost unthinkable, looking between Marin's
legs. It is blasphemy.

Nella ducks her head under the hot fug of the petticoat and looks hard at what she can see. It is the most extraordinary thing she has ever laid eyes on. Neither fish nor fowl, nor godly nor human, and yet strangely all these things at once. At that moment, it seems like something coming from another land. A small thing stretched giant, a huge mouth stoppered with a baby's head.

Nella sees a tiny crown, retches in the heat of the sheets, and pulls her head up into the air. 'I can see it,' she says, elated.

'You can?' asks Marin weakly.

'You have to push now,' says Nella. 'When you see the top of the baby's head you have to push.'

'I'm too tired. He has to make his own way out.'

Nella ducks under the hem of the petticoat again and reaches out to feel the baby. 'His nose isn't out, Marin. He won't be able to breathe.'

'Push, Madame, you have to push,' Cornelia cries.

Marin bellows and Nella places a twig between her teeth. 'Now push again!' she says.

Driving her molars into the wood, Marin begins to push, gargling behind the stick. She spits it out. 'He's ripping me,' she gasps. 'I can feel it.'

Nella pulls up the petticoat and Cornelia covers her eyes. 'You're not ripping,' she says, but she can see a red fissure in that purple hairiness, and yet more blood. She keeps this to herself. 'He's coming,' she calls. 'Keep pushing, Marin, keep pushing.'

Cornelia stands by the window and begins a long and feverish prayer. *Our Father, which art in* – but Marin begins to ululate, a high, unending moan of excruciation, of epiphany.

It is a sound that would flay off skin – but without warning, bird-sudden, the full head of the child breaks through. It comes facing down, its nose towards the sheets, its head a wet dark mass of hair.

'His head is out! Push, Marin, push!'

Marin screams, piercing the women's ears. A lot more blood comes, rushing out hot and wet, soaking the bed. Nella feels queasy, unsure whether there should be this much or not. Marin nearly pulls Cornelia's hand off in the effort to expel the child. Its head turns a quarter circle, and Nella watches in amazement as the little thing appears to try and wriggle itself free.

A shoulder emerges, and again Marin bellows. The baby turns his head back towards the bed.

'Push, Madame, push,' urges Cornelia.

Marin pushes harder, giving herself up to the agony, resisting it no longer, accepting it as her very being. Then she stops, exhausted, unable to move, gasping for air on the bed. 'I can't,' she says. 'My heart.'

Cornelia places a tentative hand on Marin's chest. 'It's jumping like a bird, Madame,' she says. 'It's hammering.'

The room becomes still. Nella on her knees, Cornelia by the pillow, Marin splayed out like a star with her knees drawn up. The flames of the fire lie low, the last logs in need of stoking. Outside, there is only the sound of the rain. Dhana scratches at the door, desperate to be let in.

The women wait. The other shoulder, tiny as a doll's, appears through Marin's widened morass. Marin starts to heave again, and as Nella reaches for the baby's shoulders, its teacup head, its body slithers out onto her surprised hands with a final gush of blood. Her fingers soaked, Nella feels the dense loaf weight of it, eyes closed like a philosopher, limbs wet and bluish, covered in white paste patches, folded tight upon her shaking palms. She checks. Marin's pilgrim of pain is a baby girl.

'Oh, Marin,' she says, lifting up the baby. 'Marin, look!'

Cornelia cries in joy. 'A girl!' she says. 'A little girl!' The long cord attaching her is metallic and muscular, and it snakes back up into Marin's insides. 'Get a knife,' Nella tells Cornelia. 'We need to cut this.'

Cornelia rushes away. Marin is breathing heavily, trying to pull herself up onto her elbows so she can see. She collapses back, barely able to speak. 'My girl,' she says, her voice half-crazed and hollow. 'Is she alive?'

Nella looks at the child, covered in the crust of drying fluid and her aunt's bloodied handprints. Her hair is dark and matted, her eyes still closed, as if now is not the moment to make herself known.

'She's not making a noise,' says Marin. 'Why isn't she making a noise?'

Nella reaches for a warm damp cloth from the pail of water and begins to rub down the baby's floppy arms, its legs and chest. 'Do you know what you're doing?' Marin asks.

'Yes,' Nella replies, but she is making it up. *Wake up, baby*, she thinks. *Wake up.*

Cornelia appears with a carving knife. Still the baby remains quiet, and the room is deathly silent too, everyone waiting, praying with every inch for one small sound of life.

Nella hands Cornelia the child and tries to cut the cord, but for all its human substance, it seems stronger than oak. She has to saw through it, and blood spatters over the sheets and onto the floor. Dhana, who has slunk into the room, trots up, examining the possibility of a meal.

Perhaps it is the arrival of the whippet, perhaps it is the clumsy ministration on her cord – but the baby begins to cry.

'Thanks be to God.' Cornelia bursts into tears.

Marin draws a lengthy ragged breath ending in a sob.

With the child now cupped in Nella's hands, Cornelia ties a dark blue ribbon on the short stub of cord by its abdomen. The stub flops onto the baby's stomach, the little girl finally victorious in battle.

Nella rubs the baby harder with a wet cloth, watching in fascination as the blood begins to pump through the deep-layered lace of veins. Cornelia, who has been standing close by, leans in. 'Can't you see?' she whispers.

'See what?' asks Nella.

'Look,' says Cornelia, pointing at the baby. '*Look.*'

'Thea,' says Marin, making them jump. Her voice is raw and heavy. 'Her name is Thea.' She shifts restlessly in her bed. Her end of the cord is still attached inside her, flowing blood. She tries to put her arms up, but is too exhausted.

'Thea,' echoes Cornelia, staring at the baby as Nella puts her onto Marin's chest. The child moves with her mother's ragged breathing. Marin's fingers tremble over Thea's back, feeling the little rump, the kitten curve of spine. Tears start in her eyes and she weeps again whilst Cornelia soothes her, stroking her forehead. She clutches her child, who nestles her head in the crook of her mother's neck. Marin wears an astonished expression, a mingling of triumph and pain. 'Nella?' she says.

'Yes?'

'Thank you. Thank you both.'

They hold each other's gaze as Cornelia bundles up the massacre of linen. Marin's breath rattles slightly, a sound to make your skin contract and prickle. She turns away to the window to look out into the fallen darkness of the canal. The rain has finally ceased. Above the narrowly divided rooftops, the weathervanes and gables, the moon is high in the star-streaked sky, an uneven half of shining light.

Turning to the closed velvet curtains of the cabinet, it occurs to Nella that Johannes missed something out when he ordered its dimensions. For where is Marin's room – where is her cell of seed pods and maps, her shells and specimens? There are the two kitchens, the study, the salon, bedrooms, even the attic. Perhaps he was protecting her, or perhaps he never thought to have it built. The miniaturist sent no comment on Marin's little space. Her secret room has evaded definition.

The Tale-Teller

Nella and Cornelia try and catch sleep, upright in two of the rosewood chairs dragged up from the salon. They twist uncomfortably as Marin sighs and moans in the bed.

When Nella wakes, the bells are ringing eight o'clock. There remains a disturbing scent in the room; organs exposed, faeces, blood and vulnerable flesh. The fire is out. Around it are the futile scatterings of weak lavender heads, the silver ewer knocked on its side in Marin's agonies. She realizes she is an hour late for her husband.

Frantically, she pulls the curtains apart. Cornelia opens her eyes, springing towards the bed. 'I have to go to Johannes. Now.'

'You can't leave me,' Cornelia pleads. 'I don't know what to do.'

Marin's pillow is soaked in sweat, and Thea, wrapped in a blanket, is asleep on her chest. At the sound of their voices the new mother flicks her eyes open. Beneath the salt-sheen, her skin still smells faintly of nutmeg, and Nella breathes it in. She must go to the Stadhuis, but she feels uneasy leaving Marin like this.

'Nella, go and tell me what they're doing to him,' Marin says, her voice even weaker than the night before. '*Go*. Cornelia, stay with me.'

Cornelia takes Marin's hand and kisses it with the intense affection of a child. 'Of course, Madame. Of course I will.'

Nella goes round to the foot of the bed. The cord is still inside Marin, the end coiled upon the mattress. She tries to pull it, as if that will unstopper something – this sense of dread, but it is stuck, and Marin moans with pain.

'She needs to sleep,' says Cornelia. 'We should leave her.'

'I know you want to call for someone, Nella,' Marin whispers. 'But nobody must know.'

Marin's stomach is a little deflated now that Thea has made her escape, but there is still a lump inside it. When Nella presses it, Marin flinches. This isn't right, Nella thinks; none of this is right. The lump is hard, unyielding, and for a moment she wonders if there is a second child in there, a quieter twin, reluctant to emerge into the chaos. She wishes she knew more, she wishes her mother was there. Never has she felt more powerless.

The breath catches in Marin's throat. Cornelia swoops Thea away as Marin ravages her lungs. 'Madame?' says Cornelia, but Marin bats the air with her hand, a visual echo of her brother.

Thea, on hearing her mother's extraordinary sounds, begins to make more of her own. They are heartbreaking, exhilarating; short, homing squeals of a brand-new voice. Under the cover of the cries, Nella motions Cornelia to join her in the corner. 'Look, Madame, *look*,' the maid whispers, peering miserably at Thea. 'What are we to do?'

'What do you mean?'

'It doesn't seem possible. It cannot be true!'

'Find *Smit's List*,' Nella hisses, ignoring her. 'And bring a wet-nurse, a midwife – anyone who might understand what's happening to her.'

Cornelia looks at the baby in terror. 'But Marin will kill me.'

'Cornelia, just do it. Johannes keeps guilders in the chest in his study. Give the woman whatever it takes to keep her quiet. And if there isn't enough, then – sell the silver.'

'But, Madame—'

Nella flees the room, too desperate to stop.

Running to the Stadhuis, breathless and red-faced, she arrives to find the gallery already full and proceedings underway, and has to take a seat at the back. Drained and delirious, her head aches, her eyes so tired and dry, her fingernails rusty with the residue of Marin's blood. Nella wants to shout to Johannes what Marin has achieved, what magic lies waiting for him back in his house, but she knows she can't. What kind of world do we live in, she wonders, where I might cause Thea harm by announcing her very existence?

She looks over the heads of the gallery spectators, down into the chamber. Johannes is holding his racked body very still upon a chair, with his head held high. Slabbaert is at his desk, the *schepenbank* lined up by his side. Jack is now among the spectators downstairs, watching Frans Meermans perched upon a chair in the centre of the flagstones.

Why isn't Agnes there with him? What have I missed? She spies the back of Pastor Pellicorne's head, his body inclined; excited, anticipating. 'Did Agnes Meermans give her testimony?' she asks the woman next to her.

'At seven o'clock, Madame. Trembling, she was. I thought she was never going to let go of the Bible.' The woman shakes her head as Slabbaert's voice comes to Nella. The Schout is already in full flow.

'Your wife has told us simply what she saw that night of the twenty-ninth of December, Seigneur Meermans,' he says. 'I would never offend a woman's sensibilities, but now it is your turn to speak, I would like to probe deeper. Tell us what you witnessed, Seigneur Meermans.'

Meermans, looking pale and large in his chair, nods. 'We walked round the back of the warehouse and could hear voices. Seigneur Brandt had pushed this young man against the side of the building. The boy's face was pressed against the brick-work. Both of them had their breeches round their ankles, their hats knocked off.'

There are sharp intakes of breath at this; an image of indignity and forceful desire rolled into one. 'Jack Philips – as I now know him to be – was begging to be set free. He saw us and called for help. My wife, you understand, was highly distressed. She had entertained this merchant at her table.'

Meermans' shaking voice fills the room, and to Nella it seems the Stadhuis walls are closing in.

'Go on,' says Slabbaert.

'We heard the cry of Brandt's disgusting release,' Meermans says. 'I left Agnes and as I came near, I could see the lust in Brandt's eyes. He scooped up his breeches as I approached, and began to beat Mr Philips – rapidly, ferociously. There was a dagger. I saw him stab Jack's shoulder. It nearly went into the man's heart – he isn't lying. No woman should have to witness that. No man either.'

The chamber is captivated by Meermans' account. Johannes has bowed his head, hunching his creaking body into a position of resistance.

'Frans Meermans,' Slabbaert says, 'you have known Johannes Brandt for many years. Despite this moment you witnessed – despite your good wife's Bible-sworn testimony – now is your chance to confirm there may be good in this man.'

'I understand.'

'Brandt has said that you knew each other well.'

'As young men, we worked together.'

'And what kind of man was he?'

Meermans seems to be struggling. He cannot even look at the curve of Johannes' back, preferring to stare instead into the pointed black cone of his own hat. 'Astute,' he says. 'Prone to his own philosophies.'

'Johannes Brandt was selling your stock, is this correct?'

Nella feels a slowing sensation inside her, as if her heart has begun to leak the last of its strength. Yet another accusation is going to fall at Johannes' feet – lazy trading, no small crime in Amsterdam.

'It is correct,' says Meermans.

'And with regard to that deal, was the sugar well kept – was Brandt doing his job?'

Meermans hesitates. 'Yes,' he says. 'He was.'

Nella sits up. Why has Meermans said such a thing? According to this account, the sugar in its entirety is pristine. As a couple of the men from the *schepenbank* write something down, she realizes that Meermans has no desire to reveal his anger at Johannes. By concealing the issue of the unsold sugar, Meermans denies Johannes the chance of exposing it as a motive for his revenge. He is blocking the channels of Johannes' defence. Meermans wants this to seem a clean case of unholy behaviour against God and the republic, nothing else. And it is unlikely, she supposes, that Johannes would admit to a sluggish sale. To do so would make him the author of his own damaged reputation.

Nella has not thought Meermans would be so calculating. And yet, she thinks, glancing over at Arnoud Maakvrede – with this very public assurance that the whole crop is good, Meermans may have handed the Brandts a gift for selling it in the future. Guilty for this feather-tip of pleasure, Nella tries to concentrate on the moment in hand.

'So you would say that he was a good merchant?' Slabbaert asks. Meermans takes a deep breath. 'You have sworn an oath to tell the truth,' Slabbaert presses. 'Well?'

'Under oath, I – would question that description.'

'You think he is a *poor* merchant?'

'Historically, I think his reputation has masked a self-centredness. His successes are not all deserved.'

'And yet you employed him to sell your stock?'

'My wife . . .' He trails off.

'What has your wife got to do with this?'

Meermans drops his hat on the floor and retrieves it. Johannes lifts his head, never taking his eyes off his old friend.

'Brandt has always pursued his will with a defiant insistence,' Meermans says, turning to Johannes. 'But I didn't realize how defiant you really were. The bribes you gave, the debts you grew – not just to me but to guilds, to clerks and friends—'

'Who are these men?' Johannes says. 'Is that a formal accusation? Show them to me. Show me their ledgers.'

'It is your soul I am here for today—'

'I have no debt to you, Frans. Nor any man—'

'But God has spoken to me, Johannes.'

'*God?*'

'He has told me that my silence is no longer enough.'

Even as Meermans speaks he sounds surprised, as if he has caught himself in the act, overwhelmed, by his own compulsion, by the bitter relish everyone can taste in his performance.

'You have never been silent, Frans, when it comes to denigrating me.'

'My old friend needs salvation, Schout Slabbaert. He is broken. He is living in the shadow of the Devil. I couldn't see what I saw that evening and remain silent. No citizen of Amsterdam could.'

His speech over, Meermans lifts his head as if expecting relief – but there is none, just Johannes in front of him, his face a picture of disgust. Slowly, Johannes straightens his back in agony. Even from above, Nella can hear the clicks of his bones.

'We are all of us weak, Frans,' Johannes says. 'But some are weaker than others.'

Meermans bows his head; the hat slips from his hands and this time he leaves it where it lies. The sight of his heaving shoulders keeps the crowd in mute suspense. Johannes is a mirror for Meermans to look at himself, and the man has seen a dark hole in place of a reflection. No one touches Meermans, no one comes forward to console or congratulate him for what he's done.

'Frans,' says Johannes. 'Have you not netted a sodomite, a rapacious taker of what he pleases – haven't you helped cleanse these canals and city streets? Why is it, then, that all you can do is cry?'

The chamber erupts into shouts and whistles. Slabbaert calls for quiet so that he and the *schepenbank* can decide their verdict.

'No!' Johannes calls loudly, his gaze breaking away from Meermans and turning to the Schout. 'That is not right.'

The court hushes, the gallery craning to see this man with his glamour and his dangerous nature, who has ripped open their neatly ordered community. Johannes stands up with immense difficulty, leaning on the chair. 'It is customary that the accused may speak.'

Slabbaert clears his throat, looking at him with unconcealed loathing. 'You wish to speak?'

Like a bird with broken wings, Johannes lifts his arms as far as they will reach. Jack lets out a cry as the drapes of Johannes' dark cloak fall crookedly to the floor.

'You put on that costume in the morning, Pieter Slabbaert,' Johannes says. 'As do you, Frans Meermans – and you both hide your own sins and your weaknesses in a box under your beds, and you hope we'll forget them in the dazzle of your robes.'

'Talk of yourself, Johannes Brandt, not me,' says Slabbaert.

Johannes looks at him. 'Am I the only sinner in this room?' he asks, turning round, looking up at the rows of the gallery. 'Am I?'

No answer comes. A stillness has descended on the crowd. 'I have worked for this city,' Johannes says, 'from the moment

I was old enough. I sailed to lands I didn't think existed, even in my dreams. I saw men fight and die and work for this republic, on hot beaches and high seas, risking their lives for a glory greater than the one they'd been handed at birth. Striving, building, never once complacent. *Schout* Slabbaert picks on my African servant, a man from Dahomey. Does the Seigneur even know where Dahomey is, as he drinks his sugared tea, or eats his little buns? Frans Meermans criticizes my freedoms but suffers no guilt enjoying his own. Find a map, Seigneurs, and learn.

'We took in an orphan girl. I sponsored apprentices, worked tirelessly against the drowning waves. And the waves will drown us all, Seigneurs. I have seen the ledger books, I have seen how the VOC is crumbling into the waters – but I have exploited no man's need in the process, I have never perjured a soul with bribes. I tried to make my wife happy, as in the times we spent together, she made me. But the problem is, Seigneurs – Mesdames – those with no horizons want to pull yours down. They have nothing, only bricks and beams, not one jot of God's great joy.' He looks at Jack. 'I pity them, truly. They will never hold the republic in the glory I have seen.'

Walking like an old man, Johannes approaches Meermans. He lifts his hand, and Meermans flinches, expecting a blow. Johannes touches his shaking shoulder.

'Frans,' he says. 'My forgiveness is all yours.' Meermans seems to sag under the force of his touch. 'And you, Jack Philips?'

Jack lifts his gaze and meets Johannes' eye. 'Me?'

'You are a stone, thrown upon a lake. But the ripples you create will never make you still.'

'Get him out!' shouts Slabbaert, pointing at Johannes.

The men of the *schepenbank* stare at the prisoner in mystification, as if, like a giant among men, his mere touch has the power to crumple. The chamber becomes a cacophony of mutterings and tuts, and Pellicorne looks sick with excitement. Death is hovering in the air, hinting at them all, its terror or its bliss beyond. They don't want Johannes to go, they want to keep him here. Rich men have tried to silence them before, but not a single one has ever worn his power so lightly, or pointed out a magistrate's false teeth and raised a laugh.

But Johannes is taken out, and the *schepenbank* gather round Slabbaert in a half-circle as Meermans stumbles to a distant chair, white and shaken. The power of the state is about to exercise itself and people's bodies are tense. Nella is no different. She feels a pressure between her legs, as if she might wet herself with fear.

Minutes pass. Ten, then twenty, thirty. It is horrific to watch these men decide Johannes' fate. There is always the chance of pardon, Nella thinks – but Slabbaert, squatting in the middle of their crescent, keeps up his murmur in the other men's ears.

Eventually they break apart, returning to their chairs. The Schout lumbers into the main square of flagstones and calls for Johannes Brandt to be brought forth once more. Unaccompanied, the prisoner walks slowly back in, dragging his damaged feet. Johannes stops opposite the Schout, and looks straight into his eyes. Nella stands up in the shadows and raises her arm. I'm here, she whispers, but Johannes is focused on

Slabbaert's face, and Nella finds no louder voice to beat her terror.

'You have been caught,' Slabbaert says. 'The crime of sodomy seeks to destroy the holiness and integrity of our society. You are so swollen with your self-belief and wealth that you have forgotten your God. Your pleasure was overheard and witnessed, but so was your sin.'

Slabbaert circulates the centre square of the chamber. Johannes holds his hands behind his back. Something is rising inside Nella; she chokes on the effort of keeping it in.

'Death comes to all of us,' Slabbaert intones. 'It is the only sure thing in this life.'

No, Nella thinks. *No, no, no.*

'For the foul crime you have committed, let it be heard today, the ninth day of January 1687, that I, Pieter Slabbaert, Schout of Amsterdam, and these six members of this city's *schepenbank*, find you, Johannes Matteus Brandt, guilty on the count of the sodomitic attack on Jack Philips, guilty of assault and subsequent bribery. Therefore, I declare your just punishment is to be weighted down at the neck, and to be drowned in the sea, this Sunday at sundown. Let the new baptism of Johannes Brandt be a warning to you all. And may God have mercy on his sinning soul.'

There is a moment – one split-hair second of time – when the chamber falls out of Nella's reach. Free of a body, of a mind, she grapples with the air, trying to stop her crashing world. Then, as Johannes collapses to the floor, the pain Nella has tried to keep at bay floods through her. The chamber becomes shrill with noise, swamping her, pushing her under. She tries to resist, forcing herself past the people on her aisle, knowing only that she must escape this room before she faints. Already they are pulling Johannes up, dragging him out, his feet lifting from the flagstones.

'Johannes,' she calls. 'I will come for you!'

'*No,*' says a voice. Nella is sure she hears it – a woman's voice, coming from the top of the gallery stairs. She turns, searching blindly for its owner. Then she sees it – the sudden movement, the unmistakeable dip and flash of a pale blonde head.

Daughters

Her blood singing notes so high she doesn't think them possible, Nella runs from the Stadhuis. She runs faster than she has ever run in her life, faster than when she was a girl, chasing Carel or Arabella through the woods and fields. People turn to watch her, this mad young woman with her mouth wide open, her eyes streaming – with the wind, they suppose. *Where is she*, Nella thinks, *where has she gone? The burgomasters haven't got her yet.* There was no sign of her when Nella had stumbled to the bottom of the gallery steps, so she ran up the Heiligeweg and is now on the Kalverstraat. Nella, always nimble, propelled by a force that lets her fly.

But when she reaches the miniaturist's house, she stops dead.

The door is still there, but the sign of the sun has gone. The rays of the heavenly body have been roughly hacked from the brickwork, the motto is half vanished, all that is left is *For A Toy*. Mounds of brick dust pile up on the step and the door has been left ajar.

Finally – today of all days – Nella can go inside. She looks up and down the street. The wool-seller opposite is nowhere to be seen. Let them put me in the Spinhuis for trespassing, she thinks, let them drown me too.

Nella pushes the door open and slips into a small room. It

is shockingly bare, the floorboards scratched and dirty, empty shelves on exposed walls. How Cornelia would love to attack this place with her vinegar and beeswax. It looks as if it's never been inhabited.

There is another room at the back, but that looks stripped of life as well. Nella moves silently up a wooden staircase, thinking her ribs will barely cage her heaving lungs.

When she gets to the top, her breath stops in her throat. A wide worktop has been built, running round all four walls; another square room, the floorboards dusty, the windows smeared with streaks of rain. But on the worktop, a world.

Tiny, unfinished pieces of furniture scatter across one part of the bench. Half-sawn and abandoned – oak, ash, mahogany, beech – chairs and tables, beds and cots, even a coffin, dressers, picture frames. There are enough pieces here to furnish ten, twenty cabinets, a lifetime of supplies. In a charred-out hearth, minuscule copper pans and imperfect pewter saucers spill like foreign currency, and the arms of a shrunken candlestick reach out like tiny tendrils.

And then the dolls. Rows and rows of puppet citizens – old men, young ladies, priests and militiamen, a herring-seller, a boy with a bandage on his eyes – and is that Arnoud Maakvrede, with his apron and a round red face? Some headless, others legless, some with blank faces, others with their hair elaborately curled, small hats the size of moths' heads.

With trembling fingers, Nella sorts through the city of Amsterdam for a new Johannes, for one last desperate hope that he will live. *Sunday at sundown* – the three words wreathe in her mind like a never-ending curse. She spies a baby, no larger than her thumbnail, curled up, eyes closed with a small smile.

Then she cries out. Before her is a miniature house, small enough to sit in her palm. It is her house – nine rooms and five human figures carved within, the woodwork considered and intricate. Each room contains a miniature of the miniature she was sent, the green chairs, the lute, the cradle. Astonished, she encloses her life in the centre of her fist.

Nella puts it in her coat pocket with the baby, and after some hesitation she takes Arnoud too. The old residue of Cornelia's superstition about idols is difficult to shake off, but Nella grips them tight, desperate for some comfort in the absence of any miniature Johannes.

Stacked up neatly and clipped with a peg, a pile of letters lies to Nella's left. Her hands still shaking, she picks them up and begins to flick through the sheaf. One: *Please – I have come to see you several times, but still you do not answer.* Another: *I received your miniature. Are you saying I shouldn't marry him?* Another: *My husband threatens to stop this, but then I cannot bear to live.* Another: *You sent my twelve-year-old a cat; I must ask you to desist.* Another: *Thank you. He has been dead ten years and I miss him every day.* Another: *How did you know? I feel a madness creeping in.* Some are merely lists: *Two puppies, black and white, but one must be a runt. A looking-glass, holding a beautiful face.*

Nella rifles for her own, and there it is, the first one written in October last year when she was newly arrived, when Marin stirred the silt and Cornelia could not yet be counted on as a friend. *I cannot guess,* she'd written, *but that you are trained in the art of small things.* How long ago that feels.

All this time, she thinks, I have been watched and guarded, taught and taunted. But never has she felt more vulnerable. Here she is – hidden in the middle of so many of Amsterdam's women, their secret fears and hopes. She is no different. She is Agnes Meermans. She is the twelve-year-old. She is the woman who will miss her husband every day. We are legion, we women; in thrall to the miniaturist. I thought she was stealing my life, but in truth she opened its compartments and let me look inside.

Wiping her eyes, she finds all her other notes – including the long missive she lost the day Jack turned up in the hall, in which she requested the board game *verkeerspel*. It is still attached to the promissory note of five hundred guilders. *Let that be the oil on your front door's stubborn hinges*, she had written, but the miniaturist hadn't even exchanged it. She hadn't taken the money.

She must have been watching me in the Old Church that day, Nella thinks – when Otto went to pray and Agnes grabbed me by the sleeve. Surely the only way she would have known I wanted a *verkeerspel* board was to creep up and pick my pocket? They say that watchers are always watched in Amsterdam, even those who cannot see.

Yet all this smacks too much of Cornelia's spy, and not enough of Nella's prophetess. She inhales the papers, as if to catch the miniaturist's scent – a Norwegian pine perhaps, or the cooling scent of lakeside mint. But there is only dry paper, smelling vaguely of Nella's own room. This letter was intended for the miniaturist, and somehow she received it.

There are annotations down the side of her letters. *Parakeet – green. Husband – yes, Johannes Brandt. She fights to emerge.*

Many doors without a key, and more than one explorer. The dog. The sister, the servant. Maps that cannot span their world. A constant searcher, a tulip planted in my soil who won't have space to grow. Don't go back. Loneliness. Talk to the English boy. Try and make him see.

A tulip planted in my soil, Nella repeats.

Someone is downstairs, closing the front door, clomping around in heavy boots. Nella looks desperately for somewhere to hide, and scurries along into the upper back room. The only thing in it is an unmade narrow bed. Crawling under its frame, she waits.

'Are you up there?' calls a voice. It is a man's voice, soft and slightly querulous. He sounds strange to Nella's ears, not from this city. 'I've come,' he says. 'There've been too many letters. I warned you again and again not to do this.'

He waits, Nella waits. The dust from the floor gets into her nose and before she can stop it, she sneezes. The sound of the boots becomes louder. He's coming up the wooden stairs. Now he begins shuffling around the workshop, tutting as he picks things up and places them back down, muttering as he rummages through the miniaturist's handiwork. 'Such a talent,' Nella hears him say. 'Such a waste.'

He stops. Nella freezes, barely breathing.

'Petronella, why are you hiding under the bed?' he calls through the other room. Nella doesn't move, a chill creeping through her, blood pounding in her head. Her throat constricts, her eyes feel hot. *How does he know my name?*

'I can see your feet,' he goes on. 'Come on, child. We haven't time for this.' This last comment makes him chuckle. Nella thinks she might vomit from the terror.

'Come, Petronella. Let us discuss your strange events.'

His voice is not unkind. Although Nella would rather spend the rest of this awful day hiding under the miniaturist's slovenly bed than face the world – his invitation, delivered so gently, so temptingly, makes her crawl out from her hiding place.

On seeing an old man before her, she cries out in surprise. He is so small, she feels twice his size. 'Who are you?' she asks.

His rheumy eyes widen, and he backs away. A solitary puff of white hair rests on top of his head like an afterthought. 'But you're not Petronella,' he says, mystified.

'Yes I am,' Nella says, her panic beginning to rise. You *are* Petronella, she tells herself. Of course you are. 'Who are you?' she demands again, trying to make her voice a challenge.

The old man looks at her suspiciously. 'I'm Lucas Windel-breke.' Nella sinks onto the bed. 'She's gone,' he says sadly, looking around the corners of the room. 'I know it.'

'The miniaturist?'

'Petronella.'

Nella shakes her head, as if to knock her own name out of her ears. 'Petronella? Seigneur – the woman who lived here was called Petronella?'

'Indeed she was, Madame. In our tongue, is it such an uncommon name?'

Nella supposes not – her own mother shares her name, and Agnes made the same observation back at the silversmiths' feast. 'But she's from Norway,' Nella says, trying to control her confusion. 'She's from Bergen.'

A cloud passes over Lucas Windelbreke's face. 'Her mother was from Bergen. Petronella grew up with me in Bruges.'

'But why?'

'Why?' echoes Windelbreke, looking forlornly round the room. 'Because Petronella is my daughter.'

Nella hears the last word he utters, but it doesn't make sense. It seems impossible to call the miniaturist *daughter* – it conjures Assendelft, a mother, a strange safety, the comfort of human flaw. 'I don't believe you,' she says. 'She's the miniaturist, she doesn't—'

'We all have to come from somewhere, Madame,' Windelbreke says. 'Do you think she was born from an egg?'

The question jars in Nella's mind. She's sure she's heard it before. 'Her mother's family wouldn't have her,' he says.

'Why not?'

Windelbreke says nothing, looking away.

'I wrote to you, Seigneur,' Nella says, feeling dizzy, sitting back down on the bed.

'If you did, your letter was one of many.'

Nella's eyes flick to the pile of letters, visible on the worktop through the other room. 'It was because your daughter was beginning to frighten me,' she says. 'But she never replied, and neither did you. I wanted to know why she was sending me these pieces.'

'In all honesty, Madame, I haven't seen her for years.' He clears his throat and worries his puff of hair, patting his skull as if to keep in the grief quivering up towards the surface. 'All these letters kept arriving, and then I discovered she'd placed this notice in *Smit's List*. "All, and yet nothing".'

'But—'

'It is hard for me to believe that Petronella was trying to frighten you.'

Nella thinks of Agnes, her bitten-down nails, her strange, distracted manner. 'I imagine she frightened many of us, Seigneur.'

He frowns. 'My daughter has a great wonder for the world, Madame. But I concede; she is often greatly dismissive of the way it presents itself to her. She always said there was something beyond her reach and she called it "the fleeting forever".' He sits at the end of the bed, his feet not touching the floor. 'If only she'd been happy with clocks!' he exclaims. 'But Petronella long desired to live outside the boundaries of measured time. Always wayward, always curious. She mocked the way people clung to their timepieces, how everything had to be in order. My work was too restrictive for her, and yet the creations she put together in my workshop would barely sell. I admit – they were extraordinary, but I was loath to put my name to them and claim them as my own.'

'Why ever not?'

He smiles. 'Because they didn't tell the time! They measured other things – things people didn't want to be reminded of. Mortality, a broken heart. Ignorance and folly. Where numbers should have been, she painted customers' faces. She sent them messages that sprang out of the clock when the hand reached twelve. I had to beg her to stop. She said it was because she could see into their souls, their inner time, a place that paid no heed to hours and minutes. It was like trying to tame a cat.'

'Did you believe that she could see into people's souls?' Nella asks. 'She seemed to know so much that was going to happen to me.'

Windelbreke rubs his chin. 'Did she?' he says. He looks towards his daughter's workshop. 'You sound as adamant as all those other women who wrote to me. So keen to give up self-dominion.'

'No! If anything, Seigneur, she has helped me take it back.'

She is silenced by the truth of this, her protestation. Windelbreke spreads his hands. 'She gave you back your own possession.' He smiles, looking shyly pleased. 'All I can tell you is this, Madame. My daughter believed readily that what she was doing had purpose. But I tried to teach her that her gift of observation could only go so far. Other people would have to choose to see what she saw too, or she'd wear herself to nothing. If she didn't reply to you, perhaps she felt you'd understood. You saw what she was trying to say.'

Nella can feel tears coming. 'But I don't understand,' she says.

'But I wonder if you do.'

Nella stares at the lines on her palms, leading off her skin, directing her to places she cannot see. She clenches them, rolling up these maps of her self. 'Perhaps I do,' she says. Windelbreke unnerves her with his probing questions. She wants to run home to the Herengracht, to be with Marin and Cornelia and Thea, to sit with Dhana and stroke her ears. But they will ask about Johannes and she will have to tell them. *Sunday at sundown.* She doesn't know if she has the strength.

'I don't know what she's been doing all these years – what

strange skills she's picked up or the company she's kept,' Lucas Windelbreke says. 'She's the cleverest person I ever knew. But if you see my daughter, Madame, please tell her to come home.'

⟨❦⟩

Nella leaves Windelbreke, a daughter missing, slowly packing her beautiful handiwork into a set of boxes. 'It can't stay here,' he says. 'But I'm not throwing it away. Perhaps she'll come to Bruges and retrieve it.' He sounds unconvinced.

Nella thinks of the women throughout Amsterdam waiting for their next delivery. Some in trepidation, many in hope, others with the glazed eye of those who cannot live without something else to support them, without the miniaturist and her quality so elusive. They will wait for their happiness. And when it doesn't come – when the pieces stop, as they stopped for Nella – what will they do then? These women gave her their letters, and the miniaturist exchanged them for the currency of themselves. They own themselves, to barter, hoard or spend.

Nella walks back down the Kalverstraat, oblivious to the calls of shopkeepers. *Sunday at sundown.* How will I tell them? she asks herself. How will I tell them that Johannes is going to have a stone put round his neck before being thrown into the sea?

Numbly, she keeps walking through the streets, onto the Golden Bend. Cornelia is standing at the door, waiting, and at the sight of her, Nella's news of Johannes, and the secret of Lucas Windelbreke and the miniaturist, dies in her throat.

The girl is pale and sombre. She looks so much older than her years.

'We did something wrong,' is all Cornelia says. 'We did it wrong.'

A Closing Door

Time, in these instances, is not easy to measure. Nella ploughs the freshest of her memories – leaving Marin awake, running to the Stadhuis and then to the Kalverstraat in search of a salvation that was never going to come. All of it on this self-same day – but Slabbaert's sentence, Windelbreke's secrets – they feel as if they happened last year. Marin has swallowed time, and on the map of her pale skin, Nella cannot find the clue of when she sank and how she disappeared.

Marin's cleverness has endured until the end, enabling her to leave unseen. Her spirit has slipped through their fingers. Even in her final breath has she evaded, keeping for herself the moment of her death.

'No,' Nella chokes. 'No. Marin, do you hear me?'

But Nella knows that she is no longer there. Standing with Cornelia at the side of the bed, they touch Marin's face. She is covered in a sheen of moisture, as if she's been lying in the rain.

Shaking, Cornelia gathers up Marin's solitary legacy from her inert breast. She lifts Thea up, her entire hand cupping the baby's tiny skull. Cornelia has swaddled her with so many lengths of cotton, only her nutshell face peeps through. Nella and Cornelia remain at the bed, still obedient to Marin in their shock.

'It isn't possible,' Nella breathes.

'There was nothing I could do,' says a voice at the open door. Nella jumps, turning in horror to see a large woman walking towards them, sleeves rolled up, built like an Assendelft cow-herd.

'Who—'

'Lysbeth Timmers,' the woman interrupts. 'Your maid found me in *Smit's List*. You should take that child out of here immediately.'

'She was the nearest,' Cornelia mutters to Nella, her voice hoarse as she holds Thea tight. 'You *told* me to, Madame.'

Nella stares at this Lysbeth Timmers, shielding Marin's prone body from the stranger's shrewd observance. In this odd, held calm, she wonders how she could have been so reckless, telling Cornelia to throw open their doors and expose their secrets. A fox in the hen house, Lysbeth stands with her hands on her hips.

'She's a wet-nurse,' Cornelia whispers. 'But she didn't pass the midwife examination.'

'I birthed four children of my own,' Lysbeth answers equably, overhearing. She strides towards them, plucking Thea out of Cornelia's arms.

'No!' Cornelia cries as Lysbeth carries the child to the threshold, where she pulls up a chair. The wet-nurse examines the baby back and front, as if Thea were a suspect vegetable at market. After running her reddened fingers over Thea's tight little cap, without further ado she pulls down her loosened corset and shirt. She hikes Thea onto her dark pink nipple and lets the child feed. 'You've done a bad job,' she observes.

'What do you mean?' Cornelia says. Nella hears the inexplicable panic in her voice.

Lysbeth looks up at her. 'Swaddling her like this.'

Exhausted, Nella bristles. 'We're not paying you for your criticism, Mrs Timmers,' she says.

'Look,' says Lysbeth, unruffled. 'Their limbs are like wax at this age. If you bind them wrong, you'll have a crooked spine and twisted legs by the time she's one year old.'

She pulls Thea off her breast and begins unravelling her like a parcel. In a second, she has whipped off the child's cap.

Cornelia takes a step forward, tense, alert.

'What's the matter?' Nella asks. In the rush to the Stadhuis, she had barely looked at the child the morning after the birth. But now, as she remembers Cornelia's agitation – *It doesn't seem possible. It cannot be true* – her own eyes see what the astonished maid was trying to tell her.

With her head of dark hair, so black for a Dutch baby, Thea's newly washed skin is the colour of a candied walnut. The baby's eyes have opened, and her irises are small pools of night. Nella comes closer; she cannot stop staring.

'Thea,' Cornelia breathes. 'Oh, Toot.'

As if she has heard this, Otto's daughter turns to the maid. She offers a newborn's gaze; a world entirely of herself.

Lysbeth looks up at Nella, waiting for her to speak. As the silence in the room thickens, Marin's words begin to race around Nella's head. *This child will be far from convenient. If he survives, this child will be stained.* Surely Lysbeth can hear her hammering heart? Beside her, Cornelia seems paralysed.

'You will be amply rewarded – for all your help. A guilder

a day,' Nella manages to say, a tremor in her voice revealing the shock at what she's seeing; a face in a face, a secret rising. *From back to front, I love you.*

Lysbeth puffs out her cheeks in contemplation, her rough hand gently patting Thea's black hair. The illegal wet-nurse takes in the paintings, the pendulum clock, the silver ewer. Her eyes focus on the huge cabinet holding their miniature lives, standing so opulent, so redundant, that Nella feels ashamed.

'I'm sure I will, Madame,' Lysbeth finally observes. 'I'll take four guilders a day.'

Nella is still too astonished to say much, but she's been in Amsterdam long enough to know that one barters as soon as breathes. Generally, she feels relieved that Lysbeth seems to desire their money more than their secrets, but perhaps the woman is enjoying her sudden luck too much. I will not be beholden, Nella tells herself. The wet-nurse seems to know the chaos that swirls beneath the surface, but unfortunately she also knows her price.

Maybe Johannes was right – even abstracts such as silence can be negotiated as one might a haunch of deer, a brace of pheasant, a handsome slab of cheese. She thinks of Johannes' dwindled chest of guilders. You must go and see Hanna, she reminds herself. All that sugar needs to sell. But when? Things are already spilling over, just as Otto said they would.

'Two guilders a day, Madame.'

Lysbeth Timmers wrinkles her nose. 'Given the unusual circumstances I'm sure you'll understand. Three.'

I nearly told Frans Meermans that Marin had birthed his child, Nella thinks, inwardly wincing at what might have happened had he caught that secret too. 'So be it, Mrs Timmers,' she says. 'Three guilders a day. For *all* your help.'

Lysbeth nods, satisfied. 'You can rely on me. I'm not interested in the burgomasters.'

'I'm sure I don't know what you mean, Mrs Timmers.'

Lysbeth grins. 'Like that, is it? Well, a father's a father in my world. All the same. And she's a pretty one, make no mistake.'

'No mistake,' echoes Nella, trying to take control of her daze. Does Otto even know? she wonders. Did Marin ever tell – is that why he ran away? Cornelia looks as if she's going to faint, and Nella wonders if the maid ever suspected this extraordinary truth. How determinedly she told the tale of Marin and Frans Meermans, how she boasted of her credentials as a keyhole queen! Otto was Cornelia's friend, her equal in this house. She has lost her crown.

'They like it, you know,' Lysbeth says.

'What on earth do you mean?' snaps Cornelia.

'The tightness of the swaddling,' observes Lysbeth drily, blinking away Cornelia's provocation. 'It reminds them of the womb.'

Grief and confusion spreads over Cornelia's face. When she thinks of Johannes in the Stadhuis and what has been indicted on his head, Nella knows it will be almost impossible to tell Cornelia another truth.

In Marin's room, amid the seeds and feathers, Lysbeth proceeds to demonstrate the correct order of the swaddling bandages. Thea is pliant and half-asleep. She then feeds her again, and the child rouses, holding on for life, with an intensity of purpose that reminds Nella of Marin, poring over the ledger book or staring at one of Johannes' maps. She stands peering at the wonderful conundrum, the peach toffee glow of Thea's skin. Thea makes a little snuffle and curls her fingers to a fist. In the pattern of her newborn face, she has clearly claimed her father, but it is too early to tell exactly how far on one side the coin will fall.

Cornelia, moving as if in a dream, begins to light oil burners through the house, keeping the smell of death at bay. She turns all the mirrors to the wall, making sure her mistress's spirit finds its way to Heaven. They do not want Marin stuck in the chimneys; they want her soul to fly through the clouds above the Amsterdam roofs.

They will have to move Marin's body very soon, Lysbeth tells them. The bad airs will not be good for Thea. 'Put a plain sheet on her, Madame.'

'A plain sheet?' says Nella. 'I think not. Marin deserves the finest damask.'

'She'd probably prefer the plain,' comes Cornelia's small voice.

Once the child is asleep, Lysbeth collects her three guilders, tucking them into her apron pocket. 'Call for me when she wakes. I'm not far.'

Making her way through the kitchen door, under Nella's insistence – no front door for Lysbeth Timmers, however much she's being paid – she stops again and turns to her new employer. 'What's that thing you've got up there?' she asks. 'The big cupboard in the corner. I've never seen anything like it.'

'It's nothing,' Nella says. 'A toy.'

'Quite a toy.'

'Mrs Timmers—'

'You must get the child baptized. Be quick, Madame. These early days are dangerous.'

Nella's eyes fill with tears. She thinks of Slabbaert's last words. *Let the new baptism of Johannes Brandt be a warning to you all.*

Lysbeth looks at her with a mixture of pity and impatience. 'Just keep her cap on, Madame,' she whispers. 'I dare say it's beautiful hair, but the poor child does have to live in these streets.'

As she says it, Nella wonders how that will even be possible. But Cornelia will never let the child go.

Cornelia is huddling by the cradle. Her face is waxen, blank. She looks wizened, and Nella is reminded of their first ever encounter in the hallway, her cockiness, her confident eye-balling of the new arrival. It does not seem possible that this is the same girl.

'I tried, Madame.'

'You did everything you could.'

Nella pauses, listening to the house. In the garden, a bundle of stiff browned sheets burns to light flakes, charred cotton fibre floating in the sky. Amongst the flames, Nella sees the sewn square of a cushion, a colourful bird's nest in foliage. *Cornelia has embroidered too much.* Every moment, Marin's voice.

'We're going to keep Thea, aren't we, Madame?' Cornelia whispers. 'She's safest here.'

'We're already bribing new people to keep our latest secret.

When will it ever stop?' Nella says. It'll stop when the money runs out, the voice in her head replies.

'I will die before I let anything happen to this child.' Cornelia's eyes are fierce.

'Cornelia, even if it means taking her out of here to Assendelft, I promise you we won't be giving her away.'

Now it is Assendelft which feels as far away as Batavia, not Amsterdam, as Agnes once said. Nella hears Marin again, her voice clear as a bell, grey eyes lighting up with scorn. *There's nothing to do in the countryside.*

Cornelia nods. 'Thea can wear a cap for her hair outside, and leave it free when she's indoors.'

'Cornelia—'

'And we will have to tell Pastor Pellicorne about Madame Marin. We can't just have her buried anywhere. I don't want her put in St Anthonis'. It's too far. I want her here, within the city walls—'

'Let me make you something to eat,' says Nella, sensing the maid's rising hysteria. 'Some cheese and bread?'

'Not hungry,' Cornelia replies, jumping to her feet. 'But we must make something and take it to the Seigneur.'

Nella sits, depleted in the face of Cornelia's mania, unable to find the words to explain what has happened today at the Stadhuis. She longs to see Johannes, but they will have to do something about Marin, first thing tomorrow morning, after some sleep. Today is Thursday. By Sunday at sundown, she, Cornelia and Thea will be in freefall, Lysbeth Timmers hanging on to their hems. It seems as easy to take a life in this city as it is to lift a counter off the *verkeerspel* board.

There may never have been a baby like this in the whole of

Amsterdam. There are the Sephardi Jews, of course – the dark Lisboa boys and girls, and the mulattos brought by Portuguese merchants, who wait outside the synagogue on the Houtgracht, reserving seats for their mistresses. There are the Armenians fleeing the Ottoman Turks – and who knows what happens out in the Indies – but in Amsterdam, people keep to their own, they do not mix. It's why people always stared at Otto. Yet here is a pure combination of the republic's opposites, born not thousands of miles away, but in the secret folds of the fatherland, on the richest part of the Golden Bend. Thea is even more scandalously unique to these cobbles and canals than her father.

From back to front, I love you. Otto and Toot, full circle, the notes and the child he left behind a reflection of himself. Nella remembers the whisperings at night, the closing doors, the blank face of Cornelia when in the mornings Nella would ask her if she'd been up late. Marin, in tears at the Old Church. Otto, terrified, weeks later in the same pew. Had Marin told him then?

The only thing Nella may ever understand about Otto and Marin is Thea, who in turn will be a secret to herself; her mother dead and father missing. Nella thinks of another mother, in Bergen, and another frustrated child, growing up in Bruges with an elderly father. Why was the miniaturist taken away? I am crazed for lack of sleep, Nella tells herself, trying to look backwards, to signs she might have missed about Otto and Marin, or the other Petronella. She cannot be sure if a new day will make any of it easier to understand.

Cornelia peers at Thea's face. 'I wanted it to be Seigneur Meermans,' she says in a quiet voice. 'I wanted it to be him.'

'Why?'

But Cornelia doesn't reply; this is the stretch of her confession. She had been so determined about the identity of Marin's secret love, the gift of salted piglet and Agnes' wifely jealousy. *I should have given Cornelia more chores*, said Marin, grumbling about her propensity to embroider stories. Meermans' gaze would linger on Marin, true; but Marin herself never presented any proof. And what did she say when questioned over her affections? You're carrying his child, Nella had said to her. *I have taken things from Johannes that were not mine to take*, was her reply. Elliptical Marin, as ever, living in the shadows between lies and truth.

'I want things to be the way they were,' Cornelia says.

'Cornelia,' Nella says, reaching for her hand. 'I have to tell you about Johannes.' She feels her grief bloom, an unwieldy rose dropping its petals too quickly. Clear-eyed, quiet, the maid sits on the bed.

'So tell me,' Cornelia says, not letting go.

Nella thinks the walls will break with the force of Cornelia's tears. Thea wakes of course, and Nella lifts the crying newborn from her cloud of cotton. The child is mesmerizing, their little crotchet wrapped in white, her lungs a tiny pair of bellows calling to the room.

'Why has God punished us, Madame? Did He always plan this?'

'I don't know. He may have posed the question, but we are the answer, Cornelia. We must endure. For Thea's sake, we must emerge from this.'

'But how? How will we live?' Cornelia asks, burying her face in her hands.

'Fetch Lysbeth,' Nella says, 'Thea needs to feed.'

Calmed by the need to calm, Cornelia quietens at the baby's noise. Blotchy-faced and numb, she leaves Nella on the bed, with Thea squalling in her arms. Lying back with the child, something digs into the top of Nella's spine, and when she feels under the pillow, her fingers find a small, hard object.

Otto, she breathes, looking at his doll, his real daughter weighing the crook of her other arm. Nella hadn't noticed he'd been taken from the cabinet. Did Marin sleep here, night after night with him hidden beneath her, a comfort that failed to conjure him home?

'Where are you?' Nella asks, as if her words will bring him back where the doll has so miserably failed. Thea cries for milk, their noisy cherub of a brave new world. This child has a beginning, just as Johannes and Marin have been handed an end.

Quietly, in the midst of the baby's chaos, Nella utters a particular prayer. Back in Assendelft, bereft at the death of his father, Carel had written a summons to God. It was defiant and childish, in the best sense of the words. It comes back to Nella now, the words etched in her heart, and she murmurs it into the shell of Thea's tiny ear. A call for comfort, a desire for resurrection. A never-ending hope.

Empty Rooms

Lysbeth Timmers sleeps in the kitchen. The next morning, Friday, her face looks misted with the room's damp air. 'The lady's body,' she says. 'You'll need some help.'

Nella feels a surge of gratefulness. She hears Johannes' voice in her head, questioning his sister. *Marin, do you think this house is run by magic?* Not by magic, Nella thinks, but by people like Cornelia and Lysbeth Timmers.

Cornelia, whose fingers barely brushed Marin in life, now has to handle her mistress and hold her tightly. 'She always hated to be touched,' the maid says. Presented with the reality of Thea, Nella wonders how true this statement can really be.

'This one.' Cornelia holds up a long black skirt. She is talkative today, as if her voice will banish the demons calling from the Stadhuis, the words *Sunday at sundown* now spiralling in her head too. The fabric panels of the corset they select are lined with lengths of sable and squirrel, and a strip of velvet runs along the spine. 'It will suit Madame Marin perfectly,' Cornelia says.

Nella feels as if she is standing on wet sand that could sink at any moment. Her armpits are wet with sweat, her bowels feel loose. 'So it will,' she replies with a weak smile.

Lysbeth frowns. 'Clothes are all very well,' she says. 'But we must prepare her first.'

This is the hardest part.

They sit Marin up, and Lysbeth uses a sharp knife to cut off the petticoat and cotton blouse. Nella steels herself as the fabric parts in two, trying to focus solely on the task in hand. It is almost too painful to look at the empty, sagging pouch where Thea has lived for nearly nine months – and unavoidable to see Marin's rounded, ready breasts. Between her legs the birth cord still remains, the thing they couldn't get out.

Cornelia gulps for air, from grief or repulsion, Nella cannot tell. The entrance Thea made into the world seems sealed up, but Nella dares not go too close, fearing she may dislodge more blood. Instead, they rub the remainder of the lavender oil into other parts of Marin's body, smothering her gradually intensifying smell, so strangely sweet.

Nella and Lysbeth stagger as they lift Marin; Cornelia gently puts on the skirt, tying it with shaking fingers. As Nella leans her forward, Marin's head thuds to her chest. Cornelia threads an arm through the corset. 'I haven't dressed her for years,' she says, her voice light and high, skimming on her breath. 'She always did it herself.'

Cornelia rolls on woollen stockings, and a pair of rabbit-skin slippers embroidered with the initials *M* and *B*. Nella washes Marin's face, dabbing it reverently with fresh towels. Lysbeth unbinds her hair and re-plaits it, tucking it in a neat white cap.

'Wait,' Nella says. She runs to Marin's small room, where Thea lies sleeping in her oak cradle. Nella pulls down the map of Africa, still annotated with its unanswered questions – *Weather? Food? God?*

'We should put more of her collections in with her,'

says Cornelia, when she sees what Nella has brought. 'The feathers and spices – those books.'

'No,' says Nella. 'We're going to keep them.'

'Why?'

'Because one day they'll be Thea's.'

Cornelia nods, looking overwhelmed by the logic and melancholy of such an idea. Nella imagines Cornelia in four years' time, showing the little girl the wider world her mother once so assiduously, no doubt lovingly pieced together. As the maid's blue eyes take on an absent look, Nella wonders if Cornelia is thinking of that future too – Thea, dangling her little legs over the bed, shown this strange inheritance by the maid who loved her mother. Nella wants Cornelia to cling to the image, a future boon to drag her from the horror of today.

'She looks peaceful,' says Cornelia.

But Nella sees the familiar furrow on her sister-in-law's brow, as if she was doing a mildly taxing sum, or thinking of her brother. Marin does not look peaceful. She looks as if she didn't want to die. There was still so much to do.

Whilst Lysbeth and Cornelia go to Marin's room to tend to Thea, Nella walks downstairs to Otto's tool cupboard, where his implements are laid out on a tidy shelf, ever ready, neatly oiled and sharpened. She finds what she's looking for. Assendelft farmers used to call them bludgeoners, and she watched them as a girl, their stocky arms swiping hardily at dying trees.

Back upstairs, the women's voices murmuring along the corridor, Nella locks her bedroom door for the first time.

She eyes it in the corner, Johannes' beautiful gift. Back in

October, he had called the cabinet a distraction, but Nella, on the threshold of a new life, had taken it as no more than an insult to her fragile status. She rejected this uninhabitable world, then gradually believed it held the answers, that the miniaturist was the one who held the light. But Johannes was right, in a way, Nella thinks. Everything about this cabinet was indeed distracting. So much happened while I was looking the other way. I was sure I'd been standing still, yet look how far I've come.

Only now is Nella sure what must be done. She approaches the cabinet and lifts up her arms, mirroring the local men who'd hacked at groaning trunks. One inhaled breath, one held moment, then down the axe comes. It drives through the tortoiseshell, it buckles the splintering elm. Pewter veins snake like plant roots, velvet curtains crumple to the ground. Nella smashes and smashes, bringing the house to its knees. The floors collapse, the ceilings cave, the craft and time, the detail and power, tumbling to her feet.

Blood pumping through her body, Nella drops the axe and reaches into the wreckage. She rips the Italian leather wall-paper, the tapestry, the glue between the marble floor. Taking the books, she tears their tiny pages. She crushes the betrothal cup in her clenched fist, and the soft metal submits to her pressure, the couple round the side flattened to nothingness. Gathering the rosewood chairs, the birdcage, Peebo, the box of marzipan, the lute, she breaks them under the sole of her shoe, all unrecognizable, for ever ruined.

With fingers like claws, Nella breaks open Meermans' body, shredding his broad-brimmed hat. She pulls Jack's head off like a dying flower. With a piece of elm, she smashes

Agnes' hand, still clutching the blackened sugar loaf. Nella does not spare Cornelia nor her own two selves – the grey and gold, one sent by the miniaturist, the other left by Agnes on the Stadhuis gallery floor. She hurls them into the pile along with Johannes' sack of money. Only Marin and Johannes does she keep intact, putting them in her pocket with Otto and the little child. Thea can have them when she's older; portraits out of time.

She feels Arnoud in her pocket and hesitates. It's just a doll, she tells herself, still astonished by the miniaturist's strange alchemy of craftsmanship and spying. It's nothing. She weighs him in her palm. Most of the sugar has not yet sold. Almost hating herself, Nella stuffs the pastrymaker hastily back into her skirt, safe and out of sight.

Emptied, exhausted, Nella can destroy no more; her wedding gift has turned into a pyre. Sliding to the floor beside it, she rests her head upon her drawn-up knees. With no one to hold her, she holds herself; her body wracked with sobs.

The Canker in the Orchard

That evening, Cornelia will not be dissuaded from going to the Stadhuis prison. In a fever of activity, she has made pasties of hen and veal, rosewater and sweetened pumpkin, cabbage and beef. They smell of home, of a solid kitchen with good utensils, a sensible cook at the helm.

'I'm going, Madame,' she says. Determination has put some colour back in her face.

'Don't tell him what's happened here.'

Cornelia draws the warm package of her food to her body, her eyes welling with tears. 'I would rather die than break his heart, Madame,' she says, burying the pies deep in her apron.

'I know.'

'But if we did tell him about Thea, a baby, a beginning—'

'It would give him more regret for the life he is about to leave. I don't think he could bear it.'

Cornelia bridles at the awful decisions they are being forced to make. Nella watches the maid's forlorn figure as she moves up the canal.

Lysbeth is in the working kitchen, folding fresh cloths for Thea. 'Will you stay with her for a couple of hours while I go out?' asks Nella.

Lysbeth looks up. 'Gladly, Madame.'

It pleases Nella that Lysbeth doesn't ask where she's going;

so unlike Cornelia. She wonders what Lysbeth might say about the carnage in her room, the damage wreaked by a child bride upon her toy. 'There's firewood upstairs,' she says to the wet-nurse. 'We should keep Thea warm.'

⋙⋘

Nella is granted entry through the door of the *kerkmeester*'s room behind the organ of the Old Church. Pastor Pellicorne is at his desk. It is for Cornelia that Nella is here. She would rather have Marin buried quietly in St Anthonis' church, away from public scrutiny. 'Wouldn't that have been what she wanted too?' she'd asked Cornelia.

'No, Madame. She'd have wanted the highest civic honour this city can bestow.' This is normality, Cornelia stilling the surface. Thus Marin's legacy lives on; that the most obsessive of Marin's preoccupations should remain alive in her maid is a bitter heartening.

Pellicorne looks at Nella, trying to bury the glint of his distaste. You know who I am, she thinks, her hatred budding. You were standing outside the Stadhuis, bellowing for all to hear. Nella has come armed in her wealth, but pearls and a silver dress feel like flimsy armour in the face of Pellicorne's disdain.

'I have come to report a death,' she says, looking straight at him, her voice clear.

Pellicorne dips his chin upon his abundant collar. 'I thought that wasn't till Sunday?' he says, pulling his bulging burial register towards him, a large leather-covered book accounting for all the bodily traffic of this city, leaving for Heaven or Hell. He dips his pen in the ink.

397

Nella steadies herself, breathing deeply. 'I've come to report the death of Marin Brandt.'

Pellicorne's pen hovers. He peers at Nella, his hard face craning forward over the ledger. 'Death?' he utters.

'Yesterday afternoon.'

The pen is laid down, Pellicorne leans back. 'May God bless her soul,' he says eventually. He narrows his eyes. 'Tell me, how did our sister Marin Brandt leave the world?'

Nella pictures Marin's corpse, the bloodied sheets, newborn Thea, then she travels back; Otto and Marin intertwined, their secret buried deep in Marin's living body.

'She died of a fever, Pastor.'

He looks alarmed. 'The sweating sickness, you think?'

'No, Seigneur. She was sick for a while.'

'True, I have not seen her in church these last weeks.' Pellicorne draws his hands together, rests his chin upon the tips of his tapering fingers. 'I had wondered if her absence was anything to do with her brother.'

'The shock would not have helped, Seigneur. She was already very weak,' Nella says quietly, hatred blooming within her, barely letting her breathe.

'It most certainly would not.' Nella keeps silent – she does not want to give this man the fuel he craves. 'Has your *gebuurte* come to help?' he asks.

She remembers her father's funeral in Assendelft, how the neighbours had come to aid her grieving mother; undressing his corpse, putting him in a nightgown, lifting his stiffening body onto an iron sheet, laying straw for leakage. Then the young unmarried females of the village, coming to lay palms and flowers, laurel leaves. There was no such *gebuurte* for

Marin, just Cornelia and herself, desolation creeping through their panic – and Lysbeth, a woman who'd never even met her alive. At least Cornelia has lit those oil burners.

Nella is pained by the lack of dignity Marin is suffering in death. There should have been a *gebuurte*, for Marin was a good person, she was strong. In another life she could have led an army. But in the end, Marin kept no friends close – only one, and he is missing.

'Yes, Pastor,' she replies. 'The neighbours have come. But we have to move her soon. We have to bring her to the church.'

'She never married,' Pellicorne says. 'A waste.'

For some of us, Nella thinks, it's a waste to be married.

It is completely dark outside. In the main body of the church, she can hear the organist practising on his pipes, torches being lit for evening prayer. The pastor stands up, smoothing his black tunic as if it is an apron. 'If you have come to bury her here,' he says, 'that is impossible.'

There is a moment of silence. Nella keeps her feet upon the floor, her back straight.

'Why, Pastor?'

Her voice is strong and reasonable, because she's made it so. She will not let it trill, or give way to emotion. Pellicorne closes the burial register and looks at her, surprised, as if he is not used to being asked to elaborate. 'We cannot have her, Madame. She is tainted by association. As are you.' He pauses, boring into her with his stony eyes. 'You have all of my pity, Madame.'

'And yet none of your mercy.'

'We are overflowing. I give my sermons to more skeletons

than flesh. Dear God, the stink,' he says to himself. 'All the perfumes of Araby cannot mask these rotting Dutchmen.' To Nella, he merely adds, 'I am sorry for her death, but I cannot have her here.'

'Seigneur—'

'Go to the men at St Anthonis', they will help you.'

'No, Pastor. Not beyond the city walls. She worshipped here.'

'Burial within the city is not an option for most these days, Madame.'

'It must be for Marin Brandt.'

'I have no more room. Do you hear?'

Nella pulls out of her pocket two hundred guilders from Arnoud and lays them on Pellicorne's register. 'If you will organize the gravestone, the coffin, the men to carry it, and the space in the church floor, I will, upon completion, double that sum,' she says.

Pellicorne looks at the money. It is money coming from the wife of a sodomite. It is money coming from a woman. It is the deep-lying root of evil, but it is a lot of money. 'I cannot accept this,' he says.

'Greed is the canker we must cut out,' Nella replies, her expression mournful.

'Precisely.' She can see he is pleased to have his sermon echoed.

'You, a man of God, are surely best placed to guard the canker,' Nella continues.

'Once it's been removed,' he replies, his eyes flicking to the guilders.

'Of course.'

'There are many alms required for our city's unfortunates.'

'And something must be done for them, or the canker begins to bloom.'

They sit in silence.

'There is a small space in the east corner of the church,' Pellicorne says. 'Room for a modest slab, nothing more.'

What a fool he is, Nella thinks. He is just a man like every other man, no closer to God than the next. She wonders how much will be skimmed off the four hundred before the pall-bearers and the alms are paid. Would Marin like it, in the corner? She spent her life in the corner, perhaps she would prefer it in the nave. But then, in the nave, people would walk up and down on her. Some citizens probably desire such an ending, so they never are forgotten, held in memory and prayed for – but to Nella's mind it is too undignified for Marin. It is better in the corner.

'I am speaking the truth, Madame,' says Pastor Pellicorne. 'We are full up. That corner is the best that I can do.'

'It will suit,' she replies. 'But I want the finest elm for the coffin.'

Pellicorne resumes his pen and opens the register once again. 'I will see to it. The funeral could be next Tuesday evening, after the normal service?'

'Very well.'

'It is easier in the night. The smell that rises when you open up the floor puts people off their prayers.'

'I see.'

'How many people will come?' he asks.

'Not many,' Nella replies. 'Her life was quite secluded.' She says this almost as a challenge, to see if he will contradict her, or offer some knowing aside regarding Marin's hidden life. The bookshops she visited, he might say. The company she kept, that Negro she paraded through the streets.

But Pellicorne merely purses his lips. Seclusion is bad; Nella knows what his expression means. Civic-mindedness, neighbourly surveillance, everyone checking up on everybody else – that's what keeps this city ticking on. Not cloistering yourself away from prying eyes. 'It will be a brief ceremony,' he says, putting the guilders into the register.

'We don't like pomp,' she replies.

'Precisely. And aside from her name and dates, what would you have inscribed on the gravestone?'

Nella closes her eyes and conjures Marin in her long black dress, the perfection of her cap and cuffs concealing so much turmoil underneath. Publicly rejecting sugar but sneaking candied walnuts, hiding Otto's love notes, annotating unvisited countries on her brother's pilfered maps. Marin, so dismissive of the miniatures, but who slept with Otto's doll beneath her pillow. Marin, who didn't want to be a wife, but who had Thea's name waiting on her tongue.

Nella feels weighed down by the pointless loss of Marin's life, the many unanswered questions. Frans, Johannes, Otto – this trio of men, did they know her sister-in-law any better than she?

'Well?' asks Pellicorne impatiently.

Nella clears her throat. '*T'can vekeeren*,' she replies.

'Is that all?'

'Yes,' she says. '*T'can vekeeren.*'

Things can change.

Degrees of Being Alive

On Saturday morning, Nella takes a pie from the pantry, thinking it's made of berries. She's starving, having barely eaten since the verdict.

The crust is deceptive, turning out to conceal a pie made of cold fish, prosaic flounder where she'd hoped for winter fruits. In Nella's nervous state, it almost feels like the food is taunting her. She wonders miserably whether Cornelia will ever candy anything again. The sight of a crystallized walnut might conjure Marin and her delicious contradictions.

Her stomach rumbling, Nella heads to Hanna and Arnoud's shop, under their sign of two sugar loaves.

'We'll take more,' says Arnoud when he sees her. 'It works well with the honeycomb, and you'll be desperate to get rid of it, no doubt.'

'*Noud*,' Hanna reprimands. 'I'm sorry, Nella. They never taught him decent manners in the Hague.'

Nella smiles. Business is business. I don't have to like you, Arnoud, she thinks – though she is fond of Hanna – clear-speaking, a diplomat in a dusted apron. As soon as this sugar's sold, Nella promises herself she will shove Arnoud's doll into a city apiary, to be covered by greedy bees.

'Come,' Hanna says, beckoning her to sit down on the polished bench in the front of the shop. Arnoud stomps to the back, banging out his trays.

'Try this new cocoa-bean drink I've been testing,' Hanna says brightly. 'I put some of your sugar loaf in, and a few vanilla seeds.'

It is truly delicious. Like a happy childhood memory, it warms Nella up. 'Have you heard?' Hanna asks.

'What?'

'The burgomasters have lifted the ban on people-shaped biscuits. Though our dogs were so popular, I'm pleased we can go back to carving people's sweethearts for those lucky enough to be young and in love. It's good news for your stock.'

Nella wraps her grateful fingers round the hot terracotta mug. It is good news, and yet, not good enough to lift the overwhelming bleakness she feels inside. 'I cannot be long away,' she says, thinking of her household; newly configured, half of whom she's only just met.

'Of course,' says Hanna, looking at her carefully.

Does she know, Nella wonders – has Cornelia finally held her tongue? 'But I thank you,' she says, 'for your friendship and your trade.'

'I would do anything for her,' Hanna says.

Nella imagines Hanna and Cornelia in the orphanage – what pacts did they swear, what blood oaths till the day they died? Hanna lowers her voice. 'Since my marriage—' She cuts herself off, looking over her shoulder at Arnoud. 'Running a business takes up every hour of my day.'

'You have Arnoud.'

'Exactly.' Hanna smiles. 'He is not a cruel man. Nor is he a selfish one. I have made my doughy bed.' She leans forward, whispering. 'We will pay you the money you need. From little seeds great flowers grow.'

Nella looks into the kitchen. 'But what will Arnoud say? I cannot sell at a low price.'

Hanna shrugs. 'There are means of persuasion. It's my money too. I earned and saved what I could before I married. My brother gambled for me on the bourse and once I'd made a profit I told him to stop. He listened, unlike some.' She sighs. 'Arnoud admires my abilities, but he seems to have forgotten the source of half his capital. He likes his new role as sugar-trader. It's brought him status in the Guild of Pastry Bakers. They might appoint him an overman. The product is good, so they think he is too.' Hanna smiles. 'New recipes, plans for expansion. He wants to go and sell the next batch of sugar in Delft and Leiden, as well as The Hague.' Hanna pauses. 'All decisions I have encouraged.'

'Will you go with him?'

'Someone has to keep the business open here. We'll take another three hundred loaves. And give you six thousand. That's fair, isn't it? Sugar crystals are more use to me than diamonds, Madame Brandt.'

What is she buying here – peace, or a moment to enjoy her own hard work? Nella glows with the sum Hanna has proposed.

'In the long run,' Hanna says, 'I believe it will benefit us all.'

Nella walks quickly from Hanna and Arnoud towards the Stadhuis. The guard lets her through the gates, she treads the same corridor, and Johannes' door is drawn back. It is three guilders this time to allow more than the usual quarter-hour. Johannes' finite existence is making him more expensive, but Nella would give ten times that if she had to. There is a distinct smell of rosewater and pumpkin wafting about the guard, Nella notices. Checking the money in his hand, he nods, closing the cell door.

Someone, maybe Cornelia, has shaved Johannes' stubble, which serves to make him more cadaverous, as if his skull is making its way inside out. I should have brought him a new shirt, she thinks, peering at her husband in the dim light. The one he's wearing is ragged and thin. Nella swallows, girding herself against the sight. He sits on the pallet of straw, head against the damp brick, long legs twisting awkwardly out of his hips.

She realizes how like Marin he looks, haughty in repose, half-handsome even now. Her throat tightens. There is excrement in the corner, covered haphazardly with straw. She looks away.

If I told him everything, Nella wonders, who would Johannes think had betrayed him more? She remembers Jack screaming at Otto – *he knows you've done something*. Johannes had once questioned Marin's piety in that argument in the salon, and later, she'd said she had taken something of her brother's that wasn't hers to take. Did Johannes know, and look away? It seems incredible but then much about Johannes' person is incredible. He and Marin often pulled Otto between themselves, claiming him like territory, arguing over who appreciated or needed him most.

The two remaining pasties lie uneaten at Johannes' side. 'You should eat those while they're fresh,' she says.

'Sit with me,' he replies, his voice quiet.

How frail he looks, the light drained from his eyes. Nella can almost feel his spirit dissolving into the air, to nothingness. She wants to grab at it and hold it in fistfuls, stop it from getting away.

'I'm selling the sugar,' she says, sitting down. 'A confectioner is helping me.'

'I don't think you'll shift it all by tomorrow,' he replies, with the shade of a smile.

Nella pushes back the instinct to sob. It seems Cornelia has kept her promise to keep quiet about Marin, but how can they not confess to him what has happened? His sister, his most beloved adversary, is dead. How is it possible he cannot tell the grief in the faces of his women?

'Meermans will never take a bribe now, anyway,' Johannes says. 'It appears that some things don't have a price after all. Marin was right, you cannot barter for abstracts. Certainly not for betrayal.'

Nella pictures Lysbeth Timmers, hustling for her silence. 'But this is Amsterdam—'

'Where the pendulum swings from God to a guilder. Frans says he's doing this to save my soul, but underneath it, he's fuming that I didn't sell the sugar overnight. He's fighting for his loaves by calling me a sodomite.'

'Is that the only reason, Johannes – revenge?'

He looks at her in the gloom, and she waits. Now, she thinks; now surely he will tell about Marin and her refusal to marry. But Johannes is loyal to the end. 'That sugar represented so much for him,' he says. 'And I mocked it with indifference.'

'Why did you do that? Because of Jack?'

'No. Because I could taste Frans' and Agnes' greed upon the air and it disgusted me.'

'But you're a merchant, not a philosopher.'

'Greed is not a prerequisite for being good at business, Nella. I crave very little for myself.'

'Just potatoes?'

He smiles. 'Just potatoes. And you are right, I am not a philosopher. I am merely a man who happens to have sailed to Surinam.'

'You said the sugar was delicious.'

He looks grimly round the room. 'And thus am I amply rewarded. The secret in business is not to care too much, to always be prepared to lose. It seems I cared both too little and too much.'

The prospect of Johannes' greatest loss to come looms large. 'I misjudged the situation. Old wounds,' he says. 'No matter now. Come, there's nothing to do. Cornelia drenched me with her tears and now you too. You could have brought me a new shirt. What a terrible wife you are,' he chides, squeezing her hand. 'You must tell Marin that she cannot come here.'

Loss washes through her; a brackish tide.

'I would not want her to see me like this,' he says.

'Johannes. Why did Jack betray you?'

He runs a hand through his silvering hair. 'Money, I suppose, and what money means. It has to be money, because any other reason I cannot counter.' The silence thickens; she senses Johannes' struggle to keep down his own fear. 'You should have heard Agnes' testimony,' he says. 'Her spirit was always brittle, but in that moment, I believe it truly snapped.'

He speaks quickly, pulling himself away from darker thoughts. 'Agnes has always loved Frans, but too much love like that can be a poison. How happy she was to do his bidding this time, I know not. She believes in her God, of course, and the sanctified order of how things should be. But there was something about her on Thursday morning. She seemed quite *dis*ordered, as if she knew perfectly well she was doing something wrong, but was going to do it anyway. She has probably never known herself better than in that moment, nor taken herself more by surprise.'

He laughs, and Nella encloses the sound inside her.

'Marin was always right about Agnes and Frans,' he continues. 'They are the type of people who see blackened sugar everywhere.'

God knows her husband has not always been the most prudent judge of character, but when it comes to Marin, Johannes has always known his sister's worth. He has years stored up of her brilliance, and her gentler moods. Perhaps he watched her change from a bright girl to a harder woman who couldn't find the path she'd plotted in her head. He is generous about her, and to Nella, it is almost as if all Marin's selves are with them, shining in the gloom of the cell.

Nella is not Jack. She will not be the one to rip Johannes' image of his sister from her frame. She can never tell Johannes what he has lost, nor, in the end, how slenderly Marin was known to them all.

'I hate them, Johannes,' she says. 'With all my soul.'

'No, Nella, don't waste yourself. Cornelia told me the work you've done with Arnoud Maakvrede. I am not surprised, but it brought me such pleasure to hear. To think, the sugar staying here in the republic!'

'Marin has been so helpful,' she says, feeling the key to his warehouse under her shirt, pressed against her skin. Falling to silence, they entwine their hands, as if the touch of flesh will keep away the dawn.

Millstone

Nella sees the hundreds of ships moored, their bodies spanning down the long, tapering jetties belonging to the VOC. Fluyts and galliots, hookers, square-sterns, various shapes and purposes all for the republic's good. Most of the masts are naked, the rigging and sails folded away, protected from the elements until it is their time to be freshly tarred, drawn up and stretched across the wood.

Those ships that have sails look as if they are in bloom, ready to catch the trade winds and take their sailors far away. The hulls creak, swollen with the irrepressible salty damp that blights every deck-hand's life. The air tangs on the tongue – the smell of bilge around the dock edge, the seagulls' detritus they couldn't quite finish, half-pecked bodies of fish. Below the diminishing light, sewage from the ships swills in the water.

The ships would normally be an impressive sight, their vast frames lilting on the waves, these vehicles of empire, dogs of war who do everyone's dirty business. But in the fading Sunday afternoon, everyone's eyes are drawn to the man with the millstone round his neck.

Whether it is a wedding or a funeral, ceremony in Amsterdam is frowned upon, ritual can be too gross, too papist, and must be avoided. But a rich man to be drowned is different, the moral juiciness, the symbolism that could be plucked out of the Bible, and of course a crowd has come. Along the jetty they stand, many other staff of the VOC, sea captains and clerks. There is Pastor Pellicorne, Schout Slabbaert, even Agnes Meermans, alone in her tatty fur collar. Her husband is not with her. There are several guildsmen, regents from the Stadhuis, their wives, other pastors, and the three solemn men who make up Johannes' guard.

Nella stands at the back of the dockside crowd. Pellicorne glides his hard gaze over her, pretending not to see. The Pastor's pall-bearers came last night to lift her sister-in-law into a coffin and take her away, and now Marin waits in the Old Church crypt for the last service she will ever attend.

Pellicorne turns back to the matter at hand. What inward glories must he be feeling now, Nella thinks. The will of the law and the will of the church are making their bloodthirsty claim, and he looks so disgustingly satisfied.

Nella has promised Johannes she would be here this afternoon, and a worse promise she has never had to keep. Last night they had sat in the dark of his cell for an hour, holding hands in silence, the guard leaving them be. That quiet, that hour, had a quality to it Nella will never experience again. In the future she will refer to it as her first wedding night, a communion where no words were needed. They lost their tangling, deceptive power, and in their place was a deeper, richer language.

When she left him, Nella stood at the door of his cell, and he smiled and looked so young – and she felt extremely old, as if somehow the silence had passed on all his grief to her. She will have to carry it whilst Johannes flies up, empty, hollow and free.

At the house, Cornelia has been sedated with a heavy sleeping draught, drawn up with frightening ease by Lysbeth Timmers, who had turned up at sunrise to feed Thea and decided not to leave. 'You might be needing me for more today,' she said. Their eyes met. Nella nodded wordlessly and now Lysbeth is in the house, waiting in the kitchen for her return.

Nella cannot be sure of the ground beneath her and she stands, trying to steady herself with her feet apart. The boisterous January wind blows through her coat, sharp as a cat's claw. She is wearing a hood, a plain brown skirt of Cornelia's. She has come in costume in order to endure this ordeal, as if the disguise might protect her from the truth.

Johannes is in a costume too. They have put him in a suit of silver satin which doesn't fit, and a preening feather in his hat that Johannes would never wear, a pointed marker to indicate that how you dress is who you are. Nella catches flashes of it through the shoulders of the crowd, a bright sleeve like armour through the dun and black. She leans suddenly on the woman next to her. The woman jumps at the contact and turns.

'It's all right, my love,' she says, seeing Nella's terror. 'Don't look if you can't bear it.'

Her kindness nearly splits Nella apart. How can good people come and watch this?

Slabbaert lays his hand on Johannes' shoulder and from then on, Nella doesn't look. She only hears, closing her eyes, the wind on her face, the sails slapping like wet laundry. She hears the millstone being dragged by the two executioners. Johannes, attached to the end of it, will by now be teetering on the edge of the jetty. The half-ton of stone makes a drawn-out, grating sound that runs under Nella's skin into the core of her bones.

As the crowd inhales, she feels the hot release of urine rush down her stockinged legs, the wool soaking it up and chafing her skin. He is speaking. She imagines him turning to look for her, for Marin, for Cornelia. *Let him see me*, she thinks. *Let him think I'm sending him a prayer.*

But the wind blows Johannes' final words off course and she does not catch them. *Johannes*, she whispers. She strains to hear, but there are prosaic mutterers around her, prayers and futile utterances. He is too weak to make his voice carry, and by the time the mutters fall to silence, the millstone has been rolled off the end of the jetty. Johannes. It smashes the choppy surface of the sea and plunges underneath.

She opens her eyes. A thick wave pushes up, crests in a white circle and disappears in seconds.

No one moves.

'He was one of our best merchants,' a man eventually says. 'We're fools.'

The crowd exhales, their hair whipping on their foreheads. 'No body to bury,' someone says. 'They're not bringing him back up.'

Nella turns away. She is alive, and she is not. She is down in the water with Johannes. Leaning against the wall, head towards the ground, her body threatens to turn her inside out. How long will it take for the sea to fill his lungs? *Be quick*, she thinks. *Be free.*

She senses something. The back of her neck prickles, her knees want to sag. Nella lifts her head, scanning the crowd for a flash of pale hair. *She's still here*, Nella thinks. *I can feel it.* She looks across the people's faces, searching for that cool, appraising gaze, a moment for the miniaturist to say good bye.

But it is not the miniaturist standing in the line of her eye.

He is thinner, dressed in the same clothes he left in, wearing that rich brocade coat. For a mad second Nella thinks her husband has come up from the water, that an angel has brought him back to life. But no, he is unmistakeable. Nella raises her hand in recognition, and, open-mouthed with grief, Otto lifts his palm. Five trembling fingers, a star shining out from the dark.

FIVE

The same evening, Sunday, 12th January 1687

Let us solace ourselves with loves.
For the goodman is not at home, he is gone a long journey:
He hath taken a bag of money with him, and will come home
at the day appointed.

Proverbs 7:18–20

Nova Hollandia

She supposes he's in shock at what he's witnessed, for she has to pull him away by the sleeve, their feet slipping on the tiles.

'Come home,' she says. 'Come home.' Nella is in agony, breathless because it hurts so much. The light has failed now, and dusk is on them. She tries to banish the image of the cresting water, the sound of Johannes being dragged beneath the surface of the sea. Her speed increases for fear grief will paralyse her, that she'll curl up in a ball on the canal path and never move.

Otto turns to her, stunned, drawing Johannes' coat tight around his body. He stops, pointing back in the direction of the docks.

'Madame, what has happened here?'

'I can't. I don't know the words, Otto. He's gone.'

He shakes his head, still stupefied. 'I did not know he'd been arrested. I thought to go to London would protect you all, Madame. I would never have—'

'*Come.*'

When they reach the Herengracht, Otto is overcome by the sight of the house. He grips the dolphin door-knocker like a prop to ward away collapse, his face a battle between agony and self-control. What he is about to discover beyond the door unfurls like a malicious flower in Nella's body, for it seems impossible that a person could withstand this double pain. She stumbles in Otto's wake at this worst of homecomings; but the peaceful interior belies the loss of Marin.

'This way.' She leads him through to the salon, where Lysbeth Timmers has indeed set a fire burning in the grate, warmer than any of them has felt for weeks, the dancing flames incongruously cheerful. Nella feels her blood brightening. At the back of the blaze, prongs of pewter bend in curtsey, panels of tortoiseshell split apart and crackle.

Lysbeth stands in the centre of the room, holding Thea tightly to her chest, eyeing Otto as he stares at the child. 'Who's this?' she asks.

Nella turns to him, wondering if he is capable of introducing himself, if he is thinking the same question of Lysbeth Timmers. As if in a dream, Otto puts out his expectant palms towards the child. Nella realizes she's seen him make that gesture before, his hands outstretched that first day she was here, when he gave her a pair of pattens against the cold.

Lysbeth shrinks away.

'Lysbeth, this is Otto. Please hand him the child,' Nella says.

Her edge of authority is so palpable that Lysbeth immediately obeys. 'Softer with her,' the wet-nurse mutters. Otto scoops Thea to his chest as if she is life itself – as if her tiny, beating heart might keep his alive. Even Lysbeth is muted, watching an introduction so strange in the midst of all this loss; so strange, and yet so natural.

'Lysbeth,' Nella murmurs. 'Go and wake Cornelia.'

As soon as they're alone, Nella knows that she must speak. 'Her name is Thea,' she says. 'Otto. I have to tell you something.'

But drawn into Thea's face, absorbed by his little mirror, it does not seem as if Otto is listening.

'Otto—'

'Madame Marin said it would be a boy,' he says.

Nella does not know how to respond. It feels impossible to speak. 'You knew, then?' she says eventually.

He nods, and as his face moves before the firelight, Nella sees his tears, how he too is struggling for the right word, any word that might support a fragment of the weight his shoulders seem to bear. He gestures suddenly to the unpolished floor, to the dusty rosewood chairs. 'She isn't here,' he says, as if these inanimate objects are comprehensive proof of loss.

'No,' says Nella. 'She isn't here.' She swallows, knowing a sob is there, worrying that to cry might be an invasion of his grief. 'I'm sorry, Otto.'

'Madame,' Otto says. His voice is raw; it cracks the simple word in two. She looks up and he holds her devastated gaze. 'You saved the child. She would have laid down her life that this little creature might survive.'

'But why did she have to?' Nella says. Her tears are coming now, she can't stop them; the effort to stop only makes them fall quicker, fuller, blurring her sight. 'She worsened so quickly. I – we could not bring her back to life. We tried, Toot, but we didn't know—'

'I understand,' he says, but from the pain on his face it is clear that he cannot. Nella feels her legs giving way and she reaches for a chair. He remains standing, staring at the top of

Thea's head. 'I never saw her more determined than when she told me she was with child,' he says. 'I was sure the world was coming to an end. I asked her, "What will this child's life be?"'

'And what did she say?'

Otto holds Thea closer. 'She said, "His life must be what he makes of it." '

'Oh, Marin.'

'I knew it might be safer if I left. But I had to come back. I had to see.'

The fact of Thea – the act of her creation – hovers in the air, life hand in hand with death. Maybe it's a secret Otto will always keep, she thinks. God knows Cornelia will help him, pretending it never happened, as if Thea was immaculate, or found growing from a tree. Perhaps one day he will tell how it started between him and Marin, and why – and whether each felt love like power or abandon, and whether their hearts were freely exchanged and full of ease, or weighed down over time.

Thea, the map of herself – she will see those plotted points of her father's face in half of hers and wonder, where is my mother? I'll give her the doll, Nella thinks. I will show her those grey eyes, those slender wrists, even the bodice lined with fur. *There must be no more secrets*, so I said. So I will show her that observed curve, the miniaturist's gift revealed. You were there, Thea. Petronella Windelbreke saw that you were coming, and she knew that it was good. She even sent you a cradle. She was telling your story before you were born, but now you must be the one to finish it.

Still tipsy from the valerian, Cornelia has been fetched from her bed by Lysbeth. She stands at the door of the salon, her face a question, its astonishment feasting on the answer before her eyes. 'You,' she breathes.

'Me,' Otto replies, nervously. 'I've been in London, Cornelia. The English called me blackamoor and lambkin. My lodging was the Emerald Parrot. I was almost going to write and tell you. I—'

Words fall on words. Otto shores up against the tide of grief before it breaks on his oldest friend's head.

Cornelia totters towards him – she touches his elbows and shoulders, his hands still full with Thea. She touches his face, anything to prove his flesh is real. She cuffs the back of his head in loving fury. 'Enough,' she says, encasing him, breathing in his presence. 'Enough.'

Still in her coat, Nella leaves them in the salon, crossing the marble tiles to the front door, which was left ajar in haste. She pulls it wide, standing on the threshold, the cooling air upon her cheeks. Sunday evening bells have started over the roofs of Amsterdam, and the churches' clanging harmonies rise high. Dhana trots up to greet her young mistress, proffering her head for a pat. 'Have they fed you, my beauty?' Nella asks the dog, rubbing the silk of her lovely ears.

As the bells call the coming night, Nella sees the small white crescent moon, like a lady's fingernail curved in the darkening sky. Cornelia passes through the hall, apron tied, head turned towards her kitchen. 'It's cold, Madame,' she calls. 'Come in.'

But Nella remains gazing along their stretch of frozen canal. A line of melting ice now runs along its edges. Warmer water has begun to fray the Herengracht's wintry hem, and it looks to her like punched lace, the lining of a giant crib.

Cornelia drops a pan in the kitchen. There is shushing from the salon as Thea sallies a cry. Lysbeth and Otto's voices float over the tiles. Nella reaches in her coat pocket to bring out the miniature house she took from the Kalverstraat, but it is no longer there. That cannot be right, she thinks, digging into the fabric. The little baby is still there – so is the miniature of Arnoud. So did I drop it, running through the city streets? Did I leave it in the workshop? You saw it, she tells herself. It was real.

Real or not, Nella has it no longer – but the five figures that the miniaturist had put inside it still remain inside this house. The young widow, the wet-nurse, Otto and Thea, Cornelia – will they come to know the secrets of each other's lives? They are all loose threads – but that has ever been the case, thinks Nella. We make a hopeful tapestry; no one to weave it but ourselves.

Dusk has slipped to night, and the smell of nutmeg wafts; Dhana's little body warms the side of Nella's skirts. The sky is a vast sea flowing between the roofs; it is too large for the naked eye to see how it began, or where it will end. Its depth, infinite to Nella in possibility, begins to draw her further from the house.

'Madame?' Cornelia calls.

She turns, inhaling the scent of spice. Stealing one last look at the air above, Nella steps inside.

A Seventeenth-Century Dutch Glossary

Bewindhebber – partner of the VOC. Often had a lot of capital invested in the company.

Bourse – between 1609 and 1611, the first Commodity Exchange (or Bourse) was built on a part of the Rokin canal. The bourse consisted of a rectangular courtyard surrounded by arcades where trading took place.

Donderbus – literally 'thunder-pipe', an early form of shotgun.

Gebuurte – a neighbourhood group, taking common care of order, safety, public quiet, assisting a neighbour in distress, being there as intermediary in domestic conflicts, providing help in upcoming deaths and in burials.

Guilder (*Gulden*) – a silver coin first minted in 1680, divided into 20 stuivers or 160 duits. Larger denominations came in note form.

Herenbrood – literally a 'gentlemen-bread' that would be eaten by the wealthy. Made with wheat flour, cleaned and ground, as opposed to a cheaper rye bread.

Hooft's *True Fool* ('Warenar') – a 1617 tragicomedy about moderation, greed and obsession. Warenar the miser has a daughter, Claartje, illegitimately pregnant by a suitor of whom Warenar does not approve. In the seventeenth century, Amsterdam developed into the centre of the international book trade, and books were not much subject to government censorship. Those that were banned in other countries were published in Amsterdam.

Hutspot – a meat and vegetable stew, everything thrown into one pot.

Kandeel – known in English as a 'caudle', a spiced drink made with wine, sometimes thickened with ground almonds, wheat starch, dried fruit, honey, sugar and egg yolks.

Olie-koecken – an early form of the doughnut. Wheat-flour with raisins, almonds, ginger, cinnamon, clove and apple, fried in oil and rolled in sugar.

Pattens – clog-like shoes that were worn inside and out, to protect the softer shoe from dirt.

Puffert – raised pancake fried in a pan.

Schepenen – if the *schout* was a sheriff or chief magistrate, the *schepenen* was a male group of magistrates. When acting in a judicial capacity, the *schepenen* were often referred to as the *schepenbank*. One of the functions of the *schepenbank* was to pass judgement on criminals, thereby functioning as a jury or magistrates' bench. As a result, the word *schepen* is often translated into English as 'magistrate' in this Dutch historical context.

Schout – this is the Dutch word for a sheriff, or bailiff. He oversaw legal proceedings of cases in the Stadhuis, rather like a chief magistrate.

Spinhuis – women's prison in Amsterdam, founded in 1597. Inmates were set to work spinning and sewing.

Stadhuis – the City Hall, now the Royal Palace in Dam Square. The testimonies and the deliberations of cases took place in the *Schoutkamer*, and the prison and the torture chamber were in the basement. The death penalty was pronounced in the basement by the *schout*, in front of the accused and in the presence of a pastor. Any audience could hear the sentence, standing in a limited space on the ground level, looking down into this sentencing room. The Amsterdam Exchange Bank was also housed in the Stadhuis cellar, holding all kinds of coins, gold nuggets and lumps of silver in safe-keeping. Depositors were credited with the equivalent amount in guilders. The Exchange Bank also carried out money transfers from the account of one client to that of another.

Verkeerspel – an early Dutch version of backgammon, often depicted in paintings to remind people not to become complacent. The word means 'game of change'.

Salary comparisons at the end of the seventeenth century in Amsterdam

By the last quarter of the seventeenth century, 0.1% of the Amsterdam rich owned about 42% of the total wealth of the city.

The Receiver General of the Republic (the top position in government) had a salary of 60,000 guilders a year in 1699.

A rich merchant like Johannes would be earning something in the region of 40,000 guilders a year, aside from his assets which accounted for a separate and substantial tranche of wealth – hugely successful merchants had been known to leave bequests of up to 350,000 guilders.

An Amsterdam *schout* or *sheriff* (a high position in the republic's machine) might earn 9,000 guilders a year.

A surgeon might earn about 850 guilders a year.

A middling or master guildsman (shoemaker, chandler, baker) might earn 650 guilders a year. (Arnoud and Hanna's income is high, but they have combined their incomes and been lucky at the Bourse.)

An ordinary labourer might earn about 300 guilders a year, or 22 stuivers a day.

Sample household costs of a wealthy Amsterdammer
in the late 1600s

A man's shirt – 1 guilder

A debt to an apothecary – 2 guilders 10 stuivers

A woman's simple skirt – 2 guilders

Widow's benefit from her husband's guild – 3 guilders a week

Small landscape or Biblical painting – 4 guilders

A house gown – 10 guilders

A debt to a surgeon – 15 guilders

A painting in a gilt frame of a sea battle – 20 guilders

A decent linen cupboard – 20 guilders

A debt to a shoemaker – 23 guilders

An Italianized hunting landscape in the style of Cuyp – 35 guilders

A coat and vest – 50 guilders

A fancy nut-wood linen cupboard – 60 guilders

A damask dress – 95 guilders

A debt to a tailor – 110 guilders

A horse and sleigh – 120 guilders

A hundred pounds of lobster – 120 guilders

Entry into one of the more exclusive guilds (such as silver and
goldsmiths, painters, wine-merchants) – 400 guilders

Twelve silver plates – 800 guilders

A house for a small-scale tradesman and his family – 900 guilders

A tapestry bought for a room in a Herengracht canal house – 900 guilders

A string of diamonds – 2,000 guilders

A miniature cabinet house, furnished with 700 items over several years – *c.* 30,000 guilders.

Thank you

The Early Readers: Jake Arnott, Lorna Beckett, Mahalia Belo, Pip Carter, Anna Davis, Emily de Peyer, Polly Findlay, Ed Griffiths, Antonia Honeywell, Susan Kulkarni, Hellie Ogden, Sophie Scott, Teasel Scott and the women of the Pageturners book group. Thank you for not saying it was rubbish and for your always kind, useful and imaginative observations. My fortune in friends indicates that in the next life I will return as a mosquito.

The Three Graces with pens and exclamation marks: my UK editor, Francesca Main, who has blended extraordinary commentary and observation with kindness and sensitivity – and my editors in the USA and Canada, Lee Boudreaux and Jennifer Lambert, whose acumen and enthusiasm have made this the most shining book it could be. Thank you so much, all three, for believing in both me and the miniaturist.

At Picador, a huge thank you to Sandra Taylor, Jodie Mullish and Sara Lloyd for all your work and good humour, to Paul Baggaley for the pastoral support, and to Nicholas Blake for your detailed eye. Thank you also to Line Lunnemann Andersen, Martin Andersen, Katie Tooke, the design team at Picador, and Dave Hopkins, who have made such a wonderful UK cover design, complete with a real miniature house. Deep thanks also to Greg Villepique and Ryan Willard at Harper Ecco.

Marga de Boer at Luitingh-Sijthoff, for her excellent observations on the infrastructure of Amsterdam, on the life of the real Petronella Oortman and her husband Johannes, and for legal and civic accuracies in late seventeenth-century Holland. Any inaccuracies and flights of fancy are mine alone, and my Nella's biography is a completely fictional creation.

For the Medical Advice: thank you to Jessica Cutler, Prasanna Puwanarajah and Victoria Scott. Again, any anomalies are the fault of my over-active imagination alone.

For the hawk-eyes: Gail Bradley.

Edward Behrens & Penny Freeman, who so kindly let me isolate myself in their respective houses, where there was no internet – just time, and peace, and quiet. And wine.

Sasha Raskin, for handling *The Miniaturist* in the USA so brilliantly.

And:

To my agent, Juliet Mushens: consigliera, champion, superstar, friend. For making this experience so fun, so wonderful – you are an exceptional agent and an astonishing human being.

To Linda and Edward, also known as Mum and Dad. For reading to me when I was little, for taking me to the library and for buying me books. For saying, 'Why don't you write a story?' when I was bored at six years old, at twelve, at twenty-seven. For always, always being there.

To Margot, for being nothing but a useless ball of fur who stamps on my keyboard.

And to Pip. I don't know how to begin. For seven years of love and friendship, thought, hilarity and wonder – thank you. You are extraordinary. My lucky soul.

picador.com

blog
videos
interviews
extracts